EVIL EXCHANGE

LORI PARIS & JOE SOLL

WingSpan Press

Copyright © 2007 Lori Paris and Joe Soll
All rights reserved.

No part of this book may be used or reproduced in any manner without written permission of the authors, except for brief quotations used in reviews and critiques.

This book is a work of fiction. Names, characters, settings and incidents are either the product of the authors' imagination or used fictitiously. Any resemblance to actual events, settings or persons, living or dead, is entirely coincidental.

Printed in the United States of America

Published by WingSpan Press, Livermore, CA
www.wingspanpress.com

The WingSpan name, logo and colophon are the trademarks of WingSpan Publishing.

ISBN 978-1-59594-135-0
First edition 2007

Library of Congress Control Number 2007922216

Dedication:
To all whose lives have been touched by adoption.

Acknowledgments:
The authors would like to thank Lisa Goldberg for her editing skills, the late John D. MacDonald whose works inspired the character of Boots Beaumont, and the late Gene Bone and Howard Fenton for the song, "Why Is It I Just Don't Belong?"

Also by Joe Soll:
Adoption Healing…a path to recovery (for adoptees) 2000
…for women who lost children to adoption 2003

Also by Lori Paris
Follow Your Heart 2002

PROLOGUE

Nardo crept toward the back of the run down house. He knew there wasn't a dog. Nardo wouldn't do a snuff and snatch if there were any dogs on the property. He hated dogs, and of course they could too easily alert neighbors. So that was something he always thoroughly checked out before hand. Tonight, everything was going according to plan, all because he had done his homework. He was good at his job. He'd been following the young woman for a week now, and knew her routine.

The sky was dark and no light came from inside. Now if the kid just wouldn't wake up while he took care of business, all would be well. He easily slipped in the back door, the lock not even worth mentioning. *Man, she lived in a piece of crap place*, he thought as he looked around the kitchen. His eyes had adjusted to the lack of light, and he could tell the place was a mess. But she was on her own, for the time being at least. No husband or boyfriend in sight. Just her and the kid. A welfare mom. Nardo was disgusted. People should work for a living. Not sit around having babies they couldn't support.

He made his way toward a narrow hallway. A floorboard creaked and he held his breath. Nothing. He continued to a small room on the right. The door was slightly ajar and he could hear soft breathing. *Let's hope she's a heavy sleeper.* Chances were pretty good as he knew the infant often kept her awake at night, and that she was exhausted. They'd only been home from the hospital for seven days.

He silently entered the room. *Shit.* He was afraid of this. The baby's bassinet was near the bed. *Oh well, not as if that had never happened before.* He'd be quick and

Evil Exchange

hopefully not disturb the child. He was a professional after all. He approached the bed, pleased to see the young woman asleep on her back. That made it so much easier. He flexed his massive gloved hands and reached out for her throat.

She never had a chance. Her eyes flew open just as his powerful hands clamped around her neck exerting enormous pressure. She thrashed ineffectually, but she was no match against Nardo. An expert was he, and naturally he took great pride in this. He didn't consider himself a cruel man, didn't care for needless suffering. Just get the job done and get out. It took only a few minutes and the woman was dead.

The next part of the program was a bit trickier. Thankfully, the baby hadn't been awakened by the struggle so he could take care of a few things first. He pulled a large garbage bag from his back pocket and went to the shabby closet. He threw in what little she had hanging there. Next was a dilapidated dresser, which held a few more of her clothes and some of the infant's tiny outfits. It all went into the bag. With his ear attuned to any noise from the bassinet he quickly checked the miniature bathroom and grabbed a few more personal items, along with a package of diapers. *Man, this woman was dirt poor.* Her few meager possessions were pathetic. The only thing left was to grab her purse and he quickly found that near the front door. It too went into the garbage bag. He could care less what was in it. That wasn't the point. Besides, it couldn't be more than a few bucks anyway, and he was paid well for his work. He didn't have to worry about a car since she didn't have one.

Back to the bedroom to grab the body. He easily hefted her over his left shoulder, and carried the bag in his right hand. He made his way to the kitchen toward the back door. Nardo quickly checked outside, but he wasn't too concerned. There were a couple of other piss-poor houses down the street, but none close by. He then backtracked through a cover of trees to where he'd left his car. Body and bag went into the trunk and he gently closed it with a muffled thunk.

Back again to the house to get the baby, and make sure he hadn't forgotten anything. Nardo was most thorough and figured he'd gotten enough of her stuff to make it look like she had taken off somewhere with the kid. That was always the best cover, and it's what the Stork and the Boss insisted upon. No sign of violence, no evidence that something malicious had happened. Make it look like she just took off with the baby, never to be heard from again. Whatever sad excuse she had for a family might go to the police, there might be some minor investigation. However the police were overworked and understaffed, so most likely nothing would come of it. She probably wouldn't be missed too much anyway.

Nardo returned to the bassinet and expertly scooped up the child. She easily fit into the crook of his arm. He made one last check of things, locked the back door, and returned to his car. He placed the still sleeping infant into a box cushioned with blankets on the floorboard of the front seat. He wouldn't dare take a chance having a baby seat in the car. It would look too suspicious. Nardo didn't exactly look like the fatherly type. Besides, the box worked just fine. He never had any problems before, and he wouldn't have the kid for very long anyway.

He started the engine and turned the heater on low. In his experience he knew if he could keep the baby warm, she'd be less likely to wake up. He drove slowly until he was a safe distance away and then sped up but kept it at the speed limit. Being pulled over in the middle of the night with a baby in a box and a dead woman in the trunk wasn't ideal. If that happened, he'd have to kill the cop too, and Nardo preferred not to do that.

But luck was on his side. No cops, no other cars. He was alone on the two-lane highway and the dumping ground he'd picked wasn't too far out of the way. *Clockwork*, he smiled to himself.

Nardo turned off the road and drove another half mile to reach the ravine. He pulled over and left the engine running while he opened the trunk. Mom tumbled over the edge of the ravine like a rag doll and the garbage bag followed. If she were ever found, it wouldn't be for a hell of a long time. He closed the trunk with a satisfying thump and lumbered back to the driver's seat.

Next would be the truck stop where he was meeting the Mule. He had no idea what her name was and he didn't care. The Stork and the Boss were in charge of the operation, but they never handled the merchandise until the final transport. Nardo always hated the meet though. The woman who exchanged the balance of his pay packet for each infant was a real bitch. It wasn't that she scared him, because nothing scared Nardo. Yet she gave him the creeps for some reason. She would speak little at each exchange and had lifeless gray eyes that stared straight through him. He could never get away from her fast enough.

He looked over at the kid. He couldn't believe she was still sleeping. She hadn't woken up once. All the better for him. Not that it mattered if she started crying, he was used to it. And, he always carried a pacifier just in case. However, it was a bonus that she slept through it all. Besides, she'd be with her new mommy and daddy soon enough, no harm.

Nardo sighed and was glad his work was almost through. After the drop-off he'd get back on the highway and head straight for home. How he hated Louisiana.

Chapter One

A trip to the Jersey shore was just what he needed. After a long work week, Todd Walters wanted to get out of Manhattan, and his new girlfriend Trina, would be the perfect companion. The two had met some weeks before at a party, and he could hardly believe the stunning blond had taken such a liking to him. Todd figured the fact they both spoke French made for an immediate connection, but after a few dates, he realized they had other things in common as well. The two were passionate Francophiles, both loved the outdoors, and shared the same sense of adventure. Their relationship seemed to be progressing nicely. She was thirty to his forty, and she made him feel like a teenager again. So on this beautiful sunny day in July, he felt it was time to take the next step. A weekend away. Just Trina and Todd. Instant bliss. That was if she agreed.

Todd picked up the phone and called her, and she said she'd be happy to join him. Thrilled by her response, he suggested she pack lightly as they would be taking the Vespa. She told him to hurry. He said no problem.

Todd eagerly grabbed a few things and put them in his backpack. He went to the closet and retrieved his helmet and the extra one he kept for passengers. After locking the front door and pocketing the keys, he walked the few blocks to the garage where he kept his scooter. He grinned when he saw it. The Vespa was a brilliant red, and on the front bumper, the previous owner had put "la grenouille" spelled out in gold stick-on letters. Todd thought "frog" described the puddle jumper perfectly. He loved his Italian scooter with the French name, it was one of the reasons why he'd bought it in the first place. He hopped on and set off for Trina's place halfway across town.

Evil Exchange

He went about a block before coming to a halt. Traffic was terrible and he realized he wasn't going anywhere anytime soon. Todd sighed and resigned himself to his weekend starting a bit later than he would prefer. You couldn't live in the city and not deal with gridlock. It was a fact of life. Naturally, his mind started to wander. Though he was trying to get away from work, he couldn't help but think about it. Another fact of life.

Todd Walters installed and repaired television stations and equipment for a living. It was not the most common of jobs, and it all started when he flunked out of college. The professors said he wasn't bright enough. Todd leaned more towards the emotional immaturity and an unwillingness to study theory explanation, still, the end result was just the same. When you flunk out of school there's not much else to do but find a job. If you want to eat that is. It didn't take him long to get lucky, and he landed a job as an engineer with Aqueduct Electric, an electrical contracting firm. Luck definitely had a lot to do with it because Todd had absolutely no experience, but was miraculously hired anyway. It just so happened Aqueduct specialized in building radio and television facilities, studios, and transmitter and antenna installations.

He fondly remembered his first assignment at the Empire State Building's 84th floor to supervise the installation of New York's first Spanish language television transmitter. He was told to supervise the electricians. Todd was more than apprehensive since he knew nothing about television, other than it was for watching his favorite programs. So once he found Tony, the foreman of the electrical crew, he quickly explained the situation with his typical candor.

"Hi, I'm Todd. I'm new to Aqueduct. They sent me over here to supervise you. So be a pal and tell me what to tell you to do?"

Tony roared with laughter and replied, "Okay kid, fair enough. How about telling me to measure this area so we can figure out which way to orient the transmitter when it gets here."

Tony was old enough to be Todd's father, and never having had a son of his own, immediately took Todd under his wing and they became fast friends. The installation of the transmitters and antenna equipment made sense to Todd and he quickly learned the how-to's of it all under Tony's expert guidance.

Within a few months, Todd was able to supervise the broadcast projects on his own, and soon after that, he was able to estimate the costs and submit his own bids on behalf of Aqueduct. His bidding and supervisory skills enabled him to finish construction projects for far less than originally estimated and therefore made bigger profits for the company. This pleased his bosses no end.

Paris and Soll

Todd loved the work but feared the monolithic Empire State. The first time he went up into the antenna tower and rising twenty stories above the 104th floor, Todd was petrified. He could swear he felt the building swaying in the wind and he thought it would just simply fall over. He sometimes had dreams about it, and once made the mistake of telling a friend about his fear. Not missing a beat, and with the most genuine concern, the friend told him he was just afraid of losing an erection. When Todd failed to see the humor, his friend clapped him on the back and told him to lighten up. Todd took his advice and walked away, feeling ever so much lighter knowing one less asshole.

No matter how many times he went up, he never did get used to it. Sometimes he felt the swaying inside the building even when he couldn't see outside. He managed it by telling himself it was all in his imagination, which usually calmed him down. At least for a little while.

Todd had a natural talent for designing the transmitter facilities and soon was in demand by the networks to design and install their transmitter upgrades. This displeased his bosses no end. They became jealous and treated him badly. He put up with it for a while, but then finally he'd had enough. Todd went to the office of the president of the company, Abraham Lincoln Hamilton (quite the mouthful), to ask for a raise. Linc, as he was known in the industry, gave Todd a standard song and dance about grooming him to one day be president of the company, and that he must be patient. The irony of this wasn't lost on Todd. He knew the stories of Linc Hamilton's notorious impatience with speeding drivers on the Taconic parkway. Linc would pull along side the offenders waving a pistol and forcing them off the road, where he then cautioned them against speeding while they sat huddled and terrified in the car. Linc got away with this maniacal behavior far longer than anyone thought possible, but eventually he got caught. Most reluctantly, Linc had to give up his patience preaching on the parkway along with his gun license, but continued to lecture at any other legal opportunity, sans pistola.

Todd figured he would show some patience all right. He had the patience to bide his time and come up with a plan. Some time later he approached Linc again, and told him since he was making the company well over a quarter of a million dollars a year in profit, he deserved either a percentage of the profits as commission, or a huge raise. The supreme boss then asked what would happen if he didn't do as Todd requested. Todd said, "Then I'd have to resign. I don't want to, but I will." Linc responded with, "You can't resign. You're fired." To no one's surprise, he pantomimed waving an empty gun in the air and the meaning was clear. Todd was not only fired, but also symbolically fired upon. It stung at first, but only until NBC offered him a job as annual inspector of their very

Evil Exchange

own television antenna on the Empire State. Buoyed by the confidence of a major television network, Todd then ventured out on his own, starting a small corporation. He sent out flyers and little by little, business picked up and Todd was happily doing the work he loved and getting well compensated for it at the same time.

His happiness was short-lived however. Not long after he left Aqueduct, Todd was in one of the Empire State's many television transmitter offices when Greg Kaplan, the shop steward of Aqueduct walked in. He grabbed Todd and put him up against the wall, telling him that he'd kill him if he did any more construction work in the building. Apparently, Greg was hard at work at his job of intimidation. Todd was very familiar with the story of the non-union electrician who was thrown out the 78th floor window of the Chrysler Building for being a scab worker, so he had reason to be nervous during this particular visit from Mr. Kaplan. Luckily for Todd, some of the staff at the station heard the threats. As soon as Greg left, Todd went to the local police precinct and gave them a written account of the threatening events, including the home address of Mr. Kaplan ripped from a local phone book. A copy of the report was issued to dear Greg, and Todd was never bothered again.

Suddenly, there was a break in the traffic. Todd followed suit and broke from his work-related reverie, and arrived shortly thereafter at his destination. He couldn't help but laugh at the memory of his first days as an electrician who barely knew how to screw in a light bulb. That was a long time ago and he'd come a long way. He was more than ready to leave work behind and concentrate on looking ahead to a weekend away with darling Trina.

When he got to her apartment, she kissed him on the cheek as he handed her the backpack. She added a few articles and Todd was secretly delighted to see a skimpy negligee among them. They said goodbye to her roommate, a shy young woman who giggled at them. They ran down the stairs filled with excitement. Todd handed her a helmet, and insisted she wear it even though she made a face. They hopped on the scooter and took off. Trina's gorgeous body pressed snugly against Todd's back, and she clasped her hands tightly around his waist. At the moment, Todd didn't think life could get much better.

About an hour into the trip, the Vespa hit a seam in the road. Todd became aware of it just as the scooter became airborne. Trina was instantly thrown clear, and instead of Todd on top and scooter on bottom, man and machine turned upside down. He hit the highway flat on his back, the Vespa now riding him, and skidded an astonishingly straight line down the center of the road. He somehow managed to stay conscious, thinking he would surely die as he realized there were cars whizzing past in both directions traveling at warp speed (or so it seems when one is on the ground), mere inches from his head. How they missed bashing his skull was a miracle, helmet or no helmet.

The slide seemed to go on forever, the moments passing in slow motion. Todd thought crazily, *this must be what it's like to be a stunt man.* Only this was no movie. Funny what can run through your mind when you're having a near death experience. He did not see any bright lights or angels however, and was just a tad disappointed in that.

He finally came to a halt, not quite believing he had survived. The scooter remained vertical for one last moment and gently toppled over, which was a great relief to Todd. That was one heavy frog. He heard the screeching of brakes and running footsteps.

"Jesus! Are you okay?"

"Oh my God! Is he all right?"

"Man, did you see that? Hey, Angie! Where's my camcorder for Christ's sake?"

Todd thought how typical that someone would want to film the accident's aftermath. The guy was probably kicking himself right now for not having the video camera on at the exact moment that Todd and Trina made like birds. Only in America. He felt arms slide underneath his shoulders, and someone asked, "Can you sit up? We've got to get you out of the road."

Todd groaned and figured it would be bad to survive an Evel Knievel flip and crash landing only to be run over by a car. He was helped to a sitting position, barely cognizant of the fact that he was now being immortalized on tape. *Hey, maybe we'll make the six o'clock news,* he said to himself, and figured he must have hit his head pretty hard, because right now he seemed to be losing his mind.

"Are you hurt?" A voice asked.

"I'm not sure," replied Todd. At least he could speak.

"Can you stand up?"

"Okay." Todd wasn't sure that was the right answer, but it was the best he could do at the moment. Obviously, his brain wasn't working right. For that matter, neither were his limbs.

He somehow made it to his feet, with help of course. Two men half-carried him to the shoulder of the highway. Someone else had righted the Vespa and walked it over to him.

"Will you look at that? Barely a scratch on the scooter."

Evil Exchange

"Yeah, but did you see his helmet? It's cracked in half."

"What about the girl?"

Todd managed to work his mouth. "Trina?"

"It's okay, buddy. She's over here."

Trina was standing on the grass shoulder staring at Todd. She'd taken her helmet off and seemed fine. It looked as if she hadn't even broken a nail. Amazing. Suddenly she burst into tears. "I could've been killed! How could you?" She yelled at him.

"Trina, I'm sorry. We hit something, it was an accident," Todd was babbling. He couldn't understand why she was so upset. *And, why was she now clinging to someone else?* A young man who had stopped to help now protectively held his arm around her.

"Hey, you need to go to a hospital pal," commented the guy on his right side. It was only then Todd became aware of a burning sensation down his back and legs. He figured the asphalt must have done some damage since he was only wearing a T-shirt and shorts. He had no idea his clothes had been ripped to shreds and that his skin looked like someone had taken a meat tenderizer to it. He was a bloody mess. His head started to throb and the scenery started to sway. Fortunately, the two men still had a hold of him as he passed out and they carefully laid him back down on the ground. Angie, the girlfriend of the amateur cameraman, picked up her cell phone and nonchalantly dialed 911 as if this were an everyday occurrence. Hopefully she wouldn't get a busy signal and an ambulance would soon be on the way.

Chapter Two

Todd was taken to a local hospital in Manasquan, New Jersey. He regained consciousness after arriving in the emergency room, remembering the accident and why he was there. But he had no idea what happened to Trina or the Vespa. The backpack did make it however, the EMT's brought it in the ambulance. After transferring to a gurney, the nurse cut off what little was left of his clothes, now just bloody rags. He was then made to lie on his stomach while awaiting medical attention. First, his wounds were cleaned, which hurt like a son of a bitch. Then one of the doctor's painted his back and legs with some nasty smelling chemical which upon contact with his skin, was so painful, he thought he might pass out again. Once the medical masterpiece was finished, he was temporarily abandoned. There seemed to be some commotion with a patient in the bed next to him, but he didn't know exactly what was going on.

Another doctor came over some time later and asked Todd where he hurt. His answer was that he hurt everywhere thanks to the artistic performance of the last doctor. The stony faced physician nodded and ordered a nurse to start an IV and to give Todd a mild sedative. Next were a series of X-rays, which caused a fresh wave of pain every time Todd had to move or be moved. Before they let him rest, they asked for a contact name. Did he want a family member or friend to be called? Todd asked to use his cell phone in his backpack, and the nurse haughtily reminded him that cell phones were off limits in the hospital. He wanted to stick his tongue out at her, but instead, gave her the number to call his brother Matt, which she jotted down efficiently on her clipboard. Then she insisted she must have his insurance information. Todd was able to rummage around in the pack, finding his wallet under the negligee. He sighed and handed it to the nurse. The wallet that is. He didn't think she'd have much of a sense of humor about the other. She seemed satisfied for the moment, having done her duty and marched off. The doctor told Todd he'd have a bit of a wait while his films were checked.

Todd floated in and out of a restless sleep. The sedative helped some, but trying not to move worked best. If he only didn't have to breathe.

When the doctor returned some time later, he told Todd how lucky he was. No broken bones. He did however have a concussion and needed to stay the night so his condition could be monitored before they would release him. Todd didn't consider almost dying, his girlfriend and scooter MIA, being in enormous pain, not to mention lying naked under a thin sheet lucky, but he was too tired to bring himself to mention it. Even though he wanted nothing more than to get back to New York, he resigned himself to the fact that it seemed to be out of the question. Eventually he was moved upstairs to a single room.

Nurses moved in and out, checking him and asking questions. *Why couldn't they just leave him alone?* One mentioned his brother had been reached at home, and would be on his way as soon as possible. Todd hoped Matt would bring him some extra clothes, as all he had in the backpack was an extra T-shirt and a swimsuit. Wouldn't be needing those now that his weekend at the shore had been so rudely interrupted. He tried to go back to sleep.

Matt arrived two hours later. Todd's younger brother was outgoing, good-looking, and instantly made friends everywhere he went. Upon his arrival, he chatted up the nurses, spoke at length with the doctor, even told a few jokes to a family in the waiting room. He was naturally charming, happily married, had two young children, and worked as a bank manager. Matt Walters was thirty-five years old and led a golden life. He and Todd, although quite different in many ways, were very close.

Todd heard Matt before he saw him. He was laughing with a nurse who followed him adoringly into Todd's room.

"Hey, big brother! Are you okay?"

"I'll live apparently." Todd wasn't in the best mood, but he was happy to see his sibling.

"Luann here was just telling me about some poor guy downstairs who came in with a moth in his ear," grinned Matt.

Luann, a slightly plump, fresh-faced young woman in uniform nodded while never taking her eyes off of Matt. "That's right," she said eagerly. "We all thought he was a nutcase when he first came in. He kept twitching and acting weird. Nurse Pritchett thought he was on drugs," she giggled.

"So they finally looked inside his ear, and sure enough," Luann prattled on.

"There's a moth in there. It took the doctor a while, but he got it out intact. Can you believe it?"

"Pretty bizarre," laughed Matt.

"Oh, that's nothing. You wouldn't believe some of the strange stuff we see. . ."

"Hey Luann, could you give my brother and me a minute here?" Todd didn't think he could take any more ER stories right now. "Maybe Nurse Rachet needs some help downstairs."

"It's Nurse Pritchett. And besides, I'm on my break," Luann huffed.

"Well, sorry. But I had an accident today, you know? Hit my head, lost half my skin. Almost died? Guess I must not be thinking straight," snarled Todd.

"Okay boys and girls, let's calm down. Luann, you can tell me some more stories later, all right? My brother's feeling a bit grouchy." Matt smiled sweetly at the nurse.

"Yeah, okay." She smiled back, then frowned at Todd and left the room.

"Grouchy?"

"Well, you know what I mean," answered Matt.

"What the hell are you doing flirting with Miss Florence Nightingale, anyway?"

The injustice of the day was catching up with Todd.

"Wait a minute, I wasn't flirting. I was just being friendly. And, FYI, big brother, she gave me all sorts of info about your accident," Matt stated triumphantly.

"Like what?" Todd eyed him suspiciously.

"Like where the Vespa is, for starters."

"Where?"

"At the police station. Safe and sound."

"Trina?"

"Well, she stayed at the scene long enough to give a police report. I guess the cops showed up when the ambulance did. All she did was cry and say how scared she was. Didn't even ask about you. Ended up leaving with some guy in a pick-up truck." Matt shrugged his shoulders.

"Great," said Todd.

Evil Exchange

"Well, you asked."

Matt became serious and sat down in a metal chair next to the bed. "So are you sure you're okay? Katy and I were pretty freaked out getting that phone call."

"Well I'll live, but it hurts," Todd admitted.

"You mean your back?"

"No, my pride. I can't believe she just left like that. And with another guy. I thought we had something good going on there."

"You *always* think that. Forget Trina." Matt quickly changed the subject. "Here, I brought you some stuff." He held up a brown paper bag. "Some old clothes of mine, and a book from Katy."

"Lemme see the book." Todd was an avid reader and often swapped books with his sister-in-law. It was also something he and Trina had in common. Well, used too anyway.

"She said it's really good."

"Boots Beaumont? Never heard of him."

"Yeah. Interesting character. I guess he's a former private investigator. After getting shot, he decided to retire and write mysteries. Katy said it's terrific."

The brothers chatted for a while. Matt had borrowed a truck from a neighbor. In the morning, he planned to pick up the Vespa from the police station, then swing by the hospital to rescue Todd. They'd be back in New York by early afternoon.

"I can't wait," sighed Todd.

"Ooooh, Mr. Walters!" Luann was back. "We really should let your brother rest now, he's had a tough day," she smiled sweetly.

Matt jumped to his feet. "Yes, boss." He saluted and added,

"I'll check in with you later, bro. There's a motel down the road, I'll hang out there."

"Bye Earthling," replied Todd.

"Boy, he really did hit his head," Luann said shaking her head.

Todd looked at the title of the book. *Near Death*. How appropriate.

Chapter Three

Matt followed through the next morning and returned to the hospital with the Vespa safely stowed in the truck bed. He was able to collect Todd with a minimum of fuss, making sure the paperwork was in order and getting necessary prescriptions filled. Todd looked fairly ridiculous in his Matt's larger clothes, but for once was spared the taunts normally thrown his way by his baby brother. Todd still looked and felt like he'd been put through a meat grinder. He moved stiffly and winced getting out of the wheelchair and into the truck. Matt found an old blanket and put it behind Todd to provide a bit of cushioning between the seat and Todd's aching back. It was time to head for home. A companionable silence passed between them until Matt spoke.

"Must you still call me 'Earthling'?"

"Why, does it bother you?"

"Luann thought you were another nutcase," Matt protested.

"Who cares? At least we didn't have to see her today, she probably would have followed you home. That might have been hard to explain to your wife," Todd smirked.

"Yeah, but . . ."

"What?"

"Well, it's just that most people don't understand what it means," Matt stated.

"Adopted people do," Todd replied.

"And, exactly how many adopted people do you know?"

"Not that many, I guess. Tanya for one, the gal who lives in my building. She says she hears it used all the time in her support group."

"You've been calling me that since we were kids though," Matt said.

"I guess I heard it from other kids at school. I was always being teased about being adopted. Everyone else was an Earthling, like I was some kind of alien from another planet."

Todd had always felt different as a kid. He didn't look anything like his parents, but he never really questioned it until Matt was born. Todd was blond and blue-eyed. Matt was dark-haired with an olive complexion, a carbon copy of their mother and father. When Matt was about two, Todd asked their mother why he looked so different from them. So at seven years of age, he learned he was adopted as a baby. According to his mother, it was some kind of minor miracle when Matt came along five years after the adoption, as Miriam and Robert Walters believed they were unable to have children.

"Do you ever think about them?" asked Matt while not looking at Todd but keeping his eyes on the road.

"Who?"

"Your real parents."

"I have *real* parents."

"You know what I mean," Matt struggled. "Your biological parents."

"Not really," Todd hedged.

"A lot of people do, you know. Wonder, I mean."

"Since when did you become an expert about all of this?"

"I've seen stuff on television, Katy's shown me articles about it."

"So?"

"Well, aren't you curious? What about Tanya? You said she's in a support group."

"I know Tanya searched and found her biological mom, they get along okay I guess." Todd looked out the window pretending to concentrate on the scenery.

"Have you gone to this group?"

"No. Tanya's tried to get me to go, but I just never felt the need. I don't want to go and talk to a bunch of strangers about being adopted."

"Maybe you're in denial," Matt said seriously.

"Who are you, my shrink? Has Katy been taping Dr. Phil again?"

Todd was quickly becoming angry. He still hurt like hell, and couldn't get comfortable in the passenger seat. His headache had subsided, but his skin felt as if it were on fire. All of this did nothing to improve his mood, much less answering all these incessant questions.

"Okay, Mr. Prickly. Sheesh. We're just talking here. Brother to brother." Matt seemed hurt.

"It just doesn't matter," sighed Todd.

"Maybe it does," answered Matt.

"No. It doesn't. Besides, my birth parents are dead. So it's all just speculation."

"How do you know that?" Matt was stunned.

"Mom told me. When I asked her why I looked so different from all of you. She said my parents had died, and that's why she and dad adopted me."

"That's not what . . ." Before Matt could finish, Todd interrupted.

"Well, we never talked about it all that much. Now will you just drop it? Change the subject," Todd warned his brother off. He'd had enough of this conversation.

Matt concentrated on driving for a while. But being a naturally chatty guy, he couldn't keep quiet for long.

"So, how do you like the book so far?" he tried for a neutral topic.

"It's good. I'm almost done with it." Todd was relieved to talk about something else.

"You're almost done?" Matt gaped at his brother.

"I didn't get much sleep last night," Todd admitted.

"Oh yeah. Kind of uncomfortable?"

"That's an understatement." Todd groused.

"Didn't they drug you up?"

"Not enough."

"What about the vicodin I got you at the hospital? Didn't you take any?"

"Not yet. I'll wait until we get home. Now will you shut up and leave me alone?"

Evil Exchange

Just as the words left Todd's mouth, he saw something out of the corner of his eye. A glint of metal caught by the sun. A car traveling on the other side of the road bounded over the median divider in a cloud of dust. It hit an SUV directly in front of Todd and Matt. There was the horrible sound of metal on metal, and the impact was deafening.

"Watch out!" yelled Todd.

Matt was speechless as he gripped the steering wheel. He couldn't believe what he was seeing. If he had been driving just a little faster, or if the other car had veered off two second later, it would have been them. He swerved, then braked hard. He pulled over just beyond the accident.

Both cars were upside down, tires spinning. A little boy, about five or six had crawled out a back window. Matt leapt out of the truck and yelled back at Todd to bring the cell phone. He reached the boy who was crying. He appeared unhurt.

"Todd! Where's that phone?" Matt called out.

"I want my mommy!" The boy wailed.

"It's okay, little guy. We'll get help for your mom." Matt spun around. *Why was Todd still at the truck? Couldn't he see he needed help with the kid?*

"Todd? Did you call?" Matt shouted.

"Battery's dead," Todd yelled back. His voice sounded strange. Flat. Detached.

"Come help me will ya?" Matt pleaded.

"I want my mommy!" The boy continued to cry.

Todd still hadn't moved. Matt looked away from him and quickly assessed the scene. A teenage boy occupied the car that had crossed over. Sadly, he now occupied the space where the front windshield had been. There was no question he was dead. The SUV held two more dead bodies. The parents. Still screaming on the side of the road, the boy was the only survivor.

Matt grabbed the boy's hand and brought him over to the truck. *What the hell was the matter with his brother?* The fact there were no other cars on the highway also struck him as odd. *Could this moment be any more bizarre?*

"Todd! Are you all right?" Matt asked but still got no reply. *Was Todd in shock? His own accident the day before, and now witnessing this tragedy. Maybe it was just too much for him.*

Paris and Soll

"Look. One of us is going to have to go for help unless someone else stops. I didn't bring my phone with me and we have to help this kid," Matt said.

Todd finally spoke. "What about . . ." he jerked his chin in the direction of the mangled cars. Matt shook his head no. There was no question. That the boy survived seemed impossible.

"There was that gas station a few miles back. Can you drive?"

Now it was Todd's turn to shake his head. Clearly, he was immobilized.

"Then I'll have to go. Stay with the kid, okay?"

Never looking at the boy, Todd took his small hand. He could not take his eyes off the twisted metal.

Chapter Four

It was a nightmarish couple of hours. Matt contacted the police. Todd was aided by another motorist who'd stopped at the scene. Fortunately, the driver was a woman who took over the supervision of the young boy, shielding him from the dead bodies. In another bizarre twist, no one else stopped. There were other cars that passed by, but they just slowed down to gawk at the accident, and then sped up to get away from the horror. Todd couldn't believe how many people just didn't want to get involved. However, there were a lot of things Todd couldn't believe. He felt absolutely numb to the core.

Once Matt returned, they had to wait for the sheriff, only then to be questioned endlessly about the accident. The officer kept going over the details again and again, until Todd thought he might go crazy. Matt finally begged for their release, using Todd's condition as an excuse. He could see how shaken his brother was and just wanted to get them the hell out of there.

They finally got back on the road. Matt drove at a reduced speed, terrified some other calamity might befall them. Todd didn't say a word for miles. Finally, Matt couldn't stand the silence anymore.

"What happened to you back there?" he asked softly.

"What are you talking about?"

"You *froze*, man. I mean, I know it was an awful thing to see, those poor people, that kid. Did you have a flashback of your accident? I could see how you'd be freaked out. Almost dying yesterday, and then barely escaping death again twenty-four hours later. That's got to do something to your head..." Matt rambled.

Todd didn't respond.

It didn't matter. Matt couldn't stop talking. His adrenaline was pumping at a dangerously high level.

"Man, you're white as a sheet. You look like you saw a ghost. Hey, you're going to get bruises," Matt pointed to his brother's lap. Todd looked down and realized he'd been gripping his thighs with such intensity he would most certainly have purple fingerprints there tomorrow. He carefully loosened his grip.

"Okay. I *did* see a ghost. And I *did* have a flashback, but not from yesterday," Todd admitted.

"What do you mean?" Matt was really getting worried now. His brother was losing it big time.

"That was how they died," Todd added.

"Focus, Todd. How *who* died?" asked Matt.

"My parents."

Now Matt was really confused. Their parents didn't die in a car crash. Bob had died of heart disease years ago. Miriam resided in an elder care facility, but she was still very much alive.

"Todd, does your head hurt? Should I take you to see a doctor? Maybe your concussion isn't better."

"My *birth parents*. They died in a car crash. I was the only survivor. That kid, he's an orphan now, just like me, except I was a baby. That's why mom and dad adopted me, because my parents were killed."

"Since when did this happen?" Matt was incredulous.

"What do you mean since when? Since forty years ago, you idiot."

"I never heard that story. That's what I was going to tell you before, but you cut me off. Your parents weren't killed. Your mother gave you up."

That got Todd's attention. His eyes tracked Matt with laser intensity.

"Mom *told* me. When I was *seven*. I *asked* her . . ."

"Okay! Okay! Christ, I'm not an imbecile! But you were seven, I was *two*. How do I know what she told you? All I'm saying is I heard differently," Matt countered.

"When was this? And what *exactly* did you hear?" Todd asked in disbelief.

"Jesus, maybe second or third grade? I don't know. You were at a friend's house. I woke up to get a drink of water and I heard mom and dad talking in their room. I looked in and they were going through a box of papers. I didn't want them to see me because I'd get yelled at so . . ."

"Get to the point," Todd said impatiently.

"Right. They kept talking about *her*. If it wasn't for *her*, they would never have you. If it wasn't for *her* making the arrangements, they couldn't have adopted you. That's what they said."

Making the arrangements? That seemed an odd way to put it. Yet, Todd was too angry to give it much thought. "You're lying," he said.

"Yeah, and fuck you too. Why would I lie? That's what I heard," Matt returned the fury.

"Well, then you were dreaming."

"No, I wasn't. It really happened," Matt insisted.

Stalemate.

Todd's jaw was clenched so hard he could have bent steel. He took a deep breath, and when that didn't help. He took one more. He tried not to scream at his brother.

"If that *is* true, and that's a big *if*, then you're saying mom lied to me. Is that right?" Todd leveled his gaze at Matt.

"Oh, no. You're not getting me to say mom is a liar," Matt shook his head.

"I'm definitely going nuts here. How come you never told me this before?"

"You just said it earlier today. We never talked about it. The family never talked about it. Did you ever talk to mom about it again, after that first time you asked her?" Matt was desperately trying to get the focus off himself.

Todd thought for a minute and then spoke.

"No. After she told me, the subject seemed off limits. It's not as if she were totally shocked that I asked. She had to figure I'd notice one day I didn't look like anyone else in the family. But I could see how uncomfortable she was telling me about it. Especially the part about my parents being killed, it made her so sad. I guess I never brought it up again because I didn't want to upset her."

"Where was dad in all of this?" asked Matt.

Todd concentrated. "All I remember is she must have mentioned it to him, because later that night he said something to me."

"What?"

"He said, 'Todd, it's good you know the truth. It's not important how you came to us, only that you did. You're our son and we love you.' It was something like that. Then he winked at me, like it was our secret. End of discussion."

"So, what are you going to do now?" Matt asked cautiously.

"Find out the truth."

"How are you going to do that?"

"Confront mom. How else?" Todd's tone indicated that for now, there would be no more discussion.

Chapter Five

It was a sweltering day. Nardo wiped his brow with an old bandanna. Sipping a Squirt, he carefully scanned the marketplace. Always busy on a Saturday, that was a given. Despite his size, he easily blended in with the crowd. Gringos were everywhere, and no one gave them a second thought. Certainly no one, Mexican or American, would dare make eye contact with him. His demeanor suggested respect be shown. His personal space would not be invaded for any reason. Even the friendly vendors selling jewelry and T-shirts while strolling through the crowd dared not approach him.

He and the Mule were once again at work. What was different about this particular job in the friendly town of Nogales, was that Nardo would not participate in the snatch itself. This time it was the Mule's job. The other difference about these jaunts to Mexico was that no one was to be killed, as long as it could be avoided. It wasn't always necessary to off the mom. All they wanted was the kid. Yet, that also meant moving around a lot. After so many years in this profession, The Stork and the Boss insisted the "acquisitions" come from many varied locations. Different cities, different states, different countries. It was vital to the operation there be no set pattern of killings or kidnappings in any one town or state. That could draw unwanted attention from the authorities. Unwanted attention would put them out of business. They were careful not to let this happen. Business was too good.

So on this particular job, Nardo was in charge of choosing the right family at the right time. Even though he and the Mule hated each other, they worked flawlessly together. Once he found the ideal situation, he would signal to her. That was her cue to try and circle around to position herself in front of the vic, while Nardo remained in the rear. Nardo would cause some kind of minor distraction or commotion, something to get the vic's attention away from the baby. Once the deed was done, the rest was easy. They'd later meet in a safe location. Nardo had an old Dodge Ram van for transportation and he would drive them back to the good ol' US of fucking A.

The only unpleasantness in all this was the Mule would ride along with him in the van. They would appear as husband and wife (which always made Nardo want to retch), obviously on their way home from an afternoon of shopping across the border. The baby would be safely tucked away in the back of the van, hidden behind a compartment that was entirely sound proof. The soundproofing was just a precaution, as they had never been questioned. They had false ID's of course, just in case. The van had never even been stopped for longer than a moment or two. Just a nod, a hello, and waved on through. Being an American certainly had its privileges.

As the marketplace became more and more crowded, Nardo scanned the area looking for the right opportunity. The Mule was playing her part as she bargained with a toothless old woman over some measly looking melons. After stubbornly shelling over a few pesos, she continued on her way. The melons would almost immediately be dumped. Nardo knew well enough the Mule always kept one eye on him, no matter what she was doing, waiting for the sign she knew would eventually come. They'd done this many times before.

It didn't take long before Nardo saw the perfect scenario. A local mother shopping alone with her children. Two young boys followed their madre who pushed a well-worn baby carriage. As they passed by Nardo, he was able to see the infant inside, perhaps six months old. The Boss preferred them a bit younger than that, but hey, you just couldn't be too choosy when it came to stealing babies. You got what you got. Nardo was hoping for a boy, not that it really mattered, but boys were always popular.

He alerted the Mule with a quick nod. Nardo followed the mother at a discreet distance, waiting for the right moment. The boys must have been hungry. As soon as they approached a man cooking chicken on a rickety looking grill, they pulled at their mother's dress, begging for some food. She parked the carriage slightly away from the grill, opened a coin purse, and counted her change. Apparently she only had enough for some warm tortillas which she ordered from the vendor and handed over to the boys. The older one seemed grateful to have anything to eat, but the younger brother felt quite the opposite. As the little boy started to cry and fuss and mama turned her attention toward him, Nardo knew it was time. A few feet away, he knelt down on one knee so that he would be at eye level with the quiet son. He fished candy out of his shirt pocket, and held it out while gesturing to the boy, motioning him to come with a slight cock of his head. The boy watched him carefully, then stuffed the rest

Evil Exchange

of the tortilla into his mouth. He was oblivious to his wailing brother. After a brief inner struggle, the boy shuffled toward Nardo. Step by step, he came closer. Nardo never said a word. He simply held the candy and waited. The boy gave a tentative smile, and Nardo smiled back. Although there were many people passing by, no one paid them any attention.

It was just about that time when mama realized one of her boys had wandered away. She called out, but spotted him before he could answer. Angry with both boys now, she marched over to her eldest, demanding to know where he'd found candy. He tried to explain about the giant gringo, but she wasn't having it. Nardo had disappeared, and she thought her son was telling a story. Still berating him, she grabbed his hand and by the time she had taken the six or seven steps back to her other son (who by now had stopped crying and was enjoying the scene between his mother and brother, glad to have the attention away from himself), the carriage was empty. By the time the mother started to scream, Nardo, the Mule, and the infant had all vanished from sight. No one in the crowd had seen anything.

Chapter Six

Matt felt guilty about telling Todd what he'd heard all those years ago. He couldn't help but feel like a traitor to both his mother and his brother. He begged Todd upon their return to at least reconsider confronting Miriam. Todd said he'd take it under advisement. However, he said it in such a way that it gave Matt the chills. Todd sounded cold and distant, like a robot. Hell, he not only sounded robotic, he *looked* robotic. His face was a rictus of pain. It was obvious Todd's wounds still troubled him, and his muscles had stiffened to the point where he looked like an unoiled Tin Man when he'd gotten out of the truck. Matt also knew it wasn't only the physical pain his brother was experiencing, it was the emotional anguish as well. The combination of these two conditions were so completely intertwined at this point, they couldn't possibly be separated. Todd Walters was one huge raw exposed nerve. The brothers had barely said goodbye.

To his credit, Todd did wait a few hours before calling his mother. During that time, sitting alone in his apartment, Todd must have picked up and put down the phone twenty times. He tried to think about what he would say. *What could he say?* He was absolutely devastated. *How could his mother, of all people, lie like that?* The person he'd loved the most, trusted the most. *How could it be?* But it wasn't just the fact that she lied. It was the impact the lie made on him. He thought about the painful survivor guilt he'd suffered believing he was the only one who lived through the car crash that killed his parents. He thought about all those years of trying to fit into his adopted family when clearly, he was so completely different from them. He'd tried so hard to please them even though they didn't require it. *Was it gratitude that drove me?* At the age of seven, learning you were adopted, that your parents had been killed, and here was this family who had taken you in. Treated you as if you were their own flesh and blood.

Evil Exchange

Was there some kind of subliminal message he was being sent while growing up? That in the back of his mind, he owed them? If not for them, wouldn't he be an orphan? His mind was spinning, his thoughts all jumbled and confused. However, the more he thought about it, and no matter how hard he tried, he still could not think of one single reason which would justify this truly shattering betrayal. Finally, he picked up the phone again, and this time he dialed.

"Hello?"

"Mom, it's Todd."

"Oh, hi son. Did you have a nice weekend? I thought you might come by . . ."

"Mom, please. I need to ask you something. Can you turn the television down? This is really important." Todd was trying to keep his blood pressure from skyrocketing. So far he was unsuccessful.

Miriam abruptly clanged the phone down. Todd could hear laughter in the background. She loved to watch inane sitcoms. The canned laugh track grated on his nerves. Everything irritated him right now. Finally, the noise died down and his mother picked up the phone again.

"What is it? I hope you know that's my favorite show."

"Mom, listen. I have to ask you something," Todd repeated.

Miriam only answered with a sigh.

"When I was a kid, and you told me my parents died in a car crash, did you lie to me?" Todd could hardly believe he'd gotten the words out.

There was a long pause.

"Yes, I did," Miriam spoke softly.

"Why?" Todd's voice trembled with anger. *So it was true.*

"Well . . . because the psychiatrist told me to say it so you wouldn't think about your other parents. That way, you would just concentrate on us as your parents," she said defensively.

What psychiatrist was this? Obviously, there were a lot of things he didn't know. Of all the dumb things in the world to tell a kid, well, it was just unfathomable. Todd's mind raced and raged. Granted, adoption wasn't discussed much forty years ago, and it was handled differently back then. He still found it incomprehensible a doctor would think this would be a healthy way for a child to be raised. Tell him his parents were killed in a car crash and he'll never think about them again? Right. Then it dawned on him that it hadn't worked anyway.

Paris and Soll

If the goal was to get him to *not* think about his birth parents, this lie he'd been told did the exact opposite. It only made him think about them all the more. Well, his birthmother anyway. With crystal clarity, Todd realized he'd thought of her every day of his life. It would be only for a second or two, because the pain was too much to bear. She had died, he had lived. He'd always felt if he thought about it any longer than that, *he* would die. He'd never told anyone. It just wasn't something he could verbalize, even if he wanted to. It wasn't even really a conscious thought, more of a constriction in his chest and a panic of his mind. He wasn't sure if he had ever fully admitted it to himself until this very moment.

"Todd? Are you there?"

Of course he never would have talked about it anyway. Not good old Todd. Todd, the obedient son who didn't want to upset mom or make dad uncomfortable. Okay, so he called his brother an Earthling. So what? Matt thought it was his brother's way of bugging him, but it wasn't, not really. Todd may have said it as a taunt, but he wished more than anything in the world that he were an Earthling too. He simply could not imagine what that would be like.

"Todd!"

Yep, good old Todd. The son who never wanted to rock the boat. Well, right now, this boat was ready to capsize. He cleared his throat and spoke in a barely contained fury.

"Were you *ever* going to tell me the truth?"

"Yes. When you were ready," Miriam stated as if he were a half-wit.

Todd couldn't help but think to himself. *When I was ready?* He was a grown man, had been for a long time. How old would he have to be to be ready?

"Don't you mean when *you* were ready?"

"Now, Todd . . . "

"Gotta go, Mom." Todd clicked the off button. It took all his self-control not to hurl the phone across the room. Not such a good son any longer, he'd never hung up on his mother in his life.

There was a tornado in his head. A buzzing in his ears. Fueled by rage, he'd been pacing while on the phone. Now, he tried to sit, but it hurt too much. It wasn't so much his body as his heart. He'd never been so wounded. He felt like he couldn't breathe. He couldn't stay still. He got up and paced again.

Remarkable how she hadn't even asked him how he found out. So, the horrible truth was in fact a horrible lie. All those years, the subconscious fear of riding in a car with anyone else driving, being afraid of a repeat performance. The fright and trauma of watching the accident today. Seeing that little boy, reliving what he thought was a primal wound from his own infancy. It was all too much. *What a waste.* The range of emotion was simply too much to bear. He could not get a grip. He felt crazed, delirious. On a scale of one to one hundred, Todd's anger was five million and rising. Todd ripped open his backpack and found the vicodin. He swallowed three of them dry. All he wanted was to make the pain, the anger, and the hurt go away. He could slide on his back on asphalt a hundred times and it would never hurt this bad. Todd's resentment may have been at the forefront, but the depth of his despair was unlike anything else he had ever known. His divorce had been a cakewalk compared to this.

His life kaleidoscoped in front of his eyes. Todd remembered when he was about nine or ten. He was at the Jersey shore. *What was it about that place, anyway?* He was swimming in the water, best day of his life, until he saw the fin. It was huge, and heading directly toward him. Panicked, he swam near another boy who had a raft and hitched a ride to shore absolutely terrified. He knew it was a shark, even though no one else had seen it. So great was his fright, he didn't go near the water for a very long time. He recalled another time, as a teenager, he'd put some homemade gunpowder in an old brass doorknob and almost blown his arm off. That was stupid and scary. And the time his date put mescaline in his drink one night? *Jesus Christ!* The hallucinations were especially terrifying considering he didn't know what was happening to him. He remembered how he'd lain on the floor of his date's apartment for hours, thinking if he let go of the carpet, he'd fall off the face of the earth. He thought she was trying to kill him. Even after it wore off, he was dizzy for a week. Later, he learned she'd given it to him for fun. Todd couldn't imagine where she'd gotten that idea.

Todd thought he might be going mad, as the frightening memories rushed back at him. There were some chilling episodes and some really bad near misses now that he really thought about it. *Too many. Way too many.* It was weird considering how always tried to keep his life low key, he had always tried not to draw attention to himself. Still, things seemed to happen to him. Yeah, he'd had some scary shit happen in his life, some very bad experiences. But compared to this weekend? He'd barely escaped death, watched people die, and found out his entire life was an enormous lie. *How was that for fucked up?* He could take every bad moment, combine it with every scare, every disappointment, every hurt he'd ever had, roll it all up into one, and it would still be minuscule in comparison to this. There was no scale for this, at least not one that had been invented yet. Exhausted from the rampage in his head, and empty from the hole in his heart, Todd found his way to bed. Sleep would be light years away.

CHAPTER SEVEN

Boots Beaumont yawned. Next to him lay Julie, a beautiful light-skinned Bahamian woman who'd been sharing his bed for some time. You would think living on the gorgeous island of Eleuthera would be absolute paradise. And it was, most of the time. At the age of fifty-five, and with a bullet still lodged in his skull, Boots Beaumont had retired from the business of being a private investigator in the city of New York. It was not a big surprise he had never lacked for work considering where he lived, but after years of tracking people down and having his fair share of dangerous dealings with shady characters, getting shot in the head seemed to be a sign to hang it all up. He also knew he wanted out of the city and the cold. He never wanted to see another winter with snow. If he had his way (which he usually did), it would be warm weather and white sandy beaches for the rest of his life.

Amazingly, Boots had somehow escaped matrimony and didn't have any kids. None that he knew of anyway. And since he'd always been a pretty frugal guy, he had some money saved up, and with it bought a primo sixty-foot motorsailer that was now anchored in the marina of the quaint town of Governor's Harbour. To some, it may have been a humble accommodation, but to Boots it was bliss. He spent some time fixing up the old gal, and when he was done, and for the first time in his life, he was absolutely bored to death. So on a whim, he bought himself a used lap top, intending to write a memoir about some of his experiences, first as a intelligence officer, and then as a private eye. Instead the book turned into a novel, which much to Boots' surprise, was picked up by the first publisher he submitted it to. Once the first book was published, he found his fingers could not stop typing, and he turned out an astonishing amount of work. His mysteries caught on with the public, and he became a rich man. He

Evil Exchange

could have lived in a mansion, but preferred a simple existence on the boat. Life was good.

The only hitch in the giddy-up was the naked woman next to him. For someone who preferred a simple life, his relationship with Julie was anything but. She was a wild woman. Of course under cover (so to speak), that was not a problem. But, outside of the bedroom, well, Julie was your basic lunatic. Their relationship was a volatile one. Julie was hot blooded, which was a big plus in some ways, Boots had to admit, but mostly it caused problems. The fact that Julie was a local, and Boots was not, also caused problems. Sure, he should know better than to be messing around with someone half his age, but he figured, what the hell? He could live with the woman's volcanic eruptions. He could live with the stony faced glares from the locals who worked at Club Med when he and Julie went out for an evening. He could live with the occasional threats that came his way from those same men. He could also live with the unspoken approval seen in the eyes of the male tourists who vacationed there as well. Julie could be a pain in the ass, but she also had certain skills. Well, let's just say that Boots was more than willing to take the good with the bad. She could love him one minute and in the next brandish a butcher knife at his throat. She came and she went when she wanted to. She was either schizophrenic, bipolar, or both. Boots didn't care. She was a challenge. She kept the excitement in his life. He never knew which Julie he would turn up. It certainly kept him on his toes. When things were good, as they were at the moment, she was best at keeping him on his back.

"Boots?" Julie purred.

"Yeah . . ."

"Tell me the story again."

"What? Oh, no baby. I've told you that story a million times," he groaned.

"I don't care, tell me again," she pouted.

Boots sighed. *What could it hurt?* After what she'd just done for him, he could indulge her one more time.

"And don't skip any parts this time," she added.

"Okay, okay. Jesus, you're demanding. Let's see, it was my first day of officer's candidate school. I'd just gotten out of my car and started towards the administration building at Camp Smith in Peekskill, New York. A stern looking soldier with icy, pale blue eyes blocked my path. 'Burp!' he said. At least I thought that's what he said and I didn't quite know how to respond. So I said, 'hi' and smiled. Then he shouted 'Urp!' and I couldn't help but wonder what he had for breakfast, or if he were speaking in some kind of code. I asked him where would I find my barrack assignment, but he shouted again. 'Urp soldier!'

"I was at a loss and told him I didn't understand. He repeated it again, 'Urp soldier!' He was getting pissed, and I was totally confused. After we stared each other down for a long minute, he finally said in a huff, 'Immediate Response Please! IRP!' So *I* said, 'okay, hi!'

'You will address me as Sir, you fucking potato ass,' he spat. As soon as I said, 'Yes, Sir!' he seemed satisfied and stormed off.

"Not a very good way to begin the day. Here I was, in the Special Forces Reserves, and our troop was sent to Camp Smith for our OCS training. We were *supposedly* an elite squad, but I didn't feel real elite after that encounter. I pretty much felt like an idiot.

"Anyway, the rest of the day was normal army FUBAR. Fucked Up Beyond All Recognition. Hurry up and wait to be told what to do. So, we waited. Finally, the soldier who had IRP'd me came to the barracks and told us he was our training sergeant. He said he must always be addressed as Sergeant or Sir. I think I had that one down. Then he put us through marching drills, close formation drills, rifle drills, you name it. He marched us almost to death. He was a sadistic bastard. So, in retaliation, we made up a special hymn for our Sarge. You know how in the army, they want you to sing while you march to keep the cadence?"

He looked over at Julie to see if she might have fallen asleep, but no such luck. She was paying attention and nodded to this as if she were hearing it for the first time, which she certainly was not. So Boots continued.

"So, we'd all be marching along and this one guy, Dennis, would sing very solemnly. 'Hymn.'

Then we'd all follow with, 'Hymn. Hymn. Fuck him!' Our Sarge never said a word, but he always had a smile on his face when he heard his hymn. At least we had a lot of spirit in our troop.

"So our training life went on like that, day after day. Toward the end of one week, we were awakened at four a.m., told to dress, and fall into formation outside. Immediately. We were divided into groups of three, blindfolded, and each group was put in a separate jeep or truck. We knew what was coming. Our survival training was about to commence. We were driven around for about an hour in what seemed like circles. All of a sudden our truck stopped. We were hustled off and told to wait until the truck was gone before we took off our blindfolds. Our mission was to figure out where we were, and to find our way back to camp.

"After we heard the truck drive away, we took off our blindfolds and found ourselves smack dab in the middle of a dense forest on a mountain top. The sun was just starting to come up. My guys looked at me and said, 'Marsh, do you know where we are?' They knew I had grown up in Stony Point, just across the Hudson from Peekskill, so I was pretty familiar with the area. I looked around, oriented myself, then pointed out the way.

"So we walked for a while and started down the mountainside. We came to a road, which I knew had to be Route 9, which curved around the majestic Bear Mountain section of the Hudson. I knew that camp was only a few miles to the east on that road. So I told the guys that we could walk back to camp in about forty minutes. I also knew that the other guys probably wouldn't make it back for hours, so I suggested to my guys that we find a spot hidden from the road and take a break. We found a sunny slope, laid down, and took a nap.

"We woke up to the smell of food. There was a hot dog vendor who had set up shop in a clearing nearby, hoping to catch some of the local traffic coming by. Not your traditional breakfast, but we thought hot dogs and soda for breakfast were brilliant."

Boots stopped again to see if Julie was still listening. He was sick to death of the damn story, but she seemed to never tire of it. She prodded him with her foot to continue. Boots sighed.

"Okay. So after we ate, we figured we'd better head back to base. We were walking along the shoulder of the highway when my right foot slipped into a crevice between two rocks. My buds tried to pull me loose, but my foot came out of my boot. For the life of me, I could not get the boot unstuck from the rocks. It was as if it had been cemented in. So I had no choice but to leave it there. I ended up taking off the other boot to walk back, which took a while since I was dodging rocks and pebbles in my socks.

"We got back to camp around noon and none of the other troops had shown up. So we headed for our barracks. Out of nowhere, our sergeant appeared. He took one look at me in my stocking feet and screamed, 'WHERE ARE YOUR BOOTS, SOLDIER?'

'Well, Sir. They had an accident, Sir.' I responded.

"He muttered 'Why me?' and wandered off. Word of the loss of my boots got around camp by the end of the day. When I got to the mess hall that night, one of my buddies said, 'Hey! Bootless is here!' Then someone else said, 'Hey Boots!'

"So from then on, it stuck. Instead of Marsh, I was called Boots. I've always kind of liked it."

"Before you told me that story, I thought your nickname had something to do with you tracking people down," Julie snuggled closer.

"Oh, you mean after the army, when I was a PI?"

"Mm-hmm." Julie was doing more than snuggling now.

Boots groaned. *Could this woman never get enough?*

"I can see you still remember something else from your days in the army," Julie giggled.

"Oh yeah? What's that?"

"You still know how to stand at attention."

"Well, parts of me do anyway," Boots answered and jumped her.

Chapter Eight

Todd stayed home for a few days recovering from his wounds. All of them. In one particularly weak moment he called Trina. He figured surely by now she would have come to her senses and be consumed with worry and remorse. He might as well have just gotten out the Morton's salt and applied it directly. The roommate answered and informed him that Trina would not speak to him, but wished him well. Oh, and by the way, would he be so kind as to drop off the negligee? Apparently she needed it. Then without taking a breath, the roomie suggested since he and Trina were obviously over, would he like to take her out? Todd was simply speechless and hung up on her, which apparently was becoming quite a trend of late. Todd couldn't believe her nerve. Was he some kind of interchangeable boy-toy? Okay, boy-toy might be going a bit too far, even he had to admit. *What was it with women these days anyway? Were they all taking some new kind of hormonal supplement that grew balls for them?* Todd was enraged and felt as if the down button had been pushed on the express elevator to rock bottom and he didn't know where the emergency off switch was. In a fit of fury, he took the negligee and gleefully jammed it down the trash chute. It didn't really make him feel better, but it did give him a twinge of satisfaction.

So he brooded. About his life, his mom, his injuries. You would think with all the venom coursing through his system, his sores would fester. Much to his dismay, he was healing quite rapidly. While his body might be in good shape, his mind had taken a deep-sea dive, and man, was it ever black down there.

Content to wallow through the muck of self-pity, Todd screened his calls. Matt called. Miriam called. The roommate called, again. *Sheesh.* Todd didn't want to talk to anyone, preferring isolation. So far, he hadn't gotten any work-related calls, but knew they'd be coming. Building and repairing television stations made you a guy who was in demand much of the time. At least he knew he wouldn't lack for work. It wasn't much consolation, but it was about all he had left at the moment.

His only diversion during those cloistered few days was reading. He'd quickly finished the book Matt had given him. Todd was absolutely intrigued by the writer. The picture of Boots Beaumont was a black and white photo on the back cover. The author looked more like a business executive than a former PI Distinguished, fifty-ish, light gray hair, lanky build. The book was a powerful story filled with twists and turns, macho characters and beautiful women. Todd was absolutely hooked. During the time at home, he only went out once, and that was only to pick up a few more of Beaumont's paperbacks. He devoured them. It was the only thing that took his mind off his troubles.

Eventually Matt gave up leaving phone messages, and started in on emails. He left Todd a message saying how concerned he was, and left the name and number of Katy's psychiatrist, just in case.

After reading it, Todd angrily shut down the computer without sending a reply. *So my brother thinks I'm a nutcase now?* Thinking things couldn't get much worse, he went back to Beaumont's *Sea of Blood*, which he had just started. Screw real life, fiction was the only thing that made sense to him right now.

It was midnight when the phone woke him out of a dead sleep. Automatically, he answered it, forgetting he wasn't speaking with anyone these days. CBS was calling, asking him to come and find a short in their television antenna, the one on top of the Empire State Building. *Great*.

By two a.m. Todd was hanging by a rope on the outside of the antenna tower, one hundred and seven stories up. Fifth Avenue sparkled below. Todd felt as if he was suspended in space, and that time did not exist. He had to work his way on the outside of the tower to reach the spot where the antenna had broken. The experience was surreal. Here he was, climbing on a tower like a kid on a jungle gym, except that it was the dead of night, and he was more than a thousand feet in the air. The air was cool and crisp, and despite the safety belt digging into his sore back, Todd felt alive for the first time in days. His work was always exhilarating, if not sometimes downright nerve-racking. Though Todd rarely admitted it to anyone, he did have a fear of heights. He didn't usually do the work of a steeplejack, but tonight was an emergency, and Simon, the head electrician who accompanied him, was too big to fit through the gap in order to get to the antenna. Actually, Todd's fear kept him alert at all times, and when a job was completed, he always felt a huge sigh of relief that he had survived and conquered gravity one more time.

Todd was able to find the short quickly. He made his repairs without too much trouble. Time to pack it in. As he made his way back around to the other side of the building, an enormous gust of wind almost blew him off the antenna. He froze in fright. He called out to Simon, but the wind whipped his words away. It was all he could do to hold on. It seemed like an eternity, but the wind finally died down. He called out to Simon again, and this time got a response. Intuitively, Simon knew to talk to Todd in such a way as to distract him from the paralyzing fear of falling, safety harness or not. Todd needed to hear his voice, to use it as a beacon to get back safely to the landing. Simon started carrying on about the Yankees and how they were going to take it all this year. The baseball litany calmed Todd just enough to make his way back in and down to the landing. He was shaking from head to toe, and close to hyperventilating. Simon kept right on talking even though he knew Todd would never remember a word he said. All Todd could think of was how he'd just cheated death again for the third time in less than a week. *What was happening to him anyway? Was this something he was bringing on himself? Was he somehow sabotaging his own safety?* Still badly shaken, Todd had plenty of questions and a shortage of answers. Maybe it was time to call a shrink.

CHAPTER NINE

His head throbbed. It certainly could be due to the fact that he was hung over, having spent the better part of the evening drinking and dancing with Julie at Club Med. Or, it could be a drop in the barometer. Boots could always tell when a storm was coming, courtesy of the bullet in his head. His unwanted souvenir from the Big Apple was never wrong, and it was a pain in the ass.

Boots slowly and carefully got out of bed, trying not to wake Julie. She was not a morning person, and if you woke her too early, well, let's just say you'd never make that mistake again. He filled the coffee maker with Blue Mountain and waited for it to brew. When it was done, he took a cup and went up on deck to check the sky. Sure enough, clouds were gathering on the horizon and the wind was starting to pick up. It was still early, but the storm would show up sometime that afternoon.

Oddly enough, when Boots was shot, it had nothing to do with his former profession. Granted, over the years he'd had some tense moments, and more than a few near misses, but nothing really life threatening. He had always carried a gun for protection though, just in case. He'd pulled it a few times, but that was always more for show than anything else. He'd never fired a shot at anyone, never had to. Of course, in self-defense, he knew he would not hesitate to pull the trigger. His philosophy was when push came to shove, he'd fire first and ask questions later. It had never happened though, thank God. However, writing about it was different. When he worked on a novel, he wrote as if it were second nature, as if he'd been killing all his life. In truth, Boots Beaumont had never taken a life, not even in the military. Of course he had combat training in the army, but he'd never seen live combat. After he became an intelligence agent, he'd trained extensively in covert operations. He knew how to kill an

Evil Exchange

enemy sixty-four different ways. Actually, he knew how to do a lot of things. He became a specialist in tracking. He learned everything he could about computers, electronics, and weaponry. He used his superior deciphering skills cracking codes. He may have been mediocre as a soldier, but he excelled at being an intelligence officer. He had a bright future. Then one day, a routine training session went horribly awry and a good buddy was killed. Beaumont may have been an expert at many things, but none of his skills or abilities could help change what happened. He could not bring his friend back to life. Unable to cope with the loss caused by a human error, and which was quickly swept under the rug by his commanding officer, Boots became disillusioned, and opted out of the military.

Once he established his life as a civilian, he decided to use his skills for private investigative work. He was well versed in surveillance. He had also developed excellent computer skills while in the army, and could easily navigate the Internet, often finding valuable information pertaining to a case or client. In the beginning of his career, Beaumont was hired on by a large firm, where he learned the ropes before striking out on his own. He quickly developed a solid reputation. He was discreet and thorough. He not only handled a lot of divorce cases, he was often hired by insurance companies to uncover fraud. He located and interviewed witnesses, investigated scams, and chased after missing persons.

Boots was a busy man for twenty-five years, and for the most part enjoyed his work. At times a particular job might be dull or routine, but overall, there was enough variety to keep his brain cells stimulated. There were also plenty of women who caused another type of stimulation, but he never had any complaints. Always the professional, Boots never dated a client until after a case was closed. He also never dated any married women as he did have an ethical code. Besides, he knew only too well what jealous husbands could do. Women found him fascinating, intriguing, and mysterious. His job was not all that glamorous, but he let them think what they wanted. He had plenty of connections, snitches, and police contacts. He didn't make a great deal of money, but as a single guy, he was comfortable. He could afford nice clothes, good investigative equipment and gadgets. Most importantly, he could afford to travel between cases, which is how he ended up in the Bahamas. He loved warm weather. Over the years, Boots had visited many islands, but when he sailed into Governor's Harbor in Eleuthera one fine spring afternoon, he knew he found nirvana. Even though it would be some years before he made it back, he knew he belonged in that magical place.

If it weren't for being shot, Boots probably would have continued working for quite a few more years in New York. He was fairly content to continue delving into the seedier side of human nature. As he approached the age of fifty, he was in good physical condition, still in demand for his services (both professionally and personally), had no debt, no baggage. He was liked and retained by men and women equally, entertained women exclusively, and had exceptional male friendships. To sum it up, Boots Beaumont was a happening guy.

However on one cold, winter night, Boots stepped outside a bar where he had just spent the evening kicking butt at the pool table with some of his buddies. He'd used up the better part of a week tailing a cheating spouse, and would be writing his final report in the morning, then taking a few well deserved days off. He'd had one too many beers while jawing with the guys, and all he wanted was to find a cab and get home to a warm bed.

As he left the bar, he didn't see a cab anywhere. He swore under his breath, and started to walk towards First Avenue. He hoped at least the frigid air might speed the sobering process along. About halfway up the block he heard a thwup, a sound of something moving rapidly through the air. Then he felt a slight painful clunk on the top of his head. Thinking someone had thrown something out a window, or that a piece of ice had fallen and hit his temple, Boots put his hand to his head and felt a wet spot. At first he thought it was water from the ice, but as he looked at his palm he realized it was blood. His hand was covered in blood. *Must have been a damn sharp icicle*, he thought. He used his other hand to wipe away some of the blood, but it was just coming too quickly. By this time, he realized he was in some serious trouble. Not only were his hands covered in blood, but half his face as well, and it was getting difficult to see.

He ran down the street and was able to flag down a car idling at the side of the curb. As he knocked on the window, the occupants looked at him in horror and locked the doors. A moment later, the car peeled away. *Where were all the good Samaritans when you needed them?* Boots was scared, confused, and afraid he would bleed to death if help didn't come along soon. The businesses in the area were closed, and all he could think about was that he needed to get to the hospital. Pronto.

He found his way to a corner, just in time to see a cab. He waved it down, and got lucky when the driver agreed to take him to the emergency room. The man was a well-seasoned taxi driver who had seen it all and then some. As far as he was concerned, as long as he got his fare, he'd pick up a customer, even if he was covered in blood. He did ask however, for the money in advance, just in case Boots passed out during the brief five-minute ride. Boots was able to pull his pool winnings out of his pocket and hand the bills over to the driver. He would have paid him anything. The driver simply nodded in return and handed him a box of tissues to help stem the crimson flow.

Evil Exchange

After being dropped off, Boots was able to make it into the hospital while still on his feet. He was surprised to find that instead of the usual question and answer routine, a nurse took one look at him and found a gurney so that he could lie down. The nurse then asked what happened, and when Boots said he was hit by a flying icicle, she shook her head in sympathy. She said the doctor would be there soon to suture him up. Much to his embarrassment, Boots asked if it would hurt. He'd always prided himself on being a tough guy, as it was part of his persona. The truth was that he hated needles, and the thought of being sewn up gave him the willies. The nurse laughed at him and said if it did hurt too much, she would sit on him to keep him quiet. Boots took one look at her and realized that not only she keep him quiet, she would kill him. She must have tipped the scales at a good three hundred pounds.

The bleeding stopped long enough for the doc to take a look and send him off for x-rays. When he got back, Boots was met by two police officers, one male, and one female. Oddly, they looked almost identical. Though he knew many of New York's finest, he didn't recognize either one of them. By this time the pain was starting to set in, and it was getting difficult for Boots to concentrate, but he tried. The male officer asked him if he'd been shot, and he said no. The female officer smirked and said, "Well you have now." Waiting for an explanation, Boots finally realized through his foggy brain, that the thwup sound he had heard was gunfire. He couldn't believe he didn't recognize the sound at the time. After all, he had heard it before. Granted it had been a long time since he'd heard live gun shots, and he couldn't recall that he'd ever heard it while walking down the street, minding his own business. He felt as if he were starting to unravel.

Tweedle-de-dum and Tweedle-de-dee informed him that the x-ray clearly showed a bullet lodged between the scalp and skull. It had entered about two inches above the right eye and traveled under the skin until it ran out of steam and settled down. It was quite a miracle the skull had not been penetrated, they said. If Boots had been looking straight ahead at the time of the shooting, he'd have died instantly. What saved him was the fact that it was as cold as a kettle of dry ice on Halloween, and his head was bent down against the weather.

Still somewhat coherent, Boots asked why the police were there. It seemed odd he was getting a medical diagnosis from the two of them rather than the doctor, but then, everything seemed weird. They explained the hospital had informed them a gunshot wound had been brought in, and by law, they had to investigate. After some further questioning and Boots telling them of the location where he was injured, they revealed that a woman had been shot in the thigh by a roof top sniper on the same block earlier in the evening. It was somewhat of a relief to Boots, not that someone else got shot, but that apparently it was just a random event. It wasn't a disgruntled client or someone he had helped put in jail. It was just another run-of-the-mill maniac loose in the city.

The fun and games were almost over for the evening. The doctor quickly stitched him up and then released him, saying it would be wise to leave the bullet where it was. It was not a danger to him in any way. The only danger could come from having it removed, he said. Removal meant surgery, and surgery always posed a risk. The twin beat cops offered to drive him home. Boots was grateful.

Little was said on the way. Even with a throbbing head, Boots was able to take a quick, but thorough inventory of his life thus far. Sadly, it didn't take long. His conclusion was one of the most basic and fundamental philosophies that existed. Life was too short. After all the years of danger and intrigue (well, that was an exaggeration, but he was allowed to take some liberties after being shot in the head), he decided he no longer wanted to be a private investigator. He no longer wanted to take risks, no matter how small, and he no longer wanted to chase after bad guys whether it was online or on the street. He no longer wanted to catch a cheating husband in bed with another woman. He no longer wanted to try and find a child who was kidnapped by a parent wounded by divorce. He no longer wanted to see, hear, or know what terrible things people would and could do to one another. He wanted out.

Snapping back to reality, he realized the coffee was long cold, and the bullet still itched as he sat on the deck. Boots didn't normally dwell on the past, unless it was an experience he could use in one of his detective novels. He wasn't the type who spent much time seeking inner peace, he'd already found it on the island. He also wasn't one to reminisce about the good old days, or what might have been. Life was what it was. He was happy doing his thing, writing blood soaked mysteries, working on his boat, and staying on Julie's good side whenever possible. Keep it simple. That was his philosophy these days. Well, almost. Julie was anything but simple. *Hell, we have to have some challenges*, he said to himself.

Boots nearly jumped out of his skin when Julie spoke. He'd been so lost in thought, he never heard her approach.

"Someone is looking for you," she said, wiping the sleep out of her beautiful eyes.

"Jesus Christ, woman. You scared the hell out of me. Who is looking for me?" Boots wanted his heart to stop hammering, and the itching was getting unbearable. *What the fuck was she talking about anyway?* His system automatically went on alert as he scouted the boat and nearby dock.

Evil Exchange

"He's not here. But he will be," Julie intoned.

This was getting freaky. Julie had done lots of weird things before, but she'd never acted like this. It was as if she were in a trance or something. Obviously, something in her brain was misfiring at the moment.

"Okay, honey. Come sit down, will ya?" Boots spoke to her as if she were a child.

"Don't talk to me that way, asshole. I am not a child, and I am not crazy."

"No, of course not . . . I just meant . . . well, *what are* you talking about?" Boots was trying to avoid a confrontation. Thank God there weren't any sharp objects nearby.

"I had a dream. I saw him in my sleep. There is a man looking for you. Well, not yet. He will be though. He will come to see you. You have to talk to him. He needs some help, and you're the only one who can help him."

Julie remained standing, with her hands on her hips. She was wide awake now. She was also naked except for some skimpy underwear. It was her natural state of dress, or undress, as often as possible. Boots rarely complained. Yet at the moment, it seemed strange to be having this conversation with her sans clothes. He found a beach towel nearby and put it around her arms. She seemed to notice the change in temperature for the first time and shivered slightly.

"Storm's coming," Boots said trying to distract her.

"Man's coming. Not yet. Not for a while, but he will. I saw him. In my dream."

"Sure babe, whatever you say," Boots sighed. He'd never had such a crazy girlfriend.

CHAPTER TEN

Thankfully work was keeping him busy. General Electric had built some new television and broadcast antennas and wanted them tested. They were erected in a field on an antenna farm in Cazenovia, New York, a suburb of Syracuse. Todd had been part of the original design team, and was to fly there with the chief engineer of the station, his assistant, and the station's engineering consultant and his assistant. Todd couldn't help but feel he should have an assistant of his own to keep up with these guys.

But he was a one-man show as he boarded the American Airlines Fokker F-100 at New York's LaGuardia airport, and he let his mind relax and wander a bit. Todd had been so focused on his job lately he conveniently and purposely forgot all about seeing a shrink. Now as he allowed himself to think about it again, he couldn't believe he'd even entertained the idea at all. After all, there was nothing really wrong with him. Despite everything, he thought he was doing all right. He could handle things. Yes, he was still pissed off at Miriam, but the sting of Trina's abrupt departure was fading. His injuries were healing, and both the accident he and Matt witnessed and his more recent scare on the Empire State building were now tucked away in a deep, dark recess of his brain. Funny how the mind can so quickly dispatch a frightening experience and then simply ignore it. The memory is there, but the brain must protect itself from reliving it time and again. So off it goes, safely stowed away in the mental attic. Todd thought of it as self-preservation, but it may have been nothing more than a good excuse not to dwell on the recent events and near misses of late. He did have to admit the anger was still pretty intense, and he knew the only way to quell it was to try and redirect it. He was working long hours, and had started jogging in the mornings. Any spare time was spent with a Boots Beaumont novel. That way he could keep himself occupied so he wouldn't have to deal with anything else. If

Evil Exchange

he were to admit it, he was still keeping the family at a distance, communicating with Matt only by email, and of course with Miriam, not at all. He knew he'd been shoving all sorts of things out of his conscious thoughts these days. He rationalized it all by deciding it would be best to think about it all later. He just needed some time and things would get back to normal. Yeah, he was kidding himself. *So what?*

Todd took a window seat and made polite chitchat with the chief engineer from G.E., Larry. The plane was designed to hold about eighty passengers, but it was only about half full. The flight attendants did their shtick as the plane taxied down the runway. The pilot came on and said to sit back and relax, they'd been cleared for departure.

Todd leaned back in his seat and looked out the window. The engines roared to takeoff power as the plane barreled down the tarmac. Jolted out of his reverie, Todd suddenly noticed the engine noise didn't sound right. He glanced over at his seatmate, and Larry stared back at him with a stunned expression. With the plane gaining speed, they both knew something was seriously wrong. The jet finally lifted off, but two seconds later, all noise stopped as the massive machine fell back to earth. Landing with a gut churning thud, there was some runway left, and fortunately, the Fokker F-100 managed to brake to a stop at the edge of a ditch.

There was absolute dead silence on the plane. A moment later, the pilot came on the PA system and said (in the irritating matter-of-fact drone that pilots seem to have) one of the engines had failed. No apology for the terrifying take-off and mind numbing landing. No expression of regret for abruptly for falling from the sky. Everyone was simply instructed to stay on the plane. Todd couldn't help but wonder what choice they had. What did the crew think they were going to do? Overpower the flight attendants, open the doors, and jump twenty feet down to the ground? The pilot said the mechanics would come take a look and fix the problem. *Oh, goody.*

During their confinement, Todd and the engineer did discuss the possibility of aborting the flight. If they weren't held captive, a train, bus, or mule would have been better form of transport as far as they were concerned. However, knowing the meeting and test they were scheduled for were of the utmost importance, they decided to leave their fate in the hands of the airline, as there seemed to be little other choice. Three times the mechanics came in to the cabin and told the pilot to "try it now." After the third test, both engines fired perfectly, and the jet was declared fit to fly. The passengers collectively held their breath, and puckered their sphincters. With extreme anxiety, they took off without a hitch. When Todd realized this time they would stay in the air, he let out a sigh of relief along with everyone else. No longer immobilized with the fear of hurtling back to earth, he truly could not believe that not one person had asked to be released from their aviation prison during the whole ordeal. Cazenovia must be a heck of a place if it was that important for all these folks to almost die to get there. He shook his head and thought how like sheep they all were. How trusting they all were to leave it up to a pilot and co-pilot they couldn't even see, and a trio of grease monkeys who slightly resembled the three stooges, with their lives. Even the flight attendants seemed calm and unaffected, as if it were no big deal and this happened all the time. He felt like slapping one of them.

During the remainder of the flight, Todd couldn't help but think that somehow the fates had decided once again to spare him an untimely death. This was becoming a frightening pattern. He felt his very existence was being threatened over and over again. Stay tuned folks for the next episode of: *Will he survive or will he perish?* Todd felt as if he were losing the precious hold on sanity he'd struggled so hard to get back as of late. Somehow, through no choice of his own, he'd gotten involved in a mind-boggling game of involuntary Russian roulette. This was some kind of horrible merry-go-round, and he wanted nothing more than to get off. *What the hell was happening, and why was it happening to him?* He contemplated that particular thought and many others while white-knuckling it to Cazenovia.

Chapter Eleven

It had been a long day for Sheila Stiles. She'd spent most of the day communicating with clients over the phone, via the Internet, and in person. The last couple who'd come into the office had been most difficult. They just couldn't understand why they were not able to request gender, eye color, hair color, nationality, etc. Sheila explained over and over again the selection was limited. They might have two options to choose from at the very most. The couple argued at the prices she was charging, they should have more of a choice, get the most out of their money as it were. $100,000 wasn't pocket change after all. Trying to be patient, Sheila reminded them when the time came and a baby was available, they would be notified. They would then be able see the child before making their final decision. Then it was a simple yes or no. Sheila also reminded them they had contacted her, not the other way around. There were plenty of prospective parents out there, just waiting for a baby to adopt. She also pointed out the fact that they were adopting here, right in the U.S. They weren't flying off to Russia or China, now were they? Stiles justified her fees by providing would be parents with babies without all the red tape, expense, and hassle of international adoption. Apparently the clients still hadn't finished whining and complaining, wanting to get in the last word. They continued with the nit-picking. Finally, Sheila could no longer take it. In a fit of fury, she stood up from her chair, put hands on hips, and raised her voice. "Do you want a baby or not?"

The corporate husband and wife quickly backed down. Of course they wanted a child they assured her. They'd already been through so much and were at the desperation point. They knew how long the waiting list was to adopt through a traditional agency. They didn't have years. She let them babble on even though she'd heard it all before. They were a fast track couple whose lifestyle had ultimately put them into this bind. After years of working and achieving success at their respective careers, they realized it was time to start a family. They couldn't be faulted for trying, tackling the job of pregnancy as if it were nothing more than another every day task. Everything else in their lives had gone according to plan, this would too. As if it were that easy. It was a stunning blow to discover making a baby wasn't just a simple undertaking. By the time they'd made it to an infertility specialist, time was in short supply. Still, they gave it their best shot. Pills, in-vitro, they tried it all. More time and money wasted without results. Mr. and Mrs. We-Deserve-To-Have-It-All simply could not believe their rotten luck, and knew there just had to be an alternative for people such as themselves. They started asking discreet questions, made some inquiries on the web, and finally connected with another couple who had retained the services of Ms. Sheila Stiles, Attorney at Law. Finally, their tale of woe came to an end, and after discussing a few more general details, Sheila shooed them out of her office, saying she would be in touch when she had something available.

Sheila Stiles had originally started her practice in general law. Drawing up wills, filing divorce papers, a personal injury case here and there, once in a blue moon. a minor criminal case or two. It was all incredibly boring. To Sheila it was not the way to make serious money, but she kept at it for it was all she knew. She continued the struggle and the tedium for a few years before representing a man of Hungarian heritage by the name of Janos Nardofsky. Nardofsky was accused of petty theft. Sheila managed to get him off without any jail time and Janos was grateful. He told her if she ever needed any extra help, or any kind of special errands, he was her man. As they parted ways, Sheila knew instinctively they would cross paths again. Janos, who insisted being called Nardo, was an unusual character whose dark side fascinated Sheila.

It wasn't until she represented a doctor for medical malpractice that an idea started to take shape. The doctor was Wendell Colby, OB/GYN. When he came to Sheila, his practice consisted of performing abortions. In his earlier years, he'd been a traditional obstetrician who monitored pregnancies and delivered babies. As time went on, the requests for termination increased, until it became the bulk of his business. Eventually, he quit the business of birthing all together and converted his medical office into an abortion clinic. He had to install security cameras and bulletproof glass in the reception area as his reputation grew and Pro-Lifers targeted his office. There was even a period of time Colby wore a bullet proof vest after some particularly vicious hate mail threatened him and his staff. He continued his work however without much interruption, other than an occasional demonstration or two. His practice was very busy. He felt justified in providing a service that was so in demand, and which of course was perfectly legal.

One day, a young Hispanic woman came to him in her first trimester. Dr. Colby performed the procedure, just as he had hundreds of times before. The young woman went home and died later that evening. She had an allergic reaction to the post surgery medication that caused the uterus to contract back to its normal size. It was an unfortunate and uncommon occurrence. Her parents, after finding out what happened, were so overcome with grief they hired a lawyer to sue Colby for negligence. A desperate Wendell needed representation, and fast. He recalled Sheila from a newspaper article he'd read about another malpractice case she'd won. The article was not the most flattering portrayal of the aggressive Ms. Stiles, but it did print her track record when it came to acquittals. Colby never hesitated for a moment and immediately hired her. She was able to get the charges dropped before the case ever went to trial. Her tactics were legal, although rather cruel, as she claimed ignorance on the young woman's part to properly fill out the medical form required by Dr. Colby's office. The parents and their attorney didn't stand a chance. The end result was that Colby became another grateful client.

After the case was closed, and the fees were paid, Colby and Stiles struck up an odd sort of friendship. They met over coffee two or three times a week, and griped to one another about life's injustices. They shared frustration at the inequality of long hours versus what they considered to be meager compensation. They both concluded that in their respective fields, they were receiving little return on large investments of time and effort. Not to mention the fact Colby lived with the threat of violence on a regular basis. Throughout their often long conversations, they also learned they shared a predilection for money. Lots of money. Status and ethics were much further down the list. Stiles and Colby were made of the same stuff. Ruthless and conniving, heartless and money hungry. Each of them was lonely and bitter, tired and jaded. Basically, although years apart in age, they were soul mates at heart. Not in the respect they felt a romantic connection, not in the slightest. Yet as friends they quickly realized they shared the same common goals. They concluded in their perfect world, they would be the ones calling the shots, not the clients. Clients were a necessary evil of course, as clients had the money. It was clear they wanted to work together, all they had to do was figure out how.

It didn't take long to reach a conclusion. Why not offer a service that so tugged at a client's heartstrings, they'd be willing to pay hand over fist for it? Why not take advantage of the opportunity to provide something which nature couldn't? By offering such a service, and with clients more than willing to pay a premium for it, Stiles and Colby would have the two things they had always wanted, wealth and control. It was just a matter of supply and demand.

It was obvious to Colby after years of doing abortions, the number of babies put up for adoption had drastically been reduced, while the demand for infants soared. Infertility was on the rise. More and more couples were delaying having a family, ignoring their biological clock until it became too late, and options ran out.

Even though there were plenty of children available for adoption, the problem was just that. They were children and not infants. Not many parents wanted to adopt an older child, or even a toddler for that matter. They were looked upon as damaged goods somehow. They couldn't be molded in the same way they naively thought an infant could. When an infertile couple adopted an infant, well, it was just somehow more like their very own, so much easier to pretend the pregnancy had just been skipped over, and *voila*, a baby. And besides, babies were so much more lovable weren't they? Both Colby and Stiles knew the reality well enough, how society worships the newborn. Constantly bombarded and surrounded by magazine ads, commercials, books, and billboards, the message was clear. Infants are revered. The smell, the innocence, the beauty of their tiny fingers and toes. There was no question babies were cherished, angelical, and miraculous.

The fact was, the more they talked about it, the more they realized what a precious commodity a baby was, not to themselves of course, but to helplessly unfruitful husbands and wives. It could be a fucking goldmine. All they had to do was find a way to make it all work.

There was a trial and error period. Colby and Stiles laid the groundwork for their new enterprise, but help was needed. Sheila had never forgotten the big Hungarian, and eventually tracked down and recruited Nardo, who of course was still grateful and only too eager to help his former attorney. After a few initial meetings, she found out Nardo was a man capable of most anything for the right price, which was certainly not much of a surprise. It became her primary reason to employ the man.

Wendell also found the proper ally. One of his assistants at the clinic was a cold-hearted woman who showed no sign of a conscience whatsoever. She was an efficient and capable helper, but never displayed any kind of emotion or empathy toward any of the women who came in. She appeared to have no feelings at all, and after she had worked for the good doctor for a while, he became intrigued by her steely exterior, and he did a bit of investigating into her background. What he discovered was most interesting and clearly explained her

Evil Exchange

frigid behavior. She was a victim of physical and sexual abuse as a child, only to grow up and marry a man who continued the vicious cycle. At one point she snapped, and retaliated to such a degree her dear husband landed in the hospital with twenty-one stitches, three broken ribs, two missing teeth, a broken nose, and a vast array of wildly colorful and terribly painful contusions all compliments of his very own Louisville Slugger. During his recovery, she packed her bags and left him for good. He, outweighing her by a hundred pounds, was too humiliated to press charges. She supported herself as a waitress while attending nursing school in the evenings, and never let anyone get close enough to hurt her again. When he'd first interviewed her, Colby knew she hid some kind of dark secret by the cold lifeless look in her eyes. But her school recommendation was excellent, her grades had been outstanding, and he could find little reason not to hire her. He had never regretted the decision. Though she never showed it, Colby knew how appreciative she was. He was her deliverer, and she would do anything for him. Talk about loyal. Leslie Steiner was as loyal as a well-fed guard dog and just as savage.

Their business was beginning to take shape. Sheila decided since they would all be involved in some covert operations, code names were in order. Nardo refused to be called anything else. Leslie was referred to as the Mule, a symbol of her determination and stubbornness. Colby was the Stork, because he would still deliver babies, just in a slightly different way. Sheila, was simply called Boss, there was no need for explanation. Nardo and Leslie were never told each other's real name, and it was for their own protection as well as Colby and Stiles. The code names also came in handy as much of their work was done over the phone.

For a while, Colby kept his clinic, but bit by bit, he reduced the number of patients he would see and procedures he would perform. Eventually, he stopped performing abortions all together and closed the clinic. He decided now that he was in the business of procuring babies for moms and dads with big bucks, he would no longer kill fetuses. Dr. Wendell Colby thought of himself as quite a stand up guy.

Sheila maintained her practice, just the clientele changed. She put out feelers via the Internet for couples who might be interested in adopting. She offered an all-inclusive package. For one fee, she provided a baby, birth certificate, assistance in the adoption process, and filing any and all pertinent paperwork. In essence, she streamlined the entire process from start to finish. Over time, the system was perfected, as everyone knew their place and their job. Once Stiles retained the clients, Nardo went to work doing the collection, the Mule aiding him whenever necessary. The Stork usually transported the infant, and then met up with the Boss who delivered the package to a waiting mom and dad. Ta-da.

Wendell was also responsible for forging the birth certificates, which could sometimes be a bit tricky. Colby filled out the application with a false birth date, parent names, and birthplaces of said parents. A local hospital would be named as place of birth. The document would then be sent to the local health department. The health department never checked to see if the baby was indeed born at the hospital stated, the paperwork just went through as is. Sometimes the adoptive parents requested their names be on the original birth certificate, but this caused problems and was potentially very risky. If the birth certificate carries the name of the adoptive parents, then there is no formal adoption proceeding, and the parents can be exposed as frauds. When there isn't an adoption proceeding, family members, neighbors, and friends can become suspicious as to how the couple came to have a baby so conveniently. So the only safe solution was to make up names of birth parents and then go through the adoption process with the assurance the birth parents did not exist and therefore could never challenge the adoption. That way, babies could be brought from another state or country to be sold, and would therefore be virtually untraceable.

Not only were Colby and Stiles adept at forgery and skirting the law, they were both excellent business people. They provided parents with children. No one ever questioned where the children came from. No one ever suspected them of any wrongdoing. It was the opposite. The clients sang their praises, and it was worth the money they crowed, every damn penny of it. Business grew by word of mouth, spread by satisfied customers. Colby and Stiles felt it prudent to keep the business low-key however. They did not advertise as they didn't need to. Stiles often ran background checks on potential clients, and if it seemed a couple was too nosy, they would be immediately red-flagged. Anyone who tried to poke around too much or ask too many questions was informed there were not any babies available at the present time, sorry and good bye.

It took a number of years of being careful and vigilant, but ultimately, Colby, Stiles, Nardo, and Steiner developed a system that brought them great reward. Lots and lots of money.

Chapter Twelve

Todd sat uncomfortably in the waiting room. He could hardly believe he'd made the appointment. Although Matt initially made the suggestion and left the name of the doctor Katy was seeing, Todd knew he didn't want to make an appointment with his sister-in-law's shrink. It just felt a little too close to home. Instead, he'd flipped through the yellow pages until he found a psychologist by the name of Claire Meyers who practiced in his area. He found the ad to be professional and straightforward, and that seemed as good a reason as any. Todd didn't mention anything to his brother about his decision to take his advice, even in part.

For some reason, Todd felt ashamed to be here. He had always prided himself on being able to handle adversity. True, over the years, he had some tough things to get through. He felt a failure when his marriage fell apart. He had difficulty dealing with the death of his father. There were times when he questioned whether he'd achieved the kind of success at work he hoped for. Many times he wondered why he hadn't remarried or managed to sustain a long-term relationship. Certainly it was common to have doubts and regrets and difficulties. Everyone felt that way at one time or another. But seeing a psychologist? Todd equated it with mental instability.

Of course the bad weather didn't help. A summer thunderstorm stalled over Manhattan and dropped buckets. Since Todd had walked to the eighty-third street office without an umbrella, he got soaked. Not that he cared much. He had so much on his mind he didn't even notice the puddles he walked through. His mood was as dark as the clouds above, and his heart felt as sodden as his feet. He was feeling sorry for himself, thinking he'd been rained on his whole life.

Paris and Soll

The door opened and a woman warmly greeted him and ushered him into an inner office. She introduced herself as they took a seat.

"Hello Todd, I'm Claire Meyers. I'm glad you could make it," she said with a smile.

"Well, I guess it was fortunate for me you had a cancellation. Sorry Ms. Meyers, I got kinda wet," Todd replied referring to his clothes while slipping off his jacket.

"Please call me Claire. Would you like a towel?"

"Okay, Claire. No, I don't need a towel. Can I just hang this up?" Todd held up the dripping mess.

Claire got up to take his jacket and hung it up on a coat rack. She turned her attention back to Todd. She noticed some faint scratches on one side of his face, and a few on his right forearm, but didn't say anything.

"What brings you here today?" She returned to her seat across from Todd.

"Well, there's been some weird sh . . . I mean stuff going on lately."

"Care to elaborate?"

Todd sighed. He was reluctant to say it, but he was here. *Might as well get it over with.*

"I had a panic attack," he finally admitted.

She raised one eyebrow, but said nothing, and waited for him to continue.

Todd quickly filled her in on his accident with the Vespa, witnessing the horrific car crash, his scare on the Empire State Building, and the frightening failed jet engine incident. For the time being, he left out the part about Miriam's betrayal. He wasn't sure he could speak of it just yet.

"I can see how terribly upsetting any one of those situations would be. So, do you believe that you had a panic attack as a reaction to so many disturbing incidents in such a short period of time?"

"I didn't have the panic attack until the falling glass two days ago," Todd replied.

This admission caused both eyebrows to raise. "Go on," she said.

Todd took a deep breath and summarized his job as a television station consultant. He told her how he did new installations, as well as repairs and maintenance of existing stations. He went on to explain what happened.

"I was on my way to look at a weather bureau installation on top of the

Evil Exchange

RCA Building, to estimate some repair work. I got off the cross-town bus, and I'm just walking along near the Time Life Building. All of a sudden I hear this sound. I didn't know what it was, but on instinct I dove between some parked cars and tried to get underneath one. Next thing I know, there's this terrible smashing sound and it's raining glass all around me, hitting the parts of me that were sticking out from the car. When the glass finally stopped coming down, I crawled out and looked up to see what happened. There was a whole bunch of people around, and I was amazed no one else had been hurt. Then someone said a pane of glass had blown out of one of the windows. Sure enough, about forty floors up, there was an open window where the glass had been. Then I realize the glass had fallen right where I was walking, and if I hadn't ducked out of the way, it probably would have sliced me up really good. Maybe even killed me."

Claire nodded her acknowledgment. His scratches were obviously a result of the glass shards that hit him. She encouraged him to continue. "Go on."

"At first I thought I was okay. I had a few nicks here and there from the glass, but nothing serious. I brushed myself off, stood around for another couple of minutes gawking with the rest of the bystanders, remembered my meeting and took off. So I made it to the RCA Building and thought I'd better go into the restroom and make sure I looked okay, wash some of the spots of blood off. And that's when it happened." Todd was feeling agitated recounting the story.

"Take your time," Claire said softly.

"Well, I started to hyperventilate. At first I thought I was winded or something, still shook up from the glass falling. I felt like I couldn't breathe. My heart was like a jackhammer in my chest. I got all sweaty, you know, clammy. Then I started getting dizzy, and sat down on the floor before I passed out. The whole time I was hyperventilating, and I still couldn't get enough air. I started to feel this tingling in my fingers and toes. I didn't know it at the time, but the EMT's told me later that it was from a lack of oxygen."

"Todd, would you like some water?"

He nodded thanks, not realizing how dry his mouth had become. Claire handed him a tall glass and he drank half of it before he felt calm enough to continue.

"So anyway, this guy comes out from one of the stalls. And here I am, smack in the middle of the rest room floor, looking like some kind of drug addict or something."

Todd went on to say that the man at least had the wherewithal to call the building's security instead of just stepping over him and leaving. In turn, security called the paramedics. By the time they reached him, he had no feeling in his hands or legs, and his breathing was shallow and rapid. They checked his pulse and took his blood pressure, and knew right away he needed oxygen. They put on the oxygen mask and instructed him to take slow, deep breaths. Todd obeyed, and within ten minutes was feeling better. His breathing became more regular and less labored. His heart rate slowed to a far less dangerous level. Some of the feeling was coming back to his hands and feet, he could tell by the pins and needles. The EMT's wanted to transport him to the hospital, but he adamantly refused. He knew for sure there was no way he wanted to see another doctor or nurse, but he wasn't about to go into telling these guys the details of why. The EMT's didn't argue much as they got another call. They made sure he was able to get on his feet, and after he promised them he'd take a taxi home, they left.

"I never did make it to my appointment. I had to reschedule," Todd finished as he wiped sweaty palms on his pants.

Claire made some notes and then set her pad aside. "And your concern is these panic attacks will continue?"

"Yeah, that's part of it I guess," Todd replied vaguely.

"And the other part?"

"Well, I just can't help but wonder if there's something that I'm doing that's causing all this to happen. "

"Explain, please."

"I don't *know* how to explain it, that's what I thought you'd help me with," Todd said in exasperation.

"Try."

"Is it me? Am I doing something that's causing these accidents to happen? Am I somehow sabotaging my own life?"

"Do you really think so?" asked Claire.

"You're the therapist, you tell me," Todd raised his voice.

Completely unaffected, Claire waited a beat before speaking. "From what you've told me, these accidents were all random events. You were not speeding or being reckless on the Vespa, were you?"

"No, of course not."

"You did nothing to cause the crash of the other two vehicles, did you?"

"Hell, no."

Evil Exchange

"Did you create the gust of wind that almost knocked you off the Empire State Building?"

"No," Todd was beginning to see her point.

"And the jet, did your presence on the plane cause the engine to fail?"

Todd shook his head no.

"Do you have superhuman powers which can cause a window to break when you walk by it?"

"This isn't funny, you know," Todd's anger flared again.

"I'm just trying to make a point. While I agree with you that it is *unusual* these incidents have occurred all bunched together, I truly believe you have done nothing to cause them."

"So the reason for these things happening would be?"

"Coincidence. Timing."

"You seem so sure," Todd sighed.

"I don't know you very well yet, but I find it hard to fathom you have some kind of miraculous ability that causes spontaneous events to occur," Claire smiled.

"But . . ." Todd couldn't believe there was such a simple answer to it all.

"Listen, Todd. Obviously you've been through a lot lately. I'm not invalidating your feelings, really. You have every right to be shaken up by these near disasters. I'm just asking you to look at this logically. For some reason you've placed the blame squarely upon your own shoulders, and I'm just trying to get you to realize you can't take on all the responsibility. Every single one of these events has an explanation. People have motor scooter accidents. People see car crashes. You admittedly work in a profession that can at times be dangerous. Mechanical failures occur, and windows do break. It is unfortunate these things happened in a relatively short period of time, but these are *random* occurrences. By the same token, your reaction to these events is clearly understandable, and I can certainly see how it could culminate in a panic attack."

"Yeah, I guess," Todd admitted.

"Would you like to explore this further? Your self-confidence and inner security may be affected, we can discuss certain coping methods." Claire noticed Todd had tuned her out, completely.

"Todd, is there something else you're not telling me?"

Paris and Soll

Todd looked at her in surprise.

"How did you know that?"

"Well, as you said, I am the therapist."

Todd stared at her hard. He couldn't tell if she were being matter of fact or making fun of him. He wasn't sure this was such a good idea. Here he was, baring his soul, and Claire seemed so detached about it all. *Wasn't she supposed to be more sympathetic?*

"To be honest, you look like you're shouldering a heavy burden," Claire said and looked quite concerned.

Todd wondered if she could read his mind, for now she seemed genuinely worried. He felt so confused and ill at ease. He realized his discomfort went way beyond the damp clothes, but he just wasn't sure he could even talk about the whole adoption issue. "Todd, we do have some more time if you'd like to tell me what else is on your mind," Claire said gently.

Todd felt as if he might have another panic attack right there and then. He gripped the cushions with his fingers while trying to force his body through the back of the couch. He felt tremendous pain, and his fear became so intense he thought he might disintegrate on the spot.

Todd steeled himself against the wave of icy cold fright. If he let himself think about it much longer, his head might explode and surely his heart would shatter into a million pieces. So, figuring he had nothing to lose, he took the plunge and quickly told Claire he was adopted. In a rush, he explained how the car crash had reawakened the memory of his biological parents being killed, how the little boy reminded him of his own survival and the tremendous guilt he felt because of it. He told her about the conversation he'd had with Matt and later Miriam's confession. How it had all been a lie. How betrayed he felt, how confused. The more he talked, the more incensed he became. He was stunned to find tears running down his face.

"Clearly, this has caused you great pain," Claire stated the obvious.

"No shit, Sherlock." Todd knew it was rude, but couldn't help himself. He angrily swiped at his cheeks.

Unruffled, Claire made a few more notes. She then said, "And you are very angry with your mother."

"SHE HAD NO RIGHT! SHE HAD NO RIGHT TO LIE TO ME!" Todd stood up as he shouted the words. His hands were clenched into tight fists, the rage and pain deeply etched on his face. He thought he must look like a lunatic, but nothing seemed to bother Claire.

"Todd, please sit down for just a moment. I want to ask you something."

Still shaking, Todd obeyed.

"I'm sorry you were lied to. It is very sad. And I agree with you. Your mother should not have deceived you. I'm not excusing her behavior, but she must have had her reasons. What I want to know is, have you had a chance to think about what this means, now that you know the truth?"

"What? That my mother is inhuman for telling me such lies? She let me suffer all those years. How could a person do such a thing?"

"This may not mean much to you right now, but perhaps she was trying to protect you," Claire suggested.

"She was just trying to protect herself." Todd countered.

"Let me rephrase the question. Now that you know, how do you feel about it?"

"I just told you!"

"No, Todd. You told me how you are feeling about Miriam. I want to know how you feel about your biological parents."

"What do you mean, how do I *feel* about them?"

"They could still be alive."

Chapter Thirteen

It was a lousy day for sun worship, but perfect for tapping on the keyboard. Boots was hard at work on his latest novel. Another storm had blown in leaving the locals to take shelter and the tourists to bitch and moan. Julie had gone off to visit her sister on the other side of the island, thankfully. They'd been spending quite a bit of time together lately, and Boots welcomed the separation. Yes, Julie kept the old proverbial juices flowing, but the woman wore him out. Especially after the dream episode, which was pretty darn creepy. *A man coming to see him?* He certainly hoped not. Boots liked his privacy and relative anonymity on the island. Sure, some people knew his occupation, but Boots tended to keep a low profile. Right off he blew that one by having a relationship with Julie, as the locals were constantly pissed off at the white man from New York who'd stolen away one of their own. In terms of his profession, and the money it brought him, it really was nobody's business. Of course, he didn't really believe her prediction. Yet with Julie, anything was possible. He put the thought out of his mind. He was determined to take advantage of the present situation. With no distractions, he should be able to hammer out at least three or four chapters.

After a few hours of non-stop clicking, Boots stretched and took a break. The book was coming along nicely. This would be his fifth novel, and was yet untitled. Typically he didn't decide on a title until a manuscript was completed. He was tossing around a few different possibilities, but nothing grabbed him so far. Boots did not write serialized novels with the same central character. Instead, he liked to write each book as a stand-alone story with a private investigator in the main role. He wrote in much the same way as John Grisham wrote books that revolved around lawyers and Joseph Wambaugh wrote about cops. Not that he put himself on the same level as those two authors, not at all. Boots realized although he'd had some success with the reading public, he knew full well as

Evil Exchange

an author he had much to learn, and would hopefully continue to improve his skills book by book. However, he figured he must be doing something right as his books were in high demand. His formula was relatively simple. Handsome, but humble PI takes on case for wronged or desperate clients. Lots of bad guys PI has to chase or be chased by. Dire situations where PI figures out how to overcome impossible odds and survive. After a myriad of copious twists and turns, PI saves the day. And last but not least, a bevy of women ready at a moment's notice to happily shed their clothes and seduce our hero. Literature? No, definitely not. Popular? Damn straight.

Living on a sailboat didn't allow Boots much room for a library. But he did have one shelf dedicated to books he had read and couldn't part with, along with first edition copies of his own work. Boots' reading taste tended toward spy stories and mysteries, not too surprising. Occasionally he read a bit of historical fiction to mix it up. Glancing at the titles, he smiled when he came across his third book, *Finding Michael*. It was his personal favorite, and he felt his best work. He pulled the book from the shelf, and sat back down to flip through it.

Finding Michael was the story of a man who, after being been beaten and robbed, was then left for dead. Found by police in an alley, the man had no form of identification, and to further complicate the situation, took such a hit on his noggin, could not remember who he was or where he lived. The police got him checked out at a local hospital where doctors cleaned him up and dressed his wounds. A search of law enforcement's computer database came up empty for a missing person that matched this John Doe's description. Running his fingerprints didn't help. He had not worked for the government or been a member of the military. He'd obviously not ever been arrested and booked for a crime. The mystery man was simply not in the system and therefore, impossible to identify until either his memory came back, or someone came looking for him. A social worker at the hospital transported him to a homeless shelter so he could have a roof over his head for the night. He would be allowed to stay for a few days until the police came up with something. The social worker was convinced a report would be filed soon, as the mystery man wore an expensive suit that even though was now torn, blood stained and filthy, meant he must be a man of some means. Surely someone would be looking for him, but no one came forward. The man stayed at the shelter for over a week, while the police scratched their heads.

One of the officers had a friend, a PI, who from time to time liked to take on challenging cases. Once the PI heard the story of Mr. Doe, he felt compelled to help him, knowing full well for all the work he did, he might never see a dime of compensation. On the other hand, the PI sensed, just as the social worker did, this man wasn't just an average guy. Although John Doe was confused as to how he got where he was, and frustrated by the temporary (for the doctor's told him it *was* temporary) amnesia, clearly Mr. Doe was an educated and refined individual. For all he'd been through, he still retained the manner and grace of a privileged person. There was no question that he was, or had been, an important fellow.

So the PI set about his quest of super sleuthing. He went out canvassing the area where his client was found by the police. It was in a downtown business area, and the amnesia victim could have worked in one of the nearby offices, or may have been having a business dinner in one of the many chic, yuppie restaurants. Armed with a photo, the PI made his way around a three block radius, hoping to find someone who recognized the man who was now reduced to living at a shelter. The PI had initially tried taking Doe with him, but as you might expect, the man was unable to recognize any familiar buildings or faces. Until he got his memory back, he was for all intents and purposes, absolutely useless.

While beating the street, the PI showed the photo to some gentlemen in a bar, who did indeed recognize the picture but did not admit to that particular piece of information. Sometime later, the PI was followed by some dangerous looking characters who cornered him in his office, beat him silly, threw him in the back seat of their car, and dropped him off at an undisclosed location. From there on out, the story was full of intrigue, a classic Boots Beaumont mystery. The PI was able to save himself, only to be drawn into a tangled web of deceit and conspiracy. What he uncovered was the botched attempt to commit the murder of a wealthy stock and bonds trader, who due to his workaholic tendencies, shamelessly ignored his wife and shunned his children. Thanks to the world wide web, the PI was able to not only solve the identity of the mystery man, but also to uncover the diabolical plot of murder for hire, exposing the greedy wife and hateful children. The case was solved, but the amnesia victim (whose name was actually Michael Shepard) discovered he didn't like the reality of his life or who he was, and most especially, the despicable plan to relieve him of his millions.

Boots replaced the book back on the shelf. He thought to himself that although the novel was his favorite, and the PI was in many ways a hero for retrieving a wealthy man's lost identity, in the end, *Finding Michael* was the story of a man who might have been better off not knowing who he really was.

Chapter Fourteen

After his first session with Claire, Todd wasn't sure he'd return, but at the time agreed to another appointment. The second appointment led to a third. During their meetings, Claire urged Todd to attend a support group for adoptees. She mentioned such groups help people search for their natural parents, as well as share their feelings, and have the opportunity to communicate directly with others who struggle for understanding and answers. Todd was violently opposed to attending such a meeting. He yelled at her for even suggesting it in the first place, stating he'd already been badgered enough by his neighbor Tanya. But Claire, always remarkably cool and calm, persisted. During the third appointment, Todd finally caved in, knowing Claire would never give up. It was easier to agree, although he did it with supremely bad manners, his way of not letting her win too easily. He was being childish he knew, but was unable to refrain. His emotions were like a form of modern art, nonsensical and abstract. He did make one rather civil gesture of accepting a couple of books she offered him. One, called *Follow Your Heart*, was a novel about an adoptees's search and reunion with her natural parents. The other, a nonfiction book called *Adoption Healing*, explained how women were coerced into giving up their babies for adoption. He told himself he would take them only to pacify her. No way was he going to read them. Of course he ended up devouring them both.

As a result, Todd was startled to discover an intense thirst for adoption related information. He cruised the web, looking up various sites, intrigued by what he read. His inner struggle still raged about attending the support group meeting. At first he thought it would mean sitting among a bunch of circus sideshow freaks, and he'd be one of them. *Would he be asked to tell his story?* He was terrified by the idea. It was one thing to discuss his feelings with Claire, whom he was just now beginning to trust, but total strangers? The very thought was chilling.

Paris and Soll

He spent hours reading articles on-line, wrestling with his thoughts. Finally, his conscience and curiosity won out, and he convinced himself he should go, and just maybe, he would be able to survive the ordeal. And he did promise Claire.

On a beautiful Saturday afternoon, Todd found himself standing across the street from the meeting location, intently watching who went inside. He was waiting for someone who looked safe, someone to walk in with. It wasn't long before an earthy looking woman with a kind face approached the door to the meeting room. Todd hurried across the street and walked in behind her. She turned to him in greeting.

"Hi, my name is Carol, welcome! Are you an adoptee?"

Instead of freezing up as he thought he might, Todd surprised himself by replying. "Yes."

"Let's get you signed up," Carol smiled.

Todd was given a nametag, and his welcome mate led him to a seat. A few more people drifted in and sat down. Two women sat behind Todd and he overheard one of them say she was there looking for the daughter she had lost to adoption. Todd was overcome with emotion, never having thought it was even possible for his mother to want to find him. He had always thought she was dead. Now that he knew the truth that his parents had not been killed, could his mother be thinking of him? He blinked back tears and painfully gripped the arms of his chair. After collecting himself for a moment, Todd turned to the woman. He didn't know what he expected to see, but there sat a very normal looking person in her early fifties, wearing a smile on her face and compassion shining from her eyes. Todd nodded at her and she responded with a gentle hello.

As Todd glanced around the group he could see that people were nice, friendly, and normal. *That makes me normal, doesn't it?* Normal and in pain, it was obvious on all the faces. Todd felt a sense of connection already. The group leader stood up and gave an introduction.

"Welcome to our support group meeting, especially those of you who are here for the first time. I would like to explain why we run the meeting the way we do, and how you can get the most out of it. Most of us, as first mothers or adopted people, are generally not encouraged by society to express our feelings about our experience. We may have been told not to be angry, or not to be sad, or not to even talk about being adopted or giving up a child for adoption. Essentially, we've been told we should not have these feelings. Unfortunately, these messages just don't work well. Feelings cannot be right or wrong, they just *are*. We need to be able to say what we feel to *validate* our experience. There are

Evil Exchange

no 'shoulds' when it comes to feelings. Can you imagine someone telling you that you are not allowed to say it's cold outside? Or that saying you are hungry is not permitted?

"The most difficult task we face is learning the language of our experience. We need to learn how to say, 'I feel sad, mad, ashamed, hurt, or afraid.' When we say things out loud, they become real in a way they can never be if left unspoken. And when they become real, we can start to understand *why* we feel *what* we feel. When we understand why, we can start to change the way our experience affects us. We begin the process of *not* being afraid of our feelings. We learn our feelings won't kill us, although it often feels like they might. When we become *unafraid* of our feelings, the world changes. Imagine being unafraid of your feelings!

"I'd also like to mention for those of you who are joining us for the first time, the mothers who have given up children to adoption, prefer to be known as 'first' or 'natural' mothers rather than 'birth' or 'biological' mothers. It is an important distinction to us. That being said, who would like to start?"

One by one, people around the room shared their stories. Adoptees and first mothers were talking and crying, expressing anger and loss. Todd was fascinated by it all. Every word resonated within his soul. When it came his turn, Todd felt comfortable enough to tell his story. He explained to the group his feelings of anger and rage. The betrayal he felt, along with all the hurt and the pain. Afterward, he felt a release he'd never known before. He felt at home. He felt a kinship with these total strangers he never knew was possible. He had to admit Claire was right about this. Maybe he'd tell her next time. *Maybe.*

During the meeting, Todd focused on all the members of the group and what they had to say. But there was one person in particular he couldn't take his eyes off of. Her name was Diana, a beautiful raven-haired woman who looked to be in her thirties. When she introduced herself she mentioned she was also new to the group. Todd felt an immediate attraction. Not only was she lovely, but she shared the same first time jitters that he did. She appeared a bit shaky, but then became quietly controlled. Todd admired her ability to express her thoughts and emotions in such a noble manner. He hoped to talk with her at the end of the session.

"Todd?" A voice called his attention.

"Yes?" he responded to a man sitting across from him.

"Hi, I'm Glen. I'm the group's search assistant. Have you given any thought to searching for your natural parents?"

"Well," Todd began slowly. "I've only just recently started thinking about it. But I have no idea what to do or where to start."

"Would there be any paperwork you might have access to?" Glen asked.

"I don't know. You see, I just found out that my natural parents weren't killed . . ."

"Yes, I understand. And, it must have been quite a shock for you," Glen replied sincerely.

"You could say that," Todd reddened. He felt the spotlight was on him while the rest of the group was listening intently.

"You're A-mom might know something. It's worth a try."

"Maybe," Todd answered through clenched teeth. It still hurt when he thought about Miriam.

"Think about it, will you? If you can find something, a name, anything. We might be able to help you get started."

Todd only nodded in reply.

A short time later the group broke up for the evening. A few people rushed off right away, eager to get home. Todd and a few others remained, including Diana. He was nervous, and more than a bit drained from the emotional evening, but Todd knew he must speak to her.

"Hi. It's nice to meet you. It's my first time," Todd said and then felt like an idiot.

"Mine too," Diana smiled at him and held out her hand. Todd took it and immediately felt a tiny jolt run up his arm. This woman had quite an effect on him. He just could not stop staring at her.

Todd felt almost tongue-tied. He usually wasn't this shy around women, but for some reason, Diana had him in knots. He knew he couldn't lose the opportunity to get to know her better.

"Would you like to have a cup of coffee with me?" he asked.

She hesitated for a moment, and Todd's heart took a dive. Then she surprised him with another dazzling smile and said yes, she would. They agreed to meet at a nearby diner.

Chapter Fifteen

On a beautiful sunny day in Dixie, Louisiana, Sheriff Nance was informed the body of a young woman had been found. Although typical for this time of the year, the weather seemed most inappropriate under the circumstances. The discovery of a dead young woman depressed him, especially when she'd been identified as Charly Farifield. Nance knew her daddy. Denny Fairfield was a mean old coot, but he didn't deserve to get such sorrowful news. His daughter's body had been found quite accidentally in a ravine and from the condition had apparently been there for quite some time. Found near her was a garbage bag full of her meager belongings, including her purse and identification. What really puzzled the Sheriff was some baby clothes and other items which were also found in the bag, but there was no sign of an infant.

A dead body at the bottom of a ravine was clearly suspicious and the medical examiner performed an autopsy. He confirmed the fact Charly's neck had been broken, but it was unclear whether that had happened before or after the fall, as her body had been ravaged by the elements as well as some local wildlife. He was able to tell she had given birth before she died. A quick call to the local hospital confirmed the fact Charly had indeed delivered a baby girl some months before. So the Sheriff had an explanation for the baby things in her possession, but what had happened to the child?

Sheriff Nance called and spoke with Fairfield, to give him the bad news and to get some answers. He was disturbed by the fact that Charly had been in the ravine for weeks and weeks, yet her father had never filed a missing person's report. He wanted an explanation, but Denny dodged some of his questions, until in a fit of frustration Nance got in his squad car and drove out to Fairfield's place. Denny gruffly accepted condolences and the Sheriff's presence. Nance then made it clear to the old man he wasn't about to leave without some kind of accounting. After throwing a fit, Denny finally came clean with the truth.

Charly had gone and gotten herself knocked up all right, the old man said. Once he had learned of her pregnancy, Denny wanted nothing to do with her. He told her he would banish her from his house, embarrassed by her condition. It wasn't so much she'd gotten herself into such a mess, hell, it happened all the time to young, ignorant girls who believed the lies young men could tell. What Denny couldn't believe was how she refused to have an abortion and actually wanted to keep the kid. "Stupid girl," he'd said. After an argument in which they almost came to blows, Denny kicked her out for good, telling her she was on her own. The only indication Denny did have a heart (as small and withered as it might be), was an envelope with some cash he gave her as some kind of consolation for cutting her loose. He made his message clear, he never wanted to see her or his own grandchild.

Charly was heartbroken, but being as stubborn as her old man, said she would never change her mind. She took the money and literally walked out with the clothes on her back. She worked some odd jobs here and there during her pregnancy. She set herself up in a dilapidated old place in a bad part of town. Once the money ran out, she went on welfare. She felt shamed by it, but had no other choice. Her daddy was the only family she had and he obviously wanted no part of her. She never quite gave up though, thinking he might change his mind someday. Pride kept her from going to see him, but she wrote to him, a letter a week, explaining it all. She knew it was probably useless, but maybe, if she kept after him, he might eventually come around and take an interest once the baby was born. The last note she wrote him was just after she had come home from the hospital, it said she'd be by in a week or so with his granddaughter. When she never showed up, Denny figured she got cold feet. Since the letters stopped coming, he thought she must have decided to take off. He said good riddance to her to her and her illegitimate child. He never knew Charly and the baby had met with foul play until the Sheriff had called him.

Once he had the facts, Sheriff Nance realized this case had broader implications than he first thought. Not only was a young woman brutally murdered, because Nance sure as shit did not believe she'd fallen into that ravine by accident, but her baby had vanished without a trace. Nance had pressed Denny for the father's name, but Denny was unable to help. Charly had never revealed the name of the boy who'd gotten her into such trouble in the first place. It was all a mystery, and too many pieces were missing to make sense of it all. Nance was a decent and hard working man, but in this sleepy nonviolent town of Dixie, this crime was out of his realm of expertise. Without hesitation, he called in the FBI.

Chapter Sixteen

Judge Harold Price sipped a martini while impatiently looking toward the door. It was not her style to keep him waiting. A moment later his irritation vanished and he smiled when he caught sight of Sheila Stiles entering the restaurant. After all these years, she was still a damn good looking woman. His attraction and eagerness weren't purely based on the physical however. They had business to attend to before pleasure.

Sheila maintained a professional air as she approached him. She slid into the booth and asked forgiveness for being tardy.

"Harry, so sorry. I got caught up in traffic. Have you been waiting long?" She expertly slid her hand under the table and caressed his knee.

"I'm always anxious to see you my dear, that's all," the judge replied magnanimously.

"Let's order, I'm famished," Sheila gave him another quick squeeze with one hand while passing him an envelope full of cash with the other. They were so well practiced at these exchanges no one would ever notice anything slip into his honor's pocket.

They talked of inconsequential things. Sheila was good at feigning interest in what the judge had to say. He was a bore, an egotistical man who loved to wield the power of his position, and Sheila knew exactly how to bolster the man's already inflated self-image. She should know, after all, they'd been playing this game for a long time. It was a well scripted routine.

Sheila first met Judge Price in his courtroom when she defended Nardo. Lawyers love to gossip, and the scuttlebutt on the judge was he had a reputation for young women, fast cars, and a gambling addiction as big as his opinion of himself. After doing some snooping and asking a few discreet questions, Sheila heard the rumors that Judge Harold Price was known to take a bribe or two upon occasion. If it were true, she definitely wanted to get to know him better.

So she'd asked him out for dinner, purely business she insisted. She played out the scenario of the young, eager lawyer searching for some pearls of wisdom from the highly esteemed and widely experienced judge. After dinner, she invited him back to her apartment for a nightcap, saying she had a case she wanted to show him. He agreed, knowing she wanted to show him much more than a case file. Although he repulsed her, Sheila quickly seduced him, praising his sexual expertise. Price was so full of himself he believed every word she said. It wasn't long before they had an arrangement. Harry would call on her every other week or so, they would have dinner, then sex. At the time, Sheila was getting nothing out of the relationship other than being sick to her stomach servicing him, but she knew her time would come.

Eventually, she'd come to ask him a favor or two, usually about a court case. At first he resisted and blustered about what an ethical man he was. Sheila simply lured him to the bedroom and rocked his world until he gave into whatever she asked. Smart enough not to ask too often, or for too big a favor when she did, Sheila bided her time. Each sexual encounter further cemented her hold over him. During that time, Sheila learned of Harry's serious penchant for gambling. He often flew off to Vegas for the weekend, winning or losing thousands of dollars at a time. Sheila accompanied him once in a while and watched him in action. She could see the dollar signs rolling in his eyes like cherries in a slot machine. Good old Harry may have demanded respect, coveted power, and lusted after Sheila, but more than anything else in the world, he loved money. Sheila was convinced it wouldn't be long before the time was ripe for her to rope him into a deal.

The perfect opportunity came some time later when Stiles and Colby went into the business of providing babies to childless couples. It was obvious to Sheila that Judge Price was the perfect person to rubber stamp the adoptions to speed the process along. At first, Sheila asked him to do it as a personal favor to her. When the business started to grow (thanks to Nardo being so competent at his job), she knew Harry would soon get suspicious of what they were really doing.

One night after a rather wild bout of love making, Sheila trusted her instincts and explained to Harry how she needed his help. She made it clear she wasn't asking for any favors this time, but how they would have a business arrangement, which would mutually benefit them both. She was doing quite well in her new entrepreneurial endeavor and was willing to offer a monetary reward to him for

Evil Exchange

expediting the adoptions. At first, Judge Price was indignant. He railed at her, and adamantly refused. It was preposterous to think he would even entertain the idea. Sheila let him have his say, let him vent his anger for the sake of his ego. In the end, she convinced him she could pay handsomely for his assistance. He would be helping people adopt babies, what could be wrong with that? Harry had never been much good at saying no to Sheila. She'd asked for little over the years, and she *was* a hellcat in bed. He also couldn't deny the fact that his last few trips to Vegas had been disastrous, and the idea of some ready cash was immensely appealing. He compromised by saying they'd try it, and Sheila knew she'd won. He could rant and rave all he wanted about his code of honor, his devotion to the law, the enormous responsibility and pressure of the noble position he held, but it wouldn't change the fact that Sheila was presenting an offer he found hard to resist.

After years of preparation, Sheila Stiles had Judge Harold Price wrapped around her little finger. Sheila told him little of her business, and Harry knew better than to ask too much. He didn't question where the babies came from because he didn't want to know the answer. The arrangement suited them both. They still had sex upon occasion, but it was Sheila who was now in the power position. As long as Harry was happy being seduced by her money, then life was just so much easier. There was no doubt Sheila was a master of manipulation, and Harry was simply one more cog in her wheel of progress.

Chapter Seventeen

Todd had to smile when he thought about his coffee date with Diana. They'd talked for two hours, getting to know one another a bit better. Although Todd was attracted to her, he kept the conversation casual and neutral. He was enormously pleased when he found out she was single, but remained cautious. After being abandoned by his last girlfriend, he wasn't ready just yet to get his hopes up with someone else. He was determined to take this slow and easy, for if nothing else, he hoped they would at least be friends. When they parted they agreed to see each other the following week at the support group meeting. Todd dearly wanted to see Diana before then, but he didn't want to push it. Besides, he had plenty of work lined up at the moment, and more importantly, his new mission was to try and find out some information about his adoption.

It was time to speak with his mother. Todd felt it best to see her rather than to have a phone conversation, considering how upsetting the last one was to them both. Besides, he wanted Miriam to know that while he may not have forgiven the lies, he still loved her and had no desire to punish her any further by his absence.

After consulting with a new client about maintenance and repair of an existing television installation, Todd knocked off work in the early afternoon. He arrived at the senior residence and found his mother in the sunroom playing cards with a friend. She was surprised and pleased to see him, but also a bit cautious. Miriam didn't know quite what to expect. Todd gave her a quick peck on the cheek and said hello to her friend. They exchanged some pleasantries for a few minutes before Miriam's friend excused herself to give them some time alone. Todd and his mother moved to a couch to chat.

"Are you still mad at me?" Miriam asked tentatively.

Evil Exchange

"I came to see you because we need to talk.." Todd wanted to avoid rehashing their last conversation.

"All right," Miriam answered and steeled herself.

"Mom, I need to find out about my first mother, to try and search for her. It has nothing to do with what you've done or haven't done," Todd said testing the water.

"If you find her, will you ever talk to me again?" Miriam's eyes filled with tears.

Todd found his eyes were leaking too. "Of course I will. Mom, this isn't about you. This is about me being adopted, thinking my parents were killed. You know it's made me crazy all my life, right?"

"I know it has," Miriam sighed.

"Well, I have to end the craziness somehow," Todd explained.

"You know, I've always wondered what wonderful people could have made you," Miriam said wistfully. More tears fell. Then Todd laughed and so did she. The tension evaporated and their strained relationship of late changed dramatically. Finally, they could actually talk about the adoption. Todd forged ahead.

"Mom, is there some paperwork from my adoption? Something that might help get me started?" Todd asked the question gently, as this was still an emotionally charged issue. Mother and son had taken the first steps toward reconciliation, and Todd wanted to proceed carefully.

With a furrowed brow, Miriam thought for a moment. "I remember a file, I think your father kept it at the office somewhere. You could ask Stuart." Her face brightened as she tried to be helpful. Stuart Tuttle was the lawyer who took over Bob Walters' practice after he passed away.

They visited for a while longer. As eager as Todd was to call Stuart's office, he didn't want to hurt his mother's feelings by rushing out the door. Their talk returned to the mundane. Family stuff, her health, his job. They stuck with safe topics that reestablished their parent-child connection. Todd said he'd come and see her again soon. Miriam seemed enormously relieved.

Once outside, he pulled out his cell phone. Not that he looked forward to speaking with Stuart, for he loathed the man. Stuart was an arrogant bastard years ago and Todd didn't think he'd changed his attitude much over time. He quickly dialed the number from memory, and immediately heard a familiar voice. It had been many years, but he still recognized Blythe's perfect diction. Todd

Paris and Soll

calculated she must have been at least a hundred and twenty years old by now. Blythe was almost a fossil when she had worked for his father, and then stayed on when Stuart took over. He could hardly believe she was still alive, much less still working. This was a good sign though since Blythe knew everything. Todd identified himself and she seemed pleased to hear from him. Todd cut to the chase and asked her if there might be an adoption folder of his lurking in the old file cabinet. Without hesitation, she said yes there was, but he would have to see Stuart about it, and he was due back from court in about an hour. Could he come by then? As the office was in Rockland County, about thirty minutes from the city, Todd would have to try and find a ride up there. He told Blythe he would try and make arrangements. After ending the call, he was a bit disappointed he wouldn't be able to deal with Blythe directly, but he knew only too well from the old days she was a professional watchdog and did nothing without her boss's permission. Her attitude hadn't changed either.

His next call was to Glen, the search assistant from the support group. He knew Glen was retired, so he hoped he might be able to catch him at home. When Glen answered on the second ring, Todd quickly explained the situation, and apologized for the short notice. Glen was pleased to help. He said it was a good idea for Todd to be with a friend anyway, considering the circumstances, as it could be an emotional experience finding out what was in the file. Better for Todd not to be alone, and he would be more than happy to drive him to Rockland. They agreed on a location, and Glen said he would pick him up.

Excited and nervous, Todd walked the six blocks to where he was to meet Glen. He needed the physical exertion, and wanted to clear his head and prepare himself for the unenviable task ahead. Stuart Tuttle made his skin crawl, but he would try and be pleasant in order to get what was rightfully his.

Thirty minutes later, Glen picked him up, and they made the drive, chatting comfortably along the way. Glen was a retired insurance salesman. He had three grown children, and five grandchildren he delighted in bragging about. Todd enjoyed his stories about the family, and it served as a distraction and helped calm his jangled nerves. Todd gave directions and the ride went by quickly. It wasn't long before they pulled up to the office of Stuart M. Tuttle, Attorney at Law. Glen said he would wait in the car, and gave a thumb's up.

When Todd walked into the familiar building, Blythe greeted him with a warm hug. Todd felt as if he were hugging a skeleton. He marveled at how the woman, who clearly was ancient, hadn't changed much. She looked almost the same as when she worked for Bob, and that was a long time gone now. Glancing around the office, he noticed not much else had changed either. It was like taking a step back in time.

Evil Exchange

Blythe buzzed Stuart and sent Todd into his inner office. *Show time*, he thought to himself. Stuart Tuttle sat behind a behemoth desk. Todd supposed it was meant to impress, but he thought it looked ridiculous. Stuart was a big man. Big, fat, and balding. He greeted Todd with a condescending smirk and nodded toward a chair. Todd sat, and noticed a manila file folder open on the desk.

"Searching is a bad idea Todd." Stuart was not a man to waste words.

"My therapist suggested it, and I intend to go forward with it," Todd replied as he held out his hand for the folder.

Stuart placed a meaty paw on top of the file. "Oh, you can't have that. I'll tell you what you need to know." Glancing at the top page Stuart read off Todd's birth name, his natural mother's name, and the hospital where he was born.

"Is that it?" Todd asked incredulously.

"That's all you need to know to find her."

Todd was stunned. It had never occurred to him that he had another name. And even though it made sense he was born in a hospital, he'd just never made the connection of coming into the world that way. He had always thought his existence started with the car crash. His head was spinning. Before he realized exactly what he was doing, he mumbled a good bye to Stuart, gave a brief wave to Blythe and walked out the door.

Todd went to the car and asked Glen if he had a piece of paper and something to write with. Glen rummaged in the glove box and found what he was looking for, pad and pen. Todd quickly wrote down the names Stuart had read to him from the file. He was so excited, he blurted the names out loud to Glen.

"My mother's name was Ruth Kelto, my name was Brad Perry, and the hospital where I was born is called Broadstreet Hospital." Glen shared the enthusiasm by giving Todd a hearty slap on the back and another thumb's up.

Todd couldn't stop reading the names over and over, absolutely enthralled by the significance they held. His name, his mother's name, and where he was born. His mother's name, Kelto, was a bit unusual, and Todd found it odd that his last name was different from his father's. Then he realized it might be her maiden name, yet that didn't make sense because his first mother and father were married weren't they? Todd sighed and realized how much he still didn't know. How he wished he'd been able to look at the folder instead of Stuart just reading the names off to him. *Oh well.*

He liked his name. Brad Perry. A solid name. Todd marveled at this link to his background, and his beginning. It was amazing how just simple letters of the alphabet, combined in a certain way could have such an impact on a human being. He felt like crying. Glen asked if he was okay, and Todd nodded. Then all of a sudden, Todd mentioned something he'd seen. He explained how he saw some letterhead in the manila folder, *his* manila folder on Stuart's desk. The letterhead looked like it had a lawyer's name on it, Max or something. But now he couldn't remember. Glen asked the obvious question, why didn't he have the folder? Realizing that Glen was right, Todd knew he shouldn't have left without it. It belonged to him after all. *Why would Stuart keep it anyway?*

Rather than going back inside, Todd pulled out his cell phone, and dialed Stuart's office. Blythe put him through. Without preamble, Todd demanded to know about the other papers in the file. Stuart shot back with a surprisingly angry response. He told Todd the papers had nothing to do with him. Todd challenged the lawyer, stating that the file belonged to him. Stuart vehemently disagreed. The file was in his father's office when Stuart took over, so it was to remain in his possession. He ended the conversation by telling Todd to stop bugging him and hung up.

Todd was furious. *How dare he?* The man was a complete idiot and a total asshole. Hearing the entire exchange, Glen suggested a plan. Nodding in agreement, Todd flipped open the cell phone one more time and pressed redial. This time he gave Blythe specific instructions to relay a message.

"Tell that smarmy son of a bitch if he doesn't give me my folder, I will report him to the bar association for withholding my property. I'll hold." Todd spoke with a barely contained fury. Without a word, she did what he asked, and Todd could hear the annoying sound of muzak. He was on hold for so long he thought Blythe might have been offended at his language and was punishing him for it. He vowed he would apologize to her. He was just so damn mad.

"Todd?" Blythe finally came back on the line.

"I'm here."

"Listen to me carefully. Mr. Tuttle will give you the entire folder for seven hundred and fifty dollars," Blythe said.

"What is the seven hundred and fifty dollars for, for Christ's sake?"

"Remember I'm only the messenger here," Blythe warned.

"Yeah, I know. Go on," Todd answered and tried to control his temper.

"He said the money is for the time he spent arguing with you. You can come back to the office with a check, but wait outside in the hallway. You and I will do the exchange. Mr. Tuttle said you are not to set foot in the office, and he does not want to see you ever again."

Evil Exchange

"Fine with me," Todd growled and ended the call. "Seven hundred and fifty bucks!" He was outraged, and vented his anger in Glen's direction. Glen nodded in sympathy at Todd's frustration and offered up one more idea. Todd grinned. He fished his wallet out of his back pocket. He always kept an extra check with him just in case. Sure enough, it was there. As Todd filled it out it refueled his rage at being treated in such a way. His face felt on fire. The nerve of the man was unbelievable. Todd knew Stuart was a scumbag, but this was beyond low. This was purely malicious. *And for what reason? What did he ever do to the guy?* Todd noticed his hands were shaking. But it didn't matter; he was getting the damn folder.

Three minutes later, he met Blythe in the hallway of the office. The exchange was silent. One check in return for one file. Todd turned to walk away, and remembered.

"Hey Blythe, sorry for my language on the phone," Todd apologized.

"Are you kidding? I've heard far worse. Happens all the time," she laughed softly and shuffled back toward the office.

"Blythe?" Todd couldn't help but ask, knowing he probably wouldn't ever see her again. "Why are you still working? Especially for such a *shit* like him?"

"Well, he's not the man your father was, that's for sure. Mostly he treats the clients that way, not me." Even at her age, Blythe still had a merry twinkle in her eye. "Besides," she shrugged. "I have nothing else. My husband died years ago, and I never had kids. If I don't work, I'll die." She waved goodbye.

Todd stared at her for a moment until she was gone, back in the safety of her work world. He felt sorry for her. There had to be more to life than working for a jerk. He clutched the folder protectively under his arm and left the building. As soon as he got outside, he had one more call to make. Implementing Glen's suggestion, Todd called his bank and put a stop payment on the check he'd just written.

Chapter Eighteen

The Mule was in charge of today's operation with Nardo assisting as driver. It was early morning, cool and cloudy. The Mule stepped out of the rental car clad in brightly colored medical scrubs. She adjusted her nurse's badge and smoothed her chin length hair. Time to get started.

Having worked for Colby so many years at the abortion clinic, she knew exactly how to blend in at the hospital. Her unremarkable looks were a plus, as she was the type of person who didn't get too many second glances. The Mule's greatest asset however, was the professional attitude and confident manner in the way she carried herself. She always avoided the staff, and the mothers never thought to question her presence or what she was doing.

She entered through the ER doors and glanced around. There were two patients being attended to, and the security guard was nowhere in sight. Having cased the small community hospital a few days before, the Mule knew the general layout of the facility, and was sure there was no more than one guard on duty at a time. She was well aware that all across the country security measures were being tightened. Most large metropolitan hospitals used strict safety procedures to insure the baby's wristband matched the mother's, thereby avoiding any potential switching mistakes, or God forbid, kidnapping. Although not common, some infant abductions did occur from time to time, and many hospitals had a "Code Pink" alert in place, which was exactly why today's snatch was carefully planned and taking place in a small rural town about an hour south of Knoxville. This particular hospital hadn't updated its security measures in the last twenty years or so, and was the perfect target.

As it was nearing shift change, the Mule knew the nurses' station would be busy. The staff, tired from working through the night, were eager to complete

Evil Exchange

their tasks and head for home. The maternity ward was on the first floor of the west side of the building, and the Mule encountered no one in the corridor. So far, so good.

She quietly slipped into a private room. A new mother was sleeping soundly, exhausted by the recent ordeal of giving birth. The infant was nearby in a tiny plastic crib on wheels, tightly bundled in a pink blanket. The Mule swiftly and silently approached, expertly lifting the baby out of the lucite container. A small cry escaped from the little girl, and mom's eyelids fluttered open.

"I'm so sorry. I didn't mean to wake you."

"Is something wrong?" asked the groggy mother.

"Not at all," whispered the Mule soothingly. "We just need to weigh her."

"But she was just weighed a few hours ago," the mother said yawning.

"I know dear, I looked at the chart. We always double check, you know, as a precaution," the Mule smiled.

"Oh, okay."

"Go back to sleep, I know how worn out you must be. I'll bring her back in a jiff, and I'll try not to wake you again. You need your rest," the Mule issued her gentle order. Mom obeyed.

Slowly opening the door, she looked up and down the hallway, no one was in sight. The side exit was just steps away. The Mule and her tiny package slipped outside. She walked from the building, quickly crossed the street to the parking lot of a nearby pharmacy where Nardo was waiting. Mission accomplished.

Chapter Nineteen

Boots turned off the laptop in a fit of frustration. He was in the middle of a chapter, and the words just weren't coming. His mind felt blank. It was unusual for Boots to come up empty, but when he did, he knew best not to fight it. It wasn't exactly writer's block, but a sign his brain wasn't going to cooperate. Usually the best thing to do was to take a break, find a distraction, and come back to it later.

He had lots of choices. He could go sailing, work on repairs, or maybe take Julie out for lunch, but then he remembered she was working later in the afternoon, so lunch was out. Nothing solo really appealed to him, and he felt like he needed some human interaction. That was a writing pitfall, it was something you did all alone. So he decided to go and visit some friends at Club Med, and see what was happening in their little patch of paradise. Even though some of the staff had changed (as Club Med employees tend to move from one exotic location to another), he still had a few friends there and enjoyed an easy camaraderie with them. He hopped on a bike, and on his way out to the village, thought back to his first time on this beautiful Bahamian island.

Boots first visited the Club Med in Eleuthera some years back when it was brand spanking new. It was early October and New York was cold and dreary. He and one of his pool playing buddies, Joe, were both unattached at the time, and the idea of spending some time in a tropical destination sounded terrific. Over the years, Boots had visited a number of Club Med villages and had always had a great time. Sometimes he went alone, but usually he and a buddy would go in search of sun, sand, warmth, and women. Since Joe had never been to a Club Med before, Boots told him the story about his first village vacation.

His first trip was to the luscious island of Martinique. Boots thought the

Evil Exchange

Martiniquese were some of the most beautiful people on the face of the earth. Plus, the setting itself was more than fantastic, and he felt he'd found heaven. At dinner that first evening, Boots sat at a table with other GM's (Gentile Members as the vacationers were called), having a grand time meeting people from around the world. As a waitress walked by, Boots heard a guest say, "Doo Doo, more coffee please." He was absolutely appalled someone would talk to a person of color (or anyone for that matter), in such a way. Just as he was about to stand up and challenge the offender, he heard it again from someone at another table. Boots couldn't believe it. *My God, if anyone said that to an African American in the states, they'd be killed.*

He whispered to a woman sitting next to him and asked what was going on. She laughed and explained that "Doo Doo" was Creole. It was short for "Douce Douce", which meant "sweet, sweet" or "sweetheart." She went on to tell him the term was only used on the islands of Martinique and Guadeloupe, which are both French states. Boots nodded in understanding, and realized he had a lot to learn. The next morning, and with great trepidation, Boots decided to get into the island spirit. As he passed by a Martiniquese woman who worked at the club, he said, "Bon jour, Doo Doo." The woman responded with a hearty, "Bon jour, Doo Doo!" and broadcast her pleasure with a dazzling smile. Boots felt as if he'd survived his first test, and from then on felt at home. It was the beginning of his love affair with the all-inclusive resort.

The Club Med Eleuthera was in a beautiful location, less than a mile across the slender island from Governor's Harbour. Upon arrival, Boots and Joe immediately hit it off with the GO's or Gentle Organizers as the staff was referred to.

The first night at the bar was rather amusing. Joe ordered a cold beer, and Boots asked for a rum and coke. Boots took a sip of his drink, and thought it tasted weak. He asked for another, and it tasted the same. Being naturally suspicious, he then asked for a snifter of rum. The bartender presented it with a flourish, and Boots realized the only liquid in the snifter was water. Without a word, he left the bar to find the resort manager, who was commonly known as the Chef de Village.

When Boots found him, he offered to buy him a drink. The Chef graciously accepted. They returned to the bar, and Boots ordered two rum and cokes. The bartender momentarily froze, but quickly recovered and reached for a different bottle of rum than before. Boots stopped him and instructed him to use the same bottle he'd poured from the first time. Once the Chef took a sip of his drink, he got red in the face, just as the bartender did. Clearly embarrassed by getting caught in their little scam, Boots never had to say another word, and the next day, all the rum bottles were actually filled with rum.

Other than that, they had a great week. Boots and Joe did a lot of sailing, played baseball, volleyball, and backgammon. They spent most evenings in the company of some rather lovely women, and the time went by far too quickly. On their last day, Boots and Joe made a pact. Since they were both doing well financially at the time, they decided to come back each month of the entire winter season.

When they showed up in November of that year, their arrival created quite a stir, as most vacationers didn't commonly return a month later. When they showed up again in December, they received a most rousing welcome from the GO's. Boots and Joe had become good friends with many staff members, and were treated as part of the family. Most of the staff were European men and women from various countries. They all spoke French, the official language of Club Med, and enjoyed teaching Boots and Joe as many words and phrases as possible.

One evening, as the two friends were sitting in the lounge, the Chef politely asked if he could join them. After the rum incident, Boots, Joe, and the Chef whose name was Kiki, had become good pals and truly enjoyed each other's company. Kiki got right to the point. He asked both men, if they would like to work at the club teaching sailing, baseball, and backgammon. Joe declined as he would soon be starting a new job, but Boots thought it a smashing idea. He was in a position where he could juggle a lighter case load, while also spending time in this lush, tropical setting, learning French and keeping tourists entertained. Boots told the Chef how flattered he was, especially because he was considerably older than most of the GO's.

So, together they worked out a plan. They agreed since he had business in New York that he had to attend to, Boots offered to work at the club two weeks on and two weeks off for the next few months. Instead of being paid for his work, all Boots asked was that Club Med foot the bill for his flights back and forth. The deal was sealed with a swig of rum. Boots left Joe to fend for himself, flew home, took care of some business, and was back on a plane in three days.

Boots settled in and was introduced to the GO's he didn't know, and was then given a brief outline of his responsibilities. First, he was assigned to the sailing team lead by a supremely tanned native by the name of Gypsy. Boots was to teach a few hours in the morning and again in the afternoon. Backgammon lessons were to be held at his discretion. As a GO, he was obligated to be at the disco each evening, to be sociable, and to alternate dining room tables at each meal to make sure that he met as many of the guests as he could.

Boots knew his first night was bound to be waterlogged. Chef Kiki had a thing about water. He found various ways to get people wet, and of course it was always just in fun. He especially liked to surprise the GO's with a devious dousing, and at times went to great lengths to catch them off guard. He'd have some of the staff rig buckets of water over a doorway, plant some sparkly beads on the ground, and as soon as a passerby reached down for the beads, the bucket was tipped and the unwitting participant soaked. Boots was surprised when he made it through most of the evening without getting drenched. He figured Kiki must have thought him special, being a tough PI from the Big Apple. Of course he was wrong.

All of the GO's were required to get on stage after the evening's entertainment and sing the "crazy signs" song. Chef Kiki led them. Boots and the others had to sing silly lyrics while moving their hands and bodies to make the crazy signs. This had to be done to the satisfaction of the Chef, who quite conveniently, was never satisfied. Whenever someone goofed, Kiki would hold up his hands. He'd bellow, "Stop the music!" Then he'd theatrically point to the miscreant and say, "In zee pool!" Either the offender jumped into the pool on his own, or was thrown in by the others. It was always a crowd pleaser.

So on this night, Kiki stood directly in front of Boots, knowing he was bound to screw up sooner or later. As soon as he did, Kiki stopped the music, and silence filled the air. Everyone was waiting to see what would happen. "Bootsa!" Kiki yelled. (He added an "a" to everyone's name.) "In zee pool!" Boots was no fool, and had secretly prepared for this eventuality. He surprised everyone when he stripped down to his bathing suit and made a mad dash for the pool. Since it was December, and rather chilly in Eleuthera, Boots expected the water to be ice cold. He was pleasantly surprised when he hit the water and realized it was still warm from the heat of the day. He was met by a female GO by the pool ladder with a towel. His audience applauded as Boots was officially initiated and was now a full-fledged member of the close knit GO group.

Boots enjoyed his various duties at the Club. He got the biggest kick from the lead sailing instructor. Gypsy was a hoot. He was fun loving, enjoyed playing innocent practical jokes, and was rarely serious about anything. Except for sharks. Gypsy hated sharks and was determined to kill as many of them as he could. Each night he set out shark traps, and each morning he checked to see if he'd caught any. One morning, as Boots arrived to give a sailing lesson, there was a dead shark lying across the dock. Gypsy was jubilant. Boots didn't care for sharks much himself, but thought it sad to see it lying there. As he walked by, the shark suddenly leapt up and snapped at his legs. It missed by mere inches, and scared the shit out of Boots. Gypsy laughed uncontrollably, and when he finally collected himself, explained to Boots how a shark's nervous system didn't always die right away, and the snapping jaws are some kind of reflexive death throe. From that moment on, Boots had a new found respect for the primal creatures, and always made sure to stay well clear of any of the sharks Gypsy caught. No matter how dead they looked.

Not only did Gypsy have a reputation for catching sharks, he also had a way of snagging the ladies. More often than not, he had a line-up of vacationing women vying for his attention. Boots was amazed to discover the male GO's slept with as many female tourists as possible. The female GO's never did. Apparently, there was some kind of mystique surrounding the male GO's and they developed a reputation (up for debate whether it was real or imagined) for being superb lovers. Boots discovered now that he was a GO at Club Med, women were falling all over him. He'd never lacked for female companionship while on vacation, but the increase was startling. The only thing that had changed was his conversion from tourist to GO. Being tanned and buff from physical activity didn't hurt either. Boots figured it was the allure of the island, the shedding of inhibitions (not to mention clothes), and the temptation of a sexual encounter with a studly stranger, which made for an irresistible combination. As inviting as it was, Boots chose not to participate in the tempting mating game. He knew many of the female tourists made a point of bedding as many GO's as they could, and the idea of a sexual merry-go-round didn't interest him. Too many diseases out there, plus the fact that it seemed, well, *sleazy*. He remained cordial and friendly to all the guests, but limited his dating to the confines of his stateside home.

The first few months were fun and carefree. He'd be on the island for two weeks, then back home for two weeks, and back again to his tropical domicile. His only frustration was the flight going back and forth. He flew on Bahamas Air. The locals referred to it as "Bahama-Mamma's Air." Whenever he was leaving the island, he couldn't help but ask if his flight was on time. He was answered each and every time with the same response. The ticket agent would always say, "Mon, our planes are *always* on time. Dey are *never* late. It's the damn schedule that keeps a-changing," and she would laugh and laugh. Boots would shake his head and settle in to wait. That was life on an island, it ran on a radically different clock.

After a while, the going back and forth, living two separate lives, one in New York, one in Eleuthera, Boots decided he'd had enough. He went to Chef Kiki and told him it had been a great experience, but he needed to back to the life of a full time PI rather than a part-time GO. A couple of months had been a blast, but the appeal was starting to wear thin. Boots knew he'd be back someday, and then he hoped it would be for good. Eleuthera had gotten under his skin unlike any other island he had ever been to.

Here I am. Boots smiled as he came back to the present. He looked forward to catching up with Kiki, still the Chef de village. He'd also be sure to check out the dock and see if Gypsy had caught any more sharks. From a distance that is.

Chapter Twenty

"Todd, you're staring at me."

"What? Oh, sorry." Todd's face reddened and he stared at his coffee cup instead.

"You were awfully quiet tonight in the group," said Diana. "How come?"

"Just thinking some things through I guess."

"Want to talk about it?" Diana smiled at him.

"It's a long story," Todd sighed.

"It's okay. I have time. You seem like you're wrestling with something. Maybe talking about it will help you figure out what you want to do. And you can look at me now," she teased.

The teasing got to him and he grinned. *She is so beautiful.* Todd was embarrassed he'd been caught staring at her like a goofy teenager. *But those eyes.* He could stare at her eyes all night. She was right, he had been quiet in the group tonight. He wasn't quite sure why.

Even though Todd was ecstatic about getting the folder from Stuart, he decided to wait until he got back to his apartment to look through it. Glen had offered to go through it with him, but for some reason, Todd wanted to do it alone. After Glen dropped him off, Todd grabbed a beer from the fridge and sat at the kitchen table. When he finally felt ready, he opened the folder gingerly, as if it were an ancient artifact and he the archeologist digging up his own past instead of someone else's.

What he found surprised, pleased, saddened, and confused him. There was a report card from the first grade. A love letter he'd written to his first sweetheart,

Evil Exchange

Abby Jane, when he was nine. Bob and Miriam's wedding certificate, letters from a slew of attorneys and adoption agencies about adoption, a photo of Todd and Matt when they were kids, and of course, his birth certificate. There was a letter or two from a Jacob Klein, and a number of letters from a Maddie Monroe, whoever the hell they were.

Rather than feeling a sense of satisfaction in having obtained the folder, he felt more conflicted than ever. So much had happened recently he just couldn't keep it all straight. His head was a raging debate over what he should do. All this conflict kept him up at night and distracted at work. He discussed it with Claire at his regular appointment, and she suggested that he not make a decision either way for a few days. "Digest it," she said. Todd thought it good advice. Which was why when he went to the support group meeting, he wanted to sit and listen, rather than speak out. Todd hoped the answer would come from within, not from other people telling him what to do. He wanted to weigh the pros and cons, he wanted to hear the experiences of others, good and bad. When the group finished for the evening, he again asked Diana out for coffee. So far, all he'd been able to do is stare at her like a dolt.

"I'm trying to decide what to do," sighed Todd.

"About?"

"Searching."

"Oh."

Todd laughed. "Well, we're quite the conversationalists, aren't we?"

Diana laughed too. When she did her eyes sparkled like gemstones. "You said it's a long story, why don't you tell me about it."

"Are you sure?"

"Todd, stop hedging. I'm full of caffeine at the moment so you don't have to worry about me falling asleep. What can it hurt?"

She was so sincere Todd couldn't possibly refuse. He started from the beginning. He told her about his accident, the car crash, all of his near misses of late. He told her about his discovery that his first parents were not killed in an auto accident as he'd been told. His spoke of his confrontation with Miriam, as well as his panic attack, and his decision to get counseling. Then there was Claire's suggestion he attend the support group. The desire to know more about his adoption, the encounter with slimy Stuart Tuttle. His joy at learning the name he was given at birth as well as his first mother's name. Basically, he pretty much told her everything that had been happening in the last couple of weeks.

Paris and Soll

"Wow," Diana said after he finished.

"I told you," Todd replied.

"I guess I'd better be careful if I'm going to keep going out with you." Diana teased him again.

"What? Oh, you mean about the accidents," Todd grimaced.

"I do love Vespas though," she confessed.

A silence fell between them. Then Todd realized what she had just said.

"You mean you'll go out with me again?"

"As long as next time it doesn't involve coffee. There are other things to do, you know," she joked. She surprised him then and took his hand in hers. "Can I tell you something about myself?"

"Anything."

"I was raised Catholic. But once I went to college, I basically started to question my beliefs. I stopped going to church, and decided I no longer wanted to be involved in organized religion. But I still believe in God. I believe things happen to us for a reason."

"Okay," Todd wasn't sure where she was going with this.

"Someone is trying to tell you something," Diana explained.

"Like?" Todd challenged.

"It's a sign, Todd. Don't you see? All these things have been happening to you for a reason."

"That's not what my therapist says," Todd reflected.

"How does she explain it?"

"Coincidence. Timing. That's all," he shrugged.

"I see it differently. Destiny is calling you."

"What does she want?" Todd quipped.

"For you to make a decision, before it's too late." Diana squeezed his hand and then let go. She stared at him, trying to decide if he got it. "Now you think I'm a kook," she frowned.

"No, really, I don't."

"What's holding you back then?"

"Well, what if . . ."

Evil Exchange

"Is *that* how you're going to live your life? '*What if?*' Okay then. Let me give you one. 'What if' you don't try and find your first parents?" Diana demanded.

"Then I'll never know," Todd was starting to get the picture.

"Exactly. Look. I'm not trying to tell you what to do. It's a very personal decision for all of us adoptees. I guess for me, I realized I didn't want to have any regrets in my life which is why I'm trying to find my first mother. That's why I'm in the group, and why Glen is trying to help me search. I grew up an only child. My parents were wonderful people, but very career driven. I had the best of everything except for what I needed the most. Time and attention. I was lonely. I started to get into trouble when I was a teenager. I was rebelling because I needed something, but I didn't know what that something was. My parents finally sent me to a shrink. He helped me realize I needed to identify my problems before I could solve them. I finally figured out I had questions no one else could answer except for my first mother. As soon as I turned eighteen, I started surfing the net, but there wasn't all that much information out there. I kept at it though. And here I am, twelve years later, I'm still trying." She smiled at him.

"You don't give up easily do you?" Todd said in admiration.

"Not when it's important to me."

They talked for another hour. Todd wanted to know more about her job. Diana managed a trendy boutique in Manhattan and she certainly dressed the part. Her parents were still among the living, but had retired and moved to Connecticut. They maintained a relationship, but at times it was strained. Diana's parents did not approve of her searching. They felt it would lead to heartbreak and disappointment. Diana explained to Todd she didn't discuss it much with them anymore, it was just easier to not bring it up. If the day ever came when she did find her natural family, she wasn't sure she would even tell her parents about it. She admitted to being headstrong and fiercely independent. She loved foreign films, which thrilled Todd to no end. She enjoyed good food and red wine. She loved the outdoors but hated to exercise. She'd had a number of long term relationships, but so far, had not married. Todd thought she was absolutely perfect.

Todd told her more about himself as well. He talked about Matt, Katy, and the kids. He mentioned his failed marriage. He didn't go into depth about it, but expressed his sorrow and disappointment that it didn't work out. Even with the caffeine boost they were both getting tired, and concluded they'd covered enough ground for one evening. Todd asked if she would have dinner with him two nights later and she agreed. They stepped outside the coffeehouse and Todd

Paris and Soll

hailed a cab. She lived across town and he wanted to see her safely home. When they arrived she did not invite him in and he did not ask. She gave him a chaste kiss on the cheek and they said their good nights. Todd gave the driver his own address. On the way home, he couldn't wipe the smile from his face. After all the calamities of late, something good was happening, and he didn't want to do anything to screw that up. He crossed his fingers, just in case.

Chapter Twenty-One

Frank Barron hated his nickname. He'd been stuck with it since he got out of Quantico, so he figured he'd have it for life. But that didn't mean he had to like it. It all started when he told a female student at the academy how his young wife Suzy was wild about Snoopy. She loved the canine character, and had started collecting just about anything that had to do with him. Maybe to some people it seemed silly, but Frank found his wife's obsession rather sweet. The day after the seemingly casual conversation, he found a Snoopy in his locker. The plastic Snoopy was dressed in aviation gear, sitting atop his doghouse, playing the role of the fearless ace pilot off to hunt down the nasty Red Baron. There was a note attached which said it was for his wife's collection. At first, Frank thought it was a nice gesture, but when word got around, everyone started calling him Red. It wouldn't be so bad if he had red hair, or if he were at least Irish. But no, he had to be called Red because of his last name, and his wife's wacky fixation with a comic character. It was embarrassing.

Frank sighed. There were worse things in life. Take the file he was holding. A young woman apparently murdered for her child in Louisiana. *What kind of sick animal does that?* Frank had been assigned to the case, but so far, there wasn't much to go on. No witnesses to the crime. No trace of the child. They didn't even have a picture of the infant, as the young woman by the name of Charly Fairfield was a welfare mother, and the hospital hadn't bothered taking an identification photo after her baby was born.

Frank knew all too well children were kidnapped and sold secretly, the practice had been going on for centuries. Occasionally, there were well-publicized trials, where individuals had been accused of such diabolical schemes, but rarely was anyone convicted. Often it was just too difficult to prove. The stories would be sensationalized by the media for a time, but then eventually drop off the radar. Most people had no idea such crimes still took place today.

Frank had worked on a similar case some years ago. A number of women in various parts of West Texas had been killed, their babies taken. The problem was again, a lack of evidence, or any concrete clues as to who the perpetrators might be. There was a full investigation by the FBI, but there weren't many leads to follow, and the outcry from the communities involved eventually died down. Then the killings stopped. Frank and his fellow agents were left with virtually nothing to go on.

Frank also knew of many kidnappings, not only in the U.S., but also in Mexico and Central America, where babies were stolen right from under their mother's nose. It happened in shopping malls, outdoor markets, sometimes even from a hospital nursery. So far, he had not been able to discern any kind of pattern to the killings or kidnappings. He still didn't know if this was the work of one operation, or a number of individuals. Typically, the information he'd gathered in the United States was sketchy. When a mother was killed there were never any eyewitness accounts. Even though it was hard to believe, when babies had been snatched from a parent whose back was turned, very few descriptions of a suspect could be garnered. The grief stricken parents could only say they had been distracted, and in the blink of an eye, their baby had disappeared. Obviously, whoever did this kind of work took precautions and planned carefully. It almost always happened in a crowd, when no one was paying any attention.

Frank shook his head. How sad it all was. The parents who had their children stolen, and some had lost their lives because of it. The children themselves, sold through some kind of baby broker to unwitting adoptive parents. The adopting parents, usually desperate, were of course discouraged to ask too many questions, and would remain tight-lipped forever for fear of someone coming and taking their child away.

"Hey Red, here's another file to add to your collection." A young agent popped into Frank's office and tossed a folder on his desk.

"Don't call me Red!" Frank shouted, but the newbie was already down the hall and out of earshot. No one listened to him anyway. It was bad enough when the others he'd gone through the academy with called him Red, but he hated it when the young ones picked up on it as well. It was his bane.

However, the anger was momentary. He flipped open the file and noticed it was a new case from a rural Tennessee hospital, where an infant had been taken from its mother's arms by a woman posing as a nurse. Great. He'd follow up on it, but he had a pretty darn good feeling the mom wouldn't be able to tell him much. It was worth a try though. Maybe he'd be able to get a description for once, or even the woman caught on a security camera. He could dream. Frank figured if he worked on these cases long enough, some clue would eventually surface that would lead to a face, a name, fingerprints, something.

For if nothing else, Frank, "Red" Barron, was tenacious. He had a vested interest in stopping the people who committed these crimes. Frank's mother had abandoned him when he was three days old, actually left him on the doorstep of a church. He entered the world of foster care, and didn't leave it until he was of legal age. Once he turned eighteen, he enlisted, spent four years in the Navy, and then applied and was accepted to the FBI academy. He figured he was cut out for that line of work. After being shuffled around from one family to another over the years, Frank's heart had hardened into stone, and he thought he would never feel anything again. Turned out he was wrong. He met Suzy, and she and her stupid Snoopy memorabilia changed him enough to care for people again. She also made him realize that in a perfect world, babies should never be separated from their mothers. Frank couldn't agree more after living all those years in the foster care void, never having a mother to call his own. So he made it his life-long pursuit to try and track down and punish those who committed such evil offenses. He was the Red Barron all right, and he was on a mission.

Chapter Twenty-Two

Over the course of the week, Todd had given a lot of thought to what Diana said about searching. They had their dinner date, and during the evening they purposely avoided discussion about anything related to adoption, or the support group, or what Todd might choose to do. It seemed there was an unspoken agreement to keep the conversation light. They just wanted to be a normal couple out on a date rather than two people who felt disconnected from the earthlings in the restaurant. So, they talked about movies, plays, and favorite books. Todd never missed an opportunity to mention his love for Boots Beaumont mysteries, and when Diana expressed an interest in reading one, Todd promised he'd bring her a copy of *Finding Michael*, one of his favorites.

They had a great time. There wasn't the awkwardness associated with a first date, maybe having gone for coffee a couple of times helped, but more importantly, Todd and Diana just clicked. Conversation came easily, and they seemed to have a natural rapport. Todd wondered if it was because they were both adopted and shared a common bond, or if it was because they were both attracted to one another, or perhaps a combination of the two. Ultimately, it didn't matter. Todd knew one thing for sure. He was falling for her big time.

Earlier in the week, Todd had been to another appointment with Claire. He'd started to become more and more reluctant about going to these regular sessions. He felt like he was really getting a handle on his life lately, and just didn't know how much longer he wanted to continue therapy. The problem was, he didn't know exactly how to bring the subject up. He feared Claire might try and talk him out of it, especially since she was so blunt and matter of fact about everything. Frankly, Todd was a bit intimidated by her. So, he simply avoided the subject by discussing the search issue with her again, and this time explained why he thought he felt ready for the next step. Much to his surprise, Claire

Evil Exchange

agreed and suggested he reach out to the support group for help, and she would remain available to him to explore his feelings and fears about such an endeavor. Never one to sugar coat or mince words, Claire also suggested they taper off the appointment schedule. She told Todd he was making good progress, he hadn't had any more panic attacks other than the original one, which had brought him to her door in the first place. Todd and Miriam had reconciled, Diana had entered the picture, and work was going well. So far (and at this point she'd even said "knock on wood" and laughed), there hadn't been any other mysterious life-threatening, near-death events either. She felt Todd was getting the emotional support he needed from the group, and keeping a regular appointment once a month for maintenance purposes would suit them both fine for the time being. Should anything change, Claire said they could adjust the schedule back again. Todd was enormously relieved. He knew seeing a therapist was the right move, but he still couldn't help but feel a bit uncomfortable about it all. He just didn't see himself as that kind of person. Going to the support group was enough of a stretch. As he made an appointment for the following month, Todd marveled at this woman's ability to know what was best for him. She seemed to know exactly what he was thinking but afraid to bring up, and she let him off the hook. The woman was incredibly intuitive.

Wednesday evening arrived in a flash. Todd clutched his file folder under his arm as he bounded up the steps to the YMCA where the support group meeting was held promptly at seven o'clock each week. He waited outside for Diana who made it just moments later. Todd had brought his copy of *Finding Michael* for her and she was delighted. She thanked him with a quick peck on the cheek and they slipped inside. On this evening, they sat together.

After a few announcements from the group leader Beth, Todd raised his hand and asked if he could address the group first. Beth said of course. Holding the folder, Todd stood and explained to everyone how he'd recovered some paperwork regarding his adoption. He left out the part about Stuart, because he knew it would just make him angry, and he didn't want to waste time going over the whole thing again. Glen and Diana both knew what he'd gone through to get the paperwork and that was good enough. He announced with great pride his birth name and his first mother's name to the group. Everyone smiled at his obvious delight in sharing this very special information. Then Todd mentioned the folder contained some correspondence between his parents and some law firms. He basically got the gist of those. His parents were inquiring about adopting a child, and most of the attorneys offered little help. However, there was one letter, the one from Jacob Klein, who mentioned he might be of assistance to his parents regarding the matter. In that letter, Mr. Klein stated he knew of a woman who upon occasion was able to match just the right baby to just the right

Paris and Soll

family. According to the glowing recommendation from Klein, the woman was an angel. She took in unwanted and abandoned infants, and arranged as many adoptions as she could for good people, such as the Walters. Mr. Klein had also mentioned he would get in touch with said woman, on their behalf. He would be more than happy to put in a good word, at no cost to them.

Those letters led to another series of letters, from the saintly woman herself, who agreed to act as the blessed miracle worker for Bob and Miriam. The correspondence consisted mostly of questions and answers, financial status, so on and so forth. There was mention of a fee involved, but no exact amount. Todd told everyone he'd read through the papers many times, but he couldn't discern much specific information about his adoption. He wasn't able to determine if his parents had adopted him from the woman who had written the letters or not. So his question to the group was how important did they think the forty-year old letters might be in helping him search for his first parents or should he just stick with the information on his birth certificate also in the file?

As Glen was the search expert, he cleared his throat and spoke first. "The more information you have to go on the better chance you'll have. Todd, you mentioned the name of Jacob Klein. But you haven't told us the name on the letters from the woman he put in touch with your parents."

"Oh right. Sorry." Todd flipped through the folder and found what he was looking for. "Um, here it is. Madeline Monroe. That's how the letters are signed."

Todd heard an audible gasp. It was Beth. "Madeline Monroe? You mean *Maddie Monroe?*" Beth covered her mouth with one hand after uttering the name as if she were going to be sick.

"Well, yeah. That's what it looks like. Why? Who is she?" Todd's skin was starting to feel prickly and a flush of heat crept up his throat. This didn't sound good.

"What year were you born?" Beth asked quickly.

"1964," Todd blurted. *What was going on?*

"May I see one of the letters, please?" Beth held out a trembling hand. *Good thing I'm only handing her paper,* Todd thought as he passed the letter over. Beth took held it between her thumb and forefinger, touching it as though it was a dead thing that might infect her on contact. As she looked it over, her eyes filled with tears.

"Oh, Todd. Oh, my God. It's her. I am so sorry," Beth was openly sobbing now and handed the letter back to him as fast as she could.

97

Evil Exchange

"Beth, please! Who is she? Why are you sorry?"

Beth tried to compose herself. She wiped some tears from her face and looked at Todd.

"Are you sure you want to know?"

"Of course I want to know," Todd was adamant. Everyone in the room was watching the exchange in stunned silence. No one knew what Beth was going to say. No one but Glen. He knew. And, his heart couldn't be any heavier for Todd.

"Maddie Monroe was an infamous baby broker for more than thirty years, up until the seventies. She sold children, Todd."

"You mean she charged for her service, right? People do that sometimes in a private adoption . . ." Todd looked around the room for confirmation. No one said a word and his stomach lurched.

"Stole *and* sold, Todd. Maddie ran a black market baby selling operation." Beth's chest heaved with another sob.

Todd's knees felt like jelly. He sat down in his seat, trying to make sense of what Beth had just said. Diana put a hand on his shoulder, but he didn't feel a thing. His mouth opened and closed a few times before any words came out. Finally he was able to ask a question.

"How do you know about all of this?"

"I had a friend named Pam," Beth said as she tried to compose herself. "She was adopted in the fifties and the arrangements were made through that woman," Beth pointed at Todd's folder. "When she tried to search for her first parents using her birth certificate, she found out all of the information had been falsified by Maddie. Not one name or date was real. Pam became obsessed with Madeline Monroe. She spent countless hours trying to find out more about her. Of course by this time Maddie had retired and her whereabouts were unknown. Pam did some digging and discovered at one point, Maddie had even gone to trial for selling babies. It was a huge scandal back then. It was sixty-seven or sixty-eight, I can't remember. She was convicted, but ended up never serving any time in prison. I don't know how she managed it, but she just paid a fine instead, end of story. She went into hiding for a while, but eventually she resurfaced, changed her name, and continued selling children."

Todd blanched. He couldn't quite believe what he was hearing. *This couldn't be true, could it?*

"Beth . . .do you think I could talk to your friend? This is all so crazy . . ." Todd stopped when he saw Beth shake her head violently.

"Impossible."

"Please, Beth. I'm begging you."

"I said I *had* a friend," Beth said softly.

Todd was confused.

"She killed herself," Beth looked away, not able to make eye contact with Todd.

The air left the room. Todd was floored. No wonder Beth had become so upset when she heard the name of Madeline Monroe.

Diana broke the silence. "But why, Beth? What happened?"

"Pam found this article on the Internet about Maddie. The article said Maddie *paid* mothers for their children, as if it were a legitimate transaction. Pam couldn't accept the fact that her mother had sold her. She was completely devastated. She thought she'd been bought and sold like merchandise, and she realized she would never know the truth about any of it since her records were false. She didn't even know if her birthday on the birth certificate was real. She felt like a ghost. She decided she couldn't live with that and took her own life. What's even more tragic is what we found out later. The article was misleading. Maddie Monroe *stole* children and then sold them for profit. Pam's mother didn't sell her. Pam was *taken* from her." Beth's eyes brimmed with fresh tears. Finally, she was able to look at Todd. She could see the toll her words were taking.

"Todd, I'm so thoughtless. I never should have told you about Pam's suicide. She was a very damaged person to begin with," Beth tried to explain.

It all fell on deaf ears. Todd bolted from the room.

Chapter Twenty-Three

Nardo sat in the rental car and waited patiently outside the pregnancy support center. He kept a low profile, but he wasn't terribly concerned about staying completely out of sight. Most people tended to steer clear of the hulking man. Besides, if someone were to approach him, he could easily explain his presence by saying he was waiting on his teenage daughter who was having a checkup. The traffic in and out of the center was what you might expect. Young women usually alone, sometimes with a friend, in various stages of pregnancy and emotional distress.

Nardo ignored most of them. His next potential victim must meet some very specific criteria mandated by The Stork. The woman must be young, but not so young she'd be living at home with mom and dad. She must be alone. She should be on foot or taking the bus so she'd be easy to follow. That the girl had to be low income or poor was a given. A middle class or wealthy young woman might either have already had an abortion, or if she were to carry a child to term, she would most likely be going to a private practice for checkups, not some rundown clinic like the one he sat in front of now.

He'd been in Alabama since morning. The envelope with this particular target area map was safely tucked away in his shirt pocket. As soon as he locked in on a likely subject, he'd destroy the envelope and its contents. Nardo knew how vital it was to be careful. Nothing was ever left behind or carelessly thrown away in the trash. He was working recognizance alone as usual, the Mule would be notified later if the operation were a go.

Nardo spotted a possible target as an expectant mother approached the center. She looked to be maybe nineteen or twenty, wearing unkempt, ratty clothes. She was stick thin, but her belly was huge with child. He noticed how she clutched her abdomen, as if the weight were unbearable. Yes, she was close

Paris and Soll

all right. Nardo had a skilled eye, and knew her baby would be coming just about any day. The girl slipped inside, and for the next hour, Nardo never took his eyes off the grimy glass doors while he waited for her to come out.

He had the routine down to a science. As soon as he zeroed in on what he was looking for, the vic would be followed home. Depending on where that might be, and if she lived alone, would determine whether he would proceed or bail. If the conditions were right, he would then settle in to wait, watching for a trip either to the hospital, or in some rare cases, for the birth to take place at home. It was usually a long arduous process, but sometimes he got lucky and things happened quickly. He had a pretty good feeling about this one.

After the girl left the center and made her way home on the bus, Nardo followed at a safe distance. She lived in a rundown trailer park, which was a bit of a red flag right there. Trailer parks often had nosy neighbors and barking dogs. He was further discouraged by the fact that she appeared to live with someone else. He could see her talking to someone inside the grungy trailer, but it was difficult to tell if it were a roommate or a boyfriend or a parent. Maybe it was just a friend. He wasn't about to give up just yet. Nardo wanted to at least check things out a little further before he decided either way. He'd give it another day or two. Even though they were some potential strikes against this one working out, he might still catch a break.

Nardo was constantly under pressure to succeed. The Stork and the Boss were relentless in the pursuit of infants. It seemed there was a never-ending queue of couples who were willing to shell out big bucks for a child of their own. Nardo and the Mule worked endlessly and traveled constantly. Each collection took careful timing and planning. They moved from state to state, crossed the border, and even flew to Central America now and then. A snuff and snatch always took a lot of planning and was quite time consuming, but the payoff there was no witnesses. Ever.

So, he wouldn't quit staking this one out just yet. He'd come back later when it was dark and see if he couldn't get a better handle on the situation.

It was late afternoon when he hit the road. He was on his way back to the motel, miles away from the shabby trailer park. Nardo always made sure he put plenty of distance between where he stayed and the vic's location, as it would eventually become a crime scene. He didn't want anyone to be able to identify him or remember he'd been in the area.

Driving along the highway, he suddenly heard a loud bang and then a violent hissing noise as a tire blew. He maintained perfect control of the vehicle and expertly slowed and steered over to the shoulder. He slid his bulk out of the

Evil Exchange

driver's seat and slammed the car door. Sure enough, the left front tire was flat. He knew he wasn't close enough to a gas station or garage to drive on the blown tire. He'd have to change it. He walked to the back and opened the trunk. At least there was a decent jack, and the spare looked okay.

Nardo was kneeling on the ground and almost finished with the tire when he heard the crunch of gravel. A state trooper had pulled up behind him and an officer stepped out.

"Need help?" The trooper called out.

"No thanks," Nardo responded politely. He ducked his head and stooped his massive shoulders to appear non-threatening. He still had his baseball cap on despite the heat and hassle of changing the tire. Nardo never took the cap off. It helped to keep his Hungarian features in shadow.

His pulse quickened a bit as the trooper approached, but as any well-trained officer will do, he kept some distance between himself and the man on the ground.

"Flat tire, huh? Sometimes those rental cars aren't worth a damn, are they?"

"It's my fault. Got the cheapest model," Nardo shook his head indicating his own stupidity. He lowered the jack. "That should do it."

"Are you here on business or pleasure?"

"Neither. Just been to see a cousin in Huntsville. Flew in yesterday. He has the cancer," Nardo spoke solemnly.

"Sorry to hear that, man." The patrol car radio sputtered in the background. "Well, as long as you don't need anything, I'd best be going. Good day, sir." The trooper gave a mock salute and started back to his patrol car.

Nardo breathed a soft sigh of relief. He didn't think the cop would remember him. He was just a guy fixing a flat. He got up from the side of the car, brushed some dirt from his pants, picked up the flat tire and the jack to stow them in the trunk.

Nardo turned to see the trooper pull away from the side of the road. The officer gave him a nod, and Nardo returned it. He knew he would have to exchange the rental car for a different model, just as a precaution. He wasn't too worried about continuing his surveillance of the girl, as he was more than thirty miles from the trailer park and he felt confident the trooper did not consider him to be suspicious. The guy seemed to buy the cancer-stricken-cousin cover story, and had only seen him from the side anyway. He hadn't even asked to see Nardo's driver's license. Still, he knew he had to be extra cautious.

Paris and Soll

What Nardo didn't know however, was the State Highway Patrol had recently installed a new camera on every trooper's car. The encounter between Nardo and the trooper, which had lasted all of two minutes and thirty-eight seconds, had all been caught on tape.

Chapter Twenty-Four

"Madeline Monroe. Do you remember that name?"

"Sounds familiar for some reason," Miriam replied. "Who is she?"

Todd rubbed his temples. He had the beginnings of a monster headache, possibly a migraine. He didn't want to upset Miriam, but it was a struggle to keep his cool after what he'd heard from Beth. As soon as he walked out of the group session, he hailed a cab and immediately went to see his mother. It was still early enough in the evening. Sure enough, when he arrived, Miriam was in her room watching television. She was happy to see him as always and immediately turned off the set. Todd knew his mother was the only one who could clear this up for him. Surely his parents had not adopted him through a purported baby seller. It was unthinkable.

"Mom, remember I told you that I went to Stuart's office, and I got my file from him? It has stuff in it about my adoption and some other stuff too. I have it with me, and I wanted you to look at some of this, okay?"

Todd's nerves were frayed. It was taking all his willpower to try and remain calm and he was trying not to jump to any wild conclusions. He knew if he lost it with Miriam, he'd never find out anything. Her health was all right, but her mental state was a different story. The last few years, Todd had seen a noticeable difference. She was not as confident as she used to be. If she were agitated or upset, she'd become confused, or as she like to put it, "confuzzled." Her memory had started to slip, or at the very least was certainly more selective. She liked to remember the good times with her darling Bob, and the joy of raising her two sons. She adored her daughter-in-law Katy, and doted on her grandchildren. Aging had mellowed her in some ways, and frightened her in others. As she aged, her self-esteem became as delicate and fragile as the skin on the back of her hands. Todd knew he had to proceed carefully.

They sat side by side on the couch in her room. Todd opened the file, and together they looked at each item. For Miriam, it was a walk down memory lane. Todd let her "ooh" and "ah" over the report card, the photo, the love letter, and the birth certificate. Her responses alternated between "I remember that," and "I'd forgotten that."

Finally they got to the letters. Miriam looked at each one, concentrating hard. Although Todd hadn't said as much, she sensed from him that she must try and remember something. It seemed to be important.

"None of this looks very familiar," she remarked. "Your father handled most of the correspondence."

"What about this one?" Todd showed her the first letter from Maddie.

Miriam squinted, but said nothing. She looked at a few more, and nodded. It was coming back.

"She's the one who arranged your adoption for us," Miriam crowed. "I remember her now."

Todd remained stone-faced, but inside, felt as if he were drowning.

"Nice enough woman. Very business-like you know. Your father and I met with her once, and she assured us she would find the perfect baby boy, just for us."

"Mom," Todd cleared his throat. "Did you pay her for me?"

"Well, heavens no! Where on earth would you get an idea like that?" Miriam seemed offended.

"There's some mention of a fee, see here? In this letter," Todd showed her the paragraph.

"Oh. That was for the expenses," Miriam stated firmly as if it explained everything.

"What expenses?"

"Well, for your natural mother. Madeline told us we would have to cover the medical fees, you know, for when she gave birth to you."

"I see," Todd said the words but didn't believe them.

"It was the least we could do," Miriam said. "Your mother was very young when she had you. She couldn't take care of you. She did what she thought was best. She gave us the greatest gift anyone could. The son we always wanted. Why wouldn't we at least help pay the bills?"

"Do you know anything else about her?" Todd pulled out the birth certificate again. "Was this her name? Did you go to this hospital to get me? Did you ever meet her?"

"Of course we never met her for heaven's sake. We were never told her name until we saw it on your birth certificate. I'd forgotten all about that one, because when your adoption became legal, then your birth certificate had our names on it as your mother and father. Besides, those things just weren't discussed back then. Madeline said it was best for all concerned if there was no contact whatsoever. She implied it would just upset your natural mother. We didn't go to the hospital. I didn't even know where it was. Madeline brought you to us at home when you were maybe a week old. That's all I know, I swear. I know I lied to you before, and I'm sorry. But right now I'm telling you the truth," Miriam put her hand over her heart for emphasis.

"Okay," Todd sighed. But it wasn't.

"It's all right there Todd. If it's on your original birth certificate, it must be true."

"Do you know anything about my father?" It was the first time Todd had even mentioned his natural father.

"No. But it's there on the birth certificate," Miriam pointed at the space which read Darryl Foster.

"Yeah. Guess I really haven't given him much thought up till now."

"Well, it's something to go on, isn't it?" Miriam asked.

Todd didn't want to tell her he feared it could all be false. They'd already been through enough drama lately, and he didn't think his mom could take any more. Obviously, Miriam and Bob thought they were doing the right thing at the time and that was forty years ago. They blindly believed everything Maddie had told them. And why not? They were trusting people. If Maddie had painted the perfect picture for them, why would they question her? She'd been recommended by a lawyer hadn't she? Todd couldn't imagine for one minute if his parents had known Madeline Monroe was running a black market baby selling operation they would have dealt with her. No way. His parents were good, honest people. They would never willingly participate in something illegal. He looked at Miriam and could tell she was getting tired. It was time to go. He thanked her for her help, and she smiled in response. He kissed her good-bye and left.

When he got home, his head was killing him, but it wasn't due to the headache.

Paris and Soll

He saw the blinking light on his answering machine, but he didn't want to listen to any messages. He went straight to his bedroom and laid down in the dark. His inner world was a maelstrom of confusion. Would he ever be able to solve the puzzle and find his natural family? And if not, could he endure the pain of never knowing where he came from? He had such high hopes of finding his natural parents, his mother at least, and now that seemed impossible. He wondered what on earth he could do to get past this hurdle. It would take a miracle now to succeed. Just before he dozed off, his last thought was whether he would ever know the truth.

Chapter Twenty-Five

After careful review of the file of the mother in Tennessee, Frank knew he needed to interview her in person. He called in a favor with one of his superiors and was able to get permission to fly out immediately rather than having to wait for the request to be processed in the more typical snail paced fashion.

Having called ahead, Frank knew it would be a difficult situation at best. The woman, Tarren Vincent, was under a doctor's care and heavily medicated since the abduction of her baby from the hospital. She was at home, but unable to care for her three-year-old son, so her husband Drew had taken a leave of absence from work to deal with his wife's depression, his rowdy little boy, and his own despair. Their baby Vanessa (who'd been named for her great-grandmother) would have completed their happy family if she had made it home. Frank received all the most recent information from Tarren's mother. He had some difficulty understanding her over the phone, as the woman could not stop crying.

He arrived at McGhee Tyson airport in Knoxville, a two hour flight from Dulles. During the flight, Frank went over the information from the Louisiana case file once again. He wondered if there might be a connection between the two abductions. If it was the work of the same group or individual, then Tarren Vincent was lucky to be alive. Not so for poor Charly Fairfield. Unfortunately, there was still little to go on in Charly's case. He'd spoken at length with Sheriff Nance about the discovery and condition of the body. He'd also interviewed the father, Denny Fairfield, over the phone, but he didn't learn anything more than what Nance had already told him. With few leads and no witnesses to the crime, Frank would keep Charly's file on active status, but did not have much confidence her crime would be solved. A young mother killed, a baby stolen, was unfortunately just another sad statistic. Frank might often get discouraged, but he would not give up. Although normally a pragmatic guy, this time he couldn't help but get his hopes up just a tad that Tarren Vincent, even in a drug induced state, just might be able to give him something to work with.

Frank rented a car and arrived at the Vincent home in the early afternoon. It was a modest home in an older neighborhood. The lawn out front was in need of a good soaking, but Drew Vincent surely had his hands full just trying to keep his family together, so the lawn would have to wait. Frank walked up to the front porch and rang the bell. He was met by Tarren's mother, Alice. Frank introduced himself and showed his credentials. Alice opened the screen door and asked him in.

Adjusting his eyesight from the blinding sun to the dimly lit interior, he entered the living room and was met by a sticky faced boy who immediately high-tailed it down the hall. Alice explained how her grandson was easily upset these days. She told Frank Drew was with his wife in the other room and excused herself to inform them he was here.

Frank waited patiently and looked around the house. Toys were scattered all over and laundry was piled high on one chair waiting to be folded. He couldn't miss the family photos as they were everywhere. The picture frames took up almost every inch of open space and were proudly displayed on the bookcase, coffee table, and mantle. Photos of mom, dad, and son in happier times. The one that really got to him was obviously recent. A shot of pregnant Tarren, her arms lovingly around her precious son. His ear was pressed against his mother's belly, listening as if his baby sister were speaking to him directly from the womb. The photo was so simple, so sweet. The picture conveyed the anticipation of the joyous occasion soon to come. Tarren's face beamed, and the excitement on her son's face was clear. Under the circumstances, it was heartbreaking to look at.

Alice returned and asked if he could speak with Drew and Tarren in the bedroom. She said they had hoped Tarren would be able to get out of bed to meet with him, but apparently she couldn't bring herself to do so. Would he mind?

Frank nodded in understanding and let Alice lead him down the hallway. More photos lined the walls. He tried not to look at them. Alice knocked and opened the door. She introduced Frank to Drew who was sitting by his wife's side. Drew let go of Tarren's hand just long enough to offer a quick, but powerful handshake. Drew Vincent was ruggedly handsome. Frank knew from a routine background check of the family that Drew had played quarterback on his high school football team. Tarren had been a song leader and straight A student. They were high school sweethearts who married not long after graduation. Drew went to work in a meat packing plant. Tarren worked at a preschool until the birth of their first child. They were nice, young people. Both were close to their families and deeply religious.

"Honey? Agent Barron is here to talk with you. Remember? I told you he was coming," Drew spoke gently to his wife.

Tarren looked in Frank's direction, but her eyes were unfocused. She looked small, almost childlike in bed. She was twenty-three, but looked much older. Losing Vanessa had taken a brutal toll. Her face looked both haunted and vacant at the same time. Drew brushed some hair from her forehead and waited for her to say something. She didn't.

"Maybe you could come sit over here?" Drew stood and indicated the chair beside the bed. The men switched places. Alice stifled a sob and went to look after her grandson.

"Hi Tarren. I'm Agent Frank Barron with the FBI. Most people call me Red, so I hope you will too." Even though he disliked his nickname, he often used it to make a person feel more at ease. People were often intimidated by the FBI, and Frank wanted Tarren to feel comfortable talking with him.

"Will you help me find my baby?" Tarren pleaded.

"I'm going to try," Frank answered. "But I'm going to need some help from you. Do you think you're up to that?"

Her eyes were tracking now, looking straight at him. She nodded.

"I know you gave a statement at the hospital. You tried to describe the woman who came in. She was dressed as a nurse?"

"Yes."

"According to the report, you said she was of medium height, medium weight, brown hair and brown eyes. No distinguishing features you can think of?"

"No, not really. She was plain. Really just average looking. And, I wasn't really paying attention, you know? The doctor had given me some pain medication, so I was pretty fuzzy."

"She'd been in labor all night, she was wiped out," Drew added in defense of his wife.

"I understand. It must be very hard to remember," Frank nodded sympathetically. He noticed Tarren's cheeks were wet with tears and that she clutched a crucifix in her right hand.

"And in the report you said that she was in medical scrubs?"

"I guess that's what you call them. It's what you see most nurses wear. You know, the cotton v-neck top and matching pants."

"Colorful."

"What?"

"You said the top was 'colorful'."

"Uh-huh."

"Design?"

"Ummm . . . animals I think. Like zoo animals. And solid colored pants. Does that mean anything?"

Frank didn't want to discourage her by saying how anyone could walk into a uniform supply store and purchase the items. So he asked another question.

"Did she wear any jewelry?"

Tarren shook her head no. Frank continued to ask questions even though it was rehashing what had been asked before. But even in her depressive state, Tarren gave the same answers she'd given the police. There weren't any inconsistencies whatsoever. Frank knew that sometimes going over and over information could upon occasion, trigger a buried memory. It was the reason he was here interviewing her today. He'd hoped he might jog her memory just enough to gain some new insight, no matter how small or seemingly insignificant. So far, that hadn't happened.

A half-hour later, he could see Tarren was visibly tiring and retreating back into her shell. Nothing more would be gained. The interview was over. Frank was disheartened, but didn't show it. He thanked the Vincents' for their time. He handed Drew a card, and said he could be reached at any time should Tarren remember anything else. The two men switched places once again, and Frank said he'd let himself out.

"Wait," Tarren said suddenly. Frank spun around.

"She had a pin. Next to her name badge. I don't remember if it had words on it, but I think I remember the design."

She released the crucifix as Frank handed her the notebook and pen he'd been using to take notes. He watched with growing excitement as she began to draw.

Chapter Twenty-Six

Todd retreated for a few days. Other than work, he didn't leave the apartment much. He knew it was becoming a bad pattern, him dropping out of sight to lick his wounds, but he couldn't seem to help it.

The temperatures had been steadily climbing, and it seemed all of Manhattan was trying to beat the heat. All Todd felt was a frostiness in his lungs and a chill in his bones, as if he'd been inside a deep freeze. He tried to come to terms with this latest bizarre development. *He was a black market baby?* Todd had trouble even grasping the concept, much less accepting the fact it had actually happened to him. His head still hurt, although it had finally settled down into a dull throb. His muscles ached and his thoughts were jumbled. He felt like a prize fighter who'd been knocked down one too many times, but like an idiot kept getting back up.

He toyed with the idea of calling Claire, but decided against it. While he knew she could help him sort through the muck that now was his life, he also had this irrational fear that if he got into the habit of calling her every time something happened, he'd become dependent on her somehow. Logic told him therapy was helpful, testosterone told him to deal with it himself. Todd compromised between the two by vowing to sort though as much of it as he could on his own, and then discuss it with Claire at their next appointment in three weeks.

He called and spoke at length with Glen, still searching for some glimmer of hope. As much as Glen wanted to help, there wasn't much he could do. Since Todd's adoption had indeed been arranged through the notorious Madeline Monroe, Glen explained it would be almost impossible to go any further.

Glen gave Todd further details about Pam's ordeal. After learning she was a victim of the black market baby selling scam, Pam sued the state of New York to release her sealed adoption records. It took time and effort, but eventually she won and got the records. It was how she learned everything was false. She didn't have a prayer to ever find out anything. That was how Maddie operated. Erroneous information was supplied on each and every adoption arranged by Monroe. The children who'd been stolen away from their mothers could never be found. Adoptees could never trace their roots, or know their true identity. Glen didn't want Todd to give up hope entirely, but chances were slim he would ever be able to find out much at all. Todd said he understood (which of course was a lie), and thanked Glen for his help. Glen urged Todd to return to the support group for their next meeting, because under the circumstances he needed them now more than ever. Todd said he'd be back when he was ready, but didn't know when that might be.

Diana left two messages on his machine. She sounded worried at first, then just plain pissed off. He finally called her back and apologized. She immediately forgave him and said she wanted to see him. She knew Todd probably wouldn't feel much like going out, so she invited him over to her place. Todd said he wouldn't be very good company, she of course said she didn't care, and after a few minutes of verbal swordplay, Diana convinced him. She would even cook dinner.

Not one to come empty handed, Todd picked up flowers and a bottle of his favorite French Bordeaux on his way over. He pushed the bell next to Diana's name in the lobby and she buzzed him up. Todd realized how much he was looking forward to seeing her, knowing her smile alone would cheer him up. As he reached the landing of the second story building, Diana opened her door to welcome him in. Todd felt a flutter in his chest. She looked great as usual. She was exactly the boost he needed after his self-imposed imprisonment.

It was his first time inside the apartment and Todd looked around with interest. When it came to decorating, Diana was a minimalist, which surprised him. She was so feminine, he thought she might land more on the frilly side of the fence, but he couldn't have been more wrong. The furniture was modern, and a number of small but expensive pieces of artwork adorned the walls. The most interesting feature of all was the telephones. Todd had never seen so many in one apartment.

Diana thanked him for the flowers, and invited him into the kitchen while she looked for a vase. After asking for a corkscrew, Todd busied himself with opening the red wine to let it breathe. The air smelled of rosemary and garlic which made his stomach growl. He hadn't had a decent meal in days. Todd couldn't help but notice there were two more phones in the kitchen.

Evil Exchange

"Do you collect phones?" Todd asked.

"Oh, those." Diana blushed and then laughed. "I'm embarrassed to say I have even more. There's two in my bedroom and one more in the bathroom. I have this friend in the building who's an electrician. He put in all these phone jacks for me, wherever I wanted."

"Don't want to miss any important calls?" Todd teased.

"Hey, you guessed it right off," Diana exclaimed.

"I did?"

"I've always had this fascination with phones. I buy them as often as some women buy shoes. Pretty weird I guess. Then one day I finally figured out why. It had to do with my wish."

Todd looked blank.

"When I was a little girl, I wished that some day, my first mother would call me. I dreamt about it, used to make up stories about it. Especially on my birthday. That's when I thought I would hear the phone ring and she would be on the other end, just waiting to tell me how much she missed me. When I became a teenager, my parents got me my own phone, and then my addiction became full blown. I especially like ones that have doodads and gadgets on them. Believe it or not, I get nervous when I'm not around one. Thank goodness for cell phones," Diana pointed at her own on the counter top. "I know, I'm strange," she shrugged.

"I think it's sweet." Todd said. "Well, I guess I won't have to worry about missing any calls," he tried to sound light hearted but failed.

Without a word, Diana set down the vase of flowers and wrapped Todd in a bear hug. Todd felt as if he'd been stranded in the desert for days and had just stumbled across a fresh water spring. He soaked up the smell and touch of her. He hadn't realized just how isolated and alone he felt until this moment when he wasn't any longer.

Diana finally pulled away and asked Todd to fill her in. She poured wine for them both and led him to the living room couch. She told him dinner wouldn't be ready for a while yet, and she wanted to hear everything.

So he told her. What he found out from his mother and what Glen had said. He was surprised at how it all came pouring out. He couldn't believe how much had happened, and how freaky it sounded once verbalized. Todd never in a million years could have predicted any of it. Now, he felt utterly hopeless that he would ever solve the mystery of his own background.

Paris and Soll

"Wait," Diana cried out. She jumped from the couch and raced to the bedroom. Todd didn't know what to do. *Was he supposed to follow her?*

Diana reappeared before Todd had a chance to make up his mind. She handed him a book.

"*Finding Michael*. You lent it to me," Diana said as if that explained it all.

Todd looked at the book. It was the Boots Beaumont novel he'd given her to read. He looked at her in confusion.

"Don't you see? As soon as you said 'mystery' I thought of it. It's perfect."

"What does this have to do with anything?"

Diana rolled her eyes in exasperation. "Remember the story? This man loses his memory and the detective helps him find his identity?"

"Okay . . ."

"Well, maybe this Boots Beaumont could help you."

"Diana, no offense. But this is fiction," Todd reminded her and handed the book back.

"I *know* that. But did you read the part at the end? Here, let me show you." She quickly riffled through the pages. "This part about the author. It says here, Boots Beaumont is a former private eye. He specialized in getting things back. He could find things that no one else could find. Hidden bank accounts, stolen property, abducted children. If anyone could help you, he could," Diana said triumphantly.

"Yeah, but he doesn't do that anymore. He writes books now," Todd said in exasperation.

"Maybe he'll come out of retirement," Diana was not about to give up.

"Yeah. And maybe I'll win the lottery."

Diana punched his shoulder. "Oh stop being so pessimistic. We can try, can't we?" Todd had to admit he liked the word "we" but thought Diana was crazy. "Besides, you don't even know where he is, how are you going to get a hold of him?" *That should stop her.*

Diana referred to the book again. "It says right here he lives on the island of Eleuthera, in the Bahamas. *And*, it gives his website address. We can email him."

"Oh good, for a minute there I thought you were going to say we could call him," Todd nodded at the phones.

Evil Exchange

This time she slugged him. "Oh, come on! What do you have to lose?"

"You are insane," Todd grinned.

"No. I'm determined."

"No. You're beautiful."

"No. I'm hungry. Let's eat."

Chapter Twenty-Seven

As much as Boots liked to give Julie crap about her psychic powers and predictions, he had to admit there was something to it. If she had any kind of vision, he knew she would pay strict attention to it. For example, he knew some years ago Julie started having plane crash visions. Most often it would happen when she was taking a nap rather than when she was asleep for the night. She would dream about a plane crash, the violence and shock of it so terrifying, it would violently wake her and she'd be drenched in sweat. At some point afterwards, it could be hours or maybe even a day later, she would hear about a plane crash on television or read the same news in the paper. Each time Julie would be horrified, as if her vision caused the real thing to occur. Over a period of two years, it happened to her five times. Each time it happened, it wasn't a small plane crash, which happens far too frequently. These were major disasters involving large commercial jets that went down due to mechanical failure or bad weather. Julie was obsessed and haunted by it. Not that she traveled much anyway, but while this was happening Julie wouldn't set foot anywhere near an airport.

Finally, when Julie couldn't take it any more, she enlisted one of her cousins to help. Shay-Shay was an expert hypnotist. Once she put Julie under, Shay-Shay was able to suppress the visions and they stopped all together, much to Julie's relief. She still retained her natural ability to foresee certain other events, and her premonitions were still very strong. But she no longer suffered from plane crash visions. Julie was immensely grateful.

Julie often had a keen sense of impending doom, and though it might sound bad, it actually came in pretty handy. Many a time Julie would sense something before it happened, and therefore be able to avoid it. She paid special attention when driving a car or riding a moped around the island. Many times it was

Evil Exchange

as simple as merely slowing down when there was an accident ahead, which of course one could argue is only common sense. Yet Julie was convinced there were many instances when her visions truly saved her. Sometimes the premonitions were so strong, Julie would refuse to even travel from one side of the island to the other. Because she didn't venture out at those times, she never knew for sure if anything would have happened, but she felt it would have, and that was enough. Julie might be wild and compulsive, but she wasn't stupid, and she did not believe in taking chances when it came to her life.

The other reason Boots believed in Julie's psychic ability was due to the fact he'd actually experienced it himself. Not to the same degree as Julie, for she had a far superior level of sensitivity, but he too had a vision.

One evening, Boots, Julie, and a group of friends from Club Med got into a discussion about ESP. Julie asked everyone if they would be interested in exploring other planes of consciousness, and they all jumped at the chance. Since everyone else wanted to try it, Boots was forced to go along with the program. Julie called her cousin, and a short time later, the eight friends descended upon Shay-Shay's home for a demonstration. Shay-Shay was a well educated and articulate woman who could have just about any job she wanted, but preferred to live on the fringe of society. Her IQ bordered on genius, but she liked to live a simple life. Every once in a while, she would put on a hypnotism show at Club Med to the delight of the guests. She also read palms (which she taught Julie to do), and tarot cards for locals and tourists alike, although she charged the tourists up the wazoo for her services. "A woman has ta make a livin'," she reasoned.

When they arrived, the cousins embraced, and Shay-Shay welcomed the group. She asked them to find a comfortable position on the floor with a pillow or cushion. She said she would put everyone under a light hypnotic state. She instructed them to close their eyes, breathe slowly and deeply, and to just let their minds go free. She had the most beautiful Bahamian lilt to her voice, and it was very soothing. She assured everyone if they felt uncomfortable or frightened in any way, they could stop by saying "three, two, one, out," and then sit up. What seemed like thirty minutes later (and in reality was only five), she brought the group out of their collective trance and asked everyone to share their experience. Each one of them said they had seen a train crash underwater. They were all excited they'd all shared the same vision, but the train crash itself didn't mean anything to anyone. Shay-Shay asked if they wanted to try again, and everyone agreed. Once again she put them under, and once again brought them back. The second time, each person had seen a funeral in the snow. This time they were startled to find there was a connection. One of their friends, Karl, had recently buried his mother in Finland in a snow-covered cemetery. He was an employee

Paris and Soll

at Club Med, and had just returned to work the week before. If Boots hadn't seen the vision first hand, he would have simply chalked it up to coincidence, or some kind of group induced phenomenon or hysteria. However it hadn't been that way at all. All eight had exactly the same vision at the same time. Shay-Shay explained how she was only helping them tap into a capability that most people possessed, but usually ignored.

As they chatted further, half the group wanted to try again, and the other half did not. Some of the participants were frightened and did not wish to continue. Boots didn't really care one way or the other and the group disbanded for the evening. Still, he found it interesting he'd actually had an experience that if someone else had described to him, he never would have believed. From that point on, he had a new respect for Julie, even though he often found her talents unnerving. He even jotted it all down in a notebook afterward, and eventually used it in one of his novels.

Just then, Julie put her arms around his neck and kissed his cheek. "Boots?"

"Yeah?"

"Have you checked your fan mail lately?"

"No. You know I hate being bothered with that stuff."

"But if you don't answer some of your fans once in a while, eventually you won't have any."

Julie was right of course. This was just a little game they played every so often. She'd bring the fan mail subject up, he'd complain about it, she'd offer to read them and perhaps answer some messages for him, Boots would say be my guest. Julie might be slightly unhinged, but she was still one smart cookie. She knew the importance of good public relations, and she delighted in electronically standing in for the famous Boots Beaumont. She answered as many emails as she could, or for as long as it held her interest. She often wrote strange and cryptic responses, which only served to heighten Boots' popularity and add to his mystique as a reclusive author.

"Why don't you look at them then? I'm busy right now," Boots responded gruffly. This was another game the twosome played. Boots liked this one the best because it always got him laid. Julie loved a challenge. The minute he acted aloof and distant, she became interested. She would let him be for a while, but then the seduction would begin in earnest. Hopping into bed any old time was boring. Julie preferred to play the role of temptress in her own impromptu script.

Evil Exchange

Julie smiled and went below. She opened the lap top, turned it on, and logged onto Boots' website. She glanced at how many had signed the guest book, then she quickly scanned the web log. Finally, she pulled up the emails. There were one hundred and thirty-two. Logic had nothing to do with which messages she read first. Julie liked to skip around. For the most part, the messages were much the same. Fans loved to name the book that was their favorite. Many asked when his next novel was coming out. Still others wanted to know if he would be participating in a book tour any time soon. Quite a few messages came from aspiring writers asking how to break into the business, and could Boots give them any advice? All in all, pretty tame and predictable stuff. Almost dull, actually. Not that there was anything wrong with it, what writer wouldn't like praise and compliments? However to Julie, it was all pretty humdrum.

She pecked out a few replies, while keeping an eye on Boots moving around the deck. She knew he was ignoring her on purpose, and it had the desired effect. She quickly tired of the fan mail, and was just getting ready to hunt down the object of her growing desire when something caught her eye. It was a message with the word "Help" in the subject line. That was rather odd, and it piqued her interest. She clicked on the message and read it through. Even though it was signed by a man, Julie knew right off a woman had something to do with the phrasing. The beginning of it started as most of them did. *Dear Mr. Beaumont, I have read all of your books and enjoy them immensely. You are a terrific writer,* blah, blah, blah. However this time Julie was getting one of those feelings, and knew she had better listen to it. So she kept reading, and finally got to the good part. A Mr. Todd Walters was in dire need of help in the search for his true identity, could Boots help in any way?

Julie knew immediately this was the man she had dreamed about. She called out to Boots.

"He wrote you!"

"What are you talking about?" Boots was scrubbing the deck and kept his back to her.

"The man I told you about. The one from my dream," Julie yelled.

"Oh, for fuck's sake woman, leave it alone, will you?"

That did it. Julie bounded up the steps to the deck while letting loose a stream of curses. She began looking for things to throw. Since he had a lot of experience with this, Boots knew exactly what to do. He got to her first, grabbed her, and pinned her arms to her sides. They struggled mightily, and in frustration, Julie bit his shoulder. Boots yelped and let her go. Their fight

Paris and Soll

stirred Julie to a new erotic level and soon they were down below in his cabin wildcatting in bed.

Later, when their lust was sated, and an exhausted Boots had fallen asleep for an afternoon nap, Julie returned to the computer. She brought up Todd's email and started tapping out a reply.

Chapter Twenty-Eight

It had been a long day. Sheila Stiles was looking forward to going home and soaking in a hot tub with a chilled glass of white wine beside her for company. *Hell, maybe the whole damn bottle.* She had one more appointment with a perspective couple, then it would be off to a well deserved, quiet night alone.

The door to her inner office was open wide so she could hear the clients arrive. Her partner, Wendell Colby, was away golfing for a few days. Things were pretty quiet at the moment. They had placed all the available children they had for the time being with the exception of just one. The infant Leslie had procured from the hospital in Tennessee was in need of new parents. Sheila had a couple all lined up when she received a last minute call from the woman who said she had just discovered she was pregnant and they would no longer need to adopt a child. *What a miracle and praise the Lord!* The woman actually said that. It made Sheila angry just to think about it. Occasionally plans did fall through. It didn't happen often, but from time to time, there was an imbalance. Either they had parents and no baby, or a baby and no parents, just as the current situation. Her faithful mule, Leslie, was tucked away in a safe location caring for the infant, waiting for the phone call from Sheila once parents had been found. It was only a matter of time.

Meanwhile, Nardo was still assigned to the pregnant mother in Alabama. Apparently she was overdue, but the last time they spoke, Nardo said he thought it would be soon. He had her trailer park home under surveillance. It turned out the mystery person involved was not a roommate or boyfriend, or even a parent for that matter. Nardo said it was an older sister who had crashed on the couch for a few days before hitting the road. The mommy-to-be was now all alone, and after a number of consultations with Sheila and Colby, Nardo was given the green light to go ahead with the snuff and snatch. Only this time, the mother's body would have to stay in the trailer home. Under the circumstances, it would be difficult enough to steal the child and get away undetected. Nardo couldn't possibly dispose of the body and take the child. This one was a bit riskier than they'd all prefer, but it was doable. Sheila had the utmost confidence in Nardo's ability to pull this one off. Leaving a dead body behind wasn't ideal, but they wouldn't be back in Alabama for a very long time. There were lots of other places to visit.

Sheila knew Nardo would be tied up for at least a few more days. Colby didn't have enough to do, and he was making her crazy with all his useless thumb twiddling and paper shuffling, so she insisted he go on a golfing trip and get out of her hair. Sheila of course had lots of work to do as she always did. Not only did she have to interview this couple who would be arriving at any moment, she also had to get started on finding parents for the new baby that would be arriving very soon according to Nardo.

Sheila heard the outer office door open and close. *Good, right on time.* She stood and smoothed the skirt of her suit and went to greet Mr. and Mrs. Pearson. After introductions and handshakes, Sheila ushered the couple into her office and asked them to sit.

"Just a few forms for you to fill out, and then we can get started. I'm sure you must be anxious," Sheila began with her standard opening pitch. She handed over the paperwork neatly arranged on a clipboard. It always fascinated her who would fill out the forms, husband or wife. Nine times out of ten, it was the wife. When it came to arranging to adopt a child, it was usually the woman's domain. It always pleased Sheila to see a perspective mother take control at this stage, establishing her role as caretaker and decision maker. The perspective fathers were usually there at their wife's insistence that a child would make them fulfilled and complete as a family unit. Women had the ability to influence their mate to make this wish a reality, and men usually took the role of provider and financier of the operation. There were exceptions of course. Once in a while the roles were reversed, but for the most part, this was the status quo.

So, naturally Sheila was surprised when Mr. Pearson grabbed the clipboard and started to examine the forms. He slipped a beautiful and expensive Montblanc pen from his jacket pocket and filled in some of the blanks. Sheila detected just a hint of embarrassment from Mrs. Pearson. An almost imperceptible tightening of her jaw was the only giveaway, but of course she kept silent. Clearly Mrs. Pearson was used to her husband's dominating behavior.

Having done a preliminary background check, Sheila chided herself for thinking Paul Pearson would let his wife Andrea, lead the interview. Paul was a thirty-something dot-commer who had the foresight to cash out before the market took a dive some years ago. He'd invested in real estate and made some very savvy moves and was currently worth a little more than five million dollars. Three years ago he married Andrea because she was a senator's daughter. Paul had political aspirations of his own, and he wanted the affiliation her family provided. Unfortunately, as it turned out, Andrea was barren. Paul was adamant they have a child. He was a shrewd man, and knew it would only help his image to be a devoted husband and father. At first, he brought up the subject of a surrogate mother. That way he reasoned, they could use Paul's sperm so the child would be biological half his, and they would be able to pick someone with a genetic background as close to Andrea as possible. And they could certainly afford the best of care for the woman during gestation. But Andrea was against the idea from the start. She couldn't stand the thought of another woman being inseminated with Paul's sperm and producing a child on demand. Andrea said none of this to her husband however. Being a senator's daughter, she knew the art of gentle manipulation. She simply told Paul that if they hired a surrogate mother, the press would have a field day. Paul realized she was right. A private adoption was a much better idea. Also, adopting a child was the ultimate proof of his loving and kind heart. He would garner sympathy and support from such an act. As soon as they adopted a child, Paul's future political career would be secure. It was the perfect plan.

Sheila knew exactly how to handle Pearson. All the years with Judge Price had taught her precisely the way to communicate with an egomaniacal pompous ass. Andrea would be a bit trickier however. Sheila decided to go with her instincts and focus her attention on Andrea, while maintaining a clear respect for Paul.

"I have a beautiful baby girl available Andrea. I think she would be just perfect for you. Would you like to see a picture of her?"

"Oh yes," Andrea replied. She was grateful just to be acknowledged.

Sheila opened her desk drawer and took out a number of photos. She handed them to Andrea.

"Oh, she's lovely. Paul, darling. Look!"

Paul examined the prints as carefully as he would the Wall Street Journal. "She's white, right?"

"Yes, Mr. Pearson. She is Caucasian," Sheila confirmed.

"Well, she'd have to be. A man in my position . . ."

"I understand," Sheila cut him off.

"What about her mother? What's her story?" Paul demanded.

"Mr. Pearson, let me assure you. Our mothers are good people and want only what's best for their babies. That's why they've chosen to put them up for adoption."

"What about medical history?"

"I can provide general medical background if you feel that is necessary."

"I want my money's worth Ms. Stiles. *That* is what's necessary. *And* I want the assurance this is completely confidential. I don't want some woman coming around years from now wanting to be a part of this child's life. No way."

"The records are sealed, which is exactly what the mother wishes. Once the papers are signed and the child is relinquished, the natural mother can make no further claim, and would never have access to the child's whereabouts. Your privacy is completely protected."

"I may be a man of means Ms. Stiles, but one hundred thousand dollars is a lot of money."

"I completely understand Mr. Pearson. However I can assure you the money is for the care of mother and child, medical costs, housing, and the like. We also provide many of our mothers with scholarships so they can further their education. We do as much as we can. I will not deny it is a difficult and emotional time for these young women who make the decision to adopt out their children. We even provide professional counseling services to help them through the process."

"It must be very satisfying to you, to help people this way," Andrea remarked.

"It is gratifying to say the least," Sheila smiled.

"And where do they come from? The mothers I mean. Surely you don't go out and recruit them or put ads in the paper," Paul questioned.

"Of course not. We are not in the business of coercion Mr. Pearson. The mothers find us through private referrals, the same way you found us."

"This facility where the mother's stay, where is it? Would we be able to see it, or talk with any of the mothers?"

The man was relentless. If Sheila didn't know better, she would think he was a cop. Shrewd was one thing, suspicious was another. She had to nip this in the bud immediately.

"Mr. Pearson. While I appreciate your interest and concern, you must realize

Evil Exchange

the mothers require the utmost in privacy and protection, as do the children. I would never divulge the whereabouts of the facility to anyone. We run a tight ship here. Our aim is to create happy families, and to offer financial aid for these mothers to get back on their feet. We provide a service, and with that come expenses, some of them quite high. You are getting your money's worth, believe me. Of course, if you aren't sure, there are other agencies and organizations you can contact. Although as you know, you'll probably be put on a waiting list, and it could be years before you can adopt. That's up to you. I don't have to solicit business. On the contrary, I often have to turn people away. You and Mrs. Pearson should consider yourselves fortunate that we have a child available for you immediately. We are well aware of the need to handle the adoption as quickly as possible so that you can get on with your new lives as parents," Sheila concluded. If the man wanted to play hardball, so be it.

"No reason to get your feathers ruffled, Ms. Stiles. You come highly recommended. Still, my wife and I need to discuss this in private, just to be absolutely sure. Can I call you tomorrow with a decision?"

"I will agree to wait twenty-four hours Mr. Pearson. After that, I will place the child with another family. I'm sure you understand."

"Of course. I will be calling you tomorrow then." Paul Pearson stood and softly reached for his wife's arm indicating that it was time to go. Andrea looked a bit shell shocked from the rapid fire discussion. As usual, she didn't have much of a say in anything. It was her husband's final decision. She felt a bit edgy about it, but was relatively sure the adoption would go ahead. She knew he wanted her to be happy, and what she wanted most was a child. And she was no fool. She was well aware Paul would benefit from having a child too, even though his motivation was vastly different from her own. She didn't care. This child was going to be more than a prop. He would grow to love the child as much as she would. More importantly, she would finally have something of her own.

As they said their good-byes, each one was left to their own thoughts.

That poor woman, married to a prize asshole. But they'll be back. Finally, I can get out of this office and go home.

I can't wait to go shopping, there's so much I need to do. A baby!

Uptight bitch. She may come highly recommended, but she's hiding something. Too slick, too sure of herself. I've got some digging to do. And I know just who can help me.

Chapter Twenty-Nine

Todd straightened up the apartment while he waited for Diana. She was on her way over and they were going to spend the afternoon at a local art gallery. He was anxious to see her. After their last evening together and the wonderful dinner she'd made for him, he wanted to be with her all the time. He'd opened up to her in a way he never had with anyone else, not even his first wife, Janette. When he talked to Diana about his innermost feelings and fears, instead of feeling vulnerable and exposed, he felt connected and safe. In addition, her enthusiasm was contagious, and her determination and resolve were most admirable. Her optimistic approach to life was infectious. She was just the kind of person that others were naturally drawn to. In her universe, Diana was the steady warmth to which all others gravitated. Todd was beginning to understand how Diana was both a comfort and a catalyst. He'd never met anyone quite so extraordinary.

He laughed to himself when he thought of the email they wrote to Boots Beaumont. He started it, but she quickly took over. He couldn't believe how brazen she was, as if asking a successful author for his help was just the most natural thing in the world. It was another thing he loved about her. She was not intimidated by anyone's status or position or celebrity. She believed everyone to be her equal, and she theirs. There were a lot of things endearing about Diana, and Todd knew exactly what was happening. He was falling in love.

Suddenly, the buzzer rang from downstairs and startled Todd from his reverie. He quickly glanced at the clock and figured she must have decided to come early. He buzzed her in. A moment later came a loud knock on the door. Todd went to open it. Matt and Katy stood before him looking lopsided as ever. Matt was tall and thin, but soft and out of shape. He had a penchant for polo shirts and khakis. Katy on the other hand, was a petite powerhouse of toned muscle and

Evil Exchange

boundless energy. Todd thought of Olympic gymnast Mary Lou Retton, every time he saw her. She might be the mother of a five-year-old and a seven-year-old, but she looked barely old enough to vote and loved to wear short skirts and midriff baring tops that showed off her great figure.

"Hey Bro! Just thought we'd stop by," Matt greeted his brother.

"Sorry to just drop by like this, but we were in the neighborhood and took a chance you might be home," Katy said as she gave him a quick peck on the check.

"Are you going to invite us in, or what?" Matt laughed.

"Come on in. I . . . well, you just surprised me that's all." Todd finally forced some words from his mouth. He was so shocked seeing his brother and sister-in-law instead of Diana, he was trying to shift gears and having a difficult time of it.

"Where are the kids?" Todd tried to find a neutral topic of conversation while getting his bearings.

"With friends for the day, swimming at the YMCA pool." Katy explained.

"So, we thought we'd come over and grab you. Go out to lunch or something. Maybe go see Mom . . . " Matt chattered away until Katy interrupted him.

"To tell the truth? We really wanted to see if you were still alive," she said.

"Guess I've been out of touch lately," Todd acknowledged with a shrug.

"Yeah, I guess you could say that," Matt joked and then turned serious. "Jesus, Todd. I've been worried about you. How many times have I called lately? You don't call me back, you don't answer my emails, what's going on anyway?" Matt might be five years younger, but right now, he sounded more like their father used to when he was concerned about one of them.

"Hello?"

All three of them jumped.

"Sorry. The door was open. I thought you heard me. Hi, I'm Diana." Diana introduced herself to Matt and Katy with a confident handshake. "I'm Todd's friend. Someone else was coming out when I came in so I didn't ring the bell."

Matt and Katy looked at each other, then at Todd.

"Diana, this is my brother Matt, and his lovely wife Katy. Normally they are joined at the hip with my niece and nephew, but somehow they escaped today," Todd said quickly.

Paris and Soll

"Nice to meet you," Diana replied.

"It's our pleasure, believe me." Matt actually winked at his brother. He was thirty-eight going on thirteen.

"Looks like we've horned in on your afternoon," Katy apologized quickly. "Matt, we should be going." She gave him the eye, the look that all wives know how to give their husbands. *Don't argue with me.* Everyone in the world knows the look.

"Oh, please don't go," Diana asked and looked at Todd. Another universal look. *Ask them to stay.*

"Come on you guys, stay. After all, you came over here to find out what's been going on with me. I might as well fill you in."

After they all found a seat, Todd began. Starting with the panic attack, Todd explained first going to see Claire, and how she encouraged him to join the support group, which was how he met Diana. Then he filled them in on the confrontation with Stuart over his adoption file, finding out about Maddie Monroe, having his worst fears confirmed by Miriam, then trying to come to grips with the knowledge that he was sold on the black market, and not knowing if he would ever be able to trace his true origin. It was a lot to cover, but he gave them the condensed version.

During Todd's account, Matt and Katy were for the most part, speechless. From time to time they would look at each other and look back at Todd. Their heads swiveling back and forth like marionettes, mouths open, eyebrows frozen in a perfect arch.

While Todd talked, Diana quietly slipped from her chair and silently went to the kitchen. She found some ice tea in the fridge, and then looked through the cupboards until she found something suitable for snacking. She gathered glasses, napkins, cheese, crackers, and olives. She found some fresh fruit and sliced it. Her movements were automatic, her intention nothing more than practical. She wasn't snooping, and she knew Todd wouldn't mind if she made herself at home. Plus, it made her feel useful. Diana liked to be productive and helpful. She unobtrusively brought the refreshments to the coffee table just as Todd was finishing his soliloquy.

There was silence for a moment once Todd concluded his narrative, and the three of them stared at the glasses of iced tea and snacks on the table as if they had magically appeared. Katy found her voice first, and thanked Diana. Matt took a long swig of his drink as if he'd been the one who'd been talking and was now suffering from cotton mouth. It didn't take long though. Matt and Katy

Evil Exchange

started in with a barrage of questions. *What did he think? How did he feel? What was he going to do?*

"That's why we sent the email," Diana interjected.

"What email?" Katy and Matt asked simultaneously.

"I hadn't gotten to that part yet," Todd admitted. "It was your idea, why don't you tell them about it?" He passed the verbal baton to Diana. He was tired of talking about himself. Todd thought he'd been asked to do far too much of it lately.

"You still have a copy on your computer don't you?" Diana asked Todd.

"Sure I do," he answered.

"Why don't you go and print it out? That way Matt and Katy can both read it," Diana suggested. Todd nodded and went to the other room while Diana explained about Boots Beaumont and why she thought he could help. She said after they'd written the email to Boots, they forwarded a copy to Todd's computer.

Matt and Katy were both incredulous. "He's the author I like!" They both said at the same time.

"I gave the book to Todd when he was in the hospital," Matt said taking full credit

"Yeah, but I gave it to you first," Katy reminded him. Then she asked. "What makes you think he will help you?"

"I don't know, really. It's just a feeling I have. Let's call it a hunch. I figured it can't hurt to try," Diana shrugged her shoulders.

Todd returned with the printout. He gave it to Matt. Diana urged him to read it out loud.

"*Dear Mr. Beaumont, I have read all of your books and enjoy them immensely. You are a terrific writer.*"

"Todd wrote that part." Diana sighed. She didn't say it, but it was obvious she thought the opening sentence rather drab and uninteresting. "And then I took over," she smiled.

Matt continued reading. "*I am in desperate need of your help. I have recently discovered I was sold in a black market baby selling scheme orchestrated by a Madeline Monroe forty years ago. This woman actually stole children and sold them to unsuspecting adoptive parents. All of the information on the birth certificate was falsified. Madeline Monroe ran her heinous operation for many years and it is difficult to determine exactly how many children*

Paris and Soll

were affected by this woman's selfish greed. She altered destinies and shattered the hope of any of us ever finding out our biological history for her own monetary gain. The bottom line is this woman played God with people's lives.

I know you are retired from the private investigating profession. But I am asking for your help anyway. You have a reputation for finding lost things. I couldn't be any more lost at this point in my life. I am in my forties, and I have no idea where, when, or even what day I was born. I have no way of finding out the names of my first parents. I know virtually nothing about my heritage or my background. My situation is basically hopeless. However if you would take my case, I might have a chance. You may suspect I want some kind of revenge or payback. I assure you that is not what I am after. All I am looking for is the truth. You are a man who has helped people find that. I am hoping you can do the same for me. Sincerely, Todd Walters."

Matt looked up from the printout. "Wow. That's really powerful. Where did you learn to write like that?" he asked Diana.

"I don't know. All I did was try to put myself in Todd's place. And I didn't want it to sound like Todd was begging. I just thought if we could appeal to Mr. Beaumont's humanity then we might have a chance," Diana explained.

"It's a long shot, but I wish you the best of luck," Katy hugged Todd.

"Yeah. We'll see," Todd replied and tried to smile.

Matt and Katy made motions they were getting ready to leave, using the kids as an excuse for their departure. Matt might not have any qualms about hanging out with them, but Katy knew better. It was clear to her these two needed some time alone. After all, Matt and Katy had gotten what they came for. They got to see Todd. He was going through a hell of a time that was for sure. He also had a new woman in his life, and Katy was thrilled to have met Diana. The foursome chatted for a few more minutes and then said their good-byes.

"I'm so glad I got to meet your brother and his wife," Diana said as she cleared some of the glasses and took them into the kitchen.

"They don't usually just drop by like that. I guess I haven't been very good about returning phone calls lately," Todd said as he picked up some plates and joined her in the kitchen Todd heard a muted musical tango coming from somewhere. Diana said it was her cell phone and went to find her purse in the other room.

Todd was putting some dishes in the sink when he heard a muffled sob. He ran to the other room to see what was wrong. Diana's back was to him and her shoulders were shaking. Her hands gripped the back of a chair in such a way that Todd was certain if she were to let go, she would fall to the floor in a heap.

Evil Exchange

"Diana, what is it? What's wrong?" Todd asked.

"He found her," Diana spun around.

"Who?"

"Glen." Diana's eyes sparkled with tears.

"Glen found?" Todd prompted.

"My mother." The tears started to fall.

"Oh my God, Diana." Todd finally realized what had just happened.

"Twelve years, Todd. I've been looking for *twelve years*. Glen did it. He found my first mother. I can't believe it." A huge sob shook her as she flew into his arms. It was a bittersweet moment for Todd. He was so happy for Diana. He knew how long she had waited for this. Yet he couldn't help but wonder if such a moment would ever be possible for him. He didn't think so. As upbeat and positive as Diana was about the email to Boots Beaumont, it wasn't likely the man was going to help him. At the same time, even though he didn't think he would ever get a reply, he wasn't giving up hope entirely. As they clung to one another, Todd's tears mingled with hers.

Chapter Thirty

Not much longer now. After waiting a week longer than anticipated, Nardo was finally going to get his chance. Do the mom, grab the kid, and get the hell out of town. Normally he wasn't this far off in his calculations. His instincts were usually right on target, just not this time. But giving birth was an inexact science. Nardo may not have gone to medical school, but even he knew that much.

The week before had been informative, frustrating, and boring. He'd kept a close eye on the young woman from the clinic. She'd been the most promising candidate, and once Nardo decided on her for sure, he started to think of her as the scarecrow. She might be swollen with child, but she looked like a walking skeleton. She had straw-colored hair and a freckled nose. After doing a bit of poking around at the county recorder's office, he was surprised to find out that the young woman was older than he first thought. She was twenty-five, but looked eighteen. He also found out that the crummy place she called home was listed in an older brother's name. Nardo surmised the brother must be letting her live there for free since she didn't have a job. What a guy.

Initially there were some major hurdles, but the more he checked out the situation, the more workable it became. His main concern at first was the trailer park itself. Situated on two dusty acres, an old weather beaten sign indicated one had now reached the end of the rainbow here at Shady Meadows. The scarecrow's rundown trailer was all the way in the back, which could have been a problem had there been a fence. Nardo was in good shape, but no way was he climbing a fence with a baby under his arm. Behind the trailer park was a shallow gully which ran parallel to the highway. Down the street there was a cement company which had seen better days, and on the other side of Shady Meadows sat a boarded up strip mall decorated with the ever popular, broken-

Evil Exchange

windows-with-walls-covered-in-graffiti look. On the opposite side of the road, there was nothing but woods. Nardo figured he would be able to park his rental car behind the strip mall, approach her trailer from the back, and proceed with his work.

There had also been the issue of the mystery guest. However once he determined it was a sister who was only visiting for a few days before moving on, the situation became even less hazardous. Before sis left though, she and her sibling had a rip roaring argument about the child's father. Nardo was able to overhear how daddy just happened to married to someone else. No wonder little miss scarecrow was on her own. Nardo may have disapproved how this young woman had seduced another woman's husband into her bed (he did have some ethics), but he was happy the baby was the result of a secret affair. Once mommy was found dead in her trailer home, suspicion would fall on daddy dearest then, wouldn't it? It was a sweet setup.

Nardo discovered the girl's next door neighbor in the trailer park was an old Vietnam vet. He was stuck in a wheelchair and drank himself into oblivion every night. Nardo wasn't concerned in the least the guy would hear anything, much less be any kind of threat. The other dilapidated homes were spaced further apart toward the front of the shabby lot, but he wasn't worried about any of the neighbors. So far he knew about the ones who worked, they did so during the day. No graveyard shift employees in this bunch. He'd spent enough nights casing the place to know virtually no one came or went in the wee hours. Quite a few senior residents lived in Shady Meadows which was a plus because they kept mostly to themselves, and generally went to sleep as soon as it got dark. There were hardly any kids around, but there were three dogs. Two of them were so old they barely tottered about and didn't concern themselves with anyone or anything. But there was a feisty little mutt who yipped and yapped at the slightest breeze. Nardo knew exactly how to take care of that one. Some ground meat packed around a tranquilizer would insure the tiny noisemaker of an uninterrupted and blissful ten hours of sleep.

So, one by one, the obstacles were checked off the list until there weren't any more left. Each night Nardo settled into his stakeout mode, waiting and watching. The baby had to come sometime. His patience was finally rewarded when at last, early one morning, the girl left her ratty residence with a small bag and walked to the street where a cab picked her up. Nardo tailed them just to be sure, but he knew where they were headed. Twelve minutes later, dumped unceremoniously at the ER entrance of the city hospital, little miss scarecrow disappeared behind hissing automatic doors. In celebration, Nardo went across town and ordered a steak and egg breakfast. If everything went according to

Paris and Soll

plan, if mommy scarecrow delivered naturally and didn't have any complications, she would be sent home in a day or two with her new bundle of joy. Then Nardo could take care of business.

Persistence does pay off, and Nardo was pleased it had all worked out. He'd invested time and effort into this particular mission. He would have been rather disappointed had it all been for nothing, not to mention being out a hefty pay packet. In only a few days, he would capture his newborn target, and then meet up with the Mule who would once again exchange payment for product. He chuckled to himself. He had a lot in common with these mothers. He could deliver too.

Chapter Thirty-One

Despite all the recent craziness, Todd fell into a fairly normal routine for a few days. Think of Diana while at work. See Diana in the evening as often as possible. Dream of Diana at night. Todd had it bad. He couldn't help but feel Diana had come into his life just at the right time. Since they had been dating, he hadn't had any further near death experiences or accidents. He was beginning to think of her as his lucky charm. So, even though he still had a great deal of personal turmoil as far as his feelings surrounding his adoption, and the whole Maddie Monroe issue, Todd thought of Diana as the perfect anchor of stability he so needed at the moment. Not only was it Diana who helped him keep things in perspective, but the members of the support group did so as well. Glen especially helped keep him grounded. He had an appointment with Claire coming up, but he was glad there was some time before that. Right now, what Todd wanted most was to let it all just simmer for a while.

In terms of the adoption revelations, his feelings and emotions were as knotted as an old gold chain tossed carelessly in a jewelry box. Time, he hoped, would help untangle his confusion. Because, when he did meet with Claire, Todd would have to rehash the most recent developments all over again. Presently, he was damn tired of talking about the whole thing. Sure, Claire might be able to give him some insight on the subject. Yet deep down, he knew it was all going to be up to him to handle, and it wasn't going to be easy. At this stage of the game, he might not have any idea of what might be down the road, or how this was all going to work out. That's why he wanted a break from it all, and maybe, that was why he was so focused on Diana. His life was too confusing to think about all the time. It was much easier, and far more pleasant, to think about her.

Todd also learned more about the story of Diana's first mom. As it turned out, Glen hadn't actually found her himself, but was the one who received an email from someone who might be her. For years Diana had tried various searching methods, all of which were unsuccessful. Diana got to the point where she was at a dead end and terribly disappointed. Her anger and frustration at the system led her to the support group. When she learned about the International Soundex Reunion Registry from Glen, she figured she had nothing to lose by signing up.

The registry provided an on-line forum for consenting participants, either natural parent or adopted adult, who wished to reunite. Each participant provided information which, when entered into a database, would then be cross-referenced against information provided by other registrants in the hopes of a possible match. When a firm match was found parties would be contacted via email addresses. That's where Glen came in. When he and Diana first sat down together to register her, Glen suggested they use his email address as the contact. That way, Glen could act as a go-between should a possible match be made. Diana thought it was the perfect solution. As strong and confident as she was, she felt less vulnerable with Glen as the point of contact rather than herself. Glen had far more experience with reunions, not to mention the fact he wasn't emotionally involved. Diana felt he could provide the needed support and clear headed decision making she would need in the event of initial contact or even a meeting. So far, all the preliminary information for Diana and the woman who claimed to be her first mother was a match, and Diana and Glen were making some tentative arrangements. Even though Diana was thrilled beyond belief she may soon be reuniting with her natural mother after thirty years of separation, she was terrified of something going wrong. Before arranging a face to face meeting, Diana wanted to be as sure as possible it was indeed her mother. Glen suggested their first step would be to email photos to one another and go from there. If there was a physical resemblance between the two combined with the personal information already established, it would certainly make for a very solid case. Diana would get an email within a day or two.

Arriving home from a consultation for a new installation, Todd went straight to the fridge for a cold beer. He couldn't stop thinking about Diana. He knew they both had a lot to juggle. Getting deeply involved with one another might not be the prudent thing to do considering the uncertainty of their lives at the moment, but who always lives their life according to common sense? Not anyone Todd knew. You had to take things as they came. Roll with the punches as the old saying goes. There was always uncertainty. There was always worry. *If worry was going to change anything, maybe I should worry more,* Todd thought. He was so lost in thought he just about jumped out of his skin when his cell phone vibrated in his pants pocket.

Evil Exchange

"Hello?" The reception wasn't very good, he thought it was Diana, but wasn't sure with all the crackling in the background.

"Todd! It's Diana. I got an email!"

She must be calling about her first mom. "What does she look like?" Todd asked.

"What? Can you hear me okay?"

Todd raised his voice and spoke slowly. "Your first mom. Does she look like you?"

"No, Todd, listen. The email isn't from Theresa. It's from Boots."

Todd wasn't sure what she said with all the damn noise. *What was she talking about?* "You bought some boots?"

"No! The email is from Boots Beaumont. He answered the one we sent him," Diana was practically shouting.

Todd couldn't believe it. Beaumont had actually replied. It was probably just a brush-off message.

"I'll read it to you," Diana practically yelled.

Todd told Diana to hold on. He moved into another part of the apartment. For some reason, the signal was much stronger when he moved away from the kitchen. The crackling disappeared.

"Okay. What does it say?"

"He said you should come see him. In Eleuthera," Diana could barely contain her excitement.

"You're sure?"

"Of course I'm sure. That's what it says. He said he would try and do what he could to help you. And you have to go there because he won't come to New York."

"Does he say when?" Todd was incredulous.

"As soon as you can. You're to make arrangements and then email him back when you'll be coming. This is so exciting!"

"I can't believe it. He's going to help me . . ."

"Todd. I have to run. I have a meeting with Glen. I'll forward the message to you so you can read it for yourself," Diana replied.

"Okay. Thanks," Todd said. "Hey, Diana?"

Paris and Soll

"What? Todd, I'm happy for you, but I gotta go."

"Want to go on a trip with me?" Before he could get an answer the phone cut out.

Chapter Thirty-Two

All the preparations were finished. The posh penthouse apartment had been thoroughly cleaned, fresh flowers scented the air, pillows were plumped, and most important of all, the nursery was ready. Andrea Pearson had orchestrated all the arrangements with aplomb, overseeing each and every detail personally. She was amazed at how much had been accomplished in such a short period of time. However, when you are the daughter of a senator as well as the wife of a wealthy man, things happened according to your timetable, not someone else's.

One week before, Andrea and Paul had given their answer to Sheila Stiles. Yes, they wanted the baby. There was no question, and certainly no hesitation on Andrea's part. Since seeing the photo, she was determined to adopt the child no matter what. No longer just a concept, the photo made it a reality and clinched the deal. This baby was real and meant to belong to her. She just knew it. If it were possible to fall in love on the spot, Andrea had. The baby had beautiful delicate features, a full head of light brown hair (a shade close to Andrea's), and gorgeous long eyelashes. One photograph and life had changed forever. Once they'd left Sheila's office that day, the deal was done, and Paul knew it from the look on his wife's face.

Paul Pearson was still a bit uncertain, but he wasn't quite sure why. Sheila Stiles did come recommended from a business acquaintance of his whom was highly trusted. Paul even asked Andrea's father, Senator Delivan Roscoe, to do some checking. It just so happened a buddy of Roscoe's, Judge Harold Price, said he knew Ms. Stiles professionally and vouched for her character. Everything seemed to be in order, and yet Paul couldn't quite shake his gut feeling something wasn't quite right. Then he got caught up in Andrea's enthusiasm and decided he was perhaps just being a bit paranoid.

Paris and Soll

For the occasion, Sheila hired a car and driver to make her delivery. Mr. Pearson had already transferred the funds from his bank account to hers as instructed. Sheila agreed to give them a week to get everything ready for the new arrival. Now, she was making her way to 1150 Park Avenue to unite the baby with her new parents. Fortunately, the child, lulled by the movement of the car, had fallen fast asleep. Sheila had some concerns at first, for Leslie complained of the child constantly crying while in her custody. Thankfully, since the Mule dropped her off at Sheila's office that afternoon, the infant had been relatively quite much to Sheila's relief.

Sheila Stiles was childless by choice. Never once in her life did she have maternal feelings. She was always awkward and impatient around children. Over time and by necessity, she'd developed the ability to appear loving when she gave a baby to its new parents, but it was all an act. And not a particularly difficult act either. All she had to do was remind herself of how much money she was making, and her performance would instantly become worthy of an academy award.

The car arrived at the classy destination and Sheila alighted with babe in arms. She briefly spoke to the doorman who was expecting her. The elevator swiftly and silently whisked her to the top floor. As the doors opened and Sheila approached the corner apartment, Andrea Pearson opened the double front doors in welcome.

"Ms. Stiles, please come in." Andrea's face glowed, and she had eyes only for the bundle cradled in Sheila's arms.

"Here she is Mrs. Pearson, your daughter," Sheila handed the child over with a certain reverence. She noticed Andrea's household staff gathered nearby for the big event.

"I'm so sorry Paul isn't here at the moment. Business, I'm afraid."

"I'm sure your husband must be a very busy man," Sheila responded solemnly.

"Oh, he is," Andrea answered automatically. "But he'll be home tonight and he'll see her then."

"It will give you time to settle in," Sheila graciously suggested.

"Yes," Andrea said still distracted.

"Oh, before I forget. Here is some information regarding medical history for the baby. I know your husband mentioned that," Sheila held out an envelope.

"Would you mind putting it on the table there?" Andrea was obviously not going to let go of her new daughter for anything.

"The adoption will be finalized in just a few weeks. I'll be in touch with you about the date."

"Oh, I thought it took much longer." Andrea seemed surprised and looked at Sheila for the first time.

"I have connections," Sheila explained. "That way you'll get the birth certificate as soon as possible. I have all the information I need for it, except for the baby's name."

"Ruby Abigail," Andrea said without hesitation.

"What a lovely name," Sheila replied.

"Ruby, because she is my gem, and Abigail means a father's joy." Andrea smiled serenely.

Chapter Thirty-Three

Todd and Diana settled in their seats. Flying on Bahamas Air from New York to Eleuthera took about three and a half hours. Plenty of time to relax, although Todd wasn't sure he'd be able to. He was definitely keyed up. First of all, the email from Boots inviting him to the island was fantastic in and of itself. Then, he asked Diana if she would join him, and when she said yes, his spirits soared to just about the same cruising level as the airplane they were flying in presently. Normally, Todd would enjoy making the arrangements himself, but time was short, and there was so much to do he asked a travel agent to help. He and Diana were going for the weekend. A short trip indeed, but Diana couldn't take too much time away from work because summer was so very busy at the boutique. Then there was the question of Diana's first mother, Theresa Croft. Digital photos had been exchanged, and the verdict was in. There was no question the two were related, the resemblance was unmistakable. They'd taken the plunge and spoken on the phone. It was a joyous occasion. Apparently, having all those phones finally paid off. Mother and daughter were most anxious to meet, but as Theresa was in Boston and had house guests visiting from Arizona, their reunion would have to wait for another week. They set a date, and Theresa insisted she be the one to make the trip and come to New York to see Diana. Glen would be there to facilitate.

From there, things had fallen into place quickly. This trip, as quick as it was going to be, was a big step for both Todd and Diana. They'd be spending nearly sixty hours together, and it would be interesting to see how they'd get along for that length of time. They'd also be sharing a significant event together. Todd would be meeting with Beaumont for the first time, and together they would forge a plan that perhaps would lead to some concrete evidence or information about his background Todd so desperately craved. And, last but not least, Todd and Diana would be expanding their relationship to the most intimate level. They'd be sharing a room *and* a bed. Being a gentleman, Todd left the decision up to Diana, but she never hesitated for a moment and told him to book one room for them both. It was time for their relationship to progress.

The first hour of the flight was smooth and uneventful. Todd and Diana fell into an easy and comfortable discussion about their respective childhoods. Because she was a lonely child, Diana had an imaginary friend who kept her entertained. Diana confided in Todd that she was timid, insecure, and painfully shy as a girl. This admission led to a further confession. One of her deepest, darkest secrets was that she sucked her thumb until she was ten. She had always been terribly ashamed of it for some reason. Todd couldn't have been more surprised, not about the thumb sucking, but about the shy and insecure part. It was hard to believe the woman sitting next to him had ever been anything else other than the confident, self-assured person she was today.

Then it was Todd's turn. He told Diana when he was a kid, he'd suffered for years from two recurrent nightmares. One had to do with masks, and the other featured a witch. Finally, as an adolescent, and desperate to be rid of the dreams, he prayed. *Please God. No more nightmares.* Todd couldn't have been more surprised when the dreams stopped. He thought it was a miracle. Then, to be fair to Diana, he felt it only right to reciprocate with a dark confession of his own, and admitted to a short lived passion for dry dog food at the age of six. The family pet, a sweet mongrel by the name of Chip, ate a brand of dry dog food that came in small crunchy bites in five different flavors. Each flavor was a different color. That's what Todd liked about it, he admitted, the colors. It became his favorite snack food until Miriam caught him in the act and just about had a heart attack. Todd and Diana had a good laugh over that one.

Naturally, talk turned to work. Todd was explaining how he'd recently bid on a television antenna installation on top of the Sears Tower. He mentioned he thought the erection of the antenna would last about seven days. At that exact moment a flight attendant walked by, and apparently all she heard was the erection part. Her face turned crimson red but she kept right on walking and never missed a step. As she reached the galley, she whispered to one of her companions and looked directly at Todd and they smothered giggles like two teenage girls. Todd cringed and could only imagine what they must be thinking.

Not much later, a light lunch was served. Just as Todd and Diana began to eat, a passenger near them began ringing his call button. The man was clearly agitated as one of the flight attendants approached him and asked what was wrong. The passenger complained his chicken was bad. The flight attendant asked him what was wrong with it. The angry man raised his voice and insisted it was just *bad*. The flight attendant remained calm and asked him if he could be more specific. Again, he raised his voice and said it was *bad*. Suddenly, the flight attendant reached down to his tray, picked up the palm-sized piece of poultry and spanked it. "Bad chicken. You're a bad chicken," she shouted. She then put it back down on his tray and walked away. The passenger sat immobilized, his mouth a perfect O. Everyone who witnessed the exchange suddenly burst into laughter and then applause.

The rest of the flight passed quickly, and soon the plane touched down at the airport in Eleuthera. Todd and Diana retrieved their carry-on bags from overhead and made their way off the plane. A blast of warm, tropical air greeted them and they went in search of the Club Med representative. The email he'd gotten from Beaumont suggested he might enjoy the Club Med for the weekend rather than a hotel. Todd asked the travel agent to make the arrangements for a weekend package, and she did. Beaumont had also suggested Todd might want to arrive a day early, enjoy the beach and the Club before meeting with him the following day. Todd just couldn't get over how helpful Boots was.

It was a short bus ride with a noisy group just in from Miami. They traveled over a two-lane dirt road jokingly referred to as the "Trans-Eleuthera Highway" and were deposited at the entrance gate to Club Med in Governor's Harbour. The well tanned GO's were dressed in skimpy bathing suits covered by brightly colored pareaus. The GO's, along with the staff, were all clapping and singing welcome songs. There was a brief orientation, and a long introduction of all the staff members. One of the GO's explained that Eleuthera stands for "freedom" and he recommended the guests take the meaning quite literally and be as free as they please. The guests were given room assignments and told to purchase a bag of bar beads so they could buy drinks at various bars around the club grounds.

Todd didn't know if he would even need alcohol as the atmosphere was intoxicating all on its own. He and Diana grabbed their bags and were off to find their room. They passed by the pool, an open air bar, a dining room, and the disco. They walked down a palm tree-lined path to their room, which was appropriately called Relax 109. Relax 109 was an end room with wide windows which overlooked a pink sanded beach kissed by turquoise surf. It was paradise. The room was simple, but spotless. There was an old heating/cooling unit underneath one window. Todd glanced at the controls and was amused to see one side of the dial read *warmth* and the other side of the dial read *coolth*. *An Eleuthera term?* He also noticed the double beds, and hoped later on in the evening they'd get pushed together. They quickly unpacked and changed into swimsuits and headed for the beach. The swim was heavenly. A walk on the beach as romantic as it could be. The unspoken acknowledgment was that the best was yet to come.

Returning to the room, it was time to change again before dinner. Diana looked so fresh and lovely now dressed in a silky, floral sheath, Todd thought her the most beautiful woman he'd ever seen. Todd was decked out in a Hawaiian shirt, shorts, and opted to go shoeless as was the custom at Club Med. They went to one of the larger bars where many of the new arrivals were drinking and chatting away. They exchanged pleasantries with one of the couples from Miami, and decided to join them for dinner when the loud speaker system trumpeted "Fanfare for the Kings Dinner," the signal dinner was served. The dining room was decorated with native plants and flowers, and the seating was communal. Besides the couple from Miami, Todd and Diana were joined by a couple from California and a couple from Germany. The food, served family style, was delicious, and the conversation lively. Everyone had a glow (or perhaps it was only sunburn) of anticipation of their days ahead at this island Shangri-la.

After dinner, Todd and Diana went to the auditorium to wait for the evening's entertainment. They talked about the meeting the next day with Beaumont. He'd written in his email that his assistant Julie, would be picking them up about one the next afternoon and deliver them to his boat. Everything was set, and even though Todd could hardly wait, he looked forward to spending the time all alone with Diana before then.

The GO's arrived and performed various skits, some were singing, some were playing instruments. There was an extravagant presentation of a scene from Cabaret with the GO's lip-synching to the sound track of the Broadway show. It was all a bit hokey, but a lot of fun. Actually, it reminded Todd of camp. Club Med was most definitely a camp for grownups.

The disco opened after the show, and Todd and Diana decided to savor the evening and dance for a while. It was packed on the dance floor, which was the perfect excuse to squeeze together as tightly as possible. It was noisy, and the vacationers were letting loose, having a great time doing as they were told and enjoying their freedom. After a while, Todd and Diana broke away from the frenzied crowd to get some air. They walked to the beach, the sand a silky runway, while the moon seemed to shine just for them. Todd couldn't remember the last time he'd been this happy. Todd took Diana in his arms and kissed her. A long, slow, deep, passionate kiss. Diana pulled away, took Todd's hand, and said it was time to go back to the room.

"Coolth," Todd murmured.

Chapter Thirty-Four

Frank Barron was surprised to get another call. Usually connections weren't made this quickly between cases. Then again, he'd entered a profile of the cases he was currently investigating into the FBI database, and law enforcement all across the country had access to it. An obvious pattern was beginning to emerge. Frank had information from Louisiana, Tennessee, and now Alabama. There was also a possibility a child snatching in Nogales was related as well. Two dead bodies, four stolen children. It was the work of a madman. Or woman.

This time he didn't need to ask permission to fly to Huntsville, he just went ahead and booked a ticket. He wanted to be there to speak with the officer in charge, and to examine the crime scene for himself. Time was of the essence. He was on a plane twenty-four hours later.

After making his way through the airport and car rental maze, Frank drove out to the small town of Piney Wood and met with the local homicide detective. After a lengthy briefing, Frank then drove a few miles further to Shady Meadows. He followed a hand drawn map, courtesy of the detective. He preferred to make the trip alone so as not to be influenced or distracted by another's take on the situation. Frank had already read the report, knew the facts, and heard all the suppositions and speculations at the police station. For now, he wanted to form his own impressions and interview some of the trailer park residents for himself.

He pulled up to a ramshackle fence out in front, or what was left of it anyway. He parked the rental car off to the side of the road. Frank wanted to walk in rather than drive. He thought he might miss something if he stayed in the car. Not much activity at the moment, but then it was noon on a Thursday, and those

Evil Exchange

that did work were at their jobs. The seniors were most likely having lunch and the war hero was probably hung over.

He took off his suit jacket. The temperature had to be pushing ninety degrees and the humidity was nearly intolerable. He could hear a barking dog inside one trailer while another dog eyed him from a rickety porch. As he approached the rear of the complex, Frank could see the yellow caution tape forbidding anyone to cross. Did cops really believe people actually obeyed instructions made from recycled plastic? However, it was standard operating procedure.

Frank spent the better part of an hour in the sweltering trailer. He examined the back bedroom carefully. Though the forensic team had gone over the room carefully, sometimes a clue, or an object was occasionally overlooked. Frank didn't see anything of importance. He found himself staring at the swayback mattress, picturing the young woman lying there dead. He'd looked at all of the photos from the file, so he knew how she was positioned. The bruises on her neck were in dark, ugly contrast to her fair skin. Little had been disturbed in the room, according to the woman's brother. Sadly, he was the one to find her. Frank knew from the report, that the older brother, Wes Stryker owned the rat trap, letting his little sister, Kerri, live there for free, her being in the family way and all. He'd come to see how she and the new baby were doing after coming home from the hospital. Though he had keys, he told the police he'd knocked to announce his arrival, and then entered the unlocked door when he received no reply. He found his sister dead in her bed, the baby gone. He used his cell phone to call 911, and had watched enough cop shows to know he should not touch anything.

After giving the arriving officer an in depth account of the situation, Stryker repeated it for the homicide detective. He admitted the trailer home was lacking in many respects, but it was better than living in a shelter, or on the street, which is where she would have been if it weren't for him. No, it wasn't much, but she always kept it neat and tidy, Stryker sobbed. *Always tidy.*

Frank had to agree. Everything looked to be in order. Nothing knocked over. No sign of a struggle. The few baby things he spotted looked horribly sad and lonely, out of place. Tragic. There was no question she'd been killed for her child. Not to Frank anyway.

After a thorough going over, Frank called it quits. New discoveries were not to be found on this day. The local police and forensic team might be inadequately staffed, but they knew how to do their job. Frank even took a moment to sit on the edge of the bed where Kerri had been killed, hoping something might come to him. Some clue, some hint, some sign. But it was not meant to be. Frank sighed and reminded himself those kinds of startling revelations usually only happened in the movies. Out of respect, he smoothed the covers where he'd been sitting. Leaving the tiny trailer, he checked his notebook. There were a few neighbors he wanted to speak to.

The interviews were short. The neighbors Frank was able to speak with did want to help, but no one heard or saw anything. One elderly woman mentioned her dog must have been slipped some kind of tranquilizer since he was comatose for ten hours straight after going out for his last potty of the evening. That wasn't news either, as it was included in the original report. Frank was striking out and getting discouraged. Whoever ran this baby stealing operation knew exactly what they were doing. The perp might as well have been a ghost since absolutely nothing had been found. Not a footprint, not a hair, not even the glimpse of a shadow moving in the night.

There was one more name on the list however, but he was hardly even worth the trouble. A Vietnam vet by the name of Nathan Hicks. Sargent Hicks had returned from his tour of duty minus his right leg, and although he was able to walk on his left and could have gotten around on crutches, his preferred mode of transportation over the last thirty-four years was a wheelchair. Yes, the cops had interviewed him, but he was for the most part incoherent due to his longtime love affair with a bottle named Stoli. As a matter of fact, the homicide detective thought Hicks had died some years before, and was astounded to discover the man was still alive. With the condition his liver must be in, surely it was a medical miracle the man hadn't passed away yet.

If Frank Barron weren't such a stickler for procedure, he might have skipped it all together. He'd come up empty so far, he figured a drunk wasn't going to provide much insight. Then again, he had come all this way, and he was a by-the-book type of guy, so he walked up the wooden ramp to the front door of the trailer and knocked. An American flag hung from a window.

"Go away!"

"FBI, Hicks. Open up," Frank stated clearly.

"Fuck off."

"Couple questions, that's all." Frank waited. He heard muffled swearing and glass breaking. "I'm not leaving," Frank said to the door.

More swearing, but the door finally opened. Frank flipped open his badge and introduced himself as Red.

"What is that? Some kind of code name?"

"Nickname. Can I come in?"

"Hell no. You can talk to me from right there. What the hell do you want, Mr. Red the Fed?"

This wasn't going well. The man reeked of cigarette smoke and booze. Dressed in faded camouflage, Hicks looked demented. Gray, wispy hair stuck straight out from his head, his mustache and beard masked swollen facial features. Surprisingly, his eyes were clear, and he looked Frank over from top to bottom.

"I'm here about your neighbor. The young woman who was killed," Frank answered the man.

"Cops already talked to me."

"I'm aware of that. Just wondered if you remembered anything since then."

"Didn't tell them a damn thing," Hicks said proudly. "Fucking pussies. They were never in the war. Never served their country." The man was rambling.

"Did the cops tell you why she was killed?" Frank tried to keep the conversation on track.

"Nope. *Why?*" Hicks asked suspiciously.

"For the baby." It must have made an impression. Frank noticed the man seemed to slump a bit in his wheelchair.

"That must have been what he was carrying then," Hicks mumbled.

"Who?" Frank demanded.

"The Hulk. I saw him ya know. Didn't tell those pussy cops. Didn't tell them shit. Like they'd believe me anyway," Hicks muttered.

"You saw the Hulk, and he was carrying the baby, is that right?" It took a supreme act of will for Frank not to roll his eyes to the heavens.

"No, you dumb ass. I didn't see the real Hulk, that guy's *green* for Christ sake. I'm just *describing* him. Big guy. Huge shoulders. Tree trunk legs. You know, a *hulk*. And he was holding something. Musta' been the kid."

"See his face? Anything else?"

"Nope. It was the middle of the fucking night. And I was drunk, just like every night. I did see him though, out my window. Saw him sneak out the back."

"But you didn't tell the police this."

"What are you deaf? I said I didn't. I fought for my country. Lost my damn leg in the war. Those assholes treat me like dirt. Let me put it this way. If one

Paris and Soll

of those guys was on fire, would I help put out the flames? Ya damn tootin'. Just so I could piss on him."

"Then why tell me? About the guy I mean," Frank couldn't help but ask.

"Like your code name, Mr. Red the Fed. Now leave me be, I've talked enough. My head is splitting and my mouth's gone dry."

"All right. I appreciate your help. I'm going to leave you my card, just in case you remember anything else," Frank pulled a card from his pocket and passed it over. Hicks grabbed it and slammed the door.

Frank shook his head and walked slowly down the ramp. Unbelievable.

"Hey! Mr. Red the Fed," Hicks called from the window.

"Yeah?" Frank turned around.

"Baseball cap. The Hulk was wearing a baseball cap."

Frank saluted the flag.

Chapter Thirty-Five

Todd woke up early. He looked over at Diana who was soundly asleep, and even more beautiful if that were possible. What a night they'd had together. Making love to her felt both new and exciting, yet warm and familiar. How easy it had been to tell her how he felt. *Diana, I love you.* No hesitation, just the most natural thing in the world to say it out loud. She'd kissed him passionately and said the same words back to him. They hadn't had much sleep, but Todd felt more refreshed than if he'd slept for a week. Love will do that.

He slipped from bed so as not to disturb the object of his desire. Throwing on a pair of shorts, Todd decided to go for a quick run on the beach. He'd been slacking a bit lately. He silently slipped outside. The air smelled salty and fresh, the temperature perfect, not too warm yet. The wet sand felt soothing and cool, the sun gently caressed his face. Todd couldn't help but think his life was finally on the receiving end again. What a run of bad luck, or karma, whatever you wanted to call it, he'd had. For a while there, Todd didn't think anything good was ever going to happen to him again. If it weren't for Diana, he might have said to hell with it all and remained unhappy, unfulfilled, and maybe even six feet under if one of those accidents had turned out differently. Instead, he now felt an optimism that had been missing for far too long. After his leisurely run and a good sweat, the endorphins started to kick in. He returned to Relax 109 to surprise Diana in the shower. She feigned indignant for all of two seconds. They took up where they'd left off only a few hours before, and it was an easy call to skip breakfast.

At one o'clock, just as the email said, Julie arrived to meet Todd and Diana in the Club Med lobby. Though they'd never met, Julie picked them out right away. They introduced themselves, and headed for the dining room to have lunch before the appointment with Boots. Todd couldn't help but stare at Julie.

Paris and Soll

Amazon was the word that came to mind. Julie was tall, thin, and stunning. Her black hair was pulled away from her face, emphasizing almond shaped eyes, a regal nose, full lips, and light mocha colored skin. She was dressed casually in shorts and a bikini top covered by a crocheted pullover, and looked like she belonged on a runway in Paris or Milan. When she first approached Todd in the lobby, he thought he might go blind from her smile. Boots Beaumont was one lucky guy.

Julie and Diana connected immediately. If someone were observing them, it would be easy to think they'd been friends for many years. The two women fell into a comfortable conversation. Some women might be intimidated by a gorgeous lady, but not Diana. Todd knew she wasn't threatened by an attractive woman, because she just didn't think that way. Diana was not insecure or competitive. She was kind, smart, funny, attractive, and sexy as hell. Todd Walters was one lucky guy as well.

Though Todd was anxious for lunch to be over so they could get on with their appointment with Boots, he enjoyed sharing the company of two beautiful women. He was content to listen to their lively conversation, and each time he thought of a question to ask Julie, it would miraculously come up, as if Julie could read his mind. Todd learned Julie worked as a singer in a piano bar from time to time, and upon occasion, filled in at a friend's restaurant as a hostess. Todd imagined if she could sing half as good as she looked, the bar would have patrons lined up around the block. Other than that, she spent time with Boots and with her family, which according to Julie was rather large. He also found out Boots Beaumont was quite disciplined about his writing, working nearly every day of the week, which is why, Julie explained, Boots was not joining them for lunch. He was hard at work finishing a chapter. After they'd eaten, Julie suggested a walk. She knew a nearby trail only the locals were familiar with. Todd stifled a pang of impatience, and said sure.

The walk turned into a bit of a hike, but it was incredible. Along the way, Julie pointed out native flowers and plants, explaining how some were used as natural remedies for common ailments. Diana complimented Julie on her vast knowledge, and Julie said it was minuscule in comparison to what her older brother knew. His specialty was nature walks for tourists. His name was Navi (short for navigator), and his excursions were booked months in advance. As they made their way back to Club Med, Todd couldn't help but wonder if Julie were stalling for some reason. She appeared to be completely at ease, not nervous in the slightest. Yet Todd couldn't shake the sense that something was just a bit off. Still, he couldn't quite put his finger on it, so he decided to chalk it up to his own anxiety.

Evil Exchange

Julie took them to the parking lot and led them to her Wrangler. As they piled in, Todd wondered what she did when it rained. There was a windshield, but no top or sides to the car. It didn't appear they'd have a problem this afternoon; there wasn't a cloud in the sky. As it turned out, Todd needn't have worried about rain, he should have worried about Julie's driving instead. She was a maniac. In Eleuthera, one drove on the left rather than the right, but Julie drove in the middle. It didn't matter if there were other cars or people along the way, it seemed likely she would run them all down. Todd didn't realize he'd shut his eyes until Julie yelled the marina was up ahead and pointed out Boots' boat. The boat was a beauty all right. Gleaming, white with one red stripe around the outside. It made Todd think of the Jamaican beer. He could barely make out the name as they came screeching around the corner. *Lost & Found*. It seemed fitting.

Julie squealed to a stop and hopped out. Todd untangled his legs and let go of the choke hold he had on the seat cushion. Even Diana, who rarely lost her composure, looked a bit pale getting out of the vehicle. Perhaps their jelly legs would make boarding the boat a bit easier.

Julie called out to Boots who was topside scrubbing something. Boots tended to be a creature of habit most of the time and his routine didn't vary much. He was either writing, cleaning, or repairing something on the boat. He spotted Julie and waved. She motioned to Todd and Diana to come aboard.

Boots stood to greet her and she introduced Todd and Diana. Boots said hello and politely shook hands. He looked a bit puzzled.

"This is the man who needs your help," Julie said to her lover.

"What kind of help?" Boots asked warily.

"Well, what we mentioned in the email, of course. Madeline Monroe? Looking for my identity?" It was Todd's turn to look confused.

"What email?" Boots' face turned dark as he looked at Julie.

"What difference does it make?" Julie shouted at him. "I told you. A man was coming. A man who needs your help. Here he is," she pointed at Todd as if it were the most obvious thing in the world.

Boots was beginning to catch on and was deeply embarrassed. "Look. I'm sorry. I think there's been a misunderstanding," he said.

It then became apparent to Todd and Diana that the email hadn't come from Boots, but from Julie instead.

"Oh, no. There's no mistake. I saw it. It's happening," Julie interrupted him. She held her ground, as defiant as Boots had ever seen her. With her hands on her hips, feet spread wide apart, she looked like a warrior princess ready to do battle.

Diana jumped in to break the tension. "Maybe we should start from the beginning," she suggested. "Would it be all right if we sat down Mr. Beaumont? We've come a long way." Leave it to Diana to defuse the situation. Boots and Julie stared daggers at each other, but apparently agreed to a silent truce for the moment. Boots gestured toward some plastic deck chairs. "Okay. Go ahead," he said when they'd all settled.

Diana started first as Todd seemed to have temporarily lost any ability to speak. Ever so diplomatic, Diana explained how they were both huge fans of his. It was because of *Finding Michael* they felt convinced if anyone in the world could help Todd, it would be Boots Beaumont. She filled him in on the email, and explained that Todd wasn't looking for any favors, that he would be more than willing to pay Beaumont for his services. Diana then managed to pull Todd into the conversation so he could take over and continue on with the exact circumstances of what he'd been through, and what he'd discovered up to this point. Haltingly at first, Todd recounted his discoveries of late. When he got to the part about Maddie Monroe and the possibility that his birth certificate was falsified, his voice grew bitter and angry. Diana reached out and took his hand as some small measure of comfort. Todd didn't notice.

When he finished, Todd looked wrung out. No one spoke. Julie looked triumphant. *I told you he needed help,* her eyes said. Diana blinked back tears. Boots appeared deep in thought, and then broke the silence.

"Look, man. I'm sorry for what's happened to you. And I wish I could help, I really do. But you must know I'm retired. I don't do investigative work anymore. Haven't for years. I write full time now. So with that, the boat, and this one over here, it keeps me pretty busy. I know Julie meant well, but she shouldn't have brought you down here under false pretenses. Premonition or not," Boots nodded in Julie's direction. He was clearly angry with her while trying to maintain his composure in front of strangers.

Julie jumped to her feet, cursing at Boots. "You have to help him, you bastard!"

"No, he doesn't," Todd yelled at her. He was now furious and didn't bother to hide it. "I don't know anything about this so called *premonition,* but you lead me to believe Boots sent the email. Now it turns out he didn't even know anything about it. I've never been so humiliated in my life. Diana, let's go.

Sorry to have wasted your time," he said to Boots. He grabbed Diana's hand and practically dragged her away.

"Let me drive you at least," Boots offered.

Without turning around Todd shook his head no. He stomped off the dock, Diana trailing helplessly behind.

Chapter Thirty-Six

Frank Barron returned to the police station after his visit to Shady Meadows. The dispatcher was working solo at the moment, apparently everyone else was either on patrol or had the day off. The homicide detective he'd met with earlier was off fishing with his son for the afternoon. Frank parked himself at an open desk to go over his notes and jot down what he'd learned from Nathan Hicks. He also made a mental note to do a bit more research on the nursing pin. So far, he hadn't been able to identify anything from the drawing Tarren Vincent had given him when he interviewed her in Tennessee.

After thirty minutes, Frank's concentration was broken by the sound of footsteps in the hallway. A state trooper walked in. He removed his hat and sunglasses. Frank couldn't help but admire the perfectly pressed uniform, the military style buzz cut, and the masculine good looks of the man who stood before him. In comparison, Frank felt as if he'd been held captive in a sweat lodge only to finally escape straight into a dust storm. He felt grimy, rumpled, wrinkled, and disheveled. Still, he tried to be professional, and straightened his tie as he rose from his seat. He introduced himself as Red and flashed his badge. For a man who hated his nickname, he sure used it a lot. It was out of habit.

The trooper, who called himself Flint (he didn't mention whether that was his first name or his last name), had stopped by to fill out a traffic incident report before his shift ended. Naturally, Flint was curious about Frank's presence in the modest little township of Piney Wood, and politely asked what he was working on. When Frank mentioned Kerri Stryker's murder and her newborn's abduction, Flint shook his head in disgust. He of course knew about the homicide, but was surprised to hear the FBI had become involved. Frank filled him in on what appeared to be a pattern of killings and child abductions which had recently taken place in some of the southern states, and how it most likely had to do

Evil Exchange

with baby selling. Flint said he couldn't believe what some people would do for money. Naturally, Frank asked the trooper if he remembered seeing anyone suspicious in the past week or so. Flint thought about it, but said he didn't think so. Most everything had been routine lately as far as he was concerned.

Frank mentioned he'd just returned from the trailer park, and spoke of what he learned from the one-legged Hicks. Flint laughed and said good old Nathan was his daddy's cousin, and how the man was crazier than a June bug in January. Frank had absolutely no idea what that particular expression meant, but found himself nodding in companionable agreement. Then Frank pointed out that even though Hicks' brain had been soaking in an alcoholic marinade for the last three decades, he did believe the man's eyeballs still functioned properly, and the hulking man wearing a baseball cap he'd spotted was not just a hallucination, but the actual perpetrator of the crime. Flint opened his mouth to say something, or perhaps to laugh again, but nothing came out.

"You say he was a big man, wearing a baseball cap?" Flint finally asked.

"That's what Hicks said. Sound like anyone you know?" Frank couldn't help but get his hopes up just a notch.

"I'm not sure. Seems familiar for some reason. Can't think of why though," Flint said in mild frustration.

"Well, maybe it will come to you." Frank tried not to show his disappointment and went back to his notes. He barely noticed when Flint excused himself.

Ten minutes later, he was just finishing up when Flint returned. The first thing Frank noticed was the smell of cigarettes. He looked up at Flint, who was grinning.

"Works every time," he crowed.

"Excuse me?"

"All I have to do is hack a butt," Flint said proudly.

Frank groaned inwardly. *Another Southern idiom?* He looked at Flint, hoping to get an explanation without having to ask for one.

"You must be a non-smoker," Flint stated.

"Oh, right."

"I know I'm not supposed to smoke on the job. Yet, when I need to remember something? It really does help. Usually, all I have to do is light up and before I'm halfway down to the filter, it comes to me."

Paris and Soll

Frank had never smoked a cigarette in his life, and was still unsure of what Flint was talking about, but nodded as if he understood.

Flint sighed and spoke to Frank as if he were six years old. "Almost two weeks ago, I see this guy on the side of the road changing a flat tire. I pull over to see if he needs help."

"Go on."

"Guy's almost done and says he's fine. We talk for just a minute or so, and then I get back in the patrol car and go on my merry way."

"Okay."

"Okay? The guy wasn't from around here. He was driving a rental car."

"Right."

Flint looked exasperated. He'd always thought of the FBI as being smarter than the average law enforcement officer. This one seemed quite dense to him though.

"The guy was *huge*. Big as a bear. And . . ." Flint said with dramatic flourish, "he was wearing a baseball cap."

"Can you give me a detailed description?" Frank asked. *Why hadn't he just said so in the first place?*

"Not really," Flint replied and shrugged his shoulders. Frank felt like Charlie Brown when Lucy pulled the football away.

"Got the tape though. Might be able to tell from that." Flint grinned.

"The tape from the dash cam?"

"Eggs-actly."

"Where?"

"In the back room."

"Can we look at it?"

"Sure."

"Now?"

"You bet."

Unbelievable. Fucking unbelievable. Maybe, just maybe, I've finally caught a break.

Chapter Thirty-Seven

To an onlooker, they could have been a coach and an umpire arguing a crucial call at a pennant game. Nose to nose, with faces lobster red and spittle flying, Boots and Julie were screaming at each another.

"How could you do something like that? Bring them all the way down here? Tell them I was going to help them, without even asking me? Damn you, woman!"

"Stop shouting at me!" Julie shouted.

"I'm not shouting at you," Boots shouted back.

"Yes, you are! But that's beside the point. You *will* help those two."

"No. I *won't* and that's final. Just who the hell do you think you are, anyway?" Boots snarled. He said it to hurt her. As if she were nothing to him, meant nothing to him. That did it for Julie. His cruel comment was a stunning blow, and she hauled off and slapped him hard across the face. Boots froze. Sure, he and Julie had their tussles. She'd bitten, wrestled, and kicked. She'd thrown dishes, brandished a knife, and jumped on his back. But never had she hit him. He couldn't believe it.

All the years of private investigating kept Boots in shape and his reflexes sharp. Though he'd become somewhat more relaxed since moving to Eleuthera and living on the boat, he maintained his good physical condition and quick reactions. His immediate response was to defend himself and hit her back. Without realizing, he'd automatically drawn his arm back, and clenched his fist ready to fire. It was sheer willpower that kept him from cold-cocking her. He'd been in many a fight, but never had he hit a woman. Though sorely tempted, he wasn't going to start now. Instead, he channeled the adrenaline and anger into his voice, and screamed at the top of his lungs. "I WON'T!" He stomped off toward the stern of the boat and stared out at the rippling water.

Fearless, Julie followed him. "You'll do it, Beaumont. You son of a bitch. You *owe* me, and you'll do it."

"Owe you? Owe you my ass," he yelled over his shoulder. *The woman has balls.*

"Have you forgotten the time your pocket got picked at the market, and I had a vision who did it? I got it back for you, didn't I? Do you remember the day you wanted to go surfing, and I had the shark premonition? You ended up not going, and one of the locals was attacked and lost an arm. Need I remind you when your idiotic cousin came to visit? You both got drunk and thrown in jail by that imbecile police chief. Who had to cancel a good paying gig that night to come and bail you out? You'd *both* still be there if it weren't for me.

"Besides, I've *seen* it. You know what that means. When I see it, it happens. You can't change the fact. I know you think I'm crazy and I don't give a shit. It's clear and unmistakable. You will do this for Todd. What the fuck is the matter with you? Are you above helping people now, Mr. Big Time Author? I'm telling you, you are his last chance. His *only* chance. You *will* help him."

Boots kept his back to her, which he knew was a risk, but he didn't think there was anything nearby that could be used as a weapon. Julie surprised him again and did not attack. Instead, she turned her back to him, furiously tapping her foot on the deck. It was a classic standoff.

"Well, Boots? I'm waiting," Julie broke the silence.

"Jesus Christ woman! Must you always win?" Boots caved. He turned around to face her. "Why don't you see if you can find them. Bring them back and I'll see what I can do," Beaumont sighed.

Julie wheeled around and threw her arms around him. "I knew you'd do it. Thanks, love." She kissed him passionately and dashed off to the Wrangler as if the last few minutes had never happened. Boots winced when he heard the squeal of tires. He stood on the deck and looked back out to sea. Shaking his head in amusement, he realized he knew all along she would find a way to convince him. Julie was unstoppable. The epitome of stubborn. The champion of sheer cussedness. He didn't know exactly how she managed to do it, but she always won these battles. Always.

Chapter Thirty-Eight

Julie's premonition frequency must have been on the blink. As she rounded a bend in the road, there was no sense of danger whatsoever, and she was completely unprepared to see a momma duck and her ducklings crossing the highway. Julie slammed on the brakes and veered off to the side, saving the babies from becoming road kill, but getting stuck in a ditch as a reward. Fortunately, she wasn't hurt, but she also wasn't going anywhere either.

She opened the glove box of the Wrangler looking for her cell phone, only to remember she'd left it on the boat. Cursing a blue streak, she tried to flag down a passing motorist, only to be ignored. In sheer frustration, she picked up a rock and hurled it at the tail end of the vehicle and earned a one-digit response for her trouble. There was not much else to do but to start walking until someone else came by who might be more of a Samaritan.

An hour later, Julie finally made it to Club Med via the bed of a pick up truck. She was pleased to see her friend, Chloe, on duty at the front desk, and asked her to ring Todd's room. Chloe frowned and said that Mr. Walters and Ms. Easton had already checked out. Quite abruptly, she added. Chloe indicated they were in a rush to get to the airport. She figured something awful must have happened since they had their room booked for another night. She went on to say that Mr. Walters appeared distraught and angry, and didn't even ask for a refund. Julie commiserated with Chloe and agreed, something awful indeed must have occurred.

As Julie walked out to the front of the facility, she felt entirely responsible for the complete and utterly disastrous turn of events. Never had one of her plans gone so terribly wrong. Many a time she'd relied on her psychic abilities as a sign, an indication of what was to come. The problem with the premonitions though, was that usually she saw only the end result of something, not the way to get there. So, most of the time she had to guess what to do next, as was the case of the email correspondence with Todd. She knew it was a bit deceitful to pose as Boots, lure Todd and Diana down to the island, and then spring it all on her unsuspecting lover. However that was all just semantics. Julie *knew* this was supposed to all work out somehow, and at the moment, couldn't figure out why it hadn't. Now it was time to get things back in proper alignment, to make things right again. But exactly how was she going to do it?

Her first break that afternoon came when she spotted her younger brother Anton, sitting in his cab. Anton often hung out at Club Med flirting with some of the female guests as he drove them around Eleuthera. Presently, he had his arm around a bikini clad young woman whose silicone breasts looked like twin pyramids draped in floral triangles. Julie opened the passenger door, hissed at the implanted jeune fille, and waited for her immediate departure. Anton could only shrug and waggle his fingers goodbye to the live Barbie. He knew if his sister wanted something from him, the thought of arguing or trying to dissuade her was absolutely hopeless.

Barbie got out as indignantly as one can with a thong up one's butt, and Julie climbed in the car and commanded Anton to drive her to the airport, quickly. Without a word, Anton pulled away from the curb, glancing in his rear view mirror. He caught a glimpse of the very angry blond, who stood staring after the cab, her mouth a perfect circle of outrage. From a distance, she resembled a plastic blow up doll. Anton thought it a terrible waste.

It wasn't a long trip to the airport, and to Anton's credit, his calm demeanor never faltered under Julie's withering gaze. He knew Julie disapproved of his sexual conquests, mainly because she felt the tourist bimbos were completely beneath him. She thought what he did for a living was beneath him as well, but Anton had little ambition other than driving his cab and getting an occasional blowjob from some wild young thing on vacation. As the baby of the family, Anton was used to having his sisters act as surrogate mothers ever since they'd all lost their real mother, Lucille, to a heart attack some years ago. Just like all her siblings, Julie could never stay mad at her baby brother for long, and finally broke the silence by telling Anton that she was sorry to ruin his "date," but it was imperative she get to the airport to find someone right away. She did not elaborate further, and he did not ask.

Anton pulled up to the entrance of the open air facility. Julie jumped out after ordering him to wait for her until she returned. The airport was very small. There wasn't much besides the terminal building, baggage area, and a small gift shop, which sold souvenirs for those last minute shoppers, as well as sodas and

Evil Exchange

candy bars. Julie went straight to the Bahamas Air ticket counter only to discover that a flight was boarding at the very moment. Since she hadn't seen them anywhere else in the terminal, Julie figured Todd and Diana had to be getting on a plane, but she was determined to find them.

She dashed to the other side of the building to the boarding gate which was an open door leading to the tarmac. She easily dodged an airline employee and shaded her eyes from the brilliant sun to scour the lineup of passengers making their way up the steps of the aircraft. She scanned the crowd with no luck. *Damn, had she miscalculated?* Her internal radar had been off today, but she still couldn't help but think this is where she would find them.

Finally, she spotted them. Todd and Diana were almost at the top of the steps, but they'd been slowed by an elderly man who juggled two overstuffed shopping bags. The gentleman appeared to be arguing with a flight attendant, and he was holding up the line. Julie called out, but her words were lost in the jet engine noise from a nearby plane. She tried again, waving her arms to attract attention. Diana turned around and saw her.

"Come back! He said he'd help you," Julie screamed at the top of her lungs.

Diana tugged at Todd's shirt to get his attention. Todd looked toward Julie as Diana pointed.

"Please don't go. Boots said he would help you. Please!"

An angry shadow crossed Todd's face. Diana spoke words to him Julie of course could not hear. It was like watching a silent movie. Todd and Diana appeared to be arguing. Julie could see Todd shaking his head. Diana seemed to be pleading, but Julie wasn't sure. The passengers on the steps below them were getting restless, they'd been patient with one delay, but they were not going to stand for another.

Suddenly, Julie felt a hand at her elbow. A security guard informed her she was in a restricted area, and that she must leave at once. "Wait," she said to the man. "WAIT," she yelled at Todd. The guard tried to gently lead her away while Julie resisted. She kept her eyes focused on Todd. *Don't get on that plane. Don't get on that plane.* She willed him to stay. Then Julie saw him say something.

"What? I can't hear you!" Julie yelled back at him. Todd repeated himself, but Julie could not make it out.

"Come on, woman. You can't be here," the guard applied more pressure.

Paris and Soll

"What did he say? Did you hear what he said?" Julie said to the man who strong armed her.

"He said 'fuck it'. Now move or I'll lose my job."

CHAPTER THIRTY-NINE

Frank was impressed with the tidiness of the video archive in the tiny storeroom. Rows upon rows of dated and labeled tapes lined an entire section of shelves. Flint searched for and found tapes from two weeks ago. He couldn't remember the exact day he had seen the motorist fixing the flat, but he knew the general time frame and said he could narrow it down from there. First, he eliminated the days he was off duty, and then pulled three tapes out and handed them to Frank. He led him into a small conference room.

Flint apologized that he would not be able to join Frank again for a while as he still had the traffic report to attend to. He promised as soon as he was done, and his shift was over, he'd be come back in. Before he left the room, Flint set up the VCR and monitor, then handed Frank the remote control. There would be hours of tape to go through, and fast forwarding while on play was the best and quickest solution.

Frank popped in the first tape and settled down to watch. The film was black and white, the texture grainy, and the viewpoint slightly nauseating as the patrol car was in constant motion. There were long stretches of highway and blurry scenery. Occasionally, there was something of interest which caused Frank to hit the pause, play, or rewind button, but for the most part it was simply plowing through the often unremarkable routine of an officer's day. He kept the audio on low since there wasn't much to hear anyway.

As he watched the minutes fly by on the bottom of the screen, Frank fell into a slightly hypnotic state. His eyes watched the screen while his mind wandered off. He reminded himself to call Suzy and let her know when he'd be home. He knew she would remind him of the long list of projects awaiting his return. Not that he minded. Frank enjoyed puttering around the house, and was always

Paris and Soll

happy to please his wife. He stopped daydreaming and when he refocused on the screen, saw Trooper Flint come into the camera frame. Frank slowed the tape down to regular speed and turned up the volume hoping this might be the flat tire episode. It was not. It was an out-of-state driver who had apparently gotten lost. Trooper Flint was giving directions to get him back on track. Frank smiled as he remembered a funny incident he had himself involving directions some years ago.

He and Suzy were in Dallas for a collector's convention. Suzy's motivation was Snoopy collectibles of course, and since neither of them had visited the great state of Texas before, they decided to make a mini vacation out of it. On the first day, while they were cruising up and down the aisles of the convention center, Frank dropped his one and only pair of glasses and broke a lens. Since he knew Suzy would be hours before she had her fill of Peanuts memorabilia, he decided he would take the rental car and go in search of a local optometrist to have the lens replaced. He inquired at the information booth and was told it was a short drive about a mile north to Bradbury Street, where Ray's Optical Solutions was located.

To his embarrassment, Frank got a bit lost finding the rental car, and by the time he found the exit out of the parking garage, he was completely turned around and disoriented. He spotted a police officer at the convention hall loading dock and asked him how to get to get to Bradbury Street. The officer thought about it for a moment and said; "Go straight to the third light, make a left and . . . no, wait. Go straight to the fourth light and make a right and . . . no, that won't work either. Hmm. Well, hell. You just can't get there from here." He slapped his thigh and started to laugh. Frank wasn't sure what was so funny, but he laughed too. Then the officer told him to go straight up the main road until he saw an overpass and to then turn left. So that's exactly what Frank did. All of a sudden, he found himself going down a one way street the wrong way. As soon as he realized his error, he made a U-turn so he'd be traveling in the correct direction and no longer be in fear of a head on collision. Before he knew it, the howl of a siren stopped him. As he looked in the rear view mirror, he saw a Texas State Police car flashing its lights. He immediately pulled over. Now, Frank could have easily avoided any hassle by whipping out his FBI identification, but he didn't like to do that when he was on vacation. As a matter of fact, he preferred to be treated like a regular guy. It was no secret people acted differently once they found out you worked for the Bureau. Either they asked idiotic questions, acted paranoid, or sometimes became downright hostile. Often police officers were the worst offenders and would become aggressive to find an agent on their own turf. Frank didn't like being interrogated, or having to explain what he was doing. So it was easier to say nothing.

Evil Exchange

So Frank chose to deal with the officer as a normal citizen would. He did a double take in the side mirror as the officer approached. She was one of the most beautiful women he'd ever seen. She walked up to the window, looked him straight in the eye and asked him what the fuck he was doing. Frank apologized and explained he was in town on vacation, and had gotten lost. "Well, then get the fuck out of here. Pronto!" She turned and strode off. Although Frank Barron was a very happily married man, he couldn't get the image of the gorgeous, garbage mouthed officer out of his head for a few days afterwards. An interesting cast of characters they had on the Dallas police force.

Almost an hour later, Flint joined Frank in the video room. Frank was on tape two by this time, and as soon as Trooper Flint saw it, he announced it was the day in question. Frank asked how he was so sure, and Flint said he remembered it was on the same day he'd stopped to remove some lumber from the highway which had fallen from the back of a pickup truck. It was what was they were looking at that very moment. Flint checked the time of day on the bottom of the screen and told Frank to fast forward through the next few hours. Frank did so without a word. They both watched the screen carefully until Flint saw the stretch of highway where he'd seen the rental car pulled over to the side, and instructed Frank to slow down. Now playing at regular speed, the dash cam showed Flint exiting his vehicle and approaching a man on the side of the road, next to his car. Although it was from a distance, Frank could plainly see the man crouched down with a tire iron in his hand. The man was very large, even in such a compact position. There was no mistaking the baseball cap.

As Flint approached, you could see the man turn his head in his direction. The baseball cap was clearly visible. Unfortunately, it was also clearly plain. No slogan, location, team name, or logo to be found anywhere on the hat. Not that it would make much difference, but it could have yielded one more clue. What was even more unfortunate was that the baseball cap, combined with the afternoon sun, made a perfect shadow across the man's features. Frank was a bit disappointed there wasn't much in the way of identifying information from this piece of tape, but it was better than nothing. It also served to help jog Flint's memory a bit. Though he hadn't been too close at the time, he did recall the man's general appearance. He said he looked European, but he wasn't sure why. The man's voice, which you could barely hear in the background as the wind whipped it away, was completely without any accent. Flint remembered the man saying he was visiting a cousin in the area, but he certainly wasn't from anywhere near Alabama, that much he was sure of. That was it. Frank continued to watch the monitor as it showed Flint walking back to the patrol car, and getting in. As he pulled away, the mystery man turned his face toward the rental car, and all the camera showed was his large and powerful back, then highway ahead.

Paris and Soll

"Let's go back," said Frank and pushed another button. The tape rewound and Flint moved backwards in slow motion. "Here," Frank paused the film. "Can you make it out?" He pointed at the back of the car, at the license plate.

"Yeah, I see it. Alabama plate, 5HY384," Flint called out. Frank pulled out a pen and small notebook from his pocket and wrote it down. "Got it. Thanks."

They watched the tape a few more times, but didn't see anything more than the first time. Frank asked if he could make a copy and Flint went off in search of a blank tape. A short time later, with VHS in hand, Agent Barron pumped the hand of Trooper Flint, thanking him for his help and cooperation. Flint was more than ready to call it a day, his shift long over, and surely craving another cigarette. However Frank Barron felt invigorated and couldn't wait to get on the phone. He had rental car companies to call.

Chapter Forty

"Julie!" Diana called from across the terminal. Julie spun around, searching for her. She saw Diana was running towards her, but she was alone.

"Where's Todd?" Julie couldn't help but ask when Diana caught up.

"He's coming. I wouldn't let him board the plane. I told him we had to give this another shot. I'll warn you though, he's pissed," Diana said slightly winded from her pursuit.

"He'll get over it," Julie smiled. The guilt she had at causing such turmoil evaporated. After all, Julie believed the destination more important than the journey. She never meant to hurt anyone on purpose. If once in a while, someone stubbornly refused to see the big picture (the big picture according to Julie that is), then it was their own fault if they got hurt. Besides, if Boots had cooperated in the first place, none of this ridiculous drama would have taken place, and Julie would not have to spend the time or the energy chasing, and then mollifying Todd Walters. She sighed and thought to herself that Boots Beaumont was lucky she put up with him. He sure could cause a lot of trouble.

Julie and Diana went to find Todd. He was in the same spot where Diana had left him. Todd had a childish scowl on his face. His arms were tight across against his chest, his back rigidly straight, and jaw tightly clenched. One look at him told Julie this was not going to be easy. She wondered, as she often did, why men had to be so complicated.

Thankfully, it was Diana who coaxed Todd out of the terminal and into Anton's cab. After a quick introduction, Julie got in the front with her brother, and they caught up on family news while Todd and Diana sat silently in the back. Diana knew well enough to leave Todd alone for the ride back to the harbor. It

Paris and Soll

had taken a great deal of persuasion and cajoling just to get him this far, and she was drained. Diana was trying her best to remain supportive and understanding. Todd had been through the wringer. Over, and over, and over again. He had a right to be angry, no question. Yet, it was time to move on and get back to being proactive. If Beaumont had agreed to help, whether under coercion or not, then Todd had to accept the offer gratefully and stop pouting.

Boots was waiting for them, although surprised to see them pull up in Anton's cab. Julie hopped out and offered a sisterly admonishment to her baby brother to keep away from the scalpel sculpted American-Tits-On-Parade. Anton laughed and flashed the same dazzling smile his sister possessed. Since Julie knew Anton would be heading back to Club Med anyway, she asked him to drop off Todd and Diana's luggage, and to inform Chloe they would be keeping their room for another night after all. Anton agreed, waved to Boots, and took off. Julie quickly boarded the boat, gave Boots a kiss, explained about the Wrangler, and then went in search of her cell phone. She said she wanted to try and find someone to pull it out of the ditch before it got dark. Boots welcomed Todd and Diana with an apology, and said he wanted to start over. Todd seemed to have thawed a bit and accepted. Boots suggested they celebrate with a margarita and went below to whip some up.

Todd and Diana settled into the deck chairs and concentrated on the harbor view. It was breathtaking. It was no wonder Beaumont loved it here. Julie came back and joined them just as Boots brought the drinks, but she turned down the salty cocktail. She had a booking at the Starfish Lounge that evening, and never drank alcohol before singing since she thought it bad for her throat. Diana asked if they could come watch her perform, that is, if Todd and Boots finished with their business in time, and Julie clapped her hands in delight. Julie said a front row table would be reserved just for them.

As the two men started talking, Diana and Julie wandered away and left them alone. Diana was happy and relieved to see Todd so animated. Bringing him back here was a gamble, but at the moment, it appeared to be paying off. Diana thought Beaumont seemed like a decent guy, and from what she could overhear of their conversation, he sounded quite enthusiastic. Hopefully, Boots would be able to help Todd unravel some of the mystery of his past.

Not wanting to waste any time, but wishing to refresh his memory, Boots asked Todd to recount his story. Todd started from the beginning, but this time condensed as much as he could. Boots mostly listened, but interrupted with a question or clarification now and then, and wrote a few things down on a legal pad. Boots told Todd he had been thinking about nothing else for the last few hours, and was already formulating a plan. He explained that although he'd been retired for some time now, he still maintained many of his contacts in New York. He'd start making inquiries as soon as possible.

"But, aren't you working on a book right now?" Todd asked.

"Yeah, but it can wait. I'll just tell my editor that I'm doing some research," Boots grinned.

As they continued to talk, Boots became more and more determined to get to the bottom of this puzzle. He listened to Todd and tried to put himself in his place. In doing so, he realized the bitter injury Todd Walters had suffered. The man had been robbed. Beaumont's increasing ire was a familiar and welcome feeling. During his years as a PI, there were plenty of cases that filled him with rage. Injustice especially made him furious. Boots Beaumont became an expert at channeling and using his emotions as fuel. It was anger that energized him. It was anger that most often solved a case.

Chapter Forty-One

Sheila Stiles had a serious addiction. Countless times a day, she would log onto her on-line bank accounts and carefully check each balance. She knew it was silly, a real waste of time. And yet, she looked. There were few things in life that gave her as much pleasure. It was a thrill each and every time, especially when she made a deposit and the amount increased. It was wonderful to see those numbers rise. Sheila kept track of five different accounts. Of course there was the business account she and Colby shared, plus four personal accounts of her own. She kept a checking account for everyday expenditures and automatic bill paying. One savings account held money for emergencies only. Another was a travel account, and the third, a retirement account, which held the largest balance of all.

Sheila knew one day, far in the future, she would retire. Retire and do what was the big question, but retire she would. Eventually. Yet now, she couldn't imagine not having a job, for she had always been a tireless worker. She was a true Type A personality, and bordered on obsession with accumulating wealth.

Growing up in the late fifties, Sheila was raised by parents who sought the American dream, which unfortunately, was always slightly out of reach. Her father worked for a large janitorial firm. Over many years, dear old dad worked his way up only a rung or two of the company's corporate ladder. This microscopic rise in the business never failed to disappoint Sheila's mother who was born, raised, and groomed to be the wife of a physician. Instead, and to her utter horror, she ended up marrying a custodian, which she simply would never have thought possible. It was all due to a wild one night stand when she'd been "slumming" with some friends, and met a quiet young man with a cute dimple in his chin. She became pregnant and a quick marriage to save her honor was the only solution.

Evil Exchange

Sheila's mother may have compromised her goals by marrying the wrong man, but she held fast to the notion that a mother should stay at home with her charge and never work outside the home. As a result, Mother and Father Stiles had to achieve their modest aspirations on one salary, which was never quite enough. They were not poor, nor were they well off.

From her earliest memories, Sheila knew about the "budget." Her father may not have been the brightest bulb, but the man did know how to follow a budget. He controlled the money since he worked for it, and everything was accounted for in a ledger. Before she was even old enough to understand, her father told her without a budget, life would be chaos.

Although Sheila was an only child, the trickle down effect did not occur in her home on a regular basis, and she often had to go without toys and books. Her father explained money was for food and clothing, to keep a roof over your head, not for extras which was really everything else. So, she learned if she wanted something for herself, it was up to her to get it. From a young age she became naturally enterprising and quickly learned which neighbors needed help with various cleaning chores, baby-sitting, yard work, pet care, or everyday errands. Sheila was willing to execute just about any task, soon earning the trust of many families, and therefore rarely lacked for jobs. As she grew up, she knew dad had done the best he could (which of course was never good enough for her mother) with very little education, and that she must do better. It was abundantly clear how bitterly disappointed mom was, having to watch every penny when she had been raised for a far better position in life. As a result, she turned to religion as an escape, and paid scant attention to her daughter. After graduating from high school, Sheila left home and put herself through college. Her parents never knew their daughter had thousands of dollars neatly rolled and stacked in an old suitcase hidden under her bed.

In college Sheila continued to work, sometimes two or three jobs while carrying a full load. She managed it all on five hours of sleep each night. Drugs certainly helped, but only over the counter kind, never illegal ones. It had nothing to do with morals, ethics, or conscience. Illegal drugs were expensive, and Sheila would never throw her hard earned money away on such things. Diet pills and caffeine tablets worked wonders and were much cheaper.

It has been said parents set examples for their children. This certainly was true in Sheila's case. She learned what she wanted, and perhaps more importantly, what she didn't want. Never living on a budget and having more money in the bank than her father ever dreamed possible, was a given. The other valuable lesson Sheila learned was twofold. Children should be wanted, and not everyone was meant to be a parent. This was basic common sense, which of course many people ignored. Sheila knew she would never (and she was absolutely sure of this) have children. Getting pregnant and having to marry beneath her was something her mother never got over. Sheila's mother never excelled at her maternal role. Whether it was because she didn't have a choice about becoming a mother, or that she simply lacked the necessary parental skills, was a toss up. Sheila never wasted much time analyzing the situation, but she considered her mother a twit for not having an abortion at the time. It would have solved all of her problems. Of course if she had had an abortion, Sheila would not exist, and she was at least grateful to her mother for that if not much else. The seed her mother planted so long ago was that children were a burden. An expensive burden. As an adult, Sheila was not about to share her money with anyone, let alone kids, so she had her tubes tied. The irony of her profession was never lost on Sheila. The fact remained, her motivation came from the income she received, not the goods she provided.

She felt the same about spouses. In her twenties, there was one terrible mistake in judgment, but she divorced him six months later. It was ever so much easier and far less trouble to be single and Sheila faithfully remained so. She never wanted to worry about what kind of reflection a spouse might cast on her image. In so many marriages, one half of the union was more prominent, dominant, smarter, or more successful. Sheila had worked too hard to ever want to live in another's shadow, or ride another's coat tails. The only person she wanted to root for, or be loyal to, was herself. She much preferred sex-only relationships, which provided physical gratification and no emotional strings. Over time she formed relationships with a few different men she enjoyed and trusted. She developed a rotation, which kept boredom at bay. She never considered the Judge to be a part of this intimate group as he was strictly business. The others were content with what she had to offer, and asked for nothing more. Anyone who did ask was immediately deleted from the roster and eventually replaced. Never one to be coy or flirtatious, Sheila was always up front about her terms and conditions. Take it or leave it. She was far too busy to waste time on romantic pursuits.

Yes, Sheila Stiles was a self-made woman who came from a working-class background. Through hard work and determination, she was well on her way to a modest goal of becoming a multi-millionaire before the age of fifty-five. She treated her partner and employees well. Her business flourished through word of mouth and satisfied customers. She was happily unattached. Free to spend or save. Able to do as she pleased, when she wanted, where she wanted, and how she wanted. Sheila did not have to share her money or the limelight. She had no one to answer to, never had to provide an explanation for anything to anyone. She could gloat about all she'd accomplished, and

Evil Exchange

check her balances as many times a day as she wished without ever having to justify it. She felt happy, complete, and fulfilled. She was absolutely certain her life was only going to get better, and her bank accounts were only going to get fatter.

Chapter Forty-Two

As Diana looked down at various shades of blue of the Caribbean waters below while the Bahamas Air jet climbed to cruising altitude, Todd retreated to his own world. He was drained, utterly and completely. He felt as if he'd just finished climbing up the side of the Empire State Building brick by brick. Like a cat up a tree and now afraid to come down, Todd felt paralyzed, not by fear, but by emotion. He just didn't have the words to describe what was he was feeling, and he searched his memory bank for some point of reference. He concentrated on a mental picture of the framed faces displayed on the wall of the support group office. There were eighteen in all, each showing a different emotion. There were the obvious ones, anger, anxiety, fear, guilt, jealousy, shame, and the like. There were also some more unusual and lesser known faces. The last one of the whole bunch was titled "whelmed." Glen said it was not an emotion per se, but a state of fear of being overcome with emotion.

Todd thought if he could see those faces on the wall in his mind, then he'd be able to tell Diana what he was feeling. He kept running through them, over and over, but he still couldn't figure it out. Growing up in a family that didn't talk much about adoption, left him unable to discuss his feelings about being adopted. It was not until he started going to the support group that Todd found out how common it is for many adoptees to be silent on the subject. With the help of the group, he was learning how to speak Adoptese, the language of adoption, but it wasn't easy. His feelings, after being bottled up for so long, were not only extremely intense, but quite frightening to identify. Glen and Carol both constantly reminded the group, *the only way to heal is to feel*. So Todd went over the faces, again and again, until he finally figured it out.

"Diana," he said while gently tapping her on the shoulder. She turned from the window and looked at him.

Evil Exchange

"I'm feeling joy, fear, sadness . . . all at the same time," Todd said as his throat constricted. "It's too much to deal with all at once."

Diana saw his hand trembling and she twisted around in her seat so she could hug him. Todd stifled a sob and gave into her comforting warmth. This simple but immensely powerful gesture calmed him enough to realize he would be all right until he got back to the support group, to share his news of the meeting with Boots. And yes, he wanted to discuss it with Claire too.

Todd felt better. This weekend may have wiped him out in many respects, but it also confirmed the way he felt about Diana. How often lately did his life feel like a shaken snow globe with everything whirling around, totally out of control? Diana proved to be the anchor, the life ring, his safety net. Diana was calm, caring, and sensible. At the same time she exuded creativity, strength, and daring. She was not afraid to take a risk, lived her life with basic common sense, and believed things will eventually work out for the best. It was no wonder he was in love with her. The question was, when she had so much to offer, why was she unattached? Before he knew what he was doing, he blurted the question out loud.

"Why aren't you married?"

"So, you're interested in some light conversation I gather," Diana laughed.

"Sorry. That didn't come out right. But you know what I mean. You're wonderful, not to mention gorgeous. Why aren't you married to some fantastic guy and making beautiful babies?"

"Life isn't that simple Todd," she replied a bit more seriously.

"It is for some people," Todd insisted.

"Maybe. Not for me though. And not for you either."

"I guess you're right," he sighed.

"I'll tell you what, you go first. You brought it up," she said mischievously.

"Fair enough," Todd answered.

He told her about his first wife, Janette. They'd met ten years ago through mutual friends and initially, had a lot in common. Janette was a dietitian and quite health conscious. She loved to exercise. But as time went by, she became more and more fanatical about it. She belonged to not one, but two gyms, and sometimes worked out for hours at a time. She had a sensational figure, and took great pride in the way she looked. Todd was very proud of his wife, even though he couldn't help but think the preoccupation with her appearance was a bit shallow. He didn't say anything about it though. Their lives were very full.

Paris and Soll

Todd was busy building his business while Janette lectured and gave classes at a local college, and of course, went to the gym. They had a busy social calendar, and Janette often commented how wonderful their life was. Todd had to agree.

But something was missing. Children. After celebrating their third wedding anniversary, Todd told his bride he wanted to start a family. His business was doing well, they were happy, life was good. Immediately, Janette became angry and defensive. Sure, it was easy for him to say she should get pregnant, he wasn't the one who had to carry the baby. He wasn't the one who had to gain weight, get hideous stretch marks, and wear horrible maternity clothes. Todd was astounded at her reaction. During their courtship she'd clearly led him to believe she wanted a family as much as he did. Now she seemed hostile about it, and she wasn't finished surprising him yet either.

They fought about it for weeks. Janette said she wasn't about to ruin her figure in order to have a child. She kept saying if she were to get pregnant and fat, Todd would no longer be attracted to her. She said he'd think of her as ugly and end up having an affair with some young hard-body. Todd thought her insane for thinking so, and did everything he could to reassure her. He told her how beautiful she would be carrying a child, how his love would only grow for her, not diminish. Nothing he said made a difference. Janette was convinced having a baby would mean losing her husband, and her self-respect.

They grew apart. They were miserable. Todd even suggested counseling, Janette refused by saying they could work it out on their own. They stayed miserable, but stayed together. Then one night, Janette told Todd she'd come up with a solution. She'd been talking with a friend from the gym who'd given her an idea. They could adopt.

Todd couldn't believe what he was hearing. *Adopt a child so Janette could stay a size four? This was the solution?* He looked at his wife, hardly believing she was human. He walked out of the room, packed a bag, and left. They were divorced a year later.

"Wow," Diana exhaled. "To treat adoption so casually, especially in front of you."

"She didn't know I was adopted," Todd said quietly.

"What?"

"I never told her I was adopted," Todd admitted.

"Why?" Diana looked aghast.

"We didn't talk about it in my family, that's all. And when I met Janette, it just didn't come up. I wasn't trying to hide anything, really. I just never talked about it, with anyone. Not until just recently anyway. Now it's different. I was always afraid to talk about it before. Like something bad would happen if I did. I guess it was the association with believing that my parents died in a car crash. And that somehow if I talked about being adopted, then I would die too. To put it simply, I equated dying with adoption. Irrational, I know, but I've felt that way my entire life. Now I know the truth. I wasn't put up for adoption because my parents died, and that's changed everything for me. I know it's okay for me to talk about it, good for me even. All those years I kept it hidden out of fear, not out of shame. That might be hard for you to understand. You're so open about it. From what you've told me, and from what you've said in the group, your parents were honest and up front with you. Some families handle it differently, that's all."

"I'm sorry. I didn't mean to sound judgmental," Diana squeezed his hand and they both became silent for a moment.

"Okay. Now it's your turn," Todd reminded her.

Diana rolled her eyes at him. "Do I have to?"

"Fair's fair."

She sighed. Todd was right. It was her turn to come clean. She told him how her failed relationships were also born of fear. Diana explained she had a history of sabotaging relationships. She didn't realize what she was doing at the time, but each time she got close to a man, she became very controlling. So controlling in fact, she could drive a boyfriend away in a matter of weeks, sometimes in just days. After the breakup, Diana would justify and rationalize how she knew all along it would never work out, and here was the proof. She told her family and friends, she'd just hadn't met the right guy yet. It became a predictable pattern which was obvious to everyone else but Diana. She'd met a great guy, they'd get close, he'd push for a commitment, she'd become a shrew, he'd say forget it. It went on for years, and Diana had absolutely no clue. The last serious relationship she had lasted almost two years. It ended the same way as all the others. Not long after the breakup, when Diana was moping about, a close friend offered to come by and keep her company. Her friend showed up lugging a bottle of tequila. After four shots on an empty stomach, she let Diana have it. She told her the truth.

At first Diana was angry, she denied having any kind of fear of commitment. *Impossible. Outrageous.* She wasn't responsible for the breakups. The man always broke up with her, not the other way around. She'd just been unlucky in love. *It wasn't her behavior, but theirs.* In a drunken fury, she asked her friend to leave, and slammed the door after her.

Paris and Soll

The next day she calmed down, called her friend, apologized, and took a good long look at herself. She had to wonder if there was some validity to the scathing observation after all. She decided to try and figure it out for herself. Diana picked up some books from the library. One of them was about the adoption triad, and she learned it was common for some adoptees to feel a genuine fear of intimacy. Apparently, it stemmed from the fear of abandonment. The basic premise was, if a mother abandoned her own child, why wouldn't everyone else abandon her as well? The closer or more intimate the relationship, the greater the risk to the adoptee should the relationship end. The chapter went on to explain how subconsciously, an adoptee often cannot tolerate this risk at all, and will do anything to stop or avoid intimacy in the first place. For Diana, sabotaging each and every romantic relationship gave her control over the ending of it.

The more she read, the more she understood. It was all starting to make sense to her. Once she joined the support group and raised the question to the others, she was amazed at the response she got. Many of them had difficulty sustaining relationships. It was a common thread among almost all the members of the group. Carol, the group leader, was on her third marriage. She said to Diana, so far it seemed to be the charm.

"So, you're the first one," Diana finished.

"The first one what?"

"The first relationship I've had since I figured this all out," she replied shyly.

"Really? I like being first," Todd said.

"Just let me know if I start getting too bossy," Diana grinned.

"I like being bossed around," Todd smiled back.

A slight commotion interrupted them. A passenger in the row ahead of theirs was loudly snapping his fingers trying to get the attention of one of the flight attendants. The man's wife hissed under her breath at him to stop. He paid absolutely no attention to her and continued to snap away. Todd could see a flight attendant near the galley who noticed the obnoxious passenger. She opened a drawer, pulled something out, and then quickly approached the man. Todd felt sorry for the poor woman having to put up with such rude behavior. She probably encountered it all the time, but why did people have to be such asses?

"Sir. If you put this between your fingers, they'll stop making that funny sound," said the flight attendant as she handed the passenger a pat of butter and then walked away. The man's wife laughed hysterically while some of the other nearby passengers applauded his humiliation.

Evil Exchange

Diana whispered to Todd. "Isn't that the same crew member we flew down with?"

"Oh, yeah, you mean the 'bad chicken' one?"

"Exactly. If she ever gets tired of flying, she could have a career doing stand-up comedy," Diana remarked. At that point, they both dissolved into uncontrollable laughter. It had been one hell of a weekend.

Chapter Forty-Three

Nardo crossed over the border and into Tijuana in the late afternoon. He'd spent the last few days in San Diego doing a bit of sightseeing after clearing it with The Boss. It was Nardo's first time in California, and he wanted to check it out. He was amazed at the casual attitude of those on foot, and the sheer madness of those on the road. Driving on the freeways wasn't nearly as confusing as he'd been told, but staying out of the way of a demented driver took far more skill than anticipated.

Once in Mexico, he could breathe a sigh of relief. Traffic was jammed which meant driving at a much slower pace. Now it was back to business. He was here to look into the possibility of this area as a viable location to acquire new merchandise. But already he could see that Tijuana wasn't going to work. The two most obvious reasons being it was too busy and too well policed. There were young people everywhere. Apparently, Tijuana was big with the college crowd, even though school was still on summer break. The young and stupid lined up everywhere for shots of tequila and frosty cold mugs of beer. He wanted nothing more than to be away from the immature idiots. The girls weren't bad to look at though.

Nardo's destination was the Mercado Hildago which wasn't frequented as much by the touristas. His assignment was to see for himself where many of the local's shopped, and to gather information for Sheila whether this place had any potential. As he entered the building, the scent of spices filled his nose and the color from hundreds of hanging pinatas assaulted his eyes. The aisles were crowded with shoppers who couldn't help but stare at the large man. Nardo felt too conspicuous and exposed, and quickly left. It was obvious he needed to stay in an area popular with other Americans so that he would not seem so out of place. He roamed the streets wanting to stretch his massive limbs after being confined in the rental car. Even though he knew his recommendation would be to cross this place off of the list of possible targets, he still had to give it a thorough examination to be absolutely sure.

Eventually, he wound up back where he left the car, and then drove to a nearby hotel. After checking in with his phony passport, he allowed a bellman to carry his small overnight bag up to his room. Nardo wanted to ask the young man a question out of earshot of the other hotel employees. Once inside the room, Nardo handed the man a generous tip and discreetly asked where he might find the nearest topless dance club. The bellman grinned and said he knew of a muy bueno establishment with mucho lindo dancers. He wrote down the name and address for Nardo and told him it was within walking distance.

He enjoyed a meal in his room before setting out for the evening's entertainment. Just about anywhere he traveled, Nardo could find a strip joint. He counted on it as a matter of fact. His work was often boring, occasionally dangerous, and undeniably lucrative. A man of Nardo's size and strength, not to mention the brutal features and intimidating presence, made for a combination which both repelled and frightened women off. The only way to be sure to get the physical attention he desired was to pay for it. Sometimes he liked to just watch them perform, but when he did want something more, he knew he could find that too. He always had enough money to buy whatever he wanted.

It was hot inside the club, but ceiling fans kept the air moving. He sat down at the bar and watched as a young senorita finished up her routine wearing only a tiny G-string and a pair of red shiny patent leather boots. She looked tired and bored. He paid her no further attention.

Two minutes later, Nardo found himself flanked by two women in halter tops and short shorts. He knew the drill, buy a drink for himself, and cokes for them. Working girls were not allowed to drink alcohol on the job, they were to keep the customers happy and entertained. It was no different in Tijuana than it was in Trenton, or anywhere else for that matter.

One of the women pulled out a cigarette from her purse and waited. Nardo found a book of matches on the bar and lit her up. Though he didn't smoke himself, he liked watching what a woman could do with her lips as she puffed away. It always gave him ideas. The woman on his right reminded him of a dancer he met not too long ago. He tried to remember where it was, but for the time being, the memory escaped him.

After a few more rounds, the girls started to get on his nerves and he shooed them away. Tonight he just wanted to sit and watch and be left alone. He picked up the book of matches again and suddenly remembered. It was in Alabama. A place called the Strip Search. He liked the name, and he liked one of the dancers there, very much. Now that he thought about it, he wondered how he could've forgotten. He was stuck in that godforsaken hick town for more than a week while waiting for the scarecrow mommy to pop the kid. He had little else to do except for hang out at the club and try to amuse himself. On the second night, he met Misty. It was kind of a dumb name, but she was gorgeous, so who cared? And could she dance. Man, oh man. Nardo had visited a lot of clubs, seen a lot of girls, but Misty was by far the best. He showered her with bills, and she joined him after her set. They got to be quite chummy.

Misty was a chain smoker, so Nardo tried to keep his pockets full of matchbooks from the club. Having Nardo light her cigarette was as close as Misty was ever going to get to being a lady, and performing the task was as close as Nardo was ever going to get to being a gentleman, but they both enjoyed playing the game. Misty thanked him each time as if it were the first, and he had to admit he liked it since it was the only time he heard those words from a beautiful woman. About the only time she didn't smoke was when she was on stage, or on top of Nardo. It turned out Misty was not only an excellent dancer, but was also quite enthusiastic and adventuresome in the sack. She loved to steal his baseball cap and wear it backwards while she rode him to exhaustion. Nardo paid her for her services of course, but toward the end of his time there in town, she became almost reluctant to take his money. He insisted, and told her she needed it as the price for a pack of smokes was going up nearly every day. She laughed at that. For whatever reason, she'd taken quite a liking to the big Hungarian and asked him to come back and see her again. He said he couldn't make any promises, but next time he was passing through, he'd be sure to look her up.

The blaring music and drunken yells from other customers sliced through his reverie. He finished his drink, laid down a tip for the bartender and decided to call it a night. After thinking about Misty, he really wasn't interested watching anyone else. Once he got back to New York, he just might have to ask The Boss when he could schedule another job in Alabama. *Yee-haw.*

Chapter Forty-Four

Paul Pearson was running late. He impatiently pulled at his shirt cuffs and smoothed the front of his jacket as his driver pulled up to the curb of the Gallerie. Paul issued some quick instructions as to when the driver should return, and then got out of the town car. He adjusted his tie, and entered the elegant building.

The Gallerie was home to a private club where members (mostly of the male variety) could come and relax, discuss business, have a drink, or play bridge. Pearson was on his way to the game room, where he would be engaging in his fondest activity. Normally, he was part of a friendly, but extremely competitive group that played on a weekly basis. But today was the start of a tournament, and he was very much looking forward to the contest.

Some men enjoyed golf or racquetball. Others preferred billiards, or a spirited game of chess. Paul Pearson was raised playing bridge. His parents played socially at monthly intervals. They were part of a group who had all attended college together, and each of the six couples hosted dinner and a bridge game twice a year in their homes. Those evenings always included their children. A baby sitter was hired to entertain the children, but Paul often snuck away and sought out his mother. She would let him sit in her lap if he promised to be quiet while she played. From a very early age, he was intrigued by the game, and followed his mother and father's every move and learned their strategy. His parents were excellent players, and unlike many of their friends, never argued with one another before, during, or after a game. As he grew older, his passion for the game remained strong. Paul sought out bridge players in college, and set up his own tournaments whenever he had the chance. His wife also enjoyed playing, and was a most competent partner. But Paul felt most comfortable in the company of men, and preferred playing at the club whenever he got the chance.

Of course bridge was not the only reason for his membership to the club. Paul did business with many of the club's members. The men were a tight-knit group and exchanged information, favors, and services. Spending the afternoon at the club today would serve two purposes. One, if he and his partner did win, they would advance toward the semifinal of this year's summer tournament, and two, it gave him the perfect opportunity to talk with his partner who was supposed to have information regarding Sheila Stiles and the adoption service she provided.

Paul's partner Lionel Jackson was a special agent-in-charge at the FBI field office in New York, and next in line to become the assistant director-in-charge of the east coast. Lionel was in charge of the CAC, crimes against children task force, and was highly respected. He'd spent many years at NCMEC (National Center for Missing and Exploited Children) in Alexandria, Virginia before transferring to New York some years ago. He and Paul met when Lionel had filled in at the last minute for Paul's regular bridge partner who'd been called away on business. The men had very little in common other than a love for bridge and well made clothes, but they played well together and became good friends.

Lionel was at the bar, sipping soda water while waiting for Paul. They had arranged to meet twenty minutes prior to their game to discuss the details of what Lionel had been able to find out.

"Well?" Paul clapped his hand on Jackson's back. "Find out anything good for me?"

"Hey, Paul. How are you? How's Andrea doing these days?"

"Good. Happy. Enough pleasantries, Lionel. What did you find out?" Paul asked impatiently.

"Not much really. Stiles appears clean. And it doesn't hurt that she has a prominent U.S. District Court judge as a personal reference," Jackson responded in his naturally clipped tone.

"Judge Price. Andrea's father knows him." Paul waved the bartender away and sat down.

"There's been some rumors over the years that he's bent, but never any concrete evidence he's actually taken any bribes. That's typical. Judges get accused of it all the time, it's like no one believes *any* of them are honorable," Jackson chuckled.

Evil Exchange

"But you think he's straight," Paul said.

"No real proof to the contrary." Jackson shrugged.

"What about the home, the facility, whatever you call it," Paul asked.

"Sheila Stiles is deeded as sole owner of a home in Congers. Apparently she inherited from her parents."

"But she doesn't live there?"

"Nope. She lives in an apartment in the city. Maybe she uses the home for the moms who adopt the kids out."

"But you don't know," Pearson frowned.

"No. I don't know. You just asked me to check out Stiles, so that's what I did. Are you suggesting surveillance of the property? For what reason? You said Andrea's father did a preliminary background check. He found nothing. A district judge vouches for the woman, I couldn't find any skeletons, what more do you want?" Jackson queried.

"I don't know. She checks out on the surface. But there's just something that nags at me, I can't explain it. I guess I should leave it alone, I mean, we got the kid already. I've never seen Andrea so happy. You'd think she gave birth to the child the way she treats her," Paul sighed.

"Have you made an official announcement yet?"

"People Magazine is coming next week to take a few photos," Paul beamed.

"Oh, really?" Jackson raised his eyebrows in admiration.

"Yes. We can thank Daddy Dearest once again," Paul laughed.

"Time to go play," Lionel checked his watch and rose from his chair.

"I'm ready. Looking forward to it," Paul tugged again at his cuffs. "Just do me a favor, would you? Keep an unofficial eye on Stiles for me, I may ask you to dig a bit deeper."

"And what am I to expect in return?"

"That you'll not only be in the semifinal, but win the whole damn tournament with me. I know how much you want to beat Lumsdaine and Treadway," Paul answered confidently.

"You got that right. Okay. You're on."

Paul immediately erased Sheila Stiles from his mind and shifted into his bridge playing mode. The competition was about to be destroyed.

Chapter Forty-Five

Frank hit it on the second try. He matched the license plate number from the video to a major rental car company, which served the Huntsville International Airport. He spoke with a supervisor and made arrangements to meet her at the service department where the car was waiting to be repaired. Fortune had shined on him once more. It was a fluke the car was out of commission rather than back on the road. Actually, Frank's luck had been pretty darn good since he arrived in Alabama. Too bad he wasn't a gambling man.

He arrived at the appointed time the next morning. The supervisor, Wanda Arquette, explained why the rental car was being serviced. She told Frank when the customer had returned the car, he mentioned the flat tire, and how he had to replace it with the spare. So, the car was immediately transferred to the service department to await a new tire. Once the mechanic removed the spare, he noticed one of the struts was leaking, and upon further investigation, concluded the strut was completely cracked. It was unusual since the car was barely a year old, but it still needed to be done. The strut had to be replaced before the car could be put back onto the lot. The part was ordered, but wouldn't arrive for one to two weeks. Apparently, this was a widespread problem with this particular make and model, and the manufacturer was scrambling to send struts out all over the country to replace the defective ones.

During his brief conference with Ms. Arquette, she provided a printout of the car rental agreement from the mystery man. Frank knew the information would turn out to be false, but he'd run it through the system anyway. If this guy was into kidnap and murder, he'd be smart enough to cover his tracks and have fake ID, no question there. Still, Frank had to wonder, did the hulk (so aptly named by the bleary-eyed but observant Nathan Hicks) get careless and leave anything behind? He was anxious to find out.

Evil Exchange

The mid-size car was parked in a back corner of the service department. Ms. Arquette gave Frank a single key, which dangled from a plastic key chain. She told him to take all the time he wanted going over the car, and to let her know when he was done. She would be in her office, and he could return the car key there.

A forensics team was on its way. The car would be dusted for prints, vacuumed, and thoroughly examined for any trace of evidence that might have been left behind. Frank pulled a pair of plastic gloves from his pants pocket. He slipped them on and got started. At first glance, there wasn't much. A paper map of the airport and surrounding areas lay folded on the passenger seat. A copy of the rental agreement occupied the glove box. Three empty Styrofoam coffee containers from a fast food restaurant littered the floor of the back seat. The trunk was empty except for the tire jack, an empty plastic bag, and a wire coat hanger. He was very careful to touch as little as possible. Time for round two.

Starting at the front again, Frank opened the driver's side door. He got down on his knees and looked under the seat. He did find a penny and a straw wrapper, but nothing else. Then he felt in between the driver's seat and the console, to see if anything might have slipped out of sight. Nada. Before moving on, he flipped the driver's seat forward and a red matchbook caught his eye. It must have fallen from someone's pocket and gotten wedged under the seat back. Frank carefully picked it up by the edges in case there might be any prints on it.

On the front cover were two words printed in bold, black type. **STRIP SEARCH.** Inside there was an address and phone number printed underneath a cartoon drawing of a topless woman with enormous breasts. Pretty easy to figure out what the place had to offer. Frank noticed quite a few of the matches were missing from the book. Obviously, someone smoked. But he was pretty sure it wasn't the guy who'd rented the car. There weren't any butts in the ashtray, and no stale cigarette smell either. Knowing he wouldn't forget the name of the club, Frank made a mental note of the address and put the matchbook on the dashboard for the forensic guys to examine. Before he could continue, his cell phone vibrated in his pocket.

"Barron," he answered.

"Hey Red, how's it goin'?"

"Omar? What's up?"

"I found a match on that nursing pin for you."

"Shoot," Frank said. The hits just kept on coming.

Paris and Soll

"Mount Saint Mary's. In New York." Omar believed in brevity.

"You sure?"

"Sure, Red. The drawing matches the pin from that school. Don't know how much help that is, but there ya go."

"Thanks."

"Welcome."

Frank ended the call. Good old Omar. Thank God for the bureau's computer geeks. So far today, things were looking good. He continued to search the car, but nothing else turned up unless you counted lint. When the forensic guys arrived, Frank let them take over.

Once back in Wanda Arquette's office, he stripped off the gloves and tossed them in the trash. He politely asked if she had a street map for Huntsville and outlying towns handy. She did. Wanda was most efficient, and Frank admired that. He looked at the street directory and found what he was looking for. He asked Ms. Arquette for the most direct route, and she frowned when she saw where he pointed. She informed him it was a bad part of town. Frank said he could take care of himself, and that she need not worry. She looked him up and down, clearly believing he couldn't harm a mouse, much less take on a street punk, but didn't offer any further advice. She simply wrote out directions and handed them over. Frank thanked her and said he'd be in touch about the car. Depending on what the techs found, it might have to be impounded. Wanda Arquette just sighed, as if dealing with the FBI was a part of her every day routine.

Frank checked his watch. It might be a bit early for the strip club. Then again, some of them were open round the clock, but he didn't think that would be the case here. Huntsville was not L.A. He'd passed a mall on his way out to the airport, and figured he might stop there for a bit. He wanted to find something to take home to Suzy. He liked picking up small gifts for her, and she always delighted in receiving them. Perhaps he could find her a bracelet or maybe even a new watch. He had to admit it would also serve to assuage his guilt. Though he wouldn't out and out lie to her, some times he did omit the truth. It was for her benefit after all. And his of course. Suzy was the sweetest woman in the world, unless she got jealous. She had a green streak that ran straight down her back and into the next county. So Frank was always careful not to look at other women while in Suzy's presence. Not that he looked at other women anyway. Frank only had eyes for his wife. But convince Suzy of that? He'd tried for years, but she never quite believed him. She believed it was a man's nature to roam. So, for that reason, there was no way in hell he was going to tell his wife he had to spend time in a strip club while working a case. She'd kill him for sure.

Chapter Forty-Six

Boots Beaumont leaned back in his chair with his feet up on the tiny computer desk. The *Lost & Found* was a fair size boat, but since space was at a premium, all the essentials were on a smaller scale than in a conventional home. Of course there were things he did without, but a desk was not one of them. His desk was just large enough to accommodate his laptop. There were two small drawers meant for writing utensils, but ended up full of odds and ends instead. He did have the one shelf for his books and reference materials. It was compact, but it was all he needed.

Boots gazed out the window on the starboard side. He didn't see the sparkling Caribbean water, or the brilliant orange sun, or the spectacular leap of a manta ray out and back into the sea. Boots was too lost in thought to see anything. He was trying to figure out the next step in his search for Todd's natural family

He was intimately familiar with the Internet having used it so much in his former line of work. And these days there were a host of sites for finding people. Yet so far, he wasn't having any luck. Kelto, Todd's mother's name on the original birth certificate, was simply not showing up anywhere. He did find a web site replete with an extensive photo album of a Finnish dog named Kelto, and he did discover that Kelto was the name of a video game character, all quasi-interesting but utterly useless information. It truly amazed him how pictures of someone's pet could fill up an entire web site. Some people had way too much time on their hands.

Whenever Boots hit a closed door, it put him in a foul mood. All his life he tended toward being proactive, not reactive. He didn't like barriers, nor was he too fond of authority either. He detested lies and deceit, which unfortunately Todd's past was full of. Although Beaumont spent years doing investigative work, he never got used to the subterfuge he'd dealt with on a regular basis. It seemed almost everyone had a secret or a skeleton from their past they wanted to keep hidden. It might be human nature to hide the darker side, but it pissed him off royally. So, it was not surprising when Boots felt this way, he preferred to be alone. At the moment he was glad Julie was off on some mysterious errand. She hadn't said so, but his best guess was it had to do with a member of her family. With that big a group, there was something always going on.

He tried to keep his feelings in check most of the time, of course Julie often made it impossible. Presently, Boots found himself rooting around the basement of his mind. His anger was just crawling around down there, in that darkest of places, looking for a way out. It didn't help to remind himself this was one of the reasons why he quit his life as a PI in the first place. *Well, that and the bullet in my head.* He lived with the anger and frustration his job caused him for years. When he moved to Eleuthera, he really did think he'd left it all behind. It was why he was so reluctant to agree to help Todd in the first place. He knew he'd end up right back here. Right back in the damn basement.

Not only was he angry at initially coming up empty with the name, but he was also angry at Todd's situation. Being sold at birth was bad enough, but then to have what seemed to be valueless information on his birth certificate was absolutely infuriating. His anger was now beginning to feel unrestrained, and it did nothing but muddle his thinking. So Boots decided to use an old trick he'd learned years ago. He talked to his anger. In his mind of course, only a crazy person would do it out loud. He ordered it to help him find a solution, and suddenly, he felt it escape his head in the shape of a dark cloud, then make its way outside to the clear water where it dissolved. He felt a sense of calm wash over his body. He now felt ready to mentally review a few facts.

He'd been in touch with a friend of his who had a contact in the New York City Health Department. The contact told him through an email message there was no record of Todd's birth under the name of Kelto. He went on to add there was virtually no one in the country with that particular name, so it was basically a dead end. Boots was however, able to find some old newspaper articles in an on-line archive about Madeline Monroe. Apparently there were rumors she changed original names around in some fashion to create the false names, which appeared on the altered documents, but it was never proven. He read that once when the police had come to arrest her for baby selling, she threw her client book to her father who then jumped out a window and escaped. Wanting to give him enough time to get away, Maddie jumped on the back of one of the policemen who tried to handcuff her, biting and scratching him before she was finally subdued. The authorities believed the book could have solved the mystery of where the babies came from and what their real names

Evil Exchange

were, but it never was found. Her father disappeared along with the evidence. Eventually, Maddie was found guilty of selling human flesh, but never went to jail. What a piece of work the woman was. Boots realized the anger had swiftly returned. *Black market baby selling. What crap!* The very idea was abhorrent to Beaumont, and he vowed right then and there he would not quit until he found Todd's family. No matter how many roadblocks he faced.

This time the anger invigorated and renewed him. He took stock. *What did he really know so far? Zip.* He needed to come at it from another angle, think of it in another way, think outside the box. He decided he was going to involve Julie. Normally, his pride would keep him from asking for help, but not this time. After all, Julie was the one who started this all in the first place. Just then, the boat stirred slightly signaling Julie's return. He felt his own stirring as he looked up at those long, luscious legs coming down the steps. Her timing was impeccable.

Chapter Forty-Seven

For the first few days after they got back from Eleuthera, both Todd and Diana were busy at work catching up. Both agreed to some time apart, although they spoke on the phone at least twice a day. Two days separation was about all they could take however, so they made plans to get together at Diana's apartment after work. A warm hug, a prolonged kiss, and things were off to a great start. Diana was dying to discuss her excitement about the forthcoming meeting with Theresa. It would be their first face to face, and Diana was a wreck over it. A nervous, excited, elated, wreck. Todd had been working since seven a.m. that morning and acted as if his day were just beginning. He was wound up as tight as barbed wire. They were happy to be together and both started talking at once.

"I have a million questions . . ."

"I heard the best story today . . ."

They both stopped talking and started laughing. "You go first," Todd offered. "No, you. I insist," Diana barely got the words out of her mouth before Todd started in.

"Well, my electrician and I were doing an inspection today. We were in the television tower on top of the Empire State Building, and Chuck says he has to leave a little early to go and get his tarantula shots. At first, I thought he said he was going to shoot a tarantula, and that didn't make sense, so I asked him what the hell he was talking about. He tells me his thirteen-year-old daughter has pet tarantulas, and he needs to get his regular anti-venom shot. You know, just to be on the safe side. I've never heard of anti-venom shots before and I'm in shock. So I ask him, 'Aren't the tarantulas in a cage?' Chuck says, no. 'They just wander around the house.' Are you freakin' kidding me? I'm totally flabbergasted. I don't know about you Diana, but teeny tiny spiders petrify me, let alone great big, humongous, hairy ones.

"So then I had to ask him how he could stand having them loose. He just laughs and says one of them is really friendly. It even rides around on his shoulder. But the other one? The other one is usually grumpy and likes to bite, and Chuck has trouble telling them apart, hence the shots. He goes on to tell me they love to hide under the blankets of his bed, so he has to be really careful when he gets ready to go to sleep. Can you imagine? I didn't know what to say to him." Todd paused long enough to take a breath.

"That's quite a story," Diana exclaimed. Truth be told, she was more surprised by Todd's behavior than she was by the story. He'd been pacing and gesturing from the moment he stepped foot in the apartment. *What was going on with him?*

"Tell me about it! He and his wife are really nice people, but if we ever get invited to dinner? I'm coming down with a permanent case of the flu," Todd shuddered for emphasis.

"My turn?" Diana asked sweetly.

"What?"

"May I speak now?"

"Uh, yeah. Sure," Todd said over his shoulder as he walked into the kitchen. Diana simply stared after him. She could hear the fridge open and close. Todd walked back in the room with a soda in his hand. "Hey, did I ever tell you about that time Chuck and I were working a job . . ."

"Stop. Sit," Diana commanded and pointed to a chair. Todd looked at her curiously, but obeyed.

"What is the matter with you?" Diana did not understand Todd's behavior at all. It was as if he were an automaton set on high speed. *Or an addict on speed.*

"Nothing. Sorry." Todd apologized automatically without any feeling. He may have been sitting, but his knee was jiggling uncontrollably.

Diana soldiered on, trying to ignore the movement. "I have so many questions to ask Theresa. Do you think it would be weird if I wrote them down and took them with me? It's just that I'm so nervous to meet her this weekend, I'm afraid I'll forget everything. But I don't want to be rude. What do you think? Todd?"

No response. Diana stepped over to Todd, put her hand on his knee to stop the bouncing. A second later, the other knee started. Diana put her other hand on that knee, leaned over him, and finally commanded his attention.

"What in the world is wrong with you?"

"Nothing!"

"Bullshit!" Diana removed her hands and turned away. Todd was up in a flash. "Look, I'm sorry. I'm just kind of hyper today, that's all. C'mon sweetie, please ."

"*Kind of* hyper? Jesus Christ, Todd. You act like you just downed five energy drinks, or did a couple of lines of coke. You walked in here without so much as a 'hi, how are you?' you tell me some bizarre story about tarantulas while you're pacing around like some guy high on PCP, you don't listen to one word I have to say, and then you say nothing is wrong?" Diana threw her hands up in exasperation.

"Look, Diana. I've just got a lot on my mind right now."

"Oh. And I don't?"

"But you're better at this than I am," Todd shrugged.

"No, I'm not. I just try and deal with it instead of letting it make me into a lunatic. You seem to be having trouble with that part," Diana accused.

"It's just that I've kept all these feelings hidden away for so long. I've never even talked about it before. My *ex-wife* didn't even know I was adopted. Now, all I do is talk about it, or hear about it, or think about it. I'm seeing a shrink about it, going to a support group about it. Now I've hired a guy to try and find out about it. It's just all making me crazy," Todd admitted in frustration.

"And now you're dating someone who constantly reminds you of it," Diana sighed. "Maybe we should have taken a longer break from each other." She wrapped her arms around herself as if she were cold.

"No. It's not that. I'm just . . ."

"What?"

"Scared. I'm scared to death. Okay?"

"You mean you're scared of what Boots will find?"

"Actually, I'm scared that he won't find anything," Todd sighed.

Chapter Forty-Eight

The Mule pulled out of the motel parking lot just slightly past dawn. She was working solo this trip which was fine with her. Normally, she and Nardo worked as a team, but he was off scoping out another potential location. Leslie had been in Texas for two days. This morning she would make her acquisition, and by this afternoon she'd be on a plane with the child heading for home. She looked forward to completing her assignment. She was tired.

She reached over and turned on the heat as it was cold in the rental car, and her nurse's uniform did little to protect her from the chill. The calendar said it was summer, but the sky was filled with swollen, gray clouds. It had been raining for the last six hours with apparently no letup in sight, and Leslie had a fitful night of sleep because of it. The motel sported a tin roof, which only served to amplify the sound of raindrops hitting the metal as if there were bullets falling from the sky. She listened to the local news this morning while getting ready, but didn't pay much attention to the flash flood warning, which had just gone into effect. According to the cheery weatherman, seasonal thundershowers were typical in Corsicana this time of the year, but this unusually heavy downfall seemed to catch both the forecasters and the public off guard. The accumulated rainfall so far was almost eight inches. Leslie would be happy to get back to New York.

The targeted hospital was only a few miles away. This time the Boss had picked a large, public hospital that was deep in debt and would be shut down in a matter of months. The operating budget had been slashed so severely, the hospital was run by a bare bones crew of doctors, nurses, technicians, and administrators. Five out of the ten security guards had been let go. The security cameras worked intermittently, and in some parts of the hospital, not at all. The maternity ward was chaotic, disorganized, and enormously understaffed. The day before the Mule had done some preliminary scouting dressed as a civilian. She'd walked around for more than an hour without ever being challenged by a staff member. She might as well have been invisible. She knew when she came back dressed in her uniform, it would be simple to perform her task, just as she'd done so many times before. She'd be in and out in a flash. It was a perfect set-up.

Leslie drove slowly as visibility was poor. There were few cars on the road, perhaps people were staying indoors until the worst of the storm was over. She could see a small river of water running along the curb of the street she traveled. Not a big deal. She looked over to the passenger seat to check the infant carrier and blanket she'd be using. She preferred to transport an infant in a soft, front pack, rather than a clunky baby seat. Strapping on the pack left her hands free, and kept the tot warm and sleepy with her body heat and soothing heartbeat. Everything was ready to go. She figured if the rain didn't let up, she'd use the baby blanket to keep dry as she dashed in a side door of the hospital, and then use it to cover up the newborn when she exited the building. Then all she would have to do is return to the motel to change clothes, and quickly pack up her belongings. She never took any identification, not even her false ID on these hospital excursions just in case she was ever detained and questioned. Not that it had ever happened, but the Mule was never one to be careless.

She came to an intersection where the storm drains had backed up to form a small lake. There was a car in front of her driving slowly through the dirty brown water, but it didn't seem too deep. She kept on going and made it safely through. Checking her watch, Leslie was pleased to see it was only a few minutes past the hour. She'd be at the hospital in no time.

She continued around a corner, and drove straight into a river of water, and before she could begin to comprehend what was happening, she felt the car being dragged. Leslie was unaware of it, but Oak Creek ran parallel to the street she was taking to the hospital. Swollen from the deluge of the past six hours, the creek had quickly risen three feet over its banks and spilled over the road with a fury. The water moved at an increasingly alarming rate, and with it, so did the rental car.

Leslie started to panic. She had no control. It was pointless to try and steer, and her foot jammed down on the brake made no difference at all. Suddenly, the electrical system quit, and the windshield wipers froze in mid-swing. The rain pelted the car with renewed vigor. The roar of water sounded like a freight train.

A dark shape loomed ahead. The car hit a huge sycamore tree with a surprisingly gentle jolt, but the flood water rushed around the trapped car as if it were being sucked by a powerful vacuum. At least she had stopped. Leslie knew she had to get out. She managed to roll down the window and was relieved to see the water hadn't yet reached the door handle. Yet. But it did look as if it wouldn't take much longer before the water would spill over into the car from the open window, so she had to make a move. She quickly pulled herself out through the window and couldn't avoid falling in the water. She felt like she'd been hit with a taser gun. The water temperature was much colder than she expected and she involuntarily gasped from the shock of it. She held onto the car as best she could, knowing that if she let go, she'd surely be swept away. Her instinct told her the only chance was to climb on top of the car and wait for help. She could barely comprehend this bizarre turn of events, it was utterly crazy, but then she didn't have time to think about it too much.

The current was unbelievably strong. She felt things hitting her body, she thought it must be branches or rocks caught up in the flow. She was no weakling, and her grip was sure and steady. She was able to swing her legs up onto the front of the car, and from there, hoisted herself to safety. She only took a moment to catch her breath, and then climbed up on the roof. The rain continued to punish her body, but at least she was out of the roiling water.

She heard someone yelling. Though she could barely see, Leslie could make out a figure about a hundred yards away. It was a man who was waving his arms and shouting something. She figured he was probably telling her to stay put. Like she had any choice. She waved back at the man to let him know she was all right. She knew she'd be okay now. The man would get help for her. She just had to wait it out. She still couldn't believe what was happening. *What kind of freakish place was this anyway?*

The man continued to yell. *What was he saying?* Leslie couldn't understand him. "Go get help, you fucking idiot!" She yelled at him. Then the man started pointing. Yelling and pointing. Leslie wiped the rain from her eyes, but she still couldn't see. The man was running now, pointing at something. She tracked him as he tried to run closer toward her trapped car. She tried to make out the words.

"Watch . . ."

Watch what?

". . . out!"

Leslie turned her head just in time to see a truck bearing down on her. There was a man and woman inside the cab, staring at her in sheer terror. Carried by the current the truck slammed into the back of the rental car knocking her

Paris and Soll

from the car. As she entered the water, Leslie's head smashed into the side of the car. As she started to lose consciousness, she wondered if the Boss and the Stork would come to her funeral. Everything went black. Water filled her lungs and she died within minutes. The couple survived the terrible ordeal without a scratch, and were later rescued by the fire department. They told their rescuers they'd been on their way to the hospital to see their daughter who'd just given birth to their first grandchild. Fate had intervened.

Chapter Forty-Nine

Frank walked into the Strip Search and waited a moment for his eyes to adjust. The interior of the club was dark and reeked of cigarette and cigar smoke. There were a few patrons sitting at the bar. A young woman dressed in only a red, white, and blue g-string and white stilettos, danced on the stage with little enthusiasm. It was one o'clock in the afternoon. Frank asked the bartender if the owner was available. The man nodded and pointed to a hallway on the other side of the room. Frank noticed a basket of matchbooks, and stuck one in his pocket.

Frank walked down the hallway, past the rest rooms, and came to a closed door marked "office." He knocked, heard a muffled reply and opened the door. The room was filled with file cabinets and an old metal desk. Behind the desk sat an enormously fat man with greasy black hair.

"Wadda ya want?" The man didn't bother looking up. His eyes were glued to a porno magazine. Apparently he didn't get to see enough naked women at work.

"FBI." Frank pulled out his badge.

"Shit." The fat man rolled his eyes. "Look buddy, I run a legitimate business here."

"I'm not here because of your business. I'm looking for a guy." Frank gave a brief description, since all he really had to work with was an alcoholic's rambling and a grainy black and white video tape which basically captured a large man in shadow.

"How do you know he came here?" The man asked suspiciously.

Paris and Soll

"Found some matches like this in his rental car," Frank held up the red matchbook and waved it. "It would have been maybe a week or so ago."

Without another word, the man picked up the phone and dialed an extension. He spoke gruffly, and then hung up.

"You need to talk to Syd. He's the one who works the front. I'm the owner, he's the manager. So, he's the one who sees who comes and goes. I'm always back here paying the bills."

"And where would I find Syd?" Frank asked.

"Bartender called in sick, so Syd's filling in for him. I told him to cooperate with you."

"Thanks."

"Always a pleasure," the fat man replied and went back to his magazine.

Syd was wiping down the bar. He was a painfully thin man with pale, wispy hair, and a complete opposite of the owner. Frank couldn't help but think of Laurel and Hardy, only these guys weren't quite that funny. He took a seat and recited the information once again. Tall white male, powerfully built, clean shaven (as far as they could tell from the video and what Trooper Flint remembered), wearing a baseball cap. Syd listened carefully and nodded as if Frank were passing along classified secrets.

"Yeah, I remember a guy like that. He was here a coupla times, at least."

"Did you catch a name?" Frank's heart rate increased.

"Nope. Misty mighta though. She was his favorite. They got pretty chummy." Syd winked.

"Misty here?"

"Nope. Too early for her. She doesn't work til later tonight. She's good, Misty is. Lotta customers like her. *A lot.*" Syd nodded and winked this time.

Frank returned to the office to get Misty's address. The owner balked at the request until Frank gently suggested it was in his best interest if he wanted his business to remain open. Frank asked the owner to jot down his name as well, and this time, received full cooperation. There was something to be said for being a federal agent. On his way out the door, Agent Barron looked at the piece of paper with Misty's address, and figured he'd stop at a gas station for directions.

Misty (whose real name was Francis) Vaughn, answered the door in pink flannel pajamas. When Frank flashed his badge, she bellowed a one-word greeting that rhymes with "duck" and disappeared down the hallway. Frank couldn't help but feel welcomed. He stepped inside and admired the interior of her home just as he had the exterior. Misty lived in a neighborhood only five miles in distance from the Strip Search, but a world away in class. Her home looked freshly painted, the yard was immaculate, her compact car sat clean and shiny in the driveway. Inside, the decor was tastefully modest and absolutely neat as a pin. He found her in the kitchen making a pot of coffee.

"Go ahead," Misty growled.

"Pardon?"

"Search the house. But I'll tell you up front, I don't hook at home, and I sure as shit don't do drugs." She defiantly turned to face Frank, arms covering her large breasts. She tried to look tough, which can be difficult in pink flannel.

"I'm not here to bust you Ms. Vaughn," Frank assured her. He explained why he was there, and Misty lost the attitude almost immediately. Once the scowl was off her face, she looked about sixteen.

"Sorry. Guess I got off on the wrong foot. I'm not exactly a morning person since I . . . oh, Christ. You know what I do."

"You mean dance?" Frank shrugged his shoulders innocently.

"Dance, yeah. And I do a little business on the side. But I only hook when I want to, understand? It's not a requirement at that fine establishment I work at, so don't be busting Nero's chops, okay?"

"Okay." Frank waited for her to continue.

"So, the guy. I know who you mean," Misty admitted. "I kinda wish he'd stuck around."

"Why?"

"He was generous," she smiled. "Why are you looking for him anyway?"

"Do you read the papers?" Frank asked.

"Yes, I read the papers. I'm not a total ditz. Sheesh," she retorted and rolled her eyes.

"Okay. Then you read about the murder and kidnapping at Shady Meadows?"

"Yeah. Fuck, that was terrible."

"I need to talk with this guy. I think he knows something about it," Frank explained. Misty's eyes grew wide. No longer looking like a teenager, she directed

Frank outside to the patio area where she kept her cigarettes and ashtray. Misty explained that she never smoked inside the house. She went back in and returned with a carafe and two mugs.

They sat down over a cup of coffee and talked. Misty told Frank she only knew the man as Bob, which she never believed for a minute was his real name. They spent quite a bit of time together at the club, and also after hours. But not at Misty's home. She was adamant about keeping her private life private. Her neighbors thought she worked nights as a nurse. Well, the women did anyway, and the husbands would surely keep the secret if they'd seen her working a shift.

Misty told Frank she and Bob had gone to his hotel room at the Ranch View three nights in a row. It was always after she'd gotten off work, and they had some laughs, some drinks, some sex, and that was it. Misty reiterated that Bob was generous, but Frank didn't push her to explain whether she meant financially or sexually, he didn't really care. How Misty earned the money for her nice home in the suburbs concerned him not at all. He did grill her about the man's physical characteristics however. She told him what she could, which wasn't much. His hair was brown, thin on top. His eyes were brown. He did not have any visible scars or tattoos, Misty was certain of that. All she could do was verify the fact he was big, strong, and someone she would never want to cross. She said his eyes looked cold and flat. Like a snake. He was surprisingly gentle with her though. Vigorous and enthusiastic in bed, but not mean or aggressive in any way. She also confirmed the baseball cap, but other than that, his clothing was nondescript. She concentrated as hard as she could, but could not remember anything else.

"He never told you where he was from?"

"No."

"Did he tell you why he was here?"

"Just passing through."

"Did he say he would be back?"

"All he said was 'if' he did come back, he would come see me at the club." Misty poured more coffee and lit her fourth cigarette. "You really think he killed someone?"

Frank didn't comment. "If he gets in touch with you, will you let me know?" He fished a business card out of his pocket and handed it to her. Misty hesitated. A woman in her line of work probably didn't like dealing with any kind of law

Evil Exchange

enforcement, let alone the FBI, unless they were a paying customer. "I think he stole the baby," Frank said sadly. He hoped it would win her over, and it did.

"Bob is a fucking asshole," Misty snarled. "Gimme the card."

Frank stood up to leave, thanking Misty for her time. She walked him to the front door.

"Can I ask you something?" Frank turned to her.

"Why do I strip? Gee, no one's ever asked me *that* before," she replied sarcastically.

Frank laughed. "I can't help it. You're a nice young woman. You're smart, there's probably lots of other things you could do."

"Who are you anyway? My dad?" Misty grumbled and then laughed. "Why the hell do you think I do it? M-O-N-E-Y. How do you think I bought this house, anyway?" She laughed again and slammed the door.

Frank got into the car, and before he could buckle up, his cell phone vibrated. He hoped it wasn't Suzy. He didn't wish to tell his wife that although he'd stopped and bought her a beautiful silver necklace, he'd also just left a strip club to go to see a hooker. She might not understand. He looked at the number. He was saved. It was Omar.

"Something of interest."

"Shoot, Omar."

"An inquiry came through the NCIC. A SAC in New York is asking if anyone knows anything about a woman named Sheila Stiles."

"And why do we care about Ms. Stiles?" Frank asked as he started the car and turned on the air conditioning.

"She arranges private adoptions in New York."

"So..."

"The SAC is doing some background investigation. He wants to know where the babies come from."

"I see."

"I thought you might want to talk to him."

"Good thinking."

Frank jotted down Lionel Jackson's name and number. He thanked Omar, disconnected, and dialed.

Paris and Soll

"Jackson," a deep voice answered.

"Agent Barron here from the DC office," Frank introduced himself.

"Make it quick Barron. I'm due in a meeting," Jackson was just shy of being rude. *How typical.* Frank quickly explained he was in Alabama and described what he was working on. Babies were being stolen.

Jackson's voice warmed considerably. "I see. I think we need to talk. I'm planning a little surveillance trip tomorrow night. You might want to join me. When can you get to New York?"

Frank checked his watch. He had one more stop to make. He wanted to visit the Ranch View to see if Bob had checked in using the same alias as he did with the rental car company. The credit card the rental car company had on file was a stolen number and therefore a dead end. Frank figured the Ranch View would be the same, but he still had to check.

"I can be there tomorrow afternoon," Frank answered. Jackson told him to call back when he had a flight and time, and he would send a car. Frank thanked him and hung up. Omar had come through once again.

Chapter Fifty

Julie woke up with her heart thumping wildly and a film of sweat covering her brow. It was just before six, and the sun was rising over the calm Caribbean. The boat was perfectly quiet. Normally she was a late sleeper, but for some reason this morning she was amped up and knew she'd never get back to sleep. She quietly slipped out of bed so as not to wake Boots, and softly padded straight towards the shower. While she washed her hair, she tried to figure out why she had woken so abruptly.

Julie knew something important must have happened in her sleep, but at the moment, she hadn't a clue as to what it was. The trick was to let it surface naturally. If she tried to force it, she'd only get frustrated and never remember anything. As the cool water revived and refreshed her, Julie suddenly thought of George Tutt. George was a local Bahamian who not only played awesome piano, but was also a talented composer and lyricist. Julie had worked with him on a number of occasions, and they'd always gotten along well. She hadn't seen him for a few months as he was off in the states collaborating on an album, so it was kind of odd she'd be thinking of him just now.

She turned off the water and stepped out of the tiny stall, reaching for her towel. As she dried off, she was struck by a vivid image. She realized it was a dream that had startled her awake, and all at once, it came flooding back. In her dream she heard a beautiful female voice (her own?) singing the words of an enchanting song that George had written a few years ago.

I talk to the wind and

My words echo back

Paris and Soll

From a mountain I cannot see

Instead of the words I sent forth

They come back

Rearranged to me

That was when she woke up. *What the hell did it mean?* Julie knew she needed coffee before she could even begin to figure it out. She threw on shorts and a T-shirt, then quickly and efficiently prepared the coffee maker and turned it on. While she waited, she tidied up the already tidy galley just to keep herself busy.

As soon as the brewing finished, she grabbed a cup and went up on the afterdeck. Julie looked out over the water and spotted an early morning fishing boat making its way out to sea. A flock of seagulls trailed behind hoping to snag a few snacks. As she sipped from her steaming cup, the chug of the boat's engine began a beat in her brain. *Kel-to, Kel-to, Kel-to.* A huge grin broke across her face.

"Morning, glory. Is that for me?" Boots asked as he came up on deck.

"Good morning. Is what for you?" Julie set her cup down and slipped her arms around him.

"That beautiful smile. Maybe you were thinking about last night," he nuzzled her neck while he slipped his hand underneath her T-shirt. Her wet hair tickled his nose and she smelled of soap.

"I was thinking about last night, but not *that*," Julie laughed and pushed him away. "Remember how you asked me to help you? Well, I did. Last night I had a dream about an arrangement."

Boots looked puzzled.

"Todd's search? I had a dream about his name. The reason you haven't been able to find anything about his mother, Ruth Kelto, is because Kelto is not the right name. The letters are scrambled. It's an anagram. I'm sure of it, Boots. I am absolutely sure."

Julie left him open mouthed on deck. She went below and fired up his laptop. A few minutes later, she googled and quickly found Andy's Anagram Solver. It just so happened to include proper names. She entered Kelto, then sat back to see what this cyberspace genius Andy would come up with.

Chapter Fifty-One

As the plane began its descent, Frank looked out the window. He was anxious to reach his destination. He'd wrapped up as much as he could in Huntsville, spent the night at a business hotel near the airport, and was up at the crack of dawn to get to the airport in plenty of time for his 7:30 flight to LaGuardia. After his visit with Misty, he'd driven straight to the Ranch View motel and interviewed the manager. Sure enough, the manager remembered good old "Bob." Unfortunately, the same stolen credit card was used for the room just as it was for the rental car. Frank anticipated as much, so unless the forensic guys came up with something, he'd be at another dead end. Frank was sorely tempted to call and check on their progress, but reminded himself it was too soon, and he would probably just end up pissing them off. Most forensic teams were overworked and underpaid, therefore on average, a pretty surly group. The techs in Hunstville seemed to be no exception. Frank understood it was a tedious process, and that the testing could take quite some time. He knew they would call him when there was something to report. Until then, he had to wait.

As much as Frank wanted to get home to see his wife, he was revved up to meet with Jackson in New York. The surveillance intrigued him, and he wanted to find out the scoop on this Stiles character. He got to the airport much too early for his flight, and didn't know what to do with himself. For a while, he paced the nearly deserted terminal, but then forced himself to sit down to try and relax. He went over his notes again, but that didn't take up much time. He called Suzy, and listened to her plans for the day, told he loved her, and smiled when she blew kisses in his ear. He checked his watch for the tenth time, and impatiently tapped his foot. He had too much nervous energy and needed to keep himself busy doing something. He decided to check in with his office for messages while he waited. It was a good thing he did.

Paris and Soll

One of the rookies answered the phone and immediately informed Frank of an alert, which had just come in from the field office in Dallas. A Jane Doe in Corsicana, Texas had been killed in a flash flood. The woman had drowned, her body horribly bruised and battered as it was swept one hundred yards away from her car. Frank listened patiently (since he didn't have anything else to do), while he stared out at the tarmac through huge plate glass windows. His plane hadn't even arrived yet. The rookie seemed to delight in the gruesome details of Doe's death, and Frank was just about to cut him off when he heard three words that galvanized him. *Nurse's uniform*, and *pin*. He sat up straight in his plastic seat and shouted at the rookie. "Slow down and repeat everything you just said."

Frank furiously jotted down some notes. "Are you absolutely sure?" he asked. The rookie assured him there was no question. The nurse's pin was from Mount Saint Mary's in New York, and matched the drawing Tarren Vincent had given him. Frank hastily gave his thanks and ended the call. He jumped up from his seat and went to find the nearest ticket agent. He needed to get on a plane right away, however not to New York, not just yet. He needed to get to the Lone Star State first.

It was a minor miracle, but he was able to arrange it all. Flashing his credentials didn't hurt. He was put on a direct flight to Dallas. After landing and getting a car, Frank went straight to the coroner's office in Corsicana. There he met with the chief medical examiner who led him directly to the morgue where he got his first glimpse of Jane Doe. Her face was relatively untouched, which was surprising considering the violent cause of death. The stone-faced medical examiner told Frank that flash floods were more common than most people realized, and yet, still seemed like a freak of nature when they happened.

Frank studied the remains carefully. Doe still awaited an autopsy, as the coroner's office was presently shorthanded and their workload was seriously backed up. She was still dressed in her uniform, and the pin was still attached to her top. *It's a miracle it didn't get ripped off from the force of the water.* There was something else about the uniform itself that niggled at Frank's brain, but he just couldn't think of what it was. Hopefully, whatever it was, it would come to him later.

Frank finished up. Time was of the essence, as he still wanted to try and make it to New York if at all possible. Earlier, he'd called and alerted Lionel Jackson regarding the change in plan and the stopover in Texas. Jackson said he understood, but if it were at all possible to make it to LaGuardia by early evening, that would be best. Frank could tell by Jackson's tone the man was itching to get started on the surveillance. Frank knew exactly how he felt. Before he left the medical examiner, he requested a copy of the autopsy report, and photos of Jane Doe to be emailed to his office as soon as possible.

Frank's good luck seemed to be holding. On his way out of the building, he was intercepted by a patrol deputy assigned to Jane Doe's case. The young officer with a serious Southern drawl brought Frank up to speed. The car had been recovered after the flood waters receded. No identification was found in the car, but a baby blanket and infant carrier were recovered. They were working on tracking down the rental car and trying to put the pieces of the puzzle together, but it was taking far longer than normal. The officer said he could not understand why a woman dressed as a nurse, carried no purse or ID, was driving a rental car that contained only a couple of baby items and nothing else. It certainly didn't make any sense to him or to anyone on the force, but then, no one had the time to think about it much. The force was stretched thin at the moment because of the havoc wrecked by the flood waters, and discovering the identity of Jane Doe was most definitely not at the top of the list. They'd gotten as far as getting her stats on the computer and out over the Internet, but that was about it.

Frank asked if they'd been able to tell where Ms. Doe might have been headed. The officer said at first they figured the woman must have been on her way to the hospital and that perhaps she was a new hire there. However when his partner called the administrator over at Navarro Memorial, they did not have a staff member who matched her description, nor did they have any no-shows at work that day. Frank's face lit up as bright as a halogen bulb. He knew the answer.

"Baby-snatching," Frank explained. The officer slowly nodded in understanding and whistled in disbelief. It was at that moment when Frank remembered what it was about the uniform. The top was colorful, *and* the pattern was of animals. Zoo animals. Exactly what Tarren Vincent had described the nurse who stole her baby from the hospital was wearing. He knew precisely where to go next.

Frank arrived at the Bricklow shortly thereafter. He had asked the officer what the closest hotel was to the hospital, and without hesitation, he said the Bricklow Inn. Frank couldn't help but notice the hotel had a metal roof and aluminum siding. Not a brick to be had anywhere. He went in search of the manager. Ten minutes later, Frank was in Jane Doe's room going through her belongings.

Once he was on his way back to the airport, Frank used his cell to call Omar. He recited the name and address from the driver's license he'd found. He also rattled off the number of the credit card found in her wallet. In his normal clipped tone, Omar said he'd get right on it.

With his good luck still holding, Frank made it to the second leg of his journey. Just before he boarded, he called to let Jackson know he'd be arriving early evening and gave him the flight number. Once he settled into his seat, he couldn't help but wonder if "Bob" was in any way teamed up with the dead nurse in Texas, whose name according to the ID was surely false. The driver's license read "Laura Branigan." *Wasn't that the name of a singer?* Frank couldn't remember. Before he knew it, he fell into an exhausted sleep, which lasted the entire flight.

Disheveled, but refreshed, Frank deplaned and went to the baggage area as he'd been instructed. There he was met by an exceedingly well-dressed man who introduced himself as Lionel Jackson. Frank was surprised the man had come by himself rather than sending another agent, but Jackson quickly explained he wanted to get out of the city and on the road to Congers pronto. Traffic would be a problem.

Along the way they stopped at a fast food place. Frank used the restroom and tried to make himself look presentable, even if it did seem pointless. After all, they were just going out on surveillance, not having dinner with the mayor. Normally, Frank could care less what he looked like. But next to SAC Lionel Jackson, he looked like a poor relation come to visit. He half expected the fashion police to burst out of a bathroom stall at any minute and cuff him on the spot.

They grabbed some food and ate on the way. Jackson never even dropped a crumb. Frank wolfed his food down. It was the first time he'd eaten all day. He tried to be careful, but got mustard on his pants. This could get him into fashion prison for life he decided.

Jackson filled Frank in on what he knew about Sheila Stiles, which didn't take long. He just explained that a friend had asked him to do some checking on the attorney who arranged private adoptions for those who could afford her exorbitant fees. They were going to check out a residence in her name, which Jackson suspected may be living quarters for some of the mothers who relinquished their babies for the sake of a better life. Jackson said he wanted to get a better idea of how the entire operation worked to make sure this Stiles woman was legit.

Frank couldn't help but wonder if Jackson knew of his foster care background. Frank figured he probably did, a Special Agent in Charge who was next in line for Assistant Director didn't get where he was by not checking out who he was interfacing with. Frank had done his own fact-finding on Agent Jackson, with Omar's help of course. Yet, Frank didn't feel the need to bring up the foster care issue, so he stayed silent on the subject. He did however fill him in on Jane Doe, as well as "Bob," along with the murder and kidnapping in Alabama. The more they talked, the more surprised and pleased Frank was to discover Lionel Jackson was truly a nice guy. He didn't seem to have the standard cattle-prod-up-the-ass demeanor like so many other SACs he'd met before. He did seem kind of obsessed with bridge playing from what Frank could tell, but other than that and the GQ persona, he came across as a pretty regular guy.

It was well after dark when they reached their destination. The large wooden house was set back far from the road and surrounded by trees. Very few other homes occupied the street. Jackson drove by slowly. There were no lights on in the house, no car in the drive. The house appeared to be empty. But to be on the safe side, they turned around in the cul-de-sac at the end of the street and cruised by again. Jackson stopped and turned off the engine. He told Frank he wanted to wait and see if there might be any activity in the house before he traipsed around the property.

They sat in the darkness and waited for two hours. Absolutely nothing happened. Finally, Frank said he needed to get out of the car to stretch his cramped legs. Jackson agreed. Both men got out and inhaled sweet, fresh air. Frank tried to ignore his wrinkled clothes while Jackson still looked impeccable. *How did the man do it?* It was getting nippy, so Frank grabbed his suit jacket from the back seat and put it on. The right pocket felt heavy, and he remembered his cell phone. He pulled it out and realized he'd never turned it back on after he'd gotten off the plane. He figured he'd better check to see if he had any messages. Apparently Jackson decided he wanted to take a closer look at the house, and said he'd be right back. He took a flashlight with him. Frank got back in the car to keep warm. He was beginning to wonder what the hell he was doing here.

His phone indicated he had one message. He called his voice mail. Omar had left a message hours ago. He said Frank's suspicion that the Laura Branigan ID was false was right on the money. He was able to trace the credit card number. The number was traced to a business account by the name of Wydex Enterprises, with a billing address in New York. Frank listened carefully and wrote it down. He repeated the message again just to be sure he had it right. He couldn't believe what he was hearing.

The car door opened, startling Frank. Jackson slid in the driver's seat, started the engine, and turned on the heat. "The house looks unoccupied," he said. "But I was able to look in a window, and I did see a portable crib with some toys inside. I also saw some garbage cans by the side of the house. An empty box of diapers was crammed into one. Newborn size."

"Where are we?" Frank asked wide-eyed.

"Congers, remember?" Jackson looked at Frank as if he were a mental patient.

"No. I mean what's the exact address here?"

"One-two-one Birch Street," Jackson recited.

Frank showed him the address he'd written down in his notebook. "This is the billing address for the credit card used by the Jane Doe who drowned in Corsicana. The one I saw in the morgue today." Frank held up the notebook, and in the soft moonlight, Jackson clearly saw the address Frank had written down. 121 Birch St., Congers, New York.

Chapter Fifty-Two

They finally managed to squeeze some time in together, and were happily lounging on Diana's couch. The couple had been very busy of late, and they hadn't been able to spend much time together. Business was going well for Todd, and he was happy to be busy. He was a bundle of nerves waiting to hear from Boots, and seemed to have boundless energy as a result. He continued to jog, made sure he made time to visit his mother, joined a club to play racquetball, and one evening joined Matt, Katy, and the kids for a cookout. He even got down on the floor and wrestled with his niece and nephew, much to their delight.

As for Diana, she never had a slow day at the boutique. Sales were brisk, especially during the summer. She'd also coordinated and provided clothes for a major fashion show, and of course did the ordering for the winter season. Fall items had been ordered months ago, and were already on the way. Work was a whirlwind of activity, and on top of it all, Diana's first mother Theresa, had come to visit.

Diana had been so nervous to meet Theresa, she thought she might faint before Glen could introduce them. She needn't have worried. From the moment the two women looked into one another's eyes, all fear and hesitation vanished. They embraced, happy tears staining their cheeks. Glen had cried too. He'd witnessed many reunions, and never tired of the emotional experience. He often likened it to being an obstetrician. No matter how many times you may have watched a baby being born, each birth was a new and unique miracle to behold. Glen felt the first moment of each reunion was like that, no matter how it all turned out later, you just couldn't help but be moved by it.

After their introduction, Diana and Theresa spent hours talking, getting to know one another. They'd only scheduled a few days together, and had wanted to make the most of it. Theresa even accompanied Diana to work one day, helping her with a new window display. Diana was impressed not only with Theresa's artistic ability, but her enthusiasm for everything she did was obvious. From unpacking boxes to steaming wrinkles from clothes, Theresa Croft worked with a special flair all her own, and always wore a smile on her face. Just like Diana. They quickly discovered they shared the same taste in fashion, color, and style. On the day that mother and daughter worked together at the boutique, countless customers asked Diana why they'd never met her sister before. Theresa could only laugh and blush at the compliment.

During that time, Todd and Diana kept up with each other by phone. Diana had asked him to meet Theresa, but he politely declined. Diana tried to be sensitive to his feelings rather than be disappointed. When he suggested he wanted mother and daughter to share their first visit together alone, and to only focus on one another, she couldn't argue with him. Besides, Todd knew he would have another opportunity to meet Theresa, and told Diana how much he would look forward to it. Diana knew he was simply trying to sort through his own emotional overload, and she respected that. She tried not to feel guilty about enjoying her time with Theresa, for she knew Todd wished he could experience the same thing for himself. And with Beaumont's help, Diana desperately hoped he could.

In the meantime, Todd had been to see Claire, and he was diligently working on sorting through all the confusion that now was his life. Diana knew Claire was far better qualified to assist Todd than she was, and she was pleased Todd was working with her, for she knew it wasn't the easiest thing for him. Although he'd made some progress, he still struggled with the fact that he was seeing a shrink. To his credit, at least he hadn't quit, even if it did make him grind his teeth at times.

He'd also made an effort at the support group. Not a hint of envy crossed his face while Diana told the group about Theresa, not even when she shared some pictures. The group asked endless questions, more tears were shed, and hugs were in plentiful supply. There was some serious discussion about the "honeymoon" period, where often those in reunion felt an initial high, only to later crash back to reality when the excitement wore off. Diana heard first hand from others how reunion could be a roller coaster ride full of highs and lows. She felt well prepared to deal with it all come what may, thanks to Glen, Carol, and the others. All she had wanted was to cherish the time with Theresa, get to know her a bit better, and lay some groundwork. They'd already made plans for their next visit when Diana would fly to Boston, to spend time with Theresa on her own turf and in her home.

"Happy?" Diana asked Todd.

"Happy to be with you," Todd stroked her hair.

"But . . ."

"But nothing," Todd replied unconvincingly.

"Why don't you call him?"

"Who?" Todd asked innocently. All it got him was a good poke in the ribs. "Ow!" he cried indignantly.

"Okay. I give you ten points for trying to be nonchalant. You seem pretty calm on the outside, but I know what your schedule's been like lately, you're a manic trying to keep yourself busy while you're waiting to hear something. So why not call him? Even if he doesn't know anything yet, it'll make you feel better just to talk to him. Please? " Diana handed Todd the portable phone. "Come on."

"Man, you're pushy." Todd smiled and took the phone. He'd committed the number to memory, country code and all. He punched in what seemed like an endless series of numbers before hearing a click, and then ringing. Todd covered the mouthpiece and said, "It's ringing." Diana rolled her eyes at him. "I can hear it, you goof!"

"Beaumont."

"Hey Boots, Todd Walters here. How's it going?"

"Todd, how are you? And how is that lovely lady of yours? What? Oh, Julie says hi."

"Tell her we say hi back." He didn't know what to say next, but Boots did.

"Enough with the fucking pleasantries. I don't have anything to report yet. But Julie and I are working on an angle." Boots always got straight to the point.

"Tell me," Todd asked.

Boots explained he'd gotten nowhere on his own. He didn't like to admit it, but he tended to be brutally honest, even with himself. He told Todd about Julie's dream and how they were working on solving the Kelto puzzle. He assured his client he felt confident they would figure it out, and as soon as they did, he would let Todd know. Immediately. The men exchanged a few more words and then ended the call. Todd repeated the conversation to Diana, who'd heard most of it already.

"That's great news!"

Paris and Soll

"What? That he doesn't know anything yet?"

"No! That Julie's helping him," Diana chirped. "That is *so* cool. *She'll* be able to figure it out. I just know it."

"What, now you're psychic?" Todd laughed. It earned him another poke. "OW!"

Chapter Fifty-Three

Sheila Stiles and Wendell Colby were at each other's throats. They'd been arguing for the better part of an hour about the sudden disappearance of the Mule. Sheila first grew concerned when Leslie failed to check in the day before. Standard procedure was to call and confirm as soon as possible after a snatch. That way, the Boss and the Stork could finish making the necessary preparations and have everything in place for the new arrival. Leslie had never failed to call in before. Never. Even if a plan were aborted at the last minute, she would call in to explain why. She had always been completely loyal and trustworthy. Stiles and Colby just couldn't figure out what was wrong. If there was anyone they could depend on, it was the Mule.

Leslie Steiner had been exceedingly grateful to Dr. Colby for hiring her all those years ago. He was the one who'd given her a fresh start. But, bastard that he was, over the years Colby took advantage of her loyalty and manipulated it into complete and utter adoration. He knew how much Leslie hated men in general, especially after everything she'd been through. Yet, even her intense hatred didn't keep her from eventually falling in love with the good doctor himself. Although he never said or did anything overt, Colby cast subtle hints in her direction. From the very beginning, he'd always had a kind word for her. Then, when he'd teamed up with Sheila and brought Leslie into the fold, his praise continued and her devotion increased. He personally congratulated her at the completion of each mission. He would make a point of driving out to the Birch Street house when Leslie was there caring for an infant waiting to be adopted, just to see how she was getting along. He spoke softly when addressing her, and he always managed to find a platonic way of touching her. A gentle squeeze of the hand, a brief fatherly hug, a warm pat on the back. He cultivated their relationship to the point where he knew, with absolute certainty, that Leslie would do anything for him. Anything at all.

It was why he and Sheila were now raging at each other. Typically suspicious and untrusting, Sheila declared Leslie a deserter. She figured the Mule had abandoned them, gone off to start her own line of business. She claimed she'd probably snatched the kid and was brokering a deal for herself, that she'd become too greedy and unreliable. Wendell exploded and said the whole idea was ludicrous. Leslie would never do such a thing. Surely, something terrible must have happened to her if she hadn't reported in, he insisted. In return, all he got from Sheila was a snort of disgust and a wave of dismissal. He wanted to throttle her.

They'd both been trying her cell phone for hours, each time hearing the same recorded message the customer was unavailable. Since each mission was secretly executed to avoid any type of complication, neither Sheila nor Wendell knew where the Mule or Nardo rented a room while on a job. They knew the city, the location of the hospitals or residence where the snatch was to take place, but beyond that, pretty much everything else was left up to the discretion of their employees.

Of course both Nardo and Leslie had the best fake ID's and passports money could buy. Sheila saw to it. As paranoid as he was, Nardo refused to use any of the phony business credit cards Sheila had set up, he always used a stolen credit card number. It was a habit from the old days Nardo just couldn't change no matter how Sheila tried to convince him her cards were safe. Once she realized he would never convert to her way of thinking, she let him be. She didn't ask how he got the stolen numbers, she really didn't care, as long as nothing could be traced back to her.

Leslie used the business credit cards when she had to, and so far, Sheila never had a reason to be concerned. They were quite a few of them, all from different companies, and she and Colby were careful to rotate the usage. Nothing was linked to the office in New York, the statements went to the old house in Congers, where they were picked up on a regular basis and paid through a separate phony business account.

Sheila and Wendell finally ran out of nasty remarks and pointed accusations as to who was to blame for this present calamity. The one thing they did agree on however, was that something had to be done, and quickly. Obviously, something was very wrong. Someone had to go on a fact-finding mission to discover what had really happened to the Mule. Their business and their livelihood were at stake. They also completely agreed that neither one of them could take a chance on making such a trip. It would be far too dangerous and foolish for either one to expose themselves in such a way. The only person who could get to the bottom of it all was Nardo.

Sheila flipped open her cell and speed dialed the Hungarian.

"Yeah."

"I want you to go to Texas," Sheila ordered.

"But Boss, I just got back from . . ."

"I don't care. I haven't heard from my friend. You know, the stubborn one. She was supposed to be home yesterday," Sheila sharply informed him.

"But can't you call her . . ."

"What the *fuck* is your problem? How *dare* you question me? I *have* called her. There's no answer. I don't *know* why she hasn't come home. That's why you need to go and *find* her," Sheila spoke to him as if he were an imbecile. Nardo bristled at her tone, but kept his mouth shut. The Boss could be a total bitch, but his job was far too lucrative to do anything to piss her off. He listened carefully as she gave him the name of the city, and the name of the hospital where the snatch was to have taken place. The rest was up to him, and she made it clear she didn't want to hear from him until he had answers.

Chapter Fifty-Four

Boots and Julie were having a little disagreement. Actually, it was a mother of a knock down, drag out fight. So very typical of their relationship. When they went at it, they went at it all the way. Boots was storming around the deck of the *Lost & Found*, and Julie was in the galley banging pots and pans. Boots could only hope she wasn't looking for any sharp objects. Though they were in separate locations, they both continued to rail at each other under their collective breaths. As Boots went by the galley window he heard Julie mumble. "Son of a bitch thinks I'm a *witch* or something," and banged a pan down hard on the stove. Boots hurled himself into the galley so fast he hit his head on the low overhead as he came down the steps. "Ouch! Damn it Julie, I heard that. And yes. Sometimes I *do* think you are a witch." Julie's hand instinctively reached for the drawer where the cutlery lay in wait. Through sheer will power, she counted to ten first (a true miracle), before she responded.

"I *told* you the letters in Todd's birth name need to be rearranged. Isn't that enough for you to figure it out? You're the private dick. Or is it just *dick*?"

"And I *told* you I found an anagram solver on the Internet. It rearranges a group of letters into known surnames, but the letters in Kelto don't show up as any known name," Boots replied nastily, as if this were her fault. He knew he was being unreasonable and could do nothing to stop himself. He was mad because he was at a dead end. He was frustrated as hell, and did what was only fair. He took it out on someone else.

"So, since *you* are the witch, the psychic, the gypsy fortune teller, or whatever it is you call yourself, you do it. You figure it out." He stomped out of the galley. In his rush to avoid the coffee mug hurtling towards him, he banged his head again. This time he saw stars. "Shit!"

Evil Exchange

The crash of the cup and the yelp from her lover satisfied her momentarily, and she grinned at his pain. *Serves him right, pigheaded American.* Then Julie reminded herself it was Todd they were trying to help, and even though she was furious with Boots, she still wanted to help him decipher the Kelto mystery. And she figured there was only one way to do it.

Julie decided to take a trip in her private plane. Oh sure, everyone thought just because she was psychic, she could find the answer to anything by just "seeing." But, it really didn't work that way. Being psychic wasn't something turned on or off at will. Being psychic meant, at least for Julie, that one often acted as a transmitter. Sometimes you received clear transmissions, other times nothing at all, or maybe just static. She couldn't chose when or where or how or why. All she could do was pay attention when it happened.

What worked best for Julie was flying. She'd been doing it for years. Whenever she had a knotty problem to solve, she would lie down on the couch, close her eyes, and imagine she was flying her own small plane. She pictured herself sitting in front of the controls where she could clearly see the cockpit instruments. She could hear the rush of air and the noise from the engine. She would look out and see the scenery of lands unknown to her. Peaceful lakes, ocean waters, enormous mountains, or sparkling sandy beaches would float by underneath her airborne chariot. She would let herself enjoy the freedom, feel totally relaxed and at peace. Her cousin Shay-Shay once suggested she might be having an out of body experience during these flights. Julie believed this might be true, but felt the most important part of it all was that when she did this, a solution to her problem always appeared as she came in for a landing. Aside from the fun of her mental flying, and the satisfaction of getting answers to her problems by doing so, there was also a third benefit which she later discovered.

The summer Julie turned twenty five, one of her older sisters came to visit. Marlene lived in Florida at the time with Ray, husband number three. Ray was a flight instructor. The man was a bore, but when he offered to give Julie some flying lessons, she took him up on it. During the first flight, her brother-in-law asked if she had taken flying lessons before. "No," Julie replied honestly. "I just practice when I'm relaxing on my couch." Ray didn't believe her for one minute and laughed. "Bullshit. No one could fly like you without some lessons and practice. You've just been keeping it a secret," and he waggled a finger at her. He had no idea how lucky he was he was to keep it attached to his hand. Julie hated finger wagglers. Yet, she didn't argue and just smiled instead. She knew he wasn't going to be around much longer anyway. She knew there would be a husband number four. She'd already had a dream about it.

Now, Julie knew it was the time for action. She went into the bedroom and

Paris and Soll

lay face down on the bed. She closed her eyes and slowed her breathing. The gentle rocking of the boat helped her instantly relax, and she was soon gliding over some beautiful Caribbean beaches in her mind. As she floated along in her plane, she saw swimmers, surfers, water skiers, and parasailers. Dolphins leapt out of the water and sunbathers jammed the shoreline. One stretch of beach was so full of people it looked like one big clog. No, that wasn't it. Not a clog, it more like a clot. Julie jumped up and yelled.

"That's it. Boots! Get in here now, you big stupid ox. Get in here!" Julie screeched.

Boots came rushing down the stairs, but remembered at the last moment to duck his head. He didn't need another lump. "For Christ's sake, what's going on?"

"Boots, I saw it while I was flying. A beach clogged with people. And clogged made me think of clot, and clot made me think of Klot, you know, with a *K*. That's when I got it." Boots stared at her. He thought *she* must have taken a whack to the head for all the gibberish she was spewing.

Julie knew the look well. She tried again. "Listen to me carefully. If you rearrange the letters in Kelto, you find the word Klot in it. Right? Go look on the Internet. Look for E. Klot. They just put the first initial and the last name together to get Kelto. I know it. I know this is right. Go on, look it up. Now. Hurry!"

Chapter Fifty-Five

Frank could hardly believe his butt was once again parked in an airplane seat, and yet, it did seem most appropriate for the Red Barron to be back in the sky. Over the last few days, the term "frequent flyer" was quickly becoming redundant. Not that he was complaining. No way. Frank was more than happy to be on his way back to Texas. Sadly, he couldn't say the same for Suzy. He'd called from the airport, apologizing for the change of plan, but his enthusiasm was evident. He told her they'd gotten a new lead. Things were starting to fall into place. She understood he could say no more about it.

Suzy always gave it her best effort, but it was never easy to mask her disappointment when Frank wasn't able to come home when planned. You'd think after all the years, Suzy would be used to her husband's schizophrenic schedule. However, it didn't matter how many times she'd been through it before. Each time would still be a letdown if he were to be away longer than expected. Of course, she would never say anything other than she missed him. Suzy knew the long hours and time away from home was part of his job, and she was immensely proud of her husband and the work he did. It was just that they only had each other, and there was no getting around the fact it was difficult for both of them to be separated for more than a few days. When Frank told her he'd be home just as soon as he could, she sent more kisses his way. When they finally hung up, they were both thinking the same thing. *I am married to the most wonderful person in the world.*

Now that they'd reached cruising altitude, Frank relaxed and thought about how quickly things had happened. The night before, Frank and Lionel Jackson had arrived back in New York City late in the evening. Jackson dropped Frank off at a hotel, and told him to get some shut-eye. They had a lot of work to do the next day.

Paris and Soll

The next thing Frank knew was someone was pounding on his door. Disoriented and confused, he stumbled out of bed and whipped open the door only to be blinded by the sun. Expecting the maid, he was surprised to see Lionel Jackson nattily attired in a three-piece suit, which probably cost the equivalent of Frank's mortgage payment. Lionel held two containers of freshly brewed java and a USA Today folded under his arm. Jackson laughed and said the blackout curtains must have worked wonders. Frank allowed him in and demanded to know the time. When Jackson told him, he simply couldn't believe it. He'd slept for twelve straight hours. Frank mumbled something about jet lag, and excused himself to slink into the shower. Ten minutes later, dressed and fully awake, Frank came out and gratefully grabbed the coffee. Jackson was seated in an armchair one leg casually crossed over the other, his tasseled loafers perfectly shined. Frank couldn't help but notice even the man's socks were expensive. SAC Lionel Jackson looked up from his paper and grinned. Even his teeth were perfect.

"Your flight leaves in two hours. We have to get to the airport ASAP. I have a car and driver waiting downstairs." Jackson said as he neatly refolded the paper.

"Very funny," Frank snorted.

"No, really." Jackson then explained Sheila Stiles was sending someone to Corsicana to look for a friend. " It's got to be Jane Doe," he said with conviction.

Frank took too big of a sip and burned his tongue. "What?" he sputtered. "How did you find this out?"

"It's my superior investigative skills," Jackson laughed. "Let's get you packed up."

On the way to the airport Frank must have asked a half dozen times how Jackson was able to get this kind of breakthrough information so fast. All he got in return were evasions. It seemed all Jackson wanted to talk about was the bridge tournament scheduled later that evening and the competition he was facing. As Jackson talked strategy, Frank tried to keep up. He knew nothing of bridge and eventually tuned out. He might have slept for twelve hours, but he felt like a zombie trying to follow the conversation and did his best to nod his way through it. When the driver pulled up to the curb at the airport, Frank remained in his seat.

"Come on. You have to tell me now. How did you find out?" He was determined to get an answer and was not above begging. Jackson laughed uproariously and picked an invisible piece of lint from his pant leg.

Evil Exchange

"Okay. I tortured you long enough. How did I find out? I overheard her on the phone," Jackson replied smugly.

"How the hell did you get a wire tap so fast?" Frank was incredulous.

"No tap necessary. I went to her office to scope things out this morning while you were imitating Rip Van Winkle. Stiles operates in an office building with a bunch of other professionals. I went because I needed to get a feel for where she works, maybe even catch a glimpse of her coming or going. It's just something I do," Jackson shrugged his Armani clad shoulders. "I thought if I did see her, I would duck into another office so she wouldn't wonder who I was, or why I was there. Anyway, I guess I didn't need to worry about it. She was so busy yelling at someone in her office, I could hear her down the hallway. I peeked in her reception area and it was empty. No secretary, nothing. She was probably scared off," Jackson laughed again before he continued. "So I just stood at the outer door. Heard everything. Word for word."

"Names?"

"Nah. But I know for sure who she was yelling at. Dr. Wendell Colby. They work together, but I'm not exactly sure what his story is. I happened across him when I was doing the background check on her. He used to have a private practice years ago. An abortion clinic. Now he spends most of his time playing golf. So I don't know if he's just part of the adoption storefront or what. But here's what I figure. We know the Jane Doe is tied to Stiles through the credit card. We saw the house with the baby stuff, and it's got to be a way station for the kids. You've got a description that matches Jane Doe and what she was wearing from the mother whose newborn was stolen right out her arms. We know of at least two murders and two kidnappings, possibly by the same guy, and I bet there's more. My hunch is Stiles and Colby are providing their clients with stolen babies. Right now, someone is on the way to Corsicana to look for the missing operative. And that someone is going to walk right into our hands." Jackson smiled and then suddenly frowned.

"And you're unhappy about what?" Frank asked bewildered.

"Well, if this all plays out the way I think it will, it's good news for us. We'll be able to catch these despicable people."

"But?"

"Bad news for my friend Paul and his wife Andrea."

"Oh, right. Man, that's the shits . . ." Frank didn't know what else to say. There really weren't words to describe the pain the couple faced. Their beautiful new daughter Ruby had been abducted. The Pearsons had bought her.

Chapter Fifty-Six

Todd finished up a proposal he'd been working on all morning. It was for a large installation, which was scheduled to begin in a few weeks, and he felt confident his bid would be accepted. He double-checked everything one final time, and then emailed it off. He hoped to get an answer by the end of the week. *Now what?* He needed a project. Todd went to check his list.

Lately, Todd had taken to making a list of household projects to work on whenever he had a spare moment. They were mostly small jobs, random stuff. Fixing a loose doorknob, cleaning out his cluttered desk, sorting through old bills and receipts. He'd become almost obsessed with keeping busy and filling up his time. Todd had always been an active, energetic guy. Yet, ever since he met with Boots Beaumont and made the decision to search for his natural mother, an urgent intensity seemed to have entered his bloodstream, invading every cell of his being.

Todd knew if they were to find her, his life would instantly and irrevocably change forever. How exactly, he didn't know. He carefully watched Diana for any obvious signs of how she'd been affected so far by meeting with her first mother, Theresa, but he hadn't noticed anything significant. Granted, mother and daughter had only gotten together once, so it was still in the early stages of their relationship, but from what he could tell, Diana seemed to be handling it all in stride. *Will I be able to do that?* He wasn't so sure. Todd and Diana may both have been adopted, but their experiences were vastly different. Todd couldn't help but wonder what the exact circumstances were surrounding his adoption through a notorious baby broker. *Did my mother know what she was doing when she gave me up? Did she know what kind of person this Maddie Monroe really was? Did she ever care about me, or was she just anxious to hand me off to someone else and be rid of me forever?*

Evil Exchange

Todd may not know much about what happened, but he did know one thing. There was a major trauma involved, for him anyway. It was a trauma which almost equaled the pain of living all that time believing his parents had been killed in a car crash. Whatever happened all those years ago, he'd been scarred from it, and it had altered the course of his life in so many ways he was just now beginning to recognize. Presently, he was looking at another life altering situation. Only this time, it would be by his own hand, not someone else's. He couldn't help but think about all the pain he'd suffered and stuffed all those years. That pain, which he'd run from, tucked away, or completely denied, now threatened to rip open the old wounds and possibly squeeze from his heart every ounce of love that ever existed there. He was amazed at how much had changed. How much *he'd* changed. Now, instead of denying, he was asking. Instead of hiding, he was seeking. He also thought he was nuts for doing such a thing. Yet now that he'd set the wheels in motion, he felt as if there was no turning back. *Did he have a choice to continue or not?* Of course he did. *Would he let fear stop him from finding out the truth?* No. *Would he be able to handle it?* He had absolutely no idea.

Todd remembered a play he saw some years ago. His neighbor Tanya had some very good friends who were talented song writers. They were working on a play, and asked Tanya to invite as many neighbors as possible to come and watch the rehearsals so the actors would have an audience to interact with. Todd went only to appease Tanya, but was blown away at the professional quality of the production. He was particularly moved by one of the songs called, "Why Is It I Just Don't Belong," and he could still remember it word for word.

Why is it I just don't belong? Why is it I just don't fit in? Fit in with anyone, any place? Why is it so?

When I look around, I've no place to go.

Why is it I don't feel related to familiar scenes I see?

I wonder why was I created to be me, only me?

Why is it I feel so alone? Why is it I feel so left out,

left out of everything, anything I want to do?

Seems false and unreal, is anything true?

Can't get into nobody's head, nobody's thoughts, are matching mine.

When I need sun, it rains instead. Why can't my day be fine?

Why is it I just don't belong?

Why is it I just don't belong?

Paris and Soll

Why is it everything goes wrong?

When all I want, all I want,

All I want is just to belong.

Though the song choked his throat and brought tears to his eyes, Todd went back every night of rehearsals, and almost every night of its three week run. Never in his life had he identified so completely with the words from a song. Todd felt as if they'd been written just for him, as they so utterly and completely explained how he felt. Thinking about those words again, he realized exactly why he wanted, no, *needed* to find his natural mother. He wanted to belong.

Todd snapped out of his reverie. This was exactly why he had to keep busy. He ended up getting bogged down in his thoughts, which only confused him further. It was why his life had been on fast forward lately. He was fast tracking to fill up time and push it forward, that much was obvious. He figured if this was what he needed to do to stay grounded then so be it. Besides, working hard at keeping busy was beneficial in so many ways. The more jobs he took on, the more in demand he was. He'd always had a good reputation in his field of work, but now? It was just getting better and better. His bank account was growing, his relationships were flourishing, and physically he was in better shape than he was five years ago. He knew what he was doing all right, and he couldn't stop himself. He felt as if there was an electrical current coursing through his body twenty-four seven. He was antsy. He was keyed up. He may have been getting a lot done, but he was also driving himself crazy with all the activity. When the phone rang, he nearly hit his head on the ceiling.

"'Lo?"

"Todd, Beaumont here."

"Hey, Boots. What's up?" Todd struggled to convey nonchalance.

"I have some excellent news, and I knew you'd want to hear it right away. I, I mean *we*, figured out the name. We have your natural mother's name," Boots reported.

"Really? That's outstanding. How'd you do it?"

Boots laughed. "Trade secret, my friend. But we came up with E. Klot. Now all we have to do is figure out what the 'E' stands for and track her down. Shouldn't be too tough," Boots explained.

"Okay . . ." Todd hesitated.

"If you're uncomfortable, we can stop right here you know," Boots reminded him.

Evil Exchange

"No. Don't stop. I've come this far and I need to see it through. That is, if you can find her."

"Oh, we'll find her all right. You just hang in there. I'll keep you posted amigo," Boots replied confidently.

"I will, thanks." Todd ended the call and set down the phone. Then he picked it up again. He wanted to tell Diana, but he didn't want to interrupt her at work. She'd been putting in a lot of hours lately. He called her home number and left a message about his conversation with Boots. He knew she'd be excited about it and call him as soon as she got home. That done, he didn't know what to do with himself. His mind reeled and his pulse raced. Distraction. He desperately needed a distraction. He went in search of his list. There were a couple of big jobs down at the bottom, ones he thought he'd never get to. Well, now was the time to find the biggest job possible. There it was, in bold script. The perfect solution. **Paint kitchen**. He found himself whistling on the way to the hardware store.

Chapter Fifty-Seven

"**B**oss. First thing I did was pick up a paper. No mention of anything 'missing' from the hospital here, so I don't think she made it to pick up the package. Then I see this big article about a flash flood a few days back. Three people killed. Yeah, crazy I know. Well, one of 'em is unidentified. So I'm thinking it's your friend maybe," Nardo reported from his cell phone. He waited for a reply, but heard only a sharp intake of breath, so he kept talking.

"So I make some calls and finally get connected to the coroner's office. So yeah, I'm pretty sure it's her. They have a Jane Doe matching her description, wearing a nurse's uniform. Then the guy got suspicious with me over the phone. He asked me who I was, was I family, could I identify her. You know, shit like that. So I hung up." Nardo took a breath and continued. "So then, I find out where the place is, the morgue I mean, and I drive by to check it out. I'm thinking maybe I can pay a visit there later or sumpin'. You know, find out for sure. Not much going on from what I can see from the parking lot, but then I see this guy. A suit. He *has* to be a Fed."

"The Feds are involved?" Sheila was incredulous.

"Guess so. Believe me, I know. This guy is definitely a Fed. I saw him go into the building."

"He could have been there for another reason Nardo," Sheila condescended.

"Maybe," Nardo retorted. He hated it when she talked to him that way. He wasn't an idiot.

"So. As *insane* as it sounds, you really think my friend died in a flash flood.

Evil Exchange

Is that right?"

"Looks that way," Nardo replied coldly. He for one could care less if the Mule had been killed in some freak accident. She gave him the creeps, and she always looked at him like he was a rapist, which he most certainly was not. He could have easily taken advantage of the young mothers before he killed them, but he never did. He didn't believe in mixing business with pleasure. Nardo always thought of himself as a stand-up guy.

He knew the Boss was flipped out about all of this. As far as Nardo was concerned, this entire chain of events would only be of benefit to him. With the Mule no longer in the picture, he would now be the main supplier, which would only increase his value, especially his pay packet.

"Nardo! Are you listening to me?" Sheila shouted at him.

"Yes, Boss." *Jesus, the woman can shriek.*

"I want you to find out for sure, do you hear me? We're not just going to *assume* it was my friend in that accident. I want you to do whatever it takes to find out. I want you to see the Jane Doe with your own eyes. I will accept nothing less. Understand? And don't let anyone see you, *especially* the Feds." Sheila terminated the call.

"Yes, always a pleasure to talk to you too," Nardo said to the dial tone. *Bitch.* Like he would ever be so careless as to let a Fed make him. Nardo started the car. He knew he wasn't going to be able to do anything until later. He'd have to wait and come back, break in, and find the body. Not too tough to do. Once he made the confirmation, he'd be able to get the hell out of Texas and back to work. Hopefully, the Boss had another job lined up for him soon. Chances were pretty damn good, he figured. Since the Mule's operation had been unsuccessful, they'd be in desperate need of new inventory. The scarecrow's baby had just been placed with a new mom and dad, so that was it for the kids they had available. So now he knew he'd be busy for a while, that much was guaranteed. Nardo whistled in delight as he pulled out of the back lot of the coroner's building. He could think of no better way to kill some time than finding a strip joint and parking his ass on a barstool.

Chapter Fifty-Eight

"Oh Andrea, she's so beautiful."

"Isn't she? I can't imagine how we ever got along without her before. Mother, here, you hold her," Andrea Pearson handed baby Ruby over with tremendous care.

"Tell me more about the adoption agency, Andrea. You haven't said much about it."

"Not much to tell," Andrea said evasively and busied herself refolding Ruby's already perfectly folded clothes.

"But do you know anything about Ruby's background? Where does her family come from? Do you know her medical history?"

"Mother, please. You sound like such a snob. I could care less where her family comes from. You and daddy may have that elitist attitude, but I certainly don't."

The words stung like a slap in the face. "That's not what I meant, dear. Not at all." Emily Roscoe was surprised her daughter would say such a thing to her. She and Delivan had raised their daughter without prejudice or class distinction. The comment was truly uncharacteristic of her. Emily couldn't help but wonder if Paul's viewpoints were rubbing off a bit too much on his wife. Emily respected Paul Pearson but didn't care much for the man personally. Obviously, her daughter saw something in him that she didn't, and Emily accepted it, for it was Andrea, and Andrea's choice alone, as to whom her husband would be. Emily never interfered. Delivan heartily approved of course, since he thought of Paul as a potential senatorial candidate. Delivan treated Paul as if he were his own son. Of course he loved and adored his daughter, but Emily knew he had secretly always wished for a son. The thought made her wince with guilt.

Emily had reservations from the very beginning about her son-in-law. Oh sure, Paul Pearson looked the part. Good family, Ivy League schools, a savvy businessman turned wealthy philanthropist with strong political ambition. He did have a bit of a superior attitude, though he hid it fairly well. More than once or twice Emily saw a brief sneer or momentary look of disdain cross Paul's face when he thought no one was looking. That was not what really bothered her though. There was something more fundamental missing. Paul lacked substance. He had no depth, no inner strength, no real foundation. He was always politically correct in public, but Emily never really knew where he stood on anything, for he was famous for skirting controversial issues. Yes, he was smart and attractive. Yes, he was charitable and involved in his church and the community. Yes, he treated Andrea with the utmost respect and showered her with love and attention. It was hard to find fault with the man. Maybe that was it. Maybe he was too perfect, at least on the surface. Emily could not entirely trust someone who appeared to have no shortcomings. To her, it showed a lack of character.

She never said a word to anyone about her misgivings, not even her husband. No, especially not her husband. Delivan Roscoe was a saint in Emily's eyes. He had literally saved her life many years ago and Emily would do anything to make him happy. And if Paul Pearson as a son-in-law made him happy, then that was fine.

Emily wasn't sure Paul made Andrea happy though. Not that Andrea mentioned anything specific to her. Still, it was a feeling. *A mother's instinct?* Emily thought she might be too protective of her daughter. It was difficult not to be, considering the circumstances, and she just couldn't help herself. And it did seem as though Andrea had become more secretive, especially over the last few months. This worried her a great deal, for Emily knew all about secrets, and the damage they can do.

Andrea had always been a delicate and emotional child, but she seemed to blossom in college, and became a strong and independent woman. She graduated with a degree in art history, and wanted nothing more than to work at MOMA for the rest of her life. Then when she met Paul, it seemed some of the insecurities crept back in, for she wanted to work and Paul wanted her to stay at home and start a family. Andrea relented, for she loved Paul immensely, and appeared content to let her career take a back seat to her husband's. When it became obvious she was having trouble conceiving, Paul sought out the finest fertility specialists. They spent years, and hundreds of thousands of dollars, all

Paris and Soll

to no avail. Andrea kept up a good front for the sake of her husband, but inside, she felt enormously inadequate.

Emily knew how withdrawn and depressed her daughter became about her infertility, but there wasn't anything she could do to help her. She tried to talk with Andrea, but was repeatedly pushed away and told it was none of her business. It made Emily's heart ache. Then, when she found out that Paul and Andrea had agreed on adopting, she could see the tremendous difference it made. Andrea became more relaxed, happier than anyone had seen her in a long time. Emily breathed a silent sigh of relief, but it was short-lived, for that was when the evasions started. Andrea would not discuss how she and Paul were going about the adoption, just that they were "going on a recommendation." Emily was terribly concerned at first, and then shocked when she found out how quickly the arrangements had been made. Surely, going through a reputable agency took time, even for someone as influential as Paul Pearson and his wife Andrea, daughter of Senator Delivan Roscoe. Paul must have made some kind of generous contribution to speed up the process. *Typical of Paul to solve any and every problem with money,* Emily mused. It wasn't right, but it was how he was.

Again, Emily kept her misgivings to herself, especially when she saw the look of excitement on Andrea's face when she talked about getting the nursery ready and bringing baby Ruby home. The baby was exactly the stability Andrea needed in her life.

"Mother? Can I have her back now, please?" Andrea laughed and gently touched her mother on the arm. It was her way of making up for the snippy remark.

"Oh, I'm sorry darling. I guess Ruby just has me mesmerized. She's so perfect," Emily reluctantly handed the baby back to Andrea.

"You had a funny look on your face while you were holding her. Are you all right?" Andrea rocked Ruby and kissed her cheek. Then she looked at her mother with genuine concern.

"Of course I'm all right. Not to worry. I was just thinking how wonderful it feels to hold a baby in my arms again." Emily looked deep in thought.

"Too bad I had to grow up, huh?" Andrea laughed, trying to keep the moment light.

"Andrea. There's something I should tell you. Something I really think you need to know."

"Oh no, Mother. Not some maternal advice, please spare me." Andrea's smile turned to a frown.

Evil Exchange

"No, darling. It's not that. It's just . . ."

Ruby started to cry. A rather loud wail from such a tiny mouth. "Oh, she's hungry. Mother, would you please go and get a bottle for me?"

"Sure," Emily immediately left the nursery and went into the kitchen. *Maybe now is not the right time. But I have to tell her sometime. I just have to.*

Chapter Fifty-Nine

Frank walked into the club and quickly scanned the room. Quite a few patrons for a week night. No one paid him the slightest attention. The stripper on stage was young, beautiful, and sported breasts so large it must be challenging to simply stand up straight. At the moment, she was lying down on the stage waiting for her musical cue. Once the music started, she went into a kind of gymnastic routine where she twisted her body in such unusual ways, Frank didn't know such positions were even possible. He'd never seen anyone quite so, limber? Agile? *Well, you learn something new every day. Add one more to my list of things not to tell Suzy.*

He took a seat in the back, and was approached by a cocktail waitress who was naked except for a pair of spandex shorts and high heels. There was a collar around her neck, and yes by God, a tail actually sprouted from her shorts. Frank couldn't believe she had black plastic whiskers glued to her cheeks, but there they were. He recalled the name of the establishment was the "Pussy" something or other, so that explained the outfit. His topless waitress appeared serious about her job, plastic whiskers and all, and enthusiastically greeted him. "Meow, I'm Kitty. Would you like a drink?" He ordered tonic water and her whiskers wiggled an acknowledgement.

It wasn't too long of a wait. Frank saw a man enter the room and make his way toward the bar. He watched as he sat down and spoke to the bartender. A moment later, a bottle of beer was served. There was no doubt it was the man he was looking for, the man from the dash cam. Frank certainly could understand why Nathan Hicks, drunk or sober, would use such a description. It was The Hulk who called himself "Bob" and he wore a baseball cap.

Five strippers and two hours later, Frank could see the man reach for his

Evil Exchange

wallet to pull out some bills. He conferred with the bartender and gave him cash. Draining his glass, he heaved his bulk from the barstool and made his way out the door. Frank threw some money on the table for Kitty and followed.

Once outside, Frank saw his quarry disappear around the side of the building. Frank knew he was headed for the parking lot in the back, and trailed slowly behind. He figured he would be able to get to his car in enough time to tail his target. He figured wrong.

As soon as Frank rounded the corner, strong, powerful hands circled his neck and started squeezing. The strength of the man was incredible. Frank Barron was six feet tall and two hundred pounds. But Frank didn't carry any extra weight. Underneath his ill fitting suits, he was lean and fit and muscular, but even he was no match against this huge Neanderthal.

Frank tried everything he could think of, he struggled mightily, all to no avail. His air supply was completely cut off, his throat was being crushed, and he felt like his eyeballs were going to pop right out of his head. The Hulk had pushed him up against the back of the building, and used his enormous body to pin Frank down. Frank couldn't use his arms or legs. He couldn't maneuver his body in any way to fight back. He could smell the beer on his assailant's breath and see the sweat dripping from his brow. His situation was getting more and more desperate, and he knew he didn't have much time left. Ten seconds later, Frank blacked out.

"Hey man, you okay?"

Frank opened his eyes and looked up at the hairiest handlebar mustache he'd ever seen. He tried to talk, but his voice box wasn't working. His throat was on fire, and the best he could do was make a harsh rasping sound.

"Here, can you try and sit up?" The mustache came closer and Frank could feel the man's arms pull him into a sitting position. "That's better. Want me to get you some water?"

"No," Frank managed. His voice was barely a whisper, but at least he could talk. "Where is he?"

"Who? Oh, that guy? He ran away. And I let him. Ya know how big he was? I mean like I'm sorry you got choked and all, but I wasn't going after him. No freakin' way. I mean, hey. I just came out to empty the trash, ya know? Then I see Godzilla out here tryin' to kill you. I guess he thought he'd better take off, so he let go of you and you dropped like a sack of . . ."

"Call the cops," Frank interrupted as best he could. Now his head was throbbing.

"Man. I was afraid you were gonna say that. See now if I did, my boss would be totally pissed. He doesn't like the cops to come here. Well, unless they come when they're off duty, know what I'm sayin'?"

"Pocket," Frank urged. *Did the man ever shut up?*

"What?" Handlebar looked at Frank reaching for his jacket pocket and understood. He obeyed and pulled out Frank's ID. "No shit. FBI? Oh, man! The boss is gonna *freak*, know what I'm sayin'?"

"Call the cops, please." Frank tried to swallow and thought he might pass out from the pain.

"Okay, okay. I'll call the cops. You stay right here and I'll go call. Boss is gonna freak. God dammit, why do these things have to happen to me," the man muttered to himself. He left Frank propped up against the wall and went back inside the building. Frank hoped he'd be back with some water, but then again, he kind of enjoyed the peace and quiet.

Chapter Sixty

"I hope this is important, my dear. I've juggled my schedule to meet you this evening, and I'm hoping you will make it worth my while," Judge Price leered at Sheila.

"Oh shut up, you old fart. I didn't ask you to meet me so we could screw around. I have a problem, and you are going to help me solve it," Sheila said with a barely controlled fury.

Judge Harold Price could not ever recall Sheila speaking to him in such a manner. Crudeness may have its place, but that was in the bedroom. Just as he was about to chastise her for being so rude, he saw how her hand trembled as she picked up her martini glass. Not a good sign.

"Whatever is the matter, my dear?"

"Nardo called me . . ."

"Ah, ah, ah! No names, remember?"

"Right," Sheila took a large gulp of her drink before setting it down and continuing. "Well, first of all, I've lost one of my best employees, she drowned. Can you believe it? And if that isn't bad enough, another one of my employees contacted me this morning to tell me that the FBI was following him. Somehow, they have discovered part of our operation," Sheila spoke through clenched teeth.

"I see," the Judge frowned and looked around the nearly empty restaurant. It was still early, and no one was in within hearing distance.

"So, when my employee realized that he was being followed, he panicked and tried to *solve* the problem on his own. Before he could conclude his business, he was interrupted, and the job was left undone. So, now he's on his way back here, and the FBI is still an issue." Sheila's voice was tight with anger.

"Well, sounds like your employee botched it all to hell. I'm sorry to hear about it, but naturally, I can't get involved," the Judge gave his standard reply.

"You don't have to get *involved* Harry. You just have to take care of it for me," Sheila drained her glass. She took a deep breath and seemed to relax slightly.

"Oh? And what exactly are you proposing *I* do?" he sneered. Now that he knew sex was not in the cards, he turned cold and distant.

"I need my employee to be terminated. Effective immediately. Do you understand me, Harry?"

"You must be insane," he hissed back at her. "What makes you think I'm going to help you?"

Sheila laughed. "Well, of course you wouldn't be doing the dirty work yourself, silly! I want you to *hire* someone to do the job. After all, a man in your position knows all sorts of unsavory characters. You send them to prison all the time, isn't that right sweetie? And sadly, some of them get out only to walk the streets and commit more crimes, don't they? It would be easy for you. And if you're worried about some crook going to the cops with a story that the honorable Judge Harold Price hired him to knock someone off, just who do you think the cops would believe? You, or some low life felon? Oh, stop puffing your chest up like a priest who's been accused of child molestation. I don't buy the 'you deeply wound me' act. Besides, I have a gift here for you that will make it worth your while. Whatever I've given you before is *nothing* in comparison to this. Just pay some asshole a couple thousand and the rest is yours, free and clear. You haven't been to Vegas for a while now, have you Harry?" Sheila patted her pocket, which contained an envelope fat with bills.

"I don't care what you say. I won't do it." Judge Price replied adamantly.

"I thought you might feel that way. Oh, Harry. I was hoping it wouldn't come to this," Sheila pulled a manila envelope from her purse. She opened it and showed him a CD along with some black and white photos made from the disc itself. She pulled the photos up just far enough so the Judge could see what they contained. Sheila watched his reaction carefully. At first, she was a bit concerned Harry might have a heart attack right there at the restaurant, but for now he was still breathing.

A few years back, as a special birthday surprise, Sheila booked a luxurious suite at The Mark. To really spice things up, she also hired a male prostitute

Evil Exchange

for the evening. The Judge had often expressed a perverse desire to watch Sheila engage in sex with another man. Sheila and the prostitute performed with so much enthusiasm in front of Harry, he lost all self-control and joined in, eventually sharing the bed with just the prostitute when Sheila tired of the fun and games. He had absolutely no idea Sheila had set up a video camera and taped the entire birthday celebration. Being a shrewd business woman, Sheila always believed in having an insurance policy, because you just never knew when it might come in handy.

"You wouldn't . . ." the Judge tried to speak. He had spittle on his lips.

"Oh darling, but I would! Yes, I know that I am on the tape also. But I don't think it would do *nearly* the damage to my reputation that it would yours. Oh, and I saved the best part for last. That young man, Phoenix, wasn't that his name? Well, he was only sixteen when we had your little birthday party, isn't that cute? They have so much stamina at that age . . ."

Harry snapped his fingers at the waiter and shook his empty whiskey glass to demand a refill.

"And make it a double," Judge Price bellowed.

Chapter Sixty-One

He was running down the corridor as fast as he could without knocking any of the other students down. He was afraid he'd be late for his final exam in electrical circuitry. Suddenly, he heard the bell ring, signaling the beginning of class. He was late. He ran faster and faster and then slipped on the floor. The bell kept ringing and ringing and ringing . . . Todd woke up startled by the harsh sound of the telephone. He reached across the still sleeping Diana to grab the portable. *Who could be calling at the ungodly hour of 8 a.m.?* Todd never got up before ten on the weekends, and he and Diana had been out late dancing until two, made love until three, then talked until four.

Todd quietly mumbled a hello into the phone and recognized Boots' voice immediately.

"Todd, wake up man, wake up! We've found her. We found your mother."

Hearing those words, Todd's heart nearly jumped out of his chest, and he prodded Diana to wake up.

"Boots, hang on a sec! I need to get something to write with. How the hell did you do it? Never mind, you don't have to answer that." Super charged with adrenaline, he was wide awake now and shouting into the phone. He raced into his office, grabbed a paper, pen, and the extension. Then he ran back to hand the extension to Diana who'd just come out of the bathroom, telling her it was important. Puzzled, and still rubbing the sleep from her eyes, she took the phone and went to the kitchen to make some coffee. Todd might not need any, but she did.

As Diana listened in, she heard Boots mention Todd's first mother, and where she lived. 357 Langston Avenue in Wilton, Connecticut. She'd been married to

Evil Exchange

the same man since she was twenty-one, and Klot was her maiden name. She had one grown daughter. Meanwhile, Todd had come into the living room and she could see him writing furiously on the pad. He was smiling as tears streamed down his face. Then she heard Boots speak again.

"Yeah, it's a pretty ritzy area where she lives, but considering who she's married too, what else would you expect? And you have a sister, isn't that great? Oh, and according to my notes, your mother used to live in Manhattan on East 74th Street between . . ."

"Boots," Todd interrupted. "Where on East 74th Street?" He was yelling and holding his breath at the same time. Not an easy thing to do.

Boots read off the address. "404 East 74th Street. Why?"

"Oh my God, I live across the street from there. In 401 East 74th. When did she live there?"

"From 1982 to 1992."

Todd could no longer speak. He let the phone slip out of his hand and drop to the floor. Diana decided she'd better step in.

"Hi, Boots, it's Diana. I've been listening on the extension. Listen, thanks *so* much. Todd is a little overwhelmed right now and I think I'd better take care of him. You know, none of us ever really know how we'll react until we actually hear the news firsthand. Say hey to Julie and we'll keep in touch. Oh, and please send the bill for all this, okay?"

"I hear ya. I have no idea how Todd is feeling right now, but I'm just glad we could help. I guess he has to figure out the next step," Boots replied. "Julie says hey back and we'll talk to you soon." He rang off.

Diana clicked the phone off and went to Todd. She hugged him until he stopped crying and then asked him why he was so upset.

"I lived across the street from my own mother for ten years and didn't know it. We could have seen each other, said hi to each other, been next to each other at the grocery store. We could have sat near each other at that Chinese place on the corner, I could have met my own sister and not known it, I could have . . ."

Diana stopped him with another hug. "Easy, my love, easy. Take a deep breath and relax a bit. It's a lot to take in all at once, I know. Let's look at the bright side, okay? We have some planning to do. You want to meet her don't you?"

"Diana! What if she doesn't want to meet *me*? Jesus Christ. Look at who she's married to. Won't it be a scandal for her to admit she had a child forty years ago and put him up for adoption? Can you imagine what people will say? I could be a *huge* embarrassment. Do you think her husband is going to welcome me with open arms? Obviously we know he's not my father, according to when they got married. See?" He held out the paper to show Diana the date Boots had given him. And almost without a breath, he continued his rant.

"And how is their daughter going to feel when *she* finds out? *If* she finds out, I should say. Maybe I'll never even get a chance to . . . Fuck! I'm so afraid of being rejected."

"Todd, stop it! First of all, you would never be an embarrassment to *anyone*," Diana said angrily. Then, realizing that she wasn't angry with Todd, she softened her tone. "Remember what Glen said about that? That we *cannot* be rejected?"

Todd dried his eyes and nodded. Finally, he took a deep breath and cleared his throat.

"Yeah, that was the paradox he was talking about. Glen said that if a mom says 'yes' to meeting, it's because they care about us. And if she says 'no,' it's all about her fear of her own feelings. Thanks for reminding me. So, I guess my only fear should be about being accepted rather than rejected."

"That's right, sweetheart. We fear if we are accepted, we will have to feel the pain of not having that love and caring all our lives. And, we also fear that once we've found the love from our first mother, it might be taken away again. But, I remember reading somewhere that our moms don't want to lose us again any more than we want to lose them. So, keep the faith, you have to *trust* her," Diana smiled and kissed him.

"You'll go with me to the support group meeting tomorrow night, right? I know Glen coaches people on how to make contact. You said he helped you before you met Theresa. I want to do this right and not screw it up," Todd pleaded.

"Well, of course I'll go with you to the meeting. I know his advice will really help put things in perspective for you. The phone call to your mother will be the most important phone call you'll ever make. You are going to *talk* with you own mother for the very first time. Believe me, this is going to change your life." Diana smiled serenely.

Chapter Sixty-Two

Nardo had never made a blunder of this magnitude before. He'd done some stupid things in his life, but those mistakes were made years ago when he was much younger and just starting out in his budding criminal career. Sure he'd been arrested, almost gone to prison even, but fortunately Sheila had helped him avoid that particular pickle. However, each blunder he experienced early on had taught him a valuable lesson, and it didn't take long for Janos Nardofsky to excel at his profession.

Until that stupid FBI agent followed him to the strip club, that is. Nardo had spotted him right off, and he was tempted to try and deal with the situation immediately, but there were just too many people around. He decided to wait until later in the evening, when he might have a better chance of getting rid of the oh-so-obvious-tail without an audience watching him do it.

Nardo still wasn't sure where or when he'd been made, but someone saw him somewhere, that much was clear. It wasn't just a coincidence the same agent Nardo saw walking into the coroner's office in Corsicana that afternoon, had then shown up at the Puss 'N Boots later the same night. The guy wasn't there for a lap dance, that much was for sure. No, the agent was there because of him. And if the FBI was hot on his trail, it was because he'd been linked to either the Mule, the Stork, or the Boss. That was certain. Not that it mattered, but he would have liked to know just out of curiosity. He knew he'd been careful, and doubted it was any slip up he might have made himself. *Damn it to hell! Why did the feds have to get involved and screw things up, just when things were going so well?*

Killing the agent seemed like the perfect solution and would have solved all his problems, if it hadn't been for that stupid hairy dipshit taking out the trash. Nardo had been so close to squeezing the very last breath from the fed, not an easy feat considering how strong the man was, when the back door banged open and the walking mustache strolls out and spots him dead on. Nardo's immediate reaction had been to cut and run. He'd instinctively loosened his grip and let the suit fall to the ground. All he thought about at the time was getting to the car and getting out of there. Of course if he had really thought it through, he could have easily taken care of both assholes, but there simply wasn't time. Too bad he'd left his gun in the car. Otherwise he would have just shot them both and been done with it. No muss, no fuss.

It was a problem. A very big problem indeed, and he'd done nothing but think about it all the way back to New York. He had hated making the call to Sheila, but he knew he had to tell her what happened. She took it better than he thought she would. She told him to lay low for a few days while she figured out what to do. She mentioned they might have to curtail their operations temporarily, but she doubted the FBI had much in the way of hard evidence against them, and she wasn't too worried about it. So typical of her. She seemed supremely confident nothing would come of this, and she treated the whole situation as if it were just a minor hiccup. She assured him she would take care of everything. Nardo believed her.

So, imagine Nardo's surprise when someone tries to off him. He's walking down the street from his apartment, minding his own business, going to the corner store to stock up on some beer for the weekend. It was still light out, but most people were in for the evening, having dinner or watching television. Suddenly, a man wearing a ski mask comes out of nowhere and puts a gun to Nardo's temple.

"Nice and easy into the alley, Bigfoot," the man instructed. Nardo heard a trace of an accent. *Russian?* He couldn't be sure. Cold steel was a most effective persuasion, and he did what the man asked while he considered his options.

"Wallet's in my pocket. It's yours," Nardo told him. The guy could have been after money for drugs, but he sure didn't act like an addict. The hand that held the gun at his head never wavered. This guy was not suffering from the shakes. On the contrary, he was calm and businesslike, merely giving instructions. He was also quite large. Nardo was able to tell just from the glimpse he got from his peripheral vision. The man was at least as big as he was. Not that it mattered. Nardo knew he could take him and not even break a sweat. He just didn't want the gun to go off accidentally.

"Don't want your money," his assailant said. "Just want you dead."

In the split second it took for the message to reach Nardo's brain and for

Evil Exchange

the trigger to fire the bullet from its chamber, Nardo did the only thing he could think of. He ducked.

The bullet grazed the top of his head while it tore the baseball cap off. It was a minor wound, but it bled like a dermal volcano spewing corpuscle magma. The ski-masked man was so startled to see his mark still upright, he froze in disbelief. It cost him big time.

Breathing heavily, Nardo wiped blood out of his eyes. He looked at the man who had tried to take his life, and was now going to lose his own as a result. It had been easy to wrestle the gun from the stunned man and down him with one shot to the forehead. Nardo then dragged the body deeper into the alley, far away from the street, and listened for any shouts or cries of alarm from nearby windows. Nothing. He took only a moment to rip the mask from the man's face, but Nardo had never seen him before. The bullet had caught him dead center, and unlike Nardo, there was no blood dripping from the wound. Just a small, neat, black hole. Nardo checked the man's pockets and found nothing in the way of identification. What he did find confirmed what he had come to suspect as soon as he heard those words, "just want you dead." The man was a gun for hire. A contract killer. And he had foolishly left a phone number in his pocket. Nardo recognized it right away. It was Sheila Stiles cell number.

Chapter Sixty-Three

Todd was standing on the mooring mast at the top of the Empire State Building, gazing out at the island of Manhattan. The 87th through the 104th floors had been an afterthought, originally added as a place to load and unload passenger dirigibles. Originally, it was a good idea in theory, until the high winds at twelve hundred feet proved to be too dangerous for such activity, and the entire dirigible idea was scraped, but the mast remained.

Todd often came up here to think. He liked the quiet, the isolation it provided. It felt as if you were actually hovering in the sky, a kind of spiritual levitation, free from earthly distractions and emotional tethers. Since he did so much work on the television and radio antennas on the tower, he had a key to the hatch in the 102nd floor observatory ceiling, which allowed him access to the forbidden floors and television antenna tower above.

It had been a week since Todd had received his mother's name, address and phone number, and he'd been mulling over how to make contact. Suddenly, a Delta 1011 came out of the clouds above as it followed the flight path to LaGuardia airport. Todd was so deep in thought, he didn't even hear it until it was directly overhead, and the sound of the screaming engines startled him so much, he grabbed one of the crossbeams of the tower structure in sheer fright. He couldn't help but be reminded of the time on top of the World Trade Center tower number one, when he was working on the antenna tower installation and a similar Delta jet had come out of the clouds. Every single construction worker up there had flattened himself on the roof in terror. Todd had always worried that a jumbo jet would smash into the twin towers and knock them down, not at the hands of a terrorist, which is of course ultimately what happened, but as an aviation disaster that somehow seemed destined to occur. He found himself

Evil Exchange

breathing heavily as he watched the Delta jet shrink in size as it turned right to begin its landing approach. The reminder of those majestic towers falling, all those innocent lives . . .

That's it, I'm not going to wait any longer. Life is so tenuous, so precious. Something could happen to her. Something could happen to me. I've certainly had enough near misses lately to know that. If I keep farting around trying to decide what to do, Emily could get hit by a bus, or have a heart attack, or God knows what. What the hell am I so afraid of anyway? C'mon Todd, take a chance, it's not going to kill you. Call her. Right now.

Todd climbed down the ladder from the tower to the 104th floor, down the steps to 103, then 102, and got in the tower elevator to go down. He changed on 86, and took the express all the way to the lobby. In just a few minutes, he walked briskly out of the building and hailed a cab to his East 74th street apartment.

By the time he got home, he was absolutely convinced he was doing the right thing, and his hand shook only in anticipation, not fear, as he dialed the number.

A soft, pleasant voice answered the phone, "Hello, this is Emily."

Todd took a deep breath and asked, "Is this Emily Roscoe?" His mind was racing and he remembered what Glen had told him. *Keep her talking. No matter what, keep her talking. Don't forget she'll be in shock when you tell her who you are, so speak softly. Stay calm.*

"Yes, this is she, who is calling?"

"My name is Todd Walters and I live in New York. Is this a good time to talk?"

"That depends Mr. Walters," Emily said with amusement. "Are you looking for me, or is it the Senator you're after? If you wish to speak with Delivan, it would be best to call his office."

"No, Mrs. Roscoe. I can assure you, it is *you* I wish to speak with," Todd tried to keep his voice steady.

"Very well, then. What's it about? I am not interested in buying anything, that's for sure," she said pleasantly.

Todd took another deep breath and crossed his fingers in his mind. *Gotta go for it.*

"I'm an adopted person, I was born on November 15th, 1964. I have been looking for my mother and my . . ." Todd heard Emily gasp and he took the final plunge, "and my search has lead me to you." There was absolute silence, and for a moment, the world froze in time.

"Oh my God, oh my God!" Emily said in a rush. "It's really you? Are you really my son? This isn't some kind of cruel joke? Please tell me it's not."

Todd heard her crying and realized that tears were streaming down his cheeks as well. It was one of the happiest moments in his life, and he simply could not stop the tears. In all his forty-three years on the planet, he'd never cried as much as he had in the last few weeks.

"Yes, Emily. I am your son," Todd said trying to swallow the massive lump in his throat. Then they both gave in to the emotion, sobbing and laughing. So much for staying calm. Finally, Todd had to say something. "I can't tell you how glad I am found you, do you have time to talk?" They both burst out laughing again.

More than two hours later, when Diana came and knocked on the apartment door, Todd and Emily were still talking. Diana took one look at his face and knew exactly what had happened. She smiled and sat down next to him, literally beaming with happiness.

CHAPTER SIXTY-FOUR

Sheila knew something was wrong. Harry couldn't or wouldn't give her a straight answer about the employee "situation." A few days ago he said it was being taken care of, but somehow, Sheila didn't quite believe him. Harry had never been good at lying, at least not to her. Although he'd never let her down before, right now she felt she couldn't count on him. Call it woman's intuition. Sheila thought it was all taking too long, and she was getting nervous. She needed to do something.

So after a brief, but very intense conversation with Colby, it was decided they'd pack it in. The business, that is. They'd had a damn good long run, but considering the unfortunate turn of events of late, it would be a most prudent time to close up shop. They might have been able to weather one problem, but not three. Losing Leslie and gaining the interest of the FBI were bad enough. Having Nardo attempt, and subsequently flub the murder of a FBI agent was a situation which simply could not be salvaged. No, the only choice she had there was damage control. Take Nardo out of the equation, lay low, and wait until things died down. Then maybe, she and Colby would search for new hires and get back to business. That was the original plan, anyway.

As the days passed, she sensed Harry was dragging his feet. She still held out hope he would follow through, for surely he knew she was serious about exposing him. Sheila never made idle threats. But so far, all Harry had to offer were excuses. "These things take time, my dear," he told her over the phone. Sheila thought it was bullshit. He kept telling her not to worry, but she could do little else. She finally realized she had made a mistake, her first in a very long time. She should have done the job herself, rather than relying on a boob like Harry. The man couldn't mastermind a trip to the zoo, let alone arrange for a murder. How he ever became a judge in the first place was beyond belief.

Paris and Soll

She wanted to give him the benefit of the doubt, since they had known one another for many years. So, Sheila really did try to quell her anxiety. She told herself that maybe the job had been done already, and Harry just didn't want to say anything over the phone. After all, there had been no sign of Nardo for a couple of days. Sheila had tried his cell phone and gotten no answer. She'd even stopped by his place, and there was no sign of him. She was sorely tempted to let herself imagine his dead body rotting away somewhere, but she just couldn't bring herself to *really* believe it. Assuming and imagining were not going to do it. Besides, until she actually had confirmation, it was all supposition anyway, and she was not good at supposition. Until she read about a murder in the paper, or saw a news report, she would not be fully convinced. Sheila sighed. *You just couldn't count on anybody to take care of business these days, could you?* She was surrounded by incompetents.

So, just this morning she called Harry and told him if he didn't get the problem solved and provide proof within twenty-four hours, she would take care of it. And if that were to happen, she'd be happy to then take care of Harry by mailing a few select photos of his honor and his teenage play date to the New York Times. Before Harry could utter a word, she hung up on him. Let the old bastard stew.

Since then, she'd been a busy little office bee, deleting, shredding, and packing. She hated giving up her client list, but she'd develop another one. A better one. Already she was thinking of California. She'd told Colby to get rid of his paperwork as well, and to his credit, he did get started, then a golf buddy called and he snuck out to play a round at Dellwood Country Club while she was down in the basement gathering a couple boxes. *Men! Did they think of nothing else but their own instant gratification?* At least Colby couldn't object to relocating to the West Coast. They had nothing but golf courses there.

Sheila was almost done. The more she thought about it, the more she realized how these last few incidents were oddly working in her favor, rather than against. It was time for a change. A nice, sunny climate, the blue Pacific Ocean, lots of wealthy childless couples . . .

"Sheila Stiles?"

"Christ, I nearly jumped a foot! Who are you? And what the hell do you want?" Sheila demanded of the two men standing in front of her. She'd been so preoccupied she never heard them approach.

"FBI, Ms. Stiles. Agents Frank Barron and Lionel Jackson. We're here to arrest you," Sheila heard the taller, but not as well dressed of the two, say. There was something wrong with his voice, it sounded strained. *Was that bruising around his neck?*

"Excuse me?" Sheila was indignant.

"For kidnapping, conspiracy, illegal placement for adoption, accessory to murder..."

Self-preservation kicked in and Sheila quickly became angry. "Do you know who I am? I'm an *attorney*, you can't just walk in here and arrest me." Sheila crossed her arms over her chest in defiance.

"Well, that's convenient. Then you don't have to call anyone, do you? You can just talk to yourself, and we do have an arrest warrant." Frank handed her a piece of paper.

Sheila looked at it and laughed in spite of her fear. "You're making a big mistake."

"Well, you can tell that to the judge. Oh, and speaking of judges, if it makes you feel any better, your good friend Judge Harold T. Price? Well, he'll also be sporting a pair of bracelets just like these right about now. And we can't forget the good doctor, now can we? Although he may a bit upset about his golf game being interrupted, nevertheless, Dr. Wendell Colby will be joining us as well," Frank said as he held out the handcuffs.

"You're bluffing. You have no proof!" Sheila smirked, but there was panic in her eyes.

"I beg to differ, ma'am. We have an eyewitness," Frank said and smiled.

"That's a good one. What eyewitness?" Sheila practically spat her sarcasm.

"Oh, you mean Mr. Nardofsky? He's been most cooperative so far."

Sheila Stiles blanched. Then she screeched like a wounded animal and lunged at Frank with her long, manicured nails. Fortunately, Lionel Jackson was close enough to stop the attack before she got too close. He quickly pinned Sheila's arms to her sides, and Frank cuffed her in seconds.

"Hey, thanks Lionel," Frank instinctively rubbed at his throat.

"No problem," Jackson adjusted his jacket and snapped his shirt cuffs smartly. Not a hair was out of place.

Chapter Sixty-Five

Langston Avenue, guarded by towering oaks, majestic maples, and fragrant orange blossom trees, wove gently through the western part of Wilton, Connecticut. It was a quiet neighborhood, but on this Sunday morning, Todd thought the pounding of his heart would surely wake the neighbors. He found number 357 and pulled into the brick-paved circular driveway. The house was colonial in style with perfectly manicured grounds. As he opened the car door, Emily came rushing out, an enormous grin on her face, tears streaming down her cheeks, and her arms outstretched. Todd looked at his mother, and thought she was the most beautiful woman he'd ever seen. She was of average height, and trim in figure. Her brown hair was loose and fell past her shoulders. Her features were elegant, but an impish quality kept her from appearing too serious. He quickly got out of the car, and without hesitation, walked directly into her arms. Almost simultaneously, they each said, "You smell so good." To anyone who might have overheard their comment, it might sound bizarre, but to Todd and Emily, it seemed the most natural thing in the world. The waterworks started up once again as they clung to each other like there was no tomorrow. Finally, Emily pulled back gently and gazed into her son's eyes.

"Let's go up to the house and talk. We have lots of catching up to do." They walked arm in arm to the veranda and sat side by side on a wide white wicker couch that seemed to just beckon them to relax.

"I can't believe I've found you. I *never* thought I would," Todd couldn't quite take it all in.

"I'd given up hope myself," Emily said as she grabbed his hand. "You know, years ago, I read an article in the New York Times about Maddie Monroe and her lawyer being arrested for selling babies. I was horrified when I recognized

Evil Exchange

the name of the attorney as the very same man who had me sign your surrender papers in 1964. I had no idea you were subsequently *sold*. I couldn't believe there was actually a black market for infants, and I was outraged. Of course, I went to an attorney and inquired about finding you. I was told searching was illegal, which of course was a lie, but I was young and didn't know any better. But he also told me if I did search and find you, it would destroy your life. I loved you so much, I could never do that to you, and I abandoned the idea of ever trying to find you."

"You cared that much? You loved me?" Todd blurted out while tears coursed down his cheeks.

"Of *course* I did, and I still do. I've never stopped." Emily reached for his other hand now grasped them both tightly in hers. Her touch was the most powerful connection Todd had ever felt. Emily never took her eyes off him and continued. "When I discovered I was pregnant at the age of seventeen, my parents told me I had to put you up for adoption, that it was the right thing to do. They told me I'd be selfish if I tried to raise you as a single parent. You see, I never told your father about you. And I never told my parents who your father was. Getting married at that age was simply out of the question. My parents said if I had you, you'd be labeled a bastard. Our family would become social pariahs, shunned by all. It may have been the sixties, but my parents were old school. And, even though I argued for months and months, they refused to even consider the possibility of me keeping you. They told me you'd be better off being adopted into a loving home, and you wouldn't suffer in any way. Eventually they wore me down and finally convinced me they just wanted what was best for you and for me. They made me feel so guilty for wanting to keep you, I finally gave in. But I never stopped wanting you. I never stopped loving you. I was devastated when I had to sign those final papers. Todd, look into my eyes. Please. The truth is right here for you to see." Emily's eyes were leaking anguished tears. Todd could clearly see the love and caring so evident there. He put his head on her shoulder, and again inhaled her scent.

"Speaking of my father . . . " Todd prompted.

"Oh, Todd," Emily's face became instantly sad. "Of course you want to know about him. And I know that I put you off when you asked me about him when we talked on the phone. I thought I'd be ready by now. I'm sorry, I'm just not there yet. It's still very painful for me. Can you be patient? I promise, I will tell you about him eventually. Just not now. Okay?"

Paris and Soll

"It's okay. I do want to know about him at some point though. Whenever you're ready. But Darryl Foster is not even remotely close to his real name, is it?"

"No. You said that was on the original birth certificate? I never saw it you know. One of those things Maddie said she would take care of." Emily sighed.

"That was the name all right," Todd nodded.

"Well, then it definitely was a fabrication on Monroe's part." Emily replied.

"Emily? I've missed you my *whole* life. My parents told me you were dead, killed in a car crash. Well, you *and* my father. I only recently found out the truth. I'd have searched for you years ago if I had known. I'm so glad I found you, I still can't believe it." Todd smiled through his tears. Emily hugged him as if she would never let go. They sat quietly for a few moments, relishing the experience of being reunited after forty years of separation. Todd wanted to remember every detail, to burn this image into his brain. This embrace of a mother and a son, the most natural thing in the world, had been missing for far too long.

"You know, I just realized something," Todd said as he broke the silence. "All my life, I've been afraid to let anyone else drive with me in the car. I was always terrified I'd die in a car crash. Since I thought you had died that way, I thought I'd die that way too. It's crazy."

"I'm so sorry you had to live with that," Emily shook her head sadly. Then she took a deep breath and wiped the tears from her face.

"We've both suffered enough. We need to concentrate on the here and now, darling. I can't wait to meet Diana, she sounds so wonderful," Emily smiled.

"She is. I know I told you a lot about her when we talked on the phone," Todd laughed remembering their marathon conversation.

"And your mother," Emily said.

"You want to meet Miriam?" Todd was startled.

"Of course I do! I want to meet the woman who raised you, and your brother, and his wife. I know, we should have a party. A celebration, what do you think?"

"Well, sure, I guess . . ." Todd stammered.

"Oh darling, I'm sorry. I don't mean to rush you. We'll talk about it, all right? I think it would be a wonderful idea. I so want you to meet my husband, Delivan. Sometimes people are intimidated by the fact that he's a senator, but please don't be. He's a wonderful man. I'm sorry he couldn't be here today, he had business to attend to. But you'll have a chance to meet him soon enough. I owe everything to him. He saved me, you know," Emily sighed.

"Well, I know you mentioned that before. But tell me how," Todd prompted.

"After I gave you up, I tried to go back to my life. Foolish of me to think I could. Everything seemed so trivial. My best friends all of a sudden seemed stupid and childish. I distanced myself from my family. Nothing was the same. I was miserable, and couldn't wait to leave home. My parents sent me off to college, a small private school in Vermont. Going away didn't change anything though. I was haunted by losing you. I kept to myself, and I became desperate and so very lonely. My heart was broken, and I knew it could never be fixed, and I thought my life was pointless to go on living. One night, I was out walking and came across a bridge, near the campus. It wasn't terribly high, but there were huge boulders down below and little water to break a fall. All I wanted was to end my misery. So I climbed over the railing, and that's when I heard this voice. 'You don't want to do that.' I turned around so abruptly, I almost fell off!" Emily laughed at the irony.

"But I hung on, and then I saw him. My Del. He was tall and thin, with a huge mass of dark, curly hair, not at all like he is now. He wasn't the most handsome boy I'd ever seen. But he had the kindest look on his face and such incredible warmth in his eyes. He was quite calm about my precarious perch. He just stood there and talked with me. He coaxed me back, and then took me for some coffee. He stayed up with me all night. He never left my side, even when I told him about you. That's right. Delivan has always known about you, Todd. He is so looking forward to meeting you," Emily patted his knee. "And he's not the only one."

"Oh?" Todd tensed a bit, not sure what was coming next.

"Your sister, Andrea. She's dying to meet you."

Chapter Sixty-Six

"I'm glad you could come with me today. I know you're anxious to get home," Lionel Jackson said.

"Well, I really wanted to be able to talk with Pearson face to face, poor bastard," Frank sighed. He was more than ready to get home to Suzy, but he needed to wrap things up here first, and it would only be one more day. He felt it wouldn't be right for Jackson to have to be the one to tell Paul Pearson such terrible news. Lionel and Paul were more than bridge partners, they were close friends.

The two men arrived at the Gallerie and went straight to the game room. Frank was happy to be in a club where people kept their clothes on. He figured he'd seen enough strip clubs to last a lifetime. The atmosphere here was elegant and refined, perfectly suited to its powerful members. Frank couldn't help but notice how Lionel Jackson fit right in, and looked more like an international businessman than a FBI agent. Frank looked down at his rumpled suit and inwardly cringed. He could tell himself a hundred times it didn't matter, that he'd been traveling for days on end, and it wasn't possible to look his best. Not that it mattered either way. Frank knew he could be dressed in his finest clothes, and still look like a hillbilly in comparison to Jackson. Not only did the man have great taste in clothes, he also had a sense of style and flair that couldn't be bought.

They stopped in the bar to find Paul waiting for them and quickly discovered he was not alone. His father-in-law was hovering nearby. Frank thought the presence of Senator Roscoe was an interesting, but not unwelcome surprise. He could see from Lionel's expression that he was not expecting the senator either.

Evil Exchange

Frank thought it was for the best though. After Paul heard what he had to say, he would need all the support he could get.

Frank had never met the senator from Connecticut before, but he'd seen him plenty of times on television and in the newspaper. In person, Delivan Roscoe was almost larger than life, and appeared quite protective of Paul. Actually, the two men seemed more like father and son than in-laws. There was even a resemblance between the two. It wasn't a physically likeness, but rather a magnetism they both possessed. *Charisma*, Frank thought. They both commanded attention and respect without saying or doing anything. As Frank studied Pearson, he could see how Lionel might look at him as a role model. Paul Pearson was exceedingly well dressed, perfectly groomed, and quite distinguished in his appearance. He looked like a celebrity, and shook hands like a prizefighter. Lionel had mentioned to Frank that Paul would soon be running for a senate seat, and if looks or the influence of his famous father-in-law had anything to do with it, he'd be a shoe-in. Of course it would hinge on whether or not he could survive this adoption scandal. Jackson made the introductions and they sat down at a table in the back corner of the room where they could speak privately.

"So, Agent Barron. Lionel tells me you have something very important to discuss with me," Paul stated neutrally.

"Please, Mr. Pearson, call me Red, most everyone does. You too, Senator," Frank nodded at Roscoe. He was stalling, and everyone knew it.

"All right, Red. Now, what do you have to tell me?" Paul asked patiently.

Frank started at the beginning. He told them how Sheila Stiles was the mastermind behind a black-market baby selling business, which had been operating for years. Frank went over how both Janos Nardofsky and Leslie Steiner stole babies from hospitals and marketplaces, and how some of the mothers had been brutally murdered for their infants, while others were left alive only to suffer the unspeakable torture of being robbed of their own flesh and blood, never knowing if their child was alive or dead. He explained how the house in Congers was a way-station for the babies while Sheila made arrangements with wealthy couples waiting to adopt a child as quickly as possible. Birth certificates were falsified and signed by Sheila's partner in crime, Wendell Colby, and how Judge Harold Price received financial kickbacks from Sheila for expediting the entire adoption process. The reference to Judge Price made Senator Roscoe visibly wince.

Paris and Soll

Frank went on to give Pearson and Roscoe the short version of his investigation and interviews, which led him to Louisiana, Alabama, Tennessee, and Texas. He told them by finding the Mule, he'd found Nardo. Frank left out the part about Nardo trying to kill him, as he felt it wasn't essential to the story. What he did feel was important though is what happened afterwards. When Nardo escaped his assassin's bullet, he knew it was only a matter of time. He was either going to be caught by the FBI, or he was going to be murdered. Prison seemed a better option than a casket. So he wasted no time in contacting the Feds. Frank made the arrangements, and brought Nardo in himself. With DNA evidence from the impounded rental car in Alabama linking him to the murder of Kerri Stryker in her Shady Meadows mobile home, Nardo wasn't going to get any kind of an immunity deal. Frank had told him the best he could hope for was to avoid the death penalty in exchange for his testimony against the others. And there was always the possibility of parole. Frank would have loved to see the Hulk fry, but he needed to make the deal in order to get to Sheila and her cohorts, and to put a stop to her horrendous transactions for good.

In going over the details, Frank emphasized how diabolical the entire operation was. He never spared Pearson's feelings or sugarcoated his words for the senator. He realized it might have been selfish on his part that his harsh narrative and blunt words caused the others to physically cringe, but he was trying to drive home his point. Frank knew how much his own foster care experience influenced his way of thinking, and he wanted justice for the innocent lives that had been destroyed. He wanted these vile baby brokers behind bars. He wanted to try and reunite at least one family even if it meant the devastation of another. All in all, Frank was telling it like it was. A horrific tale of human flesh being traded for money. It was a nauseating story of children being sold to the highest bidder, and how some desperate people who wanted what nature denied them so badly, were going to pay the ultimate price for it.

When he finished speaking, Frank looked at Paul's handsome face as it twisted into a painful mask of cruel realization. Frank couldn't imagine what the man must have been feeling, but he wasn't terribly sympathetic. Paul and Andrea Pearson used their wealth to circumvent the system, and it had backfired in the most appalling way. One thing Frank did know is that he would never forget the look on Paul Pearson's face. It would haunt him the same way Tarren's face had haunted him. Unfortunately, there would be no happy ending for the Pearsons the way there would be for the Vincents.

"Paul. I'm sorry to have to tell you all of this. But I do believe that the child you adopted, Ruby, is really Vanessa Vincent. It's a simple matter of a DNA test to be sure, but I know I'm right. We know it was Steiner who kidnapped

Evil Exchange

her from the hospital in Tennessee. It was a short time later that Sheila Stiles brought you Ruby. It all fits. Paul?" Frank knew that Pearson had tuned him out. He was staring off into space, completely immobile.

"Will there be any criminal charges brought against my son-in-law and daughter?" Delivan Roscoe demanded.

"No, Senator. There will not. I'm sure they believed they were using a legitimate private adoption agency. After all, you had Agent Jackson here do a preliminary background check. They seemed above board, at least on the surface," Frank said.

"Well, thank God for that. We can do some damage control here, Paul. . . all is not lost."

Frank looked at the senator. It was hard to tell if he were talking about Paul's race for the senate, or the well being of his daughter. Perhaps both.

"Paul?" Frank asked again.

"Hmmm?" Paul finally registered that he'd heard and looked at Frank.

"You have to give her back. You know that don't you?"

Paul Pearson looked like he'd just gone twelve rounds and lost the decision. Finally, he nodded and cleared his throat. "Yes. Of course we do. She's not ours. I know that. What I don't know, is how I'm ever going to explain this to my wife. This is going to kill her," Paul said shaking his head slowly.

"Perhaps the only consolation for your wife is that Ruby, I mean Vanessa, will be reunited with her family, where she belongs," Frank said softly.

"Where she belongs. Indeed," Paul answered.

Chapter Sixty-Seven

Todd couldn't believe how quickly the last few months had gone by. So much had happened since he met Emily, and now, he simply could not imagine his life without her. Her husband Delivan had warmly welcomed him to the family, treating him as if he were his very own son. Unfortunately, Todd hadn't been able to meet his sister Andrea yet. That was to change this evening.

Todd was in the Rainbow Room at the top of the General Electric building, one of the most dominant structures in Rockefeller Center. He looked out at the Empire State Building and realized what a different perspective it was to see it from this vantage point. Usually it was the other way around. He was looking at so many things from a different perspective these days, it seemed most appropriate.

It took some time and careful planning, but Emily's celebration had finally arrived. Todd would have preferred a back yard barbecue instead of a formal soiree provided by one of the finest caterers in the city, but Emily had insisted on a lavish affair. Being the wife of a senator, Todd supposed she was used to getting what she wanted. And he didn't mind really, he would do just about anything to please her. He laughed to himself. *It's like a coming out party, my debut.* Admittedly, he was a little nervous about it all, it would be the first time for Miriam and Emily to meet, and he didn't have any idea how that would go, but he supposed it would all work out just fine. He was really looking forward to seeing Boots and Julie. He still couldn't believe Boots had agreed to come to New York, but Julie must have worked her mojo on him, or she may have threatened him the old butcher knife routine. Either way, he probably never had a chance. Julie had always dreamed of coming to New York.

Todd was also looking forward to meeting Theresa Croft, Diana's first

Evil Exchange

mother. Emily and Diana had become close friends, and Emily insisted Theresa be included in the festivities. As a matter of fact, Emily wanted Todd to invite his entire support group, but he thought it best just to ask Glen and Beth, the group leaders, to come. They'd been so instrumental in encouraging him to search in the first place, and of course, it was where he met Diana. Since Todd wanted his supporters to come, and he wanted to include Claire, his now former therapist. He felt he owed her a debt of gratitude as well, and wanted to introduce his new family to her. She'd been invaluable in helping him sort out his feelings.

What he found most interesting about the guest list however, was the inclusion of two FBI agents. Emily said Delivan had specifically asked for them to come. Emily mentioned one of them was a friend of Andrea's husband Paul, but she didn't say much about the other one, except for the fact that he was responsible for cracking an illegal baby selling ring right here in New York. The television news, Internet, and papers had screamed headlines over it for weeks. "Babies, Incorporated" they'd dubbed it. Todd found it hard to believe that such practices still existed at all in this day and age, and he was intrigued to meet the man who almost single-handedly brought the business to a screeching halt, and exposed the ring leaders for the monsters they truly were.

Todd was stunned when Emily confided in him that his own sister Andrea fell victim to the illegal scam. Andrea and Paul were shocked to learn the baby they'd adopted was actually stolen right from the hospital, mere hours after her mother had given birth to her. When they learned the truth, they knew she must be immediately returned to her parents. Emily told Todd that one of the FBI agents had delivered the infant himself to the grateful mother in Knoxville. A DNA test was merely a formality as Tarren Vincent recognized her child immediately when mother and daughter were reunited.

Both Paul and Andrea were devastated. Andrea became severely depressed, but Emily and Delivan saw to it that she received the best medical treatment. Anti-depressants were prescribed while everyone held their breath to see if she would recover from the loss of her cherished Ruby. Paul of course was angry, ashamed to admit he had taken shortcuts to adopt a child. His excuse being that he was only thinking of his wife, wanting to make her happy. He was humiliated, but at least he put the blame squarely on his own shoulders where it belonged, rather than blaming the friends who'd also adopted from Sheila Stiles and recommended her in the first place. With Paul being in the public eye and running for office, the press and the tabloids had a field day with it all. Yet rather than retreating, Paul became even more visible, and did quite a job in turning things around. He quelled his detractors by sharing the private anguish he and his wife endured in giving up the child they had both grown to love. The return of baby Vanessa to her mother made the national news, and made Paul Pearson look like a hero. He quickly became a media darling once again, and vowed to fight for the rights of the innocent, and to put people like Stiles, Price, and Colby behind bars for good. Paul's new found role of kind, caring, and concerned husband was not an act. Not in the least. Something quite remarkable happened to Paul Pearson. Losing his adopted daughter, and nearly losing his wife to depression, changed him irrevocably. For the first time, he realized what was precious in his life. Andrea in turn, stood by her husband during the tumultuous personal exposure and the entire public ordeal, but she chose to do so in seclusion.

"Hey there handsome," Diana whispered in his ear.

"There you are, where have you been?" Todd asked and gave her a hug. Diana looked exquisite as usual.

"Oh, I was helping Emily with a few last minute details. She's still talking with the caterer. She's wonderful you know," Diana said.

"I know. I can't believe how lucky I am to have such wonderful women in my life," Todd looked deep into her eyes.

"Well, thank you," Diana blushed.

"And you do realize don't you, I'm still accident free. See how good you are for me? We were meant to be."

"So *now* you believe what I said about destiny?" Diana playfully nudged him in the ribs.

"Absolutely. And right now, my destiny is to go *par-tay* with you," Todd held out his arm.

"Todd!" Boots and Julie waved from across the room. The two couples met halfway, the women exchanging hugs and the men trading slaps on the back.

"I can't believe you're here! And all spruced up. . ." Todd said as he did a double take. Boots was dressed in a suit and actually wore shoes rather than flip-flops on his feet. He looked completely different than he did on the *Lost & Found*. Julie looked absolutely stunning which wasn't a surprise at all.

"Well, I can't believe it myself, I didn't think I'd ever come back to New York. But Julie talked me into it."

"*We* wouldn't have missed this for anything," Julie stated simply. She made it clear Boots never had a say in the matter.

They went to the bar and got a drink, and caught up on one another's lives.

Evil Exchange

Todd and Diana were thrilled to hear that Julie would be meeting with a record producer while she was in the city. Boots would be negotiating with his publisher to extend his contract for another three books. Just as the congratulations started, Emily came to join them. She was thrilled to meet the man responsible for bringing her son to her.

"I could never thank you enough," Emily hugged Boots.

"It was my pleasure. But I can't take all the credit, Julie here, is the one who figured out your name."

Emily kissed Julie's cheek. "How ever did you do it?"

"I went flying," Julie replied matter of factly, as if that was how everyone solved a problem.

"Remarkable," Emily said. "Isn't it amazing how that awful woman, Maddie Monroe, changed names around on the birth certificates? She gave me a different first name, changed my last name, made up a name for Todd, made up a name for his father. . ."

"She left the real name of the hospital though," Boots added.

"And my birthday," Todd chimed in.

"Of course you know why she did that, she never wanted anyone to be able to search. . . " Boots stopped mid-sentence as he noticed more guests arriving.

Glen came in with his wife, and Beth was joined by her sister. Todd excused himself and left the group at the bar to go and greet them, and received a warm hug from both. They were all excited to meet Emily, and Todd pointed to the bar where she was quickly becoming the center of attention. Just then, Matt and Katy walked in. Diana came to whisk the support group members over to the bar, while Todd greeted his brother and sister-in-law.

"Where's mom?" Todd asked looking around.

"Senator Roscoe cornered her in the lobby downstairs. He's bringing her up himself," Matt answered and shrugged off his coat. "She was so nervous about tonight and meeting Emily, you know? The senator treated her as if she was royalty and it really seemed to calm her down. You can imagine how much she loved the VIP treatment from him."

"How much do want to bet that was Emily's idea?" Todd said to his brother while he gave Katy an affection buss on the cheek. "You look lovely tonight."

"Flattery is not necessary, but an introduction is. I can't *wait* to meet Boots Beaumont. Where is he?" Katy was all a twitter in anticipation of meeting her favorite author. Todd pointed him out as the devilishly handsome man at the bar, and heard a sharp intake of breath from Katy.

"Oh, he's gorgeous! Who is that woman with him? Is she a model? She's beautiful," Katy gushed.

"That's his fiancee," Diana answered for Todd as she walked over to join them.

"What? They're engaged?" Todd was incredulous.

"Not officially. But it'll happen on this trip. Julie had a premonition," Diana winked. "Don't say anything, promise?"

"Well, *I* certainly won't say anything, there's still time to change his mind. I'll just convince him to run off with me. Matt can keep the house *and* the kids. Out of my way," Katy joked and made for the bar.

"Oh, Matt. You brought your camera, great idea!" Diana exclaimed.

"Yep. I'm the unofficial photographer tonight. I want to take pictures of both of Todd's families," Matt grinned and followed his wife. Todd and Diana took the opportunity for a quick, but passionate embrace. They were almost immediately interrupted by more guests. It was Claire Meyers on the arm of impressively attired and perfectly groomed man. Todd wondered if this was her husband.

"Claire, how wonderful to see you. Thank you so much for coming," Todd greeted her warmly.

"Thank you, Todd. I'm honored to be here to share in your celebration. Please let me introduce Special Agent Lionel Jackson of the FBI. We've only just met," Claire said referring to her handsome companion.

"Please to meet you," Lionel said in a warm baritone. "Senator Roscoe has told me a lot about you."

Todd looked confused and wasn't quite sure what to say.

"Sorry. I'm a friend of Paul's. The senator's son-in-law?"

"Right. You must be the agent who solved the baby selling case," Todd made the connection.

"Oh, I can't take the credit for that. I was a small part of the investigation. No, the man who holds that honor is Frank Barron. I don't see him here," Lionel looked around.

"I don't believe Agent Barron has arrived yet. I'm Diana Easton, Todd's girlfriend."

Evil Exchange

"How do you do, Ms. Easton. And this lovely lady is Claire Meyers," Lionel said. Diana suggested Claire come with her to the bar to get a drink and mingle. Once the two men were left alone, Lionel spoke quietly to Todd.

"I look forward to seeing Frank and meeting his wife Suzy. Frank is an incredibly talented and devoted agent. He worked tirelessly on that case. Believe me. As a matter of fact, he almost lost his life over it, but you'll never hear that from him. He's a very modest man, but let's keep that tidbit of information between you and me, shall we? His wife doesn't know, and she'd kill him if she ever found out that he almost died," Jackson chuckled.

Todd added another secret to his list of things not to talk about this evening. He hoped there wouldn't be any more or he'd start to lose track.

"I hope it doesn't seem too awkward. I mean, it was the senator's idea to invite him, they've become pretty good friends throughout this whole ordeal," Jackson said seriously.

"What?" Todd was perplexed.

"Well, Frank being the one who took your sister's baby back. I can see how on the surface it would look insensitive for Delivan to ask Frank to be here, but that's not how it really is," Lionel tried to explain.

"As far as I'm concerned, Delivan Roscoe is one of the most admirable men I have ever met. And I'm not just saying that because he's married to Emily," Todd smiled. "He can invite whomever he wants to this party, and I'm sure he would never do anything to make Andrea feel uncomfortable either. I know how much he loves her. Speak of the devil."

Delivan Roscoe entered the room with a flourish. On his arm, Miriam Walters glowed with pride at being escorted by such a prominent man. Todd thought she looked ten years younger.

"Todd, you never told me how utterly charming your mother is," the senator boomed in a loud voice while he whisked Miriam over to introduce her to Emily.

"Ever the politician," Lionel Jackson laughed and went to get a drink.

Todd spotted a beautiful raven haired woman walk into the room.

"Theresa," Todd recognized Diana's mother. It was their first time to meet, but Todd felt as if he'd known her for years. They'd spoken on the phone a number of times when he'd been at Diana's apartment. And Todd had seen quite a few digital photos of Theresa as well. To see her in person almost took his breath away. Yes, she was an attractive woman, but what he really couldn't get over is how much she and Diana looked alike. They were almost a mirror image of one another. The only subtle difference was that Theresa had a slightly more mature look around her eyes and mouth, but that was about it.

Theresa smiled at Todd and opened her arms wide. "Finally, I get to meet you!"

"Thank you so much for coming. How was your flight?" Todd asked as he helped her with her coat.

"Fine, uneventful. I haven't even seen Diana yet. She was still at work when I got in, and then she came straight here early to help Emily. Where is Emily? I want to thank her for inviting me. I can't wait to meet her," Theresa said.

"Then let me introduce you. You two will have a lot in common." Todd escorted her to the bar.

A lavish array of hors d'oeuvres was being served by some of the catering staff. Everyone seemed to be having a wonderful time. Diana came to get Theresa while Todd got a drink for himself and looked around. Emily and Miriam were seated together at a table, talking like old chums, Katy was pumping Boots for the release date of his next novel, Matt was snapping pictures of everyone and everything, even the food. Claire was laughing at something Lionel said, and Todd grinned when he realized they were flirting with one another. Delivan listened intently while Julie read his palm, Glen intercepted Diana and Theresa so that he could say hello and introduce them to his wife.

A sudden hush fell over the crowd as two newcomers entered the room.

"The man of the hour," Lionel Jackson broke the spell and rushed to greet Frank Barron and his wife, and then quickly brought them over to the group. The senator was first to welcome them.

"Ladies and gentlemen, for those of you who have not had to pleasure, may I introduce Agent Frank Barron, and his lovely wife, Suzy. They've come from DC just to join us this evening," Delivan explained to the partygoers.

"Please, call me Red," Frank asked the group.

"Thank you so much for inviting us," Suzy added.

Emily came to shake Frank's hand. "My husband speaks very highly of you, Agent Barron."

Frank froze for a moment. He wasn't exactly sure what to say, but figured he'd just jump right in. "Mrs. Roscoe, I can't tell you how sorry I am about what happened to your daughter. Our investigation never meant to hurt people like Andrea, only to help those who had their children stolen to get them back."

Evil Exchange

"I know that Agent Barron," Emily patted his hand.

"Red, please ma'am, " Frank said in a sigh of relief.

"All right, Red. But only if you'll stop calling me ma'am. My name is Emily," she smiled sweetly.

"Sure, Emily. And your daughter, Andrea? Is she coming? I don't see her anywhere," Frank said as he looked around.

"She is supposed to be here to meet Todd. But she's been through so much lately, I really don't know if she'll show. I hope so," Emily replied thoughtfully.

The caterers came to announce that dinner was ready. Emily excused herself from Frank and went to direct the guests to the buffet line.

An hour later, the party was in full swing and the conversation turned to the latest news about today's newspaper headlines. The three members of "Babies Incorporated" had been sentenced. Initially, Sheila Stiles pled innocent to the charges and was determined to go to trial. However, after Judge Price and Dr. Colby rolled over like two mangy dogs and plea-bargained to testify against her in order to get reduced sentences, Sheila gave up the self-righteous pretense and accepted her fate. Dr. Wendell Colby received fifteen years and lost his medical license for life. Judge Harold T. Price received an identical jail sentence and the hatred of those who were honorable magistrates. Sheila Stiles was shown no mercy by the judge who sentenced her. According to the press, he labeled her "one of the most vile and despicable attorneys to ever pass the bar exam." She was given life in prison without the possibility of parole. She barely escaped the death penalty.

Claire Meyers shook her head. The irony of the situation was hard to believe. For Todd Walters to have been sold on the black market by a baby broker back in the sixties was bad enough. But for him to find his first mother (amazing in and of itself considering all of the jumbled and false information on his birth certificate), and to then discover that her daughter, his half-sister, had also been the victim of an unscrupulous baby broker, was almost impossible to believe. They all concluded that truth was indeed stranger than fiction.

Finally, the conversation turned lighter. Katy monopolized Boots Beaumont, who didn't seem to mind having such an adoring fan. She enjoyed teasing him to no end, and startled everyone when she said: "So, are you going to keep it up?"

Never skipping a beat, Boots deadpanned. "I beg your pardon?"

"I mean, are you going to continue . . ." Katy giggled and couldn't finish.

"You mean finding people?" Boots smiled at Emily and let Katy off the hook.

"No! I mean writing books," Katy corrected him.

"Well, I'll have to check with my partner here," Boots deferred to Julie.

"You damn well better keep it up." Now it was Julie's turn to look serious. Everyone burst out laughing.

"May we join you? You all seem to be having such a grand time," Paul Pearson said as he entered the room. He was with a pale, but smiling Andrea, and another couple.

"Andrea!" Emily and Roscoe rushed to their daughter.

"Mom, Dad, please! I'm okay, really," Andrea tried to discourage her parents from hovering. She was tired of being treated like a broken doll. She was far stronger than anyone gave her credit for.

Paul gave his wife a quick squeeze and introduced their friends. "I'm sorry we've arrived so late, but we got caught in the most horrendous traffic jam. Everyone, this is Evan and Lily." Hellos were exchanged all around, and the conversations continued with enthusiasm.

"You must be Todd," Andrea went to her brother.

"I'm so happy to finally meet you Andrea," Todd hugged her carefully.

"Don't worry, I won't break," Andrea chided him. "I'm sorry I've been missing in action lately. I so wanted to meet you before, but, well, you know." She shrugged her shoulders in explanation.

"Andrea. *I'm* sorry about what happened to *you*. And to baby Ruby," Todd whispered. He couldn't imagine what she'd been going through the last few months. He had wanted to call her so many times, but both Diana and Emily suggested he wait. He watched her face carefully, not sure whether he should have mentioned the child's name or not. Andrea's eyes filled with tears, but then she surprised him and blinked them away.

"It's all right, really. It wasn't right from the beginning. She never seemed happy with me, I could just tell. She knew I wasn't her mother. Besides, it was an evil exchange. That Stiles woman deserves everything she got, and more. No one should *buy* a baby," Andrea said firmly.

"I'll agree with you there," Todd said as he looked at Miriam.

"Oh, Todd. I didn't mean . . . I feel like a total ass," Andrea looked horrified.

Evil Exchange

"Okay, now it's my turn to say 'don't worry.' Let's make a pact right now, we can speak freely with each other, sibling to sibling. How's that?"

"It's a deal. Welcome to the family. I've always wanted a big brother," Andrea smiled. "Oh, Todd. I want you to talk with my friends. You see, they have an adopted child. That's how we got Sheila's name actually, from them. They adopted a little girl from her two years ago, and in light of everything that's happened, to me and Paul, well . . . they want to find the little girl's natural mother. Lily is terrified that her child was stolen like Ruby, I mean Vanessa, was. She said she can't live with herself until she knows the truth. I put her in touch with Agent Barron, and he did some preliminary work for them, but he said he didn't know if they would ever be able to find the mother. Sheila destroyed most of her records. It seems almost impossible to try and find out where she came from, and whether the mother is even still alive. But Lily won't give up. She wanted me to ask you if you could help. I mean, you did it, didn't you? You did the impossible and found Emily. Maybe you can help Lily," Andrea pleaded.

"I don't think I can help her, but I think I know just the person who can. Come on, I'll introduce you," Todd grabbed her arm.

"Boots? Meet my sister, Andrea. She has something to ask you."

Printed in the United States
73291LV00002B/1-30